BASEBALL &
BENEVOLENCE

MARK ALLEN VALENZA

BARK PUBLISHING
Saratoga Springs, New York 12866

Published by
Bark Publishing
Bark Productions, Inc.
Saratoga Springs, New York

This is a work of fiction. All characters, events, and dialogue are imagined and not intended to represent real people, living or dead. Any reference to actual persons, names, or places is the product of the author's imagination or used fictitiously.

Copyright ©1993 by Mark Allen Valenza

Quote from *Take Time for Paradise*, copyright © 1989 by Estate of A. Bartlett Giamatti. Reprinted with the permission of Summit Books, Simon & Schuster, 1230 Avenue of the Americas, New York, NY 10020.

ISBN 0-9638257-0-4
Library of Congress Catalog Card Number: 93-73299

Cover photograph by Carol Swinger

Printed in the United States of America
October 1993

To my lovely wife Barbara and
my beautiful daughter Laura

"The gods are brought back when the people gather."
— A. Bartlett Giamatti, *Take Time for Paradise*

PART I: THE TRAGEDY

1

New York City: Winter, 1959

"LOOKS LIKE *SIR* Greco got lucky today," called Tommy from behind the bar as "Two for the Road" played on his new juke box.

Natt Greco brushed the snow from his shoulders and pulled a large wad of bills from his trousers pocket. "Scotch and soda, Tommy," said Natt. He removed a handkerchief from his blazer and wiped his red nose. "And give Two Face Pete and Little George whatever they're drinking."

"Natty, got my money?!" asked Pete as if he were talking to Santa Claus.

Natt rifled off five twenties and handed them to Pete. "What'd I tell ya, Petey?—the Knicks; I always win on the Knicks." Natt laughed and took a sip of his drink. He was feeling no pain. "Any sign of 'im?"

"Of who?" ribbed Tommy as he cleaned glasses, his droll expression awash in the pale blue glow of side bar lighting. He was bald, thick around the middle, and resembled a refrigerator wearing an apron. Tommy was well aware of who *who* was. He just enjoyed getting Natt worked up. That's the way they were together—as Natt would say, *ballbusters*. Tommy's Bar became a much more interesting place whenever Natt Greco came in for a drink.

"Who? . . . Who have I been talking about for the last month and a half. Who's coming to stay with me 'til spring training?" replied Natt, half joking and slightly annoyed. He was very sensitive about matters relating to his brother.

"Ah, your brother, the baseball player."

"Right. My brother Johney," said Natt.

"Why ya meeting 'im here? Why don't you have him come to your house? Y'know, like civilized people." Tommy sounded the bell behind the cash register as an acknowledgment of a good tip.

"Because . . . Faye, the baby . . . I thought we might have some fun."

Tommy glanced toward Two Face Pete and raised his brows. "If your brother is anything like you—"

"Hey, go easy on 'im. The kid's . . . different."

"Different? Different?" exclaimed Tommy as he swished his sizable buttocks down the length of the bar, drawing hearty laughter. Natt forced an unconvincing smile.

"No, really! I mean the kid's . . . ahh . . . naive." He would have said innocent but figured the guys would feast on that description.

"C'mon, your brother hasn't gotten laid?!" shouted Petey, feeling good, feeling rich. Money always brought out Pete's weathered sense of humor. "That's impossible," he wheezed. "He's related to you and he just spent three years in the minor leagues. Impossible! Even in Toledo!" The bar howled with drunken guffaws. Pete was on an unusual roll. He didn't win often enough to be this jovial on a regular basis.

"C'mon, you know what I mean," pleaded Natt. "He's introverted, a nice guy—plays the piano for Christ-sake. He's not like me. John's . . . all right."

"I've read his letters," grinned Tommy, trying to keep a straight face. "They've got to be stepbrothers."

"Jesus, Natty, you'd better cross your fingers he never makes it to the Highlanders," teased Pete.

Natt gave Pete and Tommy a determined look and said confidently, "He'll make it."

TOMMY'S BAR WAS not a fashionable place. It was just a bar. Nothing pretentious, nothing out of the ordinary. Just dark-stained oak and brass, all beaten, bruised, and singed from years of drinking, smoking, and heated conversation. Yet to its patrons, it was a charmed place. The clientele consisted largely of romantics, primarily dreamers who drank relatively well while discussing the big questions and devising easy money schemes. All the doorways from the front door to the kitchen, to Tommy's infamous back room were arched, like the doors of a castle or Spanish villa. They all believed it to be a taco stand before Tommy turned it into a bar. It still smelled of beer and beans and some other pungent odor that nobody could put their finger on. God knows they've spent nights trying—and drinking, and waiting for the season to begin. I suppose it was baseball that brought Tommy's Bar to life. When the season began, Tommy's became much more than a bar, it became a hopeful place. And it was hope that brought me to Tommy's, made us friends, Natt, John, Tommy, Pete, and myself.

Pete, who supported his sister Ruth and her two children as a health inspector for the City of New York, spent an exorbitant amount of time inspecting Tommy's television, primarily checking the ball game scores and testing his fate. Pete could love and hate the same team three times a week. Emotions ran high for a man who had the nerve to bet his entire paycheck on a whim or the ever popular hot tip. Two Face Pete was either elated or depressed, and there was never any doubt as to whether Pete had won or lost. Pete was the opposite of Natt who could mask his feelings as naturally as he could drink.

Natt Greco possessed a great deal of style. Had his life taken the turns he felt it should have, he might have been best friends with Frank Sinatra. Natt was confident, charming, always well-dressed, and he bore a striking resemblance to Walt Disney, which he used to his best advantage. Natt seemed always to be on the periphery of stardom, which was a location he gravely wanted to center. He concealed a quiet desperation through his good-natured affability and a firm, but thoughtful, management of other people's lives, most notedly his brother John's. "Relax," that was Natt's word, and he always used it either before or after giving what was known as *Natt-ly advice.* He gave extraordinary advice, chock-full of compassion with razor keen insight and a wise clarity of vision. Unfortunately, Natt's words only benefited others. It was as if he were unable to hear himself speak or were incapable of applying his common sense wisdom to his own circumstances. He was the sort of man who was referred to as a great guy, the sort of man who could motivate others.

Natt Greco and his brother John were good people. Only Natt was unable to believe that about himself. 'John was the good one,' he always thought. John Greco was a young man of considerable talent with a knack for walking into the best of all possible situations. He was a ballplayer capable of playing any position with a degree of competency that few could attain in just one. He could even pitch if necessary, but his strengths were at second base and catching. As Natt would say, "He's gonna go places." And once again Natt Greco was right. Natty had many opinions, but over the years he also taught John to believe in himself, to have confidence. What a wonderful gift to give his brother. It was an especially generous one after Natt became heartbroken and sickened by the rapid decline of his once great pitching arm. They say if not for Natt, John wouldn't have made the big leagues. Of course, it was Natt who spread that rumor.

In the years to come everyone would know John's story, even people who never liked baseball. John made it real hard for folks to dislike anything, especially baseball. He had a simple understanding of life that cut through the extraneous. He realized the guidance he'd received throughout his life was a blessing many go without. That recognition gave him wisdom far beyond his years, though few ever noticed that side of John Greco. In the end, John was the one who taught us all to be a little more forgiving and that you can't have too many friends.

I had to smile the first time I heard John interviewed. When asked whether he thought he had a good year, the question nearly confused him. He looked baffled, as though he truly didn't understand why the reporter had even asked. John, without any trace of sarcasm in his voice, answered as best he could, "Well . . . ah, yeah . . . I had a great year . . . I played baseball." I think with anybody else most of the bar would have fallen off their stools doubled up. But John was dead serious, and the simplicity of what he said had a dramatic effect on people. The cynics in the crowd thought he was an idiot, but we knew better.

When John walked into Tommy's that night, it was obvious Natt thought the world of his brother and vice versa.

"This kid is gonna do all the things my dead arm wouldn't let me do," declared Natt. "You wait and see. This year he'll be a Highlander, playing ball for the greatest professional organization ever. He's that good!" insisted Natt as he embarrassed the heck out of John. He then forced John to play Tommy's old upright piano and sing as if he were auditioning for Broadway. Natt wasn't trying to be mean; he was just drunk and proud and happy to see John. I suppose he wanted to show him off. Natt didn't play the piano very well, but he wasn't ashamed to sit down and play four-handed with his brother. I have to admit, Johney had a fine voice, deep and rich, a voice that made the women swoon.

"He's good. Right?" said Natt. His eyes sparkled with pride as John filled Tommy's Bar with soulful music.

When John later moved to the city, people would come to Tommy's Bar to hear and see the ballplayer with the haunting voice who played the piano. Tommy got a kick out of having a sports celebrity in his bar, so he eventually hired the young Greco to play five nights a week—the perfect off-season job for John and the perfect way for Natt to keep an eye on him, although Natt needed more surveillance than Johney ever did. Even on a slow night Natt could manage to find trouble, and most nights were slow nights at Tommy's Bar. Tommy liked it that way. He made a living. That's about as hard as he ever wanted to work. Most of the time it was just Tommy behind the bar, serving drinks to Pete and me and a handful of others. I guess Tommy really didn't want the extra business.

"I'm losing my tolerance for barroom chitchat, bullshit, and people of all walks of life," Tommy once said after his bar became fashionable for about six months. He was very much relieved when the smart set moved on to higher ground and left him alone. The older Tommy got, the more he wanted the place only for his friends and nobody else, no matter how much money he was making. The fashionable just couldn't understand Tommy's peculiar attitude. They would hand Tommy a five-dollar tip and expect free drinks, or at the very least extra service. But they never got it. Tommy wouldn't even ring his bell. He would pocket the money, barely say thank you, and go on about his business. I thought it was odd how they still tipped Tommy ostentatiously and called him by his first name, as if they were all old friends. Maybe that's what Tommy disliked the most. His friendship wasn't for sale, and he especially didn't like anybody who thought they could buy it with a five-dollar bill. Of course, he was too much of a businessman not to pocket their money anyway. "If they want to give it to me, I'll take it," he'd say.

Tommy really believed in family, tradition, and friendship; and he didn't take them lightly. Probably because he didn't have any family of his own. Funny how people tend to believe in what they don't have.   What he did have, were a few good friends with whom he considered to have a lifelong commitment. I was honored by Tommy's acceptance of me. He was a man of fierce loyalty.

My name is George. They call me Little George, because I am. Everyone sees me as a barfly, though I don't drink as much as I allow people to think. I like to keep up appearances. I couldn't do my job if I gave myself away. Most of the time I live in one room above Tommy's Bar. I have for quite awhile now. Tommy's my landlord, and I pay him a minimal sum for my dwelling, most of which I work off doing odd jobs about the bar. I'm kind of a handy man—maybe the handiest of all . . . I'm an angel.

There are many of us here with various assignments. Mine is John Greco and the preservation of his faith. By a cruel twist, John's life will not go as he worked and planned. Few ever do. But John's strength and decency are integral in keeping hope alive, and that is the one true fuel of the earth. So I came to help.

BASEBALL & BENEVOLENCE

I have a lot to tell you. This is a story that spans three decades, touches several lives, and accepts untimely death both just and unjust. I can't stop anything from happening, but if someone wants to hear me, I can guide and comfort them. My finest attribute is my ability to listen. People tell me things they would never tell anyone else. Many folks think I'm a little slow; I tend to stutter. Sometimes, due to people's assuming prejudices, such a blatant handicap can be misleading. In my case, it's helpful. People feel safe and will often share their innermost thoughts with me, and then they feel better. That is how I have come to know John Greco's story so well—he told me, and I was always there for him. I was always there.

John's path begins in 1959. It was a kind year for dreamers and the folks at Tommy's Bar. Things were looking up for America, too. The economy was strong. America led the world in most everything or, at least, everything that mattered to Americans. Cars, homes, family, and jobs—that's what mattered to Americans, pretty much in that order. In that optimistic year, NASA started the space program to combat the Soviets; the hula hoop was invented; Alaska and Hawaii became states.

Of course, for Natt every year was looking up. Each New Year's Eve Natt would say to me, "George, this is gonna be my year." And he believed it, especially after a few drinks; he was a pretty bad alcoholic. Natt believed in the power of positive thinking and that anything was possible. Those were the qualities that attracted people to him, especially women. He could never resist the women. To me, the many infidelities just highlighted his weaknesses. But on this night, in the winter of 1959, only his strengths were highlighted. Johney brought out the best in him.

"Tommy, can I have another beer?" John called from the piano.

Tommy gave Natt a look, as if to say, "What'd ya think, coach?"

Natt turned from his station at the bar and said, "Spring training," in his most authoritative and completely unnatural voice.

"C'mon, Natty, I've got a week before St. Petersburg. Where's your sense of occasion?" Natt could never resist that line. He had an overdeveloped sense of occasion. They never thought there would be a reason to stop celebrating. But the reasons would come with a crushing swiftness, and lifting a glass soon would have little to do with any kind of celebration.

I never saw Tommy more upset than on the day of the Grecos' tragedy— as it would come to be known. It was the day their luck ran out. Tommy would be devastated; so would most of the country. It went far beyond baseball. I think the whole nation felt victimized and, at the same time, maybe a bit guilty.

Nobody would understand how it could happen, including John Greco himself. I watched John that night at Tommy's as he laughed and toasted with Natt, and I thought about how years from now he would sit at that same piano and spend countless hours battling a never-ending picture show, reviewing each frame in merciless detail until it'd frustrate him to the point of near insanity. He'd play softly the way Tommy liked, though somewhat awkwardly, covering mostly old standards, only real slow and bluesy—sad stuff. Tommy liked that, too. Sometimes he'd sing in his gravelly voice. But he would only sing if the urge hit him, which usually meant when he was drunk. He didn't get drunk very often, except for during the rough years.

John would need me most during those confusing years, when he would try to remember, when he would search for answers, looking for ways to feel good about himself again and about the game he loved so deeply. I guess, in a way Johney was chasing a dream he once had about himself and the country—maybe even the world.

Some of the moments John would relive while sitting at that piano really hurt him, and some would have seemed impossible to believe, but I did. And that would ease his pain . . . and keep him searching in the right direction.

Over the years and along his path, John Greco would amass friends from all over the country. Some would know him through baseball; most would remember the misfortune that befell his family, but no one would ever forget the two incredible events of his lifetime. The miracles. That is what this story is about. Miracles. John's miracles.

2

NEW YORK CITY is a place for the hopeful with very little mercy for anyone—especially the dreamers. Natt knew if he didn't work, and work hard, the city would eventually make him pay for his indulgences. He had a family to take care of, and maybe soon, his brother as well. John's care wouldn't be financial—more like protective custody from his own trusting nature.

The Greco brothers were well acquainted with hard work. As teenagers, Natt and John sweated out the summers in their father's machine shop. The shop, appropriately named Sun Tool & Die, was really just an old garage with no air conditioning and poor ventilation. The smell of machine oil hung in the air and clung to the body like a leech. Natt said the worst thing about working in the shop was that there was no way you were going to impress a girl, smelling like that. He said you could shower for an hour and still detect the lingering malodorous scent of machine oil. He said it would have made a solid base for a powerfully bad perfume; perfect if the required effect was to repel people.

The other drawback to working in the shop was their father's partner, Ray. He was a stingy egomaniac who ran the business side of the operation. Pay was strictly minimum wage with no chance of ever making anything more. Natt and John knew their father felt bad about Ray's labor laws and worked doubly hard to help their dad out . . . and prove their worth. Mr. Greco believed in an honest dollar for an honest day's work. Something he knew his sons weren't going to get as long as Ray was around. The last straw for Mr. Greco was when Ray wanted to hire illegal immigrants at well below the minimum, a common practice at Ray's father's shop in Jersey City. Ray's dad was a well-known "bastard" in the industry, even Ray didn't like him. Of course, Ray was just like his father.

Mr. Greco had been a proud union man for twenty-five years, often working double shifts to give his family the American dream. Twenty-five years of hard work before realizing his dream—opening his own shop.

"All that, only to end up with Ray," joked Natt, bitterly.

Mr. Greco soon pulled out of his hard won goal. He felt it was hypocritical to be partners with Ray. Guy Greco was a man of true working-class principles. He didn't see his association with Ray as a good lesson for his sons.

"We liked working with our dad. It was all he ever wanted," said John.

"We would've worked for him no matter what that prick Ray said or did," stated Natt.

So Guy Greco's dream ended, but Natt and John's were just beginning. I suppose that's the way it is between fathers and sons.

NATT'S ASPIRATIONS, LIKE Johney's, began and ended with base-ball, only Natt's ended much sooner. After a disappointing season of pitching for the Buffalo Bisons, Natt was released, moved to New York City, and started his own roofing business. He was a big success, primarily because he was a relentless salesman. Eventually he became a good roofer, too, though he was never quite satisfied with just being a roofer. Natty liked to call himself an actor, though he had no training whatsoever and, to my knowledge, never actually auditioned for anything. I'm sure he would've been great, and I know he would've loved the attention. Natty was a handsome man who enjoyed making an entrance. He was always more than willing to entertain with a story or a joke. Natt looked and acted like somebody important. He paid for a good haircut and manicure, and was generous with the gratuities. A strikingly powerful man, Natt stood six-foot-three with broad shoulders from carrying fifty-pound stacks of shingles up a ladder, two at a time. He sported a healthy tan from working outdoors and looked like a movie star because of it. He had an image, and he was the only gambler I've ever met who was really good at it. Two Face Pete was always after him for the *inside lowdown*. It seemed as though that was the only time Petey ever won.

Even after John became a famous ballplayer, Natt had no problem being his brother. I would think jealousy would be common in a situation like that but not from Natt. In fact, he would use his family connection with his Highlander brother in pursuit of business . . . or pleasure . . . namely, women. He openly admitted that he got most of his roofing jobs by introducing himself to prospective clients as Natt Greco, brother of John Greco—the New York Highlander. Then he would smile, showing off his perfect teeth, maybe even making a gesture like a ballplayer tipping his cap.

On the other hand John Greco, almost six feet tall and 180 pounds, was the quiet type. Johney was easygoing, a forgiving person by nature. Like his brother before him, John made the All-State baseball team as a pitcher and lettered in three sports. He passed his senior lifesaving swimming course as a high school sophomore, making him eligible for a much more interesting summer job than his father's machine shop—lifeguard at the Mountain Edge Swim Club in Mountain Edge, New Jersey, an honored profession with beautiful scenery and a good smell.

From his magical voice to his gentle persona, Johney was different. In 1959, his looks didn't match his manner. He had hair slightly over his ears, which was long for then. He wore T-shirts and jeans and often rolled a pack of "smokes" into the sleeve of his shirt, exposing a tattoo that he had gotten as a teen down at the Jersey shore. The tattoo, a heart with a single bolt of lightening slashing through it, made him look like a tough guy, but he wasn't. It was a good look for a catcher though. When asked about the tattoo, Johney merely replied, "It sounded like a good idea at the time." He had nothing to prove that he couldn't prove on a ball field. He wouldn't flinch when a 95 m.p.h. fastball cut up and under his chin. They say he'd rather take the hit than be moved off the plate; and I've seen him take many hits.

All along, Johney proved to have the courage to face his fears and the restraint to do what's right. Some people say John Greco must have had a guardian angel. In a way, he had two. Natt was his protector and I was his confessor, his source of absolution.

The brothers had wanted one thing growing up: to someday play professional ball together. Only it didn't work out after Natt lost his lightening up in Buffalo. Natt 's share of the dream was over, but he never gave up wishing it for Johney. That's the way it should be between brothers, even men as different as the Grecos. Natt was the slick act. John was all blood and guts and heart, the real thing, a Highlander—the way the history books wanted to remember ballplayers.

3

New York City: Summer, 1959

JOHN'S CALL TO the show took everybody by surprise, even Natt. It came right after a game with the Louisville Redbirds, a game that left Johney feeling kind of queasy, having just gone for the collar (0 for 5) against a pitcher he considered to be very hittable.

"John . . . it's for you," called his landlady. She held the phone until he climbed down the stairs. Maybe she had a feeling it was good news. She gave him a sweet smile as she handed him the receiver. I think she just liked to hear him talk.

"Hello."

"John Greco?" asked a gruff, commanding voice.

"Uh-huh," replied John with no idea to whom he was speaking.

"Dillon Southwood. I'd like you to take the next train to New York. The Highlanders bought your contract."

"Yes, sir," gushed John, stunned.

"Sam Fouler just went down with a wrist injury . . . damn! We've had a lot of them! A whole rash of 'em. Injuries that is," he said, sounding very frustrated. "We need a good, solid utility man. A guy who can catch—like yourself. So, ah, get to the stadium by noon. Nick Moratta, the clubhouse man, he'll suit you up. Alright?!"

"Yes, sir! And, and, and—thank you, sir, Manager Southwood."

"Ah, just be at the stadium," said Southwood as he hung up the phone.

John swung his landlady around in a little dance. "I'm going! I'm playing for the Highlanders!"

THERE IT WAS, what he'd always dreamt about, played out just as Natt said it would. Funny, he really thought his chances were remote at best, though he wouldn't say that out loud. Natt was always the true believer. Even the guys that made it to the minor leagues only had a one-in-sixty shot of making it to the majors. Sometimes luck has a lot to do with things. A kid could have plenty of talent, say, at second base, but if his major league club had an all-star second baseman, well, that kid could rot on the vine waiting for a call. His only opportunity would be if another player had an injury or if he were traded to someplace where they needed his skills. Obviously, it would be bad luck to wish for an injury and unfortunate to have to leave the organization where you came up. John Greco's versatility put him in the right place at the right time, a very valuable quality. And he was lucky. Of course luck, as defined by Natt, meant to be prepared for the unknown.

It was on July 28th, 1959, that John Greco arrived at Grand Central Station. 'I'm a major league ballplayer now,' he thought. 'Even if they send me back tomorrow, I could say I made it to the majors.' The number four train took him directly to Ruth Memorial Stadium where he would play his first game as a New York Highlander.

In his fourth and, by far, best season in the bush, John had been praised in the local papers as a hard-nosed, versatile, fundamentally sound player. He was batting a respectable .283, with eight home runs, and 39 RBI. He'd come a long way from his shaky debut in Toledo, a bumpy start that Natt attributed more to culture shock and loneliness than anything else.

"He almost didn't make it past the first year," Natt once said. "Girl problems distracted him, ya know, first time away from home." I remember Natt flying to Toledo in the spring of 1956 to help Johney out. "He's not much of a ladies' man," Natt had added. "The first time he got laid he wanted to marry the girl." Natt had finished his martini and made a satisfying "aaaah" sound after he had eaten the liquor saturated olive. "He was eighteen," Natty had said, in between sips, with a smile. His face had been all flushed from his fifth drink in an hour. "She didn't even like him that much . . . ya know what she said?"

"No, what'd she say?" Petey had asked, dying to know.

"She said, she said, 'John who?'" The bar crowd had exploded with laughter. "You should've seen her! Tits out to here! She had her arm around another ballplayer while I was talking to her. I think he had better stats!"

It wasn't all that funny to Johney at the time, but he got over it, even laughed about it when he interrupted Natt in midstory one night. "Second time," corrected John, after Natt said it was his first.

ON THE DAY John arrived in New York to join the Highlanders, none of the gang at Tommy's even knew he was in town. It was just another night there. The game would go on at eight o'clock, about the same time all the regulars would file in, Natt included. Sometimes he'd bring Faye, but most of the time he didn't. Faye stayed home with their son Charlie. She didn't seem all that interested in socializing. I didn't get the feeling that things were going so well between them. They had a rough and unexpected start to their marriage. What a shame. They made an attractive couple. Maybe they both felt more obligated to marriage than ready for it. We all make mistakes, but Natt couldn't see how Faye might have felt trapped, too. They both needed some time and space. But then, Natt had the unfair advantage; he didn't have to stay home with the baby. And so he spent most of his time in Tommy's Bar, drinking with his buddies, doping out the horses, picking up women, while trying to figure out why he didn't feel like a father. He was a good man, with good intentions, but like most people, often misdirected by his own convenient rationale of his actions. Natty had some tough years because of it. He learned more than he wanted to know about himself, but he did learn. Of course, nobody but Natt, and maybe John, knew he was going through any kind of difficulties at all.

WHEN JOHN GOT to the ballpark, he was greeted by Nick Moratta, the clubhouse man. Nick chain smoked, laughed a lot, and had lines in his face that looked like a metropolitan road map. He was famous for his practical jokes and was in his forty-ninth year with the organization.

"You'll wear twenty-three. That's a good number," said Nick, as he handed John his uniform. John took the wool jersey and pants from Nick and mechanically sat down on the bench in front of his new locker. He always thought he'd feel something . . . joy, elation . . . something, but all he felt was numb. "You okay, kid? I usually get a bigger reaction when I hand a rookie his pinstripes," said Nick in his best grouchy old man voice. The grouchy was just an act. Folks sort of expected that from him. I guess anybody associated with the Highlanders was expected to be a bit of a character. The organization had a reputation to keep up.

"I'm fine," mumbled John, choked up. The words barely made it past his lips.

Nick grabbed him by the shoulders as if he wanted to shake some sense into him. "Could you say that again?"

"I'm okay?" John said, questioning his motives. Nick's face lit up like a Christmas tree.

"Whooooo-wee . . . shit! That's some voice you got. I hope you can hit as deep as that voice!"

"I do, too," agreed John. Nick sat down next to him as Muddy Ames walked past. Muddy gave them a slight smile.

"Hey, Mud! Say hello to the new kid, John Greco!" said Nick, playing the tricks of a seventy-seven-year-old school boy.

"Hey, John," called Ames.

John returned his greeting with, "Mr. Ames, sir," which stopped Muddy dead in his tracks. He gave the kid a look, obviously reacting to his polite manner and voice. He thought about making a wisecrack, then decided against it.

"Good luck, Greco," said Muddy, as he made his way back to his locker. Old Nick was delighted.

"You'll be fine. Just play your game," chuckled Nick, as he gave John a grandfatherly pat on the back. He grabbed a bunch of dirty jerseys and was about to leave the locker room when John called out to him.

"Nick?"

"Yeah?"

"Is there a phone—nobody knows I'm here."

"Sure, kid. It's right outside of Manager Southwood's office." John looked confused. He had no idea where the manager's office was. Nick pointed to a door. "Make a right, last door on the left . . . the phone's just outside the office."

"Thanks. Nick?"

Nick turned slowly, "Yes?"

"Where's the field?"

"You'll find it," he said, and he turned and walked away. John could tell he was laughing. But he was right; Johney did find the field and the phone and a career. What he didn't find on that midsummer day was his brother. His line was busy, so John decided to try his parents. His mom answered the phone.

"Hi, Mom. It's me. I'm calling from Ruth Memorial Stadium. I've been called up!"

There was a moment of silence while Mrs. Greco collected herself.

"I don't believe it!" she finally said. "Ooooh, Johney, I'm so happy for you!" He could tell she was starting to cry. "Let me get your father!" Before he could say another word he could hear his mom calling for his dad. 'Probably in the middle of staining furniture or something,' John thought.

"Dad! Come . . . John's on the phone! He's in New York!" called his mother with excitement.

"John?!" said Guy Greco, a little out of breath.

"Dad, I'm really here. I'm a Highlander. I might even play tonight."

"Oh, that's great, son. You did real good for yourself. I can't—"

"Dad?"

"I'm sorry. My throat is so tight. I can't believe the day finally came, John. Your mom's crying. We're just a mess here," said Mr. Greco, trying to make light of it.

"Did you call your brother?" asked Betty Greco, now on the other line.

"His line was busy, Mom. I'll try him again."

"You know how proud we are of you. And, and Natt's just gonna burst," said his dad.

"I know. Thanks. . . . I love you . . . okay?"

"We love you, too," said his mom.

"Wish me luck. I gotta get dressed and out on the field."

IT WAS ABOUT eleven o'clock at Tommy's Bar when a rookie, named John Greco, stepped up to the plate in the ninth inning to bat for the New York Highlanders. The sound on the television was turned off. The juke box played. Natt Greco sat at the bar talking to Tommy, sweating out a 2-2 tie with Cleveland while a local girl named Lucy hung all over him. He must have had a lot of money riding on the game; he was beginning to ignore Lucy. Tommy was making him another martini when Natt grabbed his wrist.

"Turn up the sound! Turn up the sound!" Natt shouted as he tightened his grip on Tommy's wrist. Tommy followed Natt's eyes to the television screen.

"Tommy, that's my brother . . . my God, it's Johney."

"Turn off the fucking juke!" bellowed Tommy. The music died, only to be taken over by the voice of Phil Rizzuto, the Highlander announcer.

"All right now . . . first game in the big leagues for rookie John Greco. Just called up from Toledo. This is his second at-bat after coming in for the injured Steve Carter at third. He's looking for his first big league hit and what a time this would be to get it. What a position for the young switch hitting Greco. Okay. We're all tied up in the bottom of the ninth at two, one out, and Muddy Ames on second. A single wins it for the

Highlanders. What a position for the young rookie. I'll tell you what— if this kid gets a hit, the whole town will be in love with 'im."

Lucy snuggled up to Natt.

"Not now," said Natt, shaking her off. "Not in front of my brother."

"What do ya mean?" snipped Lucy. "He's on TV!"

"Just that . . . never in front of my brother!" Lucy glared at him, picked up her purse, and left.

There wasn't a sound in the bar besides the game. No one could believe what they were seeing . . . well, except Natt.

"I got a hundred bucks that sez he doesn't hit," shouted Smithy Lango, shattering the quiet, stepping all over a special moment. Mr. Lango was known as a local "sleazeball" who came in every once in awhile, usually to collect from Two Face Pete. Tommy looked like he wanted to kill him, but Natt backed him off with a glance.

"I'll take that bet," said Natt, never looking at Lango. Natt's eyes stayed fixed on the television screen and his brother. Lango smiled as if he'd just made an easy hundred, though he was still angry with Tommy for turning off the juke box. Mr. Lango paced around the silent box perturbed about the attention he was no longer receiving and by Natt's self-control.

John fouled off three in a row. He was just a bit behind the major league fastball. The count went to two and two, same as the score. The pitch was a curve ball out of the strike zone that John almost went around on. The catcher asked for the appeal from the first base umpire. He flashed the safe sign. John still had life, and the count went to full.

"What bullshit! He went around!" yelled Smithy from the back of the bar. Nobody was too concerned with his opinion.

The room seemed to flinch with every swing of the bat, every wind-up and release, every motion made by the umpire. John swung at the next pitch, another curve ball that he just got a piece of, protecting the plate. The camera zoomed in on the Cleveland pitcher who faked a throw to second, spit, adjusted himself, and started into his wind-up. The pitch was a fastball, around 90 m.p.h., and fouled again.

"Shit!" shouted Smithy Lango, kicking Tommy's juke box. Tommy gave him a menacing look.

Natt sat quietly, then started talking to the television.

"Go to the dirt, Johney. Go to the dirt."

"What's 'go to the dirt' mean?" asked Tommy, mesmerized by the at-bat.

"He relaxes himself by pushing dirt around with his bat. It helps him to concentrate, clear his head. It's a timing thing."

Tommy tried to look as though he understood and said, "Uh-huh."

"It gives him something to do," whispered Natt, feeling nervous for his brother.

John called for time, stepped out, then back into the batter's box and began to stir the sandy earth with the barrel of his bat. He then cocked it back into hitting position.

"He's doing it." said Tommy, amazed.

"I know. I know," replied Natty, trying not to act surprised.

"The pitch. Fouled off again!" announced Rizzuto.

"Two hundred bucks he doesn't get a hit!" challenged Smithy Lango, swinging a bottle of beer by its neck, grinning, already spending his money.

"Fuck you!" yelled Petey. "Give the guy a break. It's his brother!"

"I'll take his bet," said Natt in a soft emotionless voice, as he continued to study every movement John made.

"You're on!" shouted Smithy. "He's not gonna hit if he's anything like his bullshit brother."

"Greco at the plate. . . . This has been a strong at-bat for the rookie. Full count; Muddy at second; one out in the bottom of the ninth inning! John's pushing some dirt around again. He sets himself. The pitch. He pulls it into left field! Muddy Ames will score! The Highlanders win! Holy cow! The rookie John Greco just up from Toledo comes up with the gamer for the 'Landers in the ninth! Make sure he gets the ball!"

The bar erupted as the camera panned to John being congratulated by his new teammates. Natt threw both arms in the air like an official making the touchdown sign.

"That's my brother! Damn-it! That's my kid brother!" he shouted at the television. "Drinks for everyone! My God, Johney's a New York Highlander!"

Tommy gladly served the drinks and declared the second round on him. I've never seen Natt happier than on that steamy, hot July night. I guess half a dream is better than none. His brother was in the big leagues and moving to New York where they could be together again. There were no words to describe just how important that was to Natt. It was as though they were two halves of the same person. Natty was so excited, he didn't notice Smithy Lango leave without paying him the two hundred dollars. On that night, he didn't care. Money wasn't important; only his brother was important.

4

JOHN FINISHED HIS half-rookie season with a respectable .286 average, 41 RBI, and to everyone's surprise 13 home runs—more power than he'd ever shown before. He was getting stronger. The Highlanders finished an uncomfortable third that year; too many injuries. But they wouldn't have to wait long before they were back in the Series.

The biggest problem John had in 1959 was a nagging toothache that he'd put off getting fixed until the end of the season. Even that worked out to his best advantage. By December the pain had grown so persistent that he had to go to the dentist. The art of dentistry was barbaric in the late fifties, and dentists in general made him weak in the knees. His fear didn't last long, because it was at the dentist's office that John met Sharon Costa.

She had long, dark brown hair with green eyes that sparkled when she smiled; a strong, athletic, perfectly proportioned body; radiant skin he wanted to touch. John couldn't keep himself from staring. He felt an attraction stronger than he ever had felt before. He was captivated by her, and, eventually, she by him. Sharon wore blue jeans that seemed to be too big for her with a lot of material gathered at the belt around her tiny waist. She also wore a sweatshirt tucked into her jeans that read Princeton in large collegiate letters. She smelled of lilacs and mint. Her fragrance seemed at odds with the antiseptic odor of the office, which smelled like most doctors' offices and grammar schools, some kind of government disinfectant issued at graduation to kill the germs of sick people and little kids. Not a romantic smell, but it was a memorable odor nonetheless with a new and vastly improved association for John.

Johney's love life wasn't as successful as his baseball career. Only once did I see him leave the bar with a woman, attractive too. Natty said John never learned how to pick up women or how to tell he was being hit on, and he wasn't fond of women liking him just because he was a ballplayer. John once told me that whenever he dated a girl who wanted to go out with a ballplayer all she wanted to do was meet other ballplayers.

"And if she did," he said, looking embarrassed, "well, that was the end of our date."

When John saw Sharon Costa, he knew things were going to be different, and that his luck was still running strong. As it turned out, Sharon wasn't all that pleased to see him at first, though it was nothing personal. She simply thought the doctor had double booked the time. John took a seat and picked up a copy of *Life* magazine. He had trouble keeping his eyes on the magazine, and he couldn't help but notice that the drilling didn't seem to bother her.

"What time is your appointment?" Sharon asked in an accusing tone.

'Is she talking to me?' John asked himself. He wasn't sure, but realized he was the only person in the room. 'So, she must be . . . Answer her,' he told himself as he reviewed the upside-down photos and print of the sizable magazine. He felt self-conscious and even more ridiculous not knowing what to do. 'What would Natt do?' —a question he often asked himself. Casually he placed the magazine down on the seat next to him, desperately trying not to draw attention to himself. It was to no avail—his motion was so stilted, and Sharon was already looking straight at him. They each pretended not to notice the magazine thing. Sharon bit her bottom lip in an effort not to laugh and at the same time suppressed the throbbing of a huge cavity.

'He's shy . . . and cute,' she noted, just as a sharp pain kicked in, limiting any further thought. John found himself in an unfamiliar situation. He really wanted to meet her.

When Sharon wasn't attending college, she lived in Astoria, Queens, with her parents and younger brother, Mark. Princeton, New Jersey, was only thirty minutes away from where John grew up, but light years away from his working-class background. Sharon was home for the Christmas holidays and some emergency dentistry. The English/Italian daughter of Mike and Joan Costa now had John's complete attention and wasn't sure what, if anything, to do about it. She was going into her last semester of college and would graduate in the spring with a degree in political science. Sharon didn't date much; she was a driven student with career ambitions every bit as serious as John's. As I already told you, Johney didn't date much either, and he had never dated a college girl, let alone an Ivy League woman. He was intimidated.

"Do you have a one o'clock appointment, too?" she asked again.

After considering his answer carefully, fearful of saying the wrong thing, John said, "Oh . . . ah, no. I'm at two o'clock."

"You're a little early," she smiled. 'Why would anyone be an hour early to the dentist?'

He smiled back, considered how crazy being an hour early sounded and did something he'd never done in his life. He started to babble.

"I always end up at places I don't want to be . . . ah, early. You know. To get it over with. That's how I do it. I throw myself . . . in—to—it. Ha! . . . The opposite of being late. I guess." 'What a stupid thing to say,' he instantly thought. John put his hand to his brow and shook his head in a self-deprecating gesture.

Sharon liked him. She thought him to be sweet, handsome, even charming in a real folksy way. But what cut through all her pain was his voice. Its rich, masculine tone gave her goose bumps and sent a rush of adrenaline through her body. There was an awkward silence. They both wanted to talk but neither one of them could think of a thing to say; two minds, two blanks . . . tie score. So, there they were with silly grins on their faces and no words on their lips to ease the awkwardness. Sharon couldn't decide if he was hitting on her or not. 'Was this a novel approach?' she asked herself. But the throbbing in her molar didn't allow these thoughts serious consideration.

"I'm sorry if I sounded aggravated. I'm in a lot of pain," she said, pointing to her mouth. She noticed herself apologizing for nothing. It was a habit she was trying to break.

"I understand. That's why I'm here," John said. "You go to Princeton? I grew up just down the street in Mountain Edge."

"It's my last year."

"That's great." 'That's great? I can't think of anything better to say than *that's great*?' John thought, beginning to feel inadequate. "I never went to college," he said in a fit of honesty.

She gave him a strange look. He visualized a stream of blood spewing from his neck. 'Honest,' she thought, a quality that ranked high on her list. "Are you an actor?"

"An actor? No. My brother is the actor in the family. What made you think I was an actor?" asked John, flattered that she thought he could be an actor and even more delighted to be engaged in a conversation.

"Well, a lot of actors don't go to college and . . . your voice. You have a very nice speaking voice."

"Thanks. I like to sing."

"So, you're a musician?" He could see she liked the idea, that she respected musicians.

"Yeah, I'm a musician. Piano, sing a little—down at Tommy's. Downtown on University?"

"I don't know it. I just turned twenty-one."

"Well, maybe you can come to Tommy's some night."

"Maybe."

"Sharon, the doctor will see you now," said the nurse.

'What am I saying? I don't know this man. I'm only home for two weeks.' She felt as though she weren't really in the room, as if she were listening and watching herself flirt from above. Apparently her mind had no control over her actions. Sharon was a very practical young woman. The loss of self-control bothered her almost as much as his voice. She got up to follow the nurse into the doctor's office. Then she watched herself turn back to John and say, "Maybe the nurse can give you my number. I don't think I'll be able to after this."

"Great, I'll call you tonight then," said John, amazed by the fortunate turn of events. That was John Greco's secret; he could make things happen, but at the time he was unaware of his instrumental ability. His joy and excitement numbed the effect of primitive dentistry. 'It would've been a good day to remove wisdom teeth,' he reasoned.

Sharon moved slowly as she passed John on her way out of the office. Her mouth full of Novocain, unable to speak, she managed only a small wave as she was about to leave.

"Sharon," John called out. She turned, trying not to reveal too much of her puffy cheeks. "The name is John . . . John Greco," he stated with all the confidence of Errol Flynn.

Sharon smiled, then pulled a small pad and pen from out of her bag and wrote, "What a Wonderful World."

"A request?" he asked.

"Mr. Greco, the doctor will see you now."

Sharon nodded her head and left for home.

BASEBALL & BENEVOLENCE

THE DAY AFTER their unexpected dentist meeting, Sharon and John had their first date—almost. Sharon found out John wasn't just a musician when he picked her up at the house in Astoria.

He had called her that same night after allowing a few hours for the Novocain to wear off. Sharon agreed to go out to dinner and maybe a drink at Tommy's afterwards. They talked a little about their families, but not much more was said. After all, they were young, very attracted to each other, and very much afraid of saying the wrong thing. The energy was in their voices, and for the moment that was all that mattered.

John tried on every shirt he had and decided that none was right. This was his first real date, the first time he'd ever asked a woman out to dinner. In anticipation, he decided to buy himself some new clothes, some nice clothes. Johney was still wearing the same stuff he had in high school. He knew they wouldn't do if he wanted to make a good impression on Sharon and her family.

Remembering Natt's favorite place to shop, he went to Barney's and bought his first suit: navy blue, double breasted, English. He looked like a real blue blood. He paid ten extra dollars for same day alterations. Then he bought himself a new white shirt and a rich looking burgundy tie with a twisting blue and grey pen stroke pattern. The salesman said it was an outstanding look. John thought it was something Natt might like. He wanted to do everything just right. As he shopped, John tried to picture Sharon's home. 'An Ivy League girl; probably lives in an old English Tudor. Her father will want to interview me in the study, possibly over a brandy and a good cigar. The smell of leather will be in the air; maybe a St. Bernard lying by the fireplace. Everybody will be well-dressed for the family dinner.' These thoughts and other equally misguided notions rambled through John's head. He obviously never had been to Astoria, Queens.

He started to get ready for the date about four hours beforehand. He spent the final two hours sitting around the apartment in his new suit. Every five minutes or so he would check himself in the mirror or brush his teeth. It seemed as though Johney's social skills had been stunted. While most men went through this stage in their teens, he was just getting around to it at the age of twenty-two, almost twenty-three. When John was a teenager, he didn't have a car or particularly like cars all that much. He thought the fixing and cleaning and maintaining took up too much time. The girls weren't impressed with his sensible logic and that didn't help his social life. He was a serious kid who did and studied what he wanted and nothing else.

"He has a one-track mind," said Guy Greco of his son, usually it wasn't meant as a compliment. Guy felt his boy might have been missing out on the youthful wonders of high school.

About two hours before the date, with his suit beginning to show signs of rumpling and his teeth sparkling, John attempted to practice conversation. He felt uncomfortable in a suit and tie. He walked like a manikin and smiled at himself in the mirror as he pretended to meet the family. He then spent a lot of time trying to think of witty things to talk about, but came up with nothing.

The date was December 16, 1959. It was twenty-eight degrees outside. The night air had a crisp, clean quality about it and John was finally on his way to Sharon's home. As he walked to the subway, Johney realized that he had neglected to buy himself an overcoat. The wind whipped around the buildings, stealing his breath and robbing him of his color. Fortunately, he was able to warm up on the ride to Queens.

When he arrived, John took a deep breath and stepped out onto the above ground Broadway subway station, which was modestly decorated in red and green holiday lights and ribbons. There was snow on the ground in Astoria, not much, just enough to give everything that quiet, muffled sound. John took this to be a good omen. Like most ballplayers he had his superstitions and snow was one of them. Snow was always a good sign. As a kid, it meant a day off from school and sleigh riding with friends. As an adult, it meant unexpected good luck.

In Queens he bought candy, flowers, and cigars, figuring he'd cover all the bases. John was sort of out of touch with the times and his own generation. He envisioned dating the way he saw it in the movies: Cary Grant in pursuit of Ingrid Bergman. Cary was sophisticated, debonair, charming, and that's what worried him. He knew that he was none of the above. John trusted in the movies. They were how he passed many long nights, watching them in small towns all across America. They helped him get by when the ball game ended and the friends left. They made him feel closer to home. Because of the movies, John thought America was as innocent as the game of baseball itself. He believed in the romantic idealism Hollywood produced through its Golden Era.

John had never been to Queens before and was surprised to find that it looked a lot like Mountain Edge, New Jersey. It was filled with regular old houses, nothing special, row after row of homes built right on top of each other with no yards to speak of and apartment buildings interspersed every so often. It was middle class. I suppose that was the real similarity. There were Christmas lights on everything from the small shrubs and trees to the street lamps, to the houses themselves, framed in geometrical patterns. Front doors were decorated as presents. Santa and his reindeer were parked on the rooftops and in the tiny yards, sometimes right along side Jesus, Joseph, Mary, the three wise men, and a flock of pink plastic flamingos. Modest electric candles burned in the windows while the apartment buildings hung evergreen wreaths with large red bows just outside of their entrances. As John walked to Sharon's house, snow began to fall ever so slightly, as if it hadn't planned to do so. It was his first snowfall of the year and in New York. Its silencing effect was magnified a thousand times in the City and made John feel very young and fortunate as he listened to the snow crunching under foot and the cry of child's play. The sounds made him think of Christmas and the mint-condition Washington Senators' Walter Johnson card he was going to give Natt. 'Natty loved to collect cards,' he thought, 'and the Johnson would be a real prize.'

I know Christmas means many things to many people. Some people can't bear its memories or tolerate its commercialism. Some folks can't help but think of old friends and family and feel regret for relationships long gone. John understood none of this. Christmas made him feel happy, like a child, as though everything were going to be all right or a slate had been cleaned by the season and the snow, making a new beginning possible. He thought about the movies and felt the urge to sing, even dance, maybe both. But his arrival at Sharon's home put an end to his romantic daydreams as he felt himself tense up.

"Hi. Is Shar—on—" John began, then stopped himself in midsentence when he saw the look of shock, or was it fear, on the boy's face. Mark, Sharon's brother, dropped his jaw, exposing an intricate labyrinth of silver braces. John wasn't sure what to do. Nobody had ever reacted to him in quite this way.

"You're—a—Highlander," extracted Mark, barely able to dig out the words.

"Well, ah . . . yeah," said John. "You're Mark, right?" John was trying to be friendly; the kid looked as though he were about to hurt himself. John extended his hand to him, more to hold the boy up than anything else.

"I'm John," he said.

"I know, John Greco! Number 23—You're going out with my sister?!" he said in disbelief, then made a screwy face.

"Is your sister Sharon?"

"Yeah."

"Afraid so," said John.

Mark turned to the staircase and screamed, "Sharon! . . . John's hereeee!!!!!"

"Can I come in?"

"Sure. What's all that stuff?" asked the boy, referring to the roses and cigars but mostly to the huge five-pound box of candy.

"Oh, ah . . . here." He handed the candy and cigars to Mark. "Would ya give these to your folks for me. The cigars are for your dad." Sharon appeared at the top of the staircase unfazed by Mark's scream.

"I see you've met my brother," she said. Mark held the boxes like two footballs, still gawking at John in amazement. Sharon looked stunning in a white cocktail dress cut just above the knee. Her hair was pulled back off her face revealing her sculpted cheekbones, dimples, and lovely neck. She wore a black onyx necklace and very little makeup. Sharon smiled graciously to John. She was very beautiful.

"Mark, tell Mom and Dad we're leaving."

"He's John Greco . . . you know! John Greco!" exclaimed Mark, unable to comprehend his sister's coolness.

"Dad! Dad!" Mark shouted as he ran into the next room. Sharon followed her normally normal nine-year-old brother with a suspicious gaze.

"He's not usually like this," she said.

"There's something I should tell you," said John, feeling a bit guilty.

At that moment Mr. Costa bellowed from the dining room, "Sharon, bring your date in to meet your mother."

The family was about to have dinner. Sharon took John by the hand and led him through the living room and into the dining room. The living room was decorated in white French Provincial furniture, the couch and matching chairs covered in plastic. There was a mismatched, uncovered love seat that seemed to clash with the wall-to-wall carpet which was an odd shade of olive green, probably a brighter shade at one time, and a bit worn. There was a piano in one corner and family photographs everywhere. John felt right at home. The Christmas tree stood in front of the bay window, the focal point of the living room. The star on top missed the ceiling by a thumbnail and the tree itself was wide and very thick, as if it meant to grow into every inch of the room. Sharon's mom, Joan Costa, had hung a light-up Santa with a bright red nose on the wall of the dining room. Sharon's dad, Mike Costa, thought it was silly, tacky, and extremely funny. Santa became a Costa family tradition. "Mom hangs Santa and Dad hangs his little cracked bell on the tree. He found it in the garbage when he was seven. They're our traditions," Sharon would later tell John.

Mr. Costa was dishing out spaghetti with clam sauce while Mark was going on about Sharon's date. He obviously didn't believe his young son, certain it was simply a case of mistaken identity. But he wanted to see for himself just the same. Mark stood by his dad hardly able to contain himself as he awaited his father's reaction. Mike was a big diehard Highlander fan. He was big period. Mr. Costa was in midsentence, something about "showing the kid Santa," when Sharon brought John into the dining room. Mike had never seen anybody famous before, in person, and he certainly had never *met* anybody famous. One glance at John Greco and the plate of spaghetti slipped through his fingers and onto the floor. The man was so embarrassed he didn't know what to do with himself. John immediately hit the floor in an effort to pick up the fallen pasta. It wasn't his intention to further embarrass Sharon's dad; it was just a natural reaction.

"Son, please don't do that," said Mr. Costa. "We'll clean it up." Mike slowly extended his hand to help John up. John handed the plate to Sharon who couldn't understand why everybody was acting so *weird.* Her father kept gazing at John as if he was an ancient idol.

"John Greco," uttered Mike Costa in a hazy, dreamy voice, all the while grinning from ear to ear.

"You know him?!" questioned Sharon, astounded by her father's reaction. Never in her life had her dad seemed so impressed by someone. 'Not an easy man to get a reaction from, and John just turned him inside out,' she thought.

"Pleasure to meet you, sir," said John. He shook Mike's hand. His tone of voice was very respectful, which helped Mr. Costa regain his composure.

"Dad, Sharon doesn't know!" insisted Mark, pulling at his father's sleeve.

Sharon handed the plate of dangling spaghetti to her mother who was also trying to figure out what was going on.

"He didn't tell you?" inquired Mike Costa of his daughter.

"Tell me? Tell me what? Is he wanted?!"

"No. I'm not wanted," John butted in. "They know me from baseball. I'm a baseball player."

"A baseball player!" laughed Mike Costa. "He's not just a baseball player. He's a New York Highlander."

"He's really great, Shar!" shouted Mark, bursting. He just had to say something. "He's a catcher most of the time, but he can play any position! He's really great!"

Sharon looked faint. John pulled out a chair for her. "I thought you said you were a musician?" she muttered.

"This is soooo cool! Can I call my friends over?!?" Mark pleaded with his visibly weakened sister.

"Sure. Call your friends. Alert the neighborhood," responded Sharon, not knowing what to make of the situation. Given dazed permission, her brother was already out the door to spread the word.

"Mark," called his father, "not the whole neighborhood—a few friends—and ask Fred Mason to come over." Mike Costa turned to John and said, "He's gonna die. He's always betting against the Highlanders. Lost a small fortune."

"I thought the name was familiar," said Joan Costa.

John pulled up a chair next to Sharon. "Listen, I play music, too. I didn't tell you about the baseball because I didn't want to sound like I was bragging. Not that . . . I'm not proud of it . . . I am . . . I would have told you tonight. I didn't think this would happen. It's my first year in New York. I guess it's hard for me to understand just how much that means, especially the popularity part."

"He damn near made rookie of the year," exclaimed her dad, as if that would make everything all right.

John gave Sharon the red roses he'd been holding the entire time. The pink and white wrapping paper was torn and battered at the stems from the thorns and his sweaty palms.

"I hope everything's okay," he sighed, worried that he had made a terrible mistake. She accepted the roses, inhaled their scent, and smiled.

"He's a good kid, Shar," said her dad. "Phil Rizzuto thinks so."

"Let me put these in some water," said her mom. Sharon absentmindedly handed the flowers to her mother, then noticed the huge boxes of chocolates and cigars. 'Five pounds of candy, fifty cigars,' she thought and broke into laughter. Her brother marched back into the house followed by five of his friends and introduced the gawking, gangling kids to John—making the whole scene even more absurd to Sharon, and at the same time, innocently sweet.

"This is John Greco the Highlander. He's my sister's boyfriend," Mark said proudly. John felt a little embarrassed, after all that was what he wanted to accomplish. Sharon gave her little brother a hug.

"He's not my boyfriend," she whispered.

"He could be," Mark replied, and she squeezed him even harder.

"Do you mind?" asked John. He gestured toward the piano in the living room. "I feel like I owe you a song."

"Please! We'd love to hear you play," said her mom, delighted.

"Yes, I think you do," replied Sharon, blushing a bit.

"I know your request." He sat at the piano and played "What a Wonderful World," covering the Louis Armstrong rendition.

Natt later said, "I knew he was in love when I heard about Armstrong."

When John finished his song, he gave Sharon a look that searched for approval. Sharon was visibly moved. Mr. and Mrs. Costa, Mark, and his five friends applauded the performance.

"Bravo! Bravo!" Mike Costa shouted enthusiastically. Then he whispered into his daughter's ear, "And he's one hell of a ballplayer, too, Shar."

The boys surrounded John wanting him to autograph their bats and baseballs and gloves, which he did. Mike Costa wanted to know what it was like to play pro ball and if his teammates were good guys. The boys wanted to know everything.

"What's it like in the minor leagues?"

"Do you know Joe DiMaggio?"

"Think you'll hit .300?"

"What's your favorite ballpark?"

"Do you always stay in the best hotels?"

Joan Costa wanted to know if they fed him well.

It was clear to Sharon that everybody wanted her accidental hero to stay and talk. And for one of the first times in John's life, he felt like talking, though he wasn't sure how that would sit with Sharon. After all, they had a dinner date.

"John, I think everybody would love if you stayed for dinner," Sharon said graciously. Her decision was a popular one. "My father and brother would never forgive me if I took you away now."

"Fine, I'd like that," said John.

"We can go to dinner tomorrow—if you want," Sharon offered sweetly. She was a family person. John liked that about her.

Sharon was falling for John. She appreciated his unassuming nature. 'He's a kind man,' she thought. Her instinctual feelings were later confirmed when her father told her stories about John and why the fans liked him so much. Her father explained, "He's like a throwback to another time. John Greco would play for free. He'd give his team everything he had." Mike Costa was absolutely right about Johney. It wasn't the money, as history would bear out. He took the contracts offered him as long as they were fair. To John, *fair* didn't seem all that hard to figure out. Some people thought he was a fool. Once a reporter called him stupid for missing out on thousands. Johney almost got angry. "They paid me enough. . . . My family lives well," was John's response. "If Mr. Harrington feels bad about how I get paid, he can send a check to my favorite charity. They can write that into my next contract, too." A year after that statement when John's contract was up, it was done. Along with a respectable raise, the Highlanders made a considerable donation to help the mentally handicapped. Johney was pleased with the deal and saw it as a good example of people just being straight with each other. From that very first night in Queens, Sharon could see the unquestionable character of this most unusual person. And she never doubted his judgment or clarity of thought. 'He might be a simple man but his priorities are in the right place.'

"Dinner smells great. I'd love to stay. We'll go out tomorrow night then?" asked John for all to hear.

"Yes, it's a date," smiled Sharon.

"I told you he was her boyfriend," Mark whispered to his friends.

Mr. Costa's best friend, Fred Mason, rang the bell. Mike thought it would be funny if John answered the door. Fred was speechless.

That night was spent over a fine home cooked meal and a great deal of wine. Mr. Costa got out the good stuff from the basement. He even poured a bottle of *unique* wine that he'd made himself. Mike was very proud of it, as he should be. They spent the night talking baseball and telling family stories. Many of the stories were about Christmas past, brought on by the season. Some of the stories were about old friends, most of whom were just memories now, but on that night they all lived again. It seems when people really feel comfortable, at ease, they get past the self and remember everyone else.

John and Sharon learned a lot about each other that night. There was so much more between them than just a sexual attraction. And there was plenty of that going on. Maybe they realized that they could be lovers and best friends, too, as though they had known each other before, under different circumstances. Maybe they each recognized the beauty from within and didn't want to live without it.

5

"WHAT DO YOU know?! One year, the Highlanders, the next year, he's married!" said Natty, smashed out of his mind.

"Here'sss to the beaut-i-ful bride. Wasn't she, Natty?" slurred Two Face Pete. He'd been drinking, too.

They were drunk, but they were good at it. Besides, it was late, and by now the newlyweds were well on their way to Niagara Falls. Me, Tommy, Natt, and Petey went back to the bar for one last drink to the bride and groom. Natt insisted, but he didn't have to insist too hard. We probably would've gone anyway. Faye went home right after the reception. She looked tired and she figured Natt would rather be alone, even though he tried his best to get her to come out and have a drink.

"Natt, it's late; I'll take care of the baby sitter," she said as they walked down Greene Street from the party. I liked Faye. She wasn't a bitter woman, though she had every reason and right to be.

"You sure? I don't have to go," he said, praying she wouldn't listen to him, and she never did.

"You wanna go. It's all right. I'm fine," and she meant it. Faye loved Natt, but she didn't want him if he only gave himself as charity.

Their marriage seemed so necessary at the beginning. At least, it was necessary to Natt. Faye regretted the idea from the day they tied the knot when Natt wanted to spend his wedding night at Tommy's. That set the tone for their marriage. Faye was three months pregnant with Charlie; the same old story, the difference was they really did care deeply about each other. Natty never stopped wanting to take Faye out. "She could turn heads," he was fond of saying. "Real smart, too." Natt said he liked that about her, but I'm not sure if he really did—never cared for that quality before. I think that was Natt's problem: after his arm lost the power, he never knew what he wanted or liked—he just tried to escape.

Natt said he wanted a family, but that was just talk. He thought he could handle a family. The truth was he never thought about it at all. He tried to make their home life seem typical. But the life of a gambler was anything but typical, and the life of a roofer was far too ordinary for Natt to endure. He always saw himself as the pitcher, the boy with the golden arm, but never the man he was now, never just plain old Natt Greco.

Natt always had a good excuse for leaving the house, even though he didn't need one for Faye. She could see how restless he had become, and in an odd way she appreciated his trying to keep up appearances. But in the end, she was just as happy to see him go. Faye wasn't a jealous woman and preferred not to know about Natt's infidelities. As long as he loved his son, and he did, Faye was okay . . . or so she said. Charlie would be three in August. With each passing year Faye and Natt seemed to grow further and further apart, each afraid of their own truths and what could have been, but hadn't come about. They had the good sense not to blame the child for their problems and conducted themselves in a parentally professional manner. It seemed to John that after Charlie was born they stopped getting to know each other. Instead, they became just Charlie's parents.

"I don't think that many changes is something you can prepare for," John said. "They're both so sad . . . yet they have everything they need."

Too bad Natt was never able to conquer his vices . . . but then old practices are hard to overcome. Guy Greco loved to tell Natt's Seaside Heights boardwalk story, a tale that seemed to set the tone for his son's life, entertaining to a point, if you didn't scratch beyond the surface.

"So, he's what? Fourteen," chuckled Guy Greco, "and wants money to go on the rides, eat junk, win garbage . . . y'know, maybe some cigarettes to smoke when I'm not looking. Huh. Like I couldn't smell them! He wants to be on his own, meet girls, that sort of thing. A lot of fourteen-year-old girls on the boardwalk wearing nothing but their bathing suits. Who could blame him? So he sez, 'Dad give me five bucks.' I say, 'Five bucks, what are you joking?' That was a lot of money back in '46. I say, 'Here's five, but I want three back.' 'Two dollars, c'mon! What if I meet a girl?!' he sez. I say, 'So, pool your money!' He gives me the look, completely disgusted. 'Give me three and I'll take Johney to get something to eat. Alright? You and Mom can eat in that nice restaurant you like—alone.' I had to hand it to him, he knew how to bargain. So we met two hours later outside the restaurant. Natt's with his buddy Jimmy and some real cute girls; they're all smiling, y'know, like they've got a secret. Natt drops Johney off with us and they're off for the rest of the night. The next day at breakfast I say, 'Natt, how'z the boardwalk?' And he sez, 'Great. I met up with Jim; we met some girls, did all the rides, won a couple stuffed animals, had some clams, burgers, taffy; saw the house of wax and the horror museum.' I say, 'Wow, you did all that on three bucks?' And he sez, 'Uh-huh.' So I say, 'Where's my change?' He sez, 'Sure, Dad.' And pulls out a wad of bills. Singles, ones and ones of dollars! And counts out five for me. I say, 'You owe me two.' He sez, 'That's okay, Dad. Maybe you'll think about this the next time I need a loan.' He's holding the wad in his hand, showing off. So . . . I say, 'Let me get this straight. You went to the boardwalk, met some girls, did all the rides, played the booths, ate . . . all on three dollars?' He sez, 'Not exactly.' 'So where did you get all the money? . . . I know you didn't have any money last night; besides what I gave you. What's going on?!' I was getting nervous. Ya know what that kid was doing? I was afraid to ask. His friend Jimmy told me. I couldn't get it out of Natt. You know the game where ya knock the three bottles off the table? They're all over the boardwalk. Well, Natt hit every one with all of his friends and Johney, too. Ya see big guys trying to knock those bottles off the table all the time. And they can't do it. It's more than speed. They're weighted and you have'ta throw a perfect strike to clear 'em. Well, it didn't take Natty long to figure out that Johney could do it two out of three times. Think of the odds. As Jimmy tells it, Natt would push his little nine-year-old brother up to the booth and say to the man, 'I'll bet a dollar on the side my little brother clears the bottles.' And they took Natt's bet every time. Jimmy said that when John missed, Natt would just double the bet or try to get the guy to go for more on his own arm. And they did, every time. Natty had a helleva arm." The thought of Natt's dead arm would change Guy's expression from amusement to heartache, but never stopped him from telling his story. "When the booth man lost enough, they'd just go to another booth. The kid made over thirty bucks and spent most of it on his friends." Mr. Greco would sit back in his chair with an odd but content look on his face, and say, "He does the same crap today."

Guy Greco was right. Natt always had an angle to make a buck, but he was generous with his money. He had a way of making what he needed and didn't mind helping a friend in need. He was that sure about his luck. I guess a lot of people owed Natt favors, but he didn't collect them like a gangster. Natty considered loaned money and advice to be his gifts, nothing more.

"It's what I'm able to do," he would say.

WHILE NATT'S LIFE appeared bleaker, more disconnected and desperate with each day, John's world couldn't have been more different.

That same autumn when Sharon and John were married, the Highlanders went to the World Series, only to lose in the seventh game against Pittsburgh. But it was a great season nonetheless. John batted .301, with 19 homers and 87 RBI. He played in his first post-season games, including the World Series. Johney was fast becoming an important part of the Highlander team, and New Yorkers loved their newly discovered, soft-spoken ballplayer.

The newlyweds rented and later bought the small townhouse at 24 East 10th Street, right off University Avenue and around the corner from Natt and Faye's townhouse and Tommy's Bar. It was just down the street from St. Raphael's where they were married.

A year later on September 3, 1961, Maya Anne Greco was born. John was so delighted with her that he took her everywhere with him. He would carry her on his back in a knapsack. It got so whenever you saw John, you'd look on his back to say hello to Maya. She was a lucky kid; she got to see a lot of her parents. While John looked after the baby in the off-season, Sharon was able to take a job working on the Mayor's re-election committee. She worked hard, excited by the hands-on experience of the campaign. When spring training started, she became the full-time parent. Their lives seemed perfect, and in many ways they were to be envied.

The '61 Highlanders had one of the greatest ball clubs ever fielded. John Greco hit 25 homers that year, and his club beat the Reds in five to take the Series. When Dillon Southwood was asked to comment on the quiet nature of his young ballplayer, John Greco, he was quoted as saying: "The kid does his talking on the field. Why don't you write about how he plays? He works real hard. He's proud to be a Highlander, and I wouldn't be surprised if he makes a contribution to the baseball history books before he's done."

AS LIFE FLOURISHED for Sharon and John, things only got tougher for Natt and Faye. Faye was in the habit of almost never going out of the house, while Natt was seldom home. If Natt wasn't working or at the track, he was doing all the shopping, and taking little Charlie to the park, doctors, school, or wherever else he needed to go.

Natt never felt sorry for himself; he played the role of good father by day and binged on his vices by night. He was a completely different person out on the town than he was in his own home. And Faye . . . she seemed to get more depressed with each passing year. She wasn't happy and neither was Natt. In a way, they weren't anything. They didn't argue; they didn't talk much; but when they did, it was usually to or through little Charlie.

By their seventh year of marriage, Natt and Faye had achieved acceptance. They were dissatisfied and did nothing to change the fact. Whereas Faye escaped by isolating herself, drawing back into her own limited world of Charlie, television and books, Natt escaped through his very social, social life which included, but was not limited to, his brother, his friends, his girlfriends, drinking, and gambling. Spending nights at Tommy's became more frequent and lasted longer, and that worried John. Natt's boundless energy and lust for the nightlife seemed unquenchable. I wasn't sure if he ever slept or if he needed to.

Everyone knew Natt's marriage was in trouble, but they didn't know about his other problems. He didn't tell a soul until it was too late. Then one night in September of '64, it became obvious Pete knew something about Natt, something terrible, but he was sworn to secrecy.

"Let's have another," said Two Face Pete. He meant a drink, which he didn't need.

Natt and Petey had been drinking hard for about five straight hours. Natt showed no effects from the alcohol with the exception of his hearing, or was it his attention span? He didn't seem to be listening to anything Pete was saying, and Petey was sloppily babbling away as the juke box played Benny Goodman's "In the Mood." Natt was thinking of the next point he wanted to make, and with any break in Petey's rhythm, Natt would jump in and babble away himself. Natt usually was a good listener, but not tonight. It was just about three in the morning, and considering what they had had to drink, it was surprising they could talk at all. There's something about drinking buddies that makes them never want to separate when they're on a roll. Only tonight was different. Most nights they would drink and tell stories about their glory days, or the glory future, or women. Sometimes it was all the same thing. Tonight they were serious, speaking in hushed tones or trying to, making sure the juke box was constantly playing to cover their words. Serious wasn't like them. Natt left serious at home. Pete, to the best of my knowledge, never achieved it.

"How can I? It would kill 'im. It would kill me. You want a drink?" questioned Natt.

"Yeah, I wanna drink. I just asked you! You're letting it get to ya. Hey,

Tommy! Two more scotch and sodas!!" shouted Petey, really ticking Tommy off. He was standing right in front of him.

"I think you've had enough," said Tommy, as he cleaned a glass in the sink. "You're going blind!"

"Last round," said Natt in a relaxed tone of voice. Tommy was already pouring.

"What's with you guys tonight? If I wanted all this intensity, I would've opened up on Wall Street."

"We're trying to decide what Petey's gonna be when he grows up," explained Natt, not expecting a laugh and not getting one. It was too late.

"Gentlemen, your nightcaps. They're free if you go home—even if ya just go and let me go home," said Tommy, serving their drinks. The place was empty but for the three of them, a couple at the other end of the bar, and me sweeping up.

"So, double up!" Petey called emphatically, thinking he was whispering, but I heard him halfway across the room.

"Shhhhh! Lower your voice," Natt hissed.

"What?! Who can hear?" Pete questioned as he pointed around the room with a shaky motion.

"Little George, what'd he say?" Natt called over.

"De-de-de-double up," I responded.

"See?" Natt dropped a dime in the juke box and made his selection. I guess he figured it would drown out Pete. Hank Williams' "Your Cheating Heart" played.

"That's not what they want," Natt said as he downed the last sip of his drink. He started to eat the ice cubes in his empty glass, looking for the last trace of alcohol that might steady his nerves. He seemed very upset.

"Tommy, one for the road. I'm buying for the house. And that means you and you and even you!" he declared as he gestured to all of us individually, now speaking in a loud but regal tone of voice. For once on this rainy, ugly, cold, and of all things, Monday night, Natt was himself again. I guess he knew he'd have to put on a show to get another drink out of Tommy.

"And give my unfortunate friend Two Face Pete a double!" he commanded.

"I'm glad none of you drive, especially you, Petey. Tonight you're wearing your shit face," said Tommy, letting out a deep, barely audible snort. He served drinks all around, even had one himself, while Sinatra came on the juke box singing, "That's Life."

"To number twenty-three, but who's counting?" Petey raised his glass in a toast. Nobody knew if he was toasting John's number or the amount of drinks Natt and he'd had, probably both. Our four glasses clinked together.

"To better days," toasted Natt.

"Amen," said Tommy.

As if on cue, the bar door swung open, letting in the damp night air. It was still drizzling at three-thirty in the morning when John walked in.

"J-Johney?" Natt stuttered. He seemed to be to trying to clear some crazy thought out of his head but couldn't. "What are you doing here?"

"Looking for you," John said. There was no anger or judgment in his tone. He was just doing what he had to do. "I figured you'd be here."

"Sit down! Sit down! Have a drink with us," called Natt. He looked deranged, almost giddy and a bit hysterical, as though he'd been caught in a lie or hiding something obscene.

"Faye called. It's Monday night. She's worried about you, Natty. She thought you were at my house."

"Well . . . I told her I might stop by your place," replied Natt. His facial muscles contorted as a chill ran down the length of his body. The alcohol had kicked in; he was helpless. His knees buckled. He had to steady himself by grabbing hold of the bar. John put his arm around his brother to comfort him and help him regain his balance.

"You're feeling restless tonight, Natty," said John, softly. Natt said nothing. He knew his brother could feel his pain. Somehow John always knew.

John held Natt's arm and walked him back to Faye and his family. The bitter air stung their faces; the sharp wind stole their breath. John had come to bring his brother home, to support him on the journey. He said he had never seen such unforgivable sadness as he saw in Natt's eyes on that night.

"The smile on his face couldn't disguise it," John said.

Faye took over at the door. She didn't scold him. She simply kissed him on the cheek and put him to bed. John said Natt looked so surprised after the kiss. Maybe he felt her love . . . or maybe he was ashamed.

6

Chicago: August, 1991

THE GAME WAS over, yet another loss in a long line of disappointing losses for the Highlanders. The Chicago White Sox had just beaten them 5 to 4, dropping their fifth straight game on the road trip. If it wasn't the pitching, which it usually was, it was the hitting. Today they did a pretty fair job of both hitting and pitching, but they still couldn't get it done. A mental mistake, a base running error, it was always something. It just wasn't meant to happen for the Highlanders in 1991. In that sense the season had a lot of consistency to it, but that didn't matter to John, especially in Chicago. He was feeling nostalgic, or as Yogi would say, "Deja vu all over again."

This was his first time at the new Comiskey Park and one of the important sights for him to see on his baseball vacation. After 1990 old Comiskey became history. It was now an empty lot, until they paved it for parking. 'At least they kept it in the neighborhood,' John thought. The only thing they saved from the old ballpark was the infield. They dug up the original infield as if it were an archaeological expedition and planted it in the new ballpark. I suppose it was an acknowledgement of tradition, an olive leaf to the past, as they moved the good spirits from one park to the other. Baseball may change, but it doesn't change easily and it never wants to jinx itself. It seems the one thing all baseball people agree on, whether they know it or not, is the precariousness of the unknown. They wouldn't dare tempt fate in a game that could go on forever. You may lose.

BASEBALL & BENEVOLENCE

John was truly anonymous in the Chicago stands. He hadn't slept in days.
The binge he was on was going strong, and no one had the slightest suspicion
that the disheveled man with sad, bloodshot eyes and scruffy beard was John
Greco. He was a loner in many ways or so he had come to believe. What he
really was was an aged ballplayer without a team. An uneasy feeling sat in
his gut as he watched the game in the present-day park. The unsettling
thought occurred to him that if Comiskey with all of its history could go, why
not Fenway . . . why not Ruth Memorial? And where would those ballparks
go? Probably not across the street. Instead of cherishing and repairing the
old ballparks and their communities, he reasoned, they'd most likely go some
place safer. History was being destroyed because of it, like the Dodgers and
Brooklyn's Ebbets Field. John believed that every move to safer ground
meant giving up on the spirit and the soul of a community, on a part of our
nation. Johney couldn't understand how things had become so cynical, so
anti-heroic and self-absorbed in the last ten years. He wondered if the greed
of a few wasn't really at the heart of this whole safety thing, and he wondered
if a country could afford to give up on so many of its citizens.

"Go! Go to a safe place!" John yelled. Several fans moved away from
him. "Make your money—" He caught himself in midsentence and the
thought occurred to him that he might be losing his mind. But he couldn't
shake the feeling that humanity was at a pivotal point in its evolution or de-
evolution. And, for an old ballplayer, any kind of change always started with
baseball. Had baseball become his religion? Driven him crazy? He wasn't
sure, but he felt that the game was a vehicle through which people had
bettered themselves, and the corruption of the institution would have dire
consequences.

John also felt like he was running, letting people down. He was uncertain
of what he could do, but searching to find some answers. Sometimes he felt
as if his mind would never rest until he found those answers. He contemplated what New York would be like without Ruth Memorial, or what the
Bronx would be like for that matter. The thought bothered him, nagged at
him. He had too much information to shake his dark mood. The ballpark had
become his last refuge, and even the game couldn't settle his thoughts.

When the White Sox game ended, John quietly said a pray for Old
Comiskey. Then he walked over to Stan's Sports Bar just a couple blocks
away. The walk over to Stan's cleared John's head a bit and put an end to his
unchecked utterances. He was sure he would meet friends there whom he
hadn't seen for a long time. Johney was growing tired of being a loner and
wanted some company . . . and a drink more than he cared to admit.

"JOHN! IS THAT you? I'll be damned, what'ya doing here!" shouted Steve Schneider, a retired major league umpire. He was a short man with a full head of thick silver hair and was built like a bowling ball. Schneider pulled up a bar stool next to John and slapped him on the back just as John was about to swallow a martini olive. John started to choke on a small piece that went down the wrong tube. Schneider took no notice of the choking and continued talking while Johney turned bright red.

"How's the hand!" howled Steve, not waiting for an answer as he looked for Harry, the bartender.

John squeaked out, "Fine."

Harry gave Steve a draft beer. "Harry! Where's my shot?!" demanded Schneider. It seemed as though Steve shouted everything, and he did. He was a little hard of hearing, a true blessing for an umpire.

"It's coming!" Harry shouted back. He was in no mood for Schneider; John could see that.

"John, what brings—Sorry to hear—Boyyy! That was a raw deal!" Steve yelped as he almost made three complete sentences. John wanted some company but this was pushing it.

"I'm on vacation," replied John.

Steve rolled his eyes and then whispered one of those whispers everybody could hear. "Does your wife know?" Schneider wasn't a bad guy but he could be irritating if you weren't in the mood. John was on the borderline.

"Yes, Sharon knows."

In another minute Steve would start talking about all the times he called John out on strikes. John wasn't sure if he could take that, so he just nodded his head and ordered another drink while Steve talked to anybody within ear shot. Schneider didn't seem to mind and, in fact, seemed content with this arrangement. It was his way of holding court.

The place was beginning to fill up with baseball people and sportswriters. John knew most of them, and the ones he didn't know Steve loudly introduced him to as if John were his best friend. A writer asked John if he had become a White Sox fan in light of his current situation.

"Cubs' fan," balked John. He got a big laugh and a few well-intended boos from the crowd that had gathered around the bar. It was obvious that many of them wanted to meet John Greco. He took a lot of ribbing about the Highlanders and about being a Highlander, but the underlying feeling was that they were glad, even honored, that he was sharing a night with them. They exchanged many exaggerated baseball stories and had plenty to drink. John was pretty drunk by the end of the night. Most of the guys had left, but

Schneider was still babbling away to anyone who would listen—something about chasing a cat off the field in the top of the fifth . . . and rain . . . and a plane to catch.

"We never got that friggin' game in. The sky opened like, like . . . I don't know what! Twenty minutes I chased that damn cat, making an ass out of myself!"

"That's better than most nights," somebody shouted from the back of the bar. The whole place broke up. Harry, the bartender, was laughing so hard you could see the veins in his head.

Steve thought they were laughing at his story, which inspired him to ramble on. ". . . rained the rest of the night. Can ya beat that, Johney? Never let up!" Steve didn't wait for a response; he just grabbed the next available ear and told the same story all over again. John had to smile. Steve was out there. 'Probably not a bad place to be,' he thought.

"Mr. Greco, excuse me," said a young man in his twenties. He wore a blue denim jacket and a ball cap with no insignia. John didn't recognize him. He must have just walked in, though he seemed to have come from nowhere. Johney was having a hard time focusing, the liquor was taking over and this was his fifth night of binging. "Can I get your autograph?" asked the man. John was surprised. Not many fans recognized him anymore, especially the young ones.

"Sure," said John as he looked for a pen, even though he knew he didn't have one.

"I have a pen . . . and a ball I'd like you to sign," said the man.

John looked a bit confused and said, "You always carry a ball?"

"Sometimes," replied the man. "You're my father's favorite player. The signature is for him."

"Thanks, that's a real compliment," said John, trying to maneuver the pen around the ball. "You're gonna have'ta hold it for me." The man smiled and steadied the ball on the bar.

"You proved his theory," he said.

"Really . . . your father, what's his theory?" asked John, as he managed to get an autograph out of his drunk hand.

"That baseball is more than just a game."

"Yeah, I think it is. Of course, I haven't a clue what else it is," John said with a nervous chuckle. After Johney gave it a little more thought, he knew he was drunk and he knew he was lying. "That's not true. I'm afraid to say what I think it is. I always have been."

"I know," said the man.

The man's self-assuredness struck John, snapping his pent-up tension. "You know? What do you know? How could you!?" exclaimed John. I felt bad that John was feeling such despondency. In fact, I was afraid he'd give into it.

"Is this some kind of a joke?" John cried, trying to quell his agitation, but he hadn't any control. "What did he think? The theory . . . his theory? Your father?!" John appeared desperate to hear the answer. Suddenly it became the most important thing in the world to him. Maybe it was the answer he'd been looking for; maybe it was nothing, but he greedily awaited the man's reply.

"He said the game contained the better part of all things in its soul."

"Yes! Yes! But-but how can it," John took a long, deep breath, "help?"

The man took the baseball from John, smiled, and said, "Thank you."

John struggled to get hold of himself. He wanted an answer. He wanted to say something, a lot of things, but nothing would come out. Finally, a release from his momentary confinement came.

"How does it help? Please tell me," he begged.

"It helps, because it is."

"Yes! And!?"

"If it wasn't, it couldn't help," said the man.

John wasn't sure if this made him feel any better; it sounded more like a riddle than a theory. The man turned to leave. John, turning his frustration inward, spun his seat back to face the bar and was about to order one more for the road when the man called to him.

"Mr. Greco. Many people love you, like my father. You're important to them. I hope you know that." And he left. His words poured over John, soothing him. A welcome calm quenched his despair.

John turned his attention back to Harry who raised an eyebrow and said with a hint of sarcasm, "I love you, too, John. You want that drink?"

"No. Thanks. That's all I can take." John left whatever money was on the bar and called it a night. He was feeling better, somehow better than he had felt in a long time.

When he got to the street, he looked in both directions for the man with the ball. Not sure what he would've done if he had seen him, but he didn't have to make that decision because he was nowhere to be found. There weren't many people out but that didn't bother John. He was so drunk his safety wasn't a factor on his walk back to the hotel. John started to sing "Because It Is" over and over again.

The fear he'd been living with was completely gone. The fear was what he fought and battled within himself. The fear was what he feared most. Then he thought, 'I'm thinking like that guy talked.' And it made him smile.

"If people knew how scared I've been all these years . . . " he said aloud. The thought hung in the air as he walked.

7

New York City: September, 1964

"JOHN, I'M THINKING about broiling the fish with a little lemon and butter. Is that okay?" Sharon called from the kitchen.

John was busy playing airplane with Maya. Sharon could hear her daughter squealing with delight.

'He didn't hear me,' she thought.

Maya's dad was on his back in the middle of the living room floor. His arms were stretched to the ceiling as he held his daughter firmly in his hands above him.

"Arms out, arms out. Do like an airplane. Arroooo!!!!" The little girl shrieked with joy as she flew over her daddy and dribbled down his shirt.

Sharon entered the living room planning to re-ask the fish question but stopped herself from interrupting. 'They look so cute,' she thought and decided to appreciate the moment instead. 'John won't care how the fish is cooked,' she told herself and started back to the kitchen, thinking she wasn't noticed.

"Shar," John called, just as she took her second step. "Broiled, lemon and butter sounds fine."

"So, you did hear me," she said, returning to her family. She picked her "baby" out of John's hands; she too wanted to hold Maya.

"I heard something. On Friday around dinner you always ask me how I want the fish cooked."

"So, I'm getting that predictable." She put Maya down next to her daddy, pinned him to the floor like a knowledgeable wrestler, kissing him all over his face. Maya giggled and clapped her hands.

"Are we ever gonna stop this fish on Friday thing? We're not very Catholic," he said, pretending to wrestle a full fifteen years ahead of the World Wrestling Federation.

"It's good for us to have fish once a week; we eat too much meat. Besides, I really wanted to know how Natt likes it cooked. I know how you like it. Is Faye coming tonight?" asked Sharon, as her thoughts hopscotched from fish to nutrition, to family.

"Faye only leaves the house on holidays."

"She'd leave if Natt asked her," said Sharon, sympathetically, knowing John agreed with her but was unwilling to be critical of his brother. "I don't understand," Sharon continued. " I know they love each other, but they can't seem to find any common ground. Those two are the strangest—" She stopped in midsentence, catching herself in a habit she wanted to break: meddling. She knew John felt powerless when it came to Natt and Faye's relationship and that it made him sad.

"I wish they'd get together," he said as he removed a strand of Sharon's hair from in front of her face. He thought to himself, 'The introvert, the extrovert—Natty and Faye.'

"Did you say something?"

"What? Are you psychic? Can you read my thoughts?"

"Sometimes," she said playfully. "What were you thinking?"

"That Natt likes lemon and butter and plenty of scotch with his fish."

"You were not!" she protested, just as the doorbell rang. It was Natt. Sharon released John from her hold. "I'll deal with you later," she smiled seductively, then took Maya by the hand and went to answer the door.

"Oh, you were having so much fun with your daddy, weren't you?" she cooed. "It's your Uncle Natt. Yes, it is!"

John turned on the radio in the living room. Bobby Darin was singing "Mac the Knife." He liked music playing when they had company. He said it made the house come to life.

"Sharon! Maya! Look at you two! You're so beeeeautiful!!!!" Natt exclaimed from the front stoop. John listened as his brother complimented Sharon's flowing peasant dress and Maya in general. He could picture Natt giving them big hugs and kisses, and heard him doing a whole routine in baby talk for Maya. She giggled at her uncle's silly faces, funny dance, and expert command of baby-ese. After Maya was adequately entertained, Natt produced a bottle of white wine for dinner and presented it to Sharon. "It's Friday . . . white with fish, right?"

"Right," she replied, always amazed by his energy.

"How's the Mayor treating—Hey! Did you ever consider running for office? City council—borough president? A smart woman like you could do this city a world of good! Huh! . . . Good idea, right?! I'll bet you could get the streets clean and the subways running!"

Natt's optimistic charm was as invigorating as a dip in a whirlpool of self-confidence. Sharon was speechless as he effortlessly and enthusiastically picked her dreams right out of her head, then gave them his wholehearted support. Natt had vision. He saw the best in people and had a way of inspiring them to develop it.

"Where's my brother?" he clamored. Maya followed him into the living room as though he were the pied piper. Natty could turn a simple family dinner into an event. He lived within the moment and knew which ones were really important.

Natt once told me he was afraid of dying because he was afraid he'd lose his friends. He was feeling sentimental that night but that was part of his appeal, because he meant every word he said. Over dinner Natt and Sharon had a playful argument about the new French fashions.

"New York is the new fashion capital of the world," Natt proclaimed as he sat back in his chair like a dictator waiting to be ousted. A look of amusement danced across his face as he added, "Although I can see the fascination with the English miniskirt."

They talked for hours after dinner that night and had a great time. Sharon said good night to her brother-in-law around midnight and went to bed.

The brothers moved into the study where John poured them each a scotch and soda and showed Natt some Highlander newspaper clippings from other cities. One article in particular, a profile piece, featured John in its story. Two lines were highlighted for Natt to read: *My big brother Natt was my biggest influence. He was a great pitcher but it just didn't work out for him. Natty did everything he could to help me get to the big leagues.*

"There's a lot of 'bigs' in that quote," said Natt, getting a bit misty. John pretended not to notice. Natt's mood went from contemplative to melancholy, to a deep lonely despair. He finished his drink in no time and got himself a refill. He stood in front of the window staring at a street lamp, trying to count the ringlets of colored light surrounding it. He didn't want his brother to see him upset.

"I thought you would like the article. It's true," said John, thinking he had reminded Natty of what could have been. "You can take it home if ya want. Y'know, read it when you get a chance."

But there was more to it than that; Natt's hands began to shake uncontrollably. He couldn't hold his drink. Sweat beaded on his forehead.

"Natty, what's wrong? I don't like seeing you like this. Whatever it is, we'll work it out—like you always do for me." Natt just stared at the lamp, not saying anything. "C'mon, let me help you for a change. There's something wrong, isn't there?" pleaded John, trying to get his brother to open up to him. "A woman? Gambling? Do you need money? I got plenty of money. You can have it. I'll make more. Please, tell me what I can do."

Natt grabbed a handful of clippings and absentmindedly flipped through them, trying his best to regain his composure.

"*Los Angeles Times*—Hey, that's a good picture," Natty said unconvincingly. John took the clippings from him and put them on his desk. Natt grabbed his scotch glass and downed whatever was remaining. He handed the empty glass to John and asked for another refill.

"Natt, the alcohol isn't helping. You're just getting numb. Honest to God, I want to help. Can I help?" he asked, phrasing the question as delicately as possible. Natt had a lot of pride.

"Johney, if it was that easy . . . I don't need your money." He put his hands to his head, rubbed his eyes, and did his best to form a smile. "I've made a bad bet or two, and maybe that's got me a little worried."

"I thought so," said John.

"You don't understand. A little worried—yes, but could it be driving me crazy?" Natt didn't wait for a response. "I've had it worse—took a second mortgage—no big deal. I did it before. I won again and I paid it off. I've done it before . . . but this!" He had his hand wrapped so tightly around the tumbler John thought it was going to crack.

"But what?"

"I think I'm going crazy."

"C'mon, you're the sanest man I know."

"I know, I know! A month ago I was the sanest man you knew." he agreed and, at the same time, looked like he wanted to bolt out the door. John took the glass out of Natt's hand, sat across from his brother, and waited for him to speak.

"Okay, okay, I don't think you can help." Natt leaned in close to his brother. "Johney, I'm hearing things."

"You're hearing things?"

"I'm really hearing things."

"Voices?"

"No, no, no, nothing like voices. Well, nobody telling me to go kill people if that's what ya'mean. Ahh . . . at first I wasn't sure. I thought I was just dreaming. Wow and what dreams," he said reflectively. "I dreamt of angels singing. Ooooh, Johney. They were beautiful dreams!"

"Angels. Real angels?" questioned John.

"Just hear me out," Natt snapped defensively, though there was no cause for it. John's tone was reserved. "It happened late at night; almost undetectable at first. I didn't think anything of it. There're a lot of strange sounds in the city. And the dreams—the sweetest I've ever had; really deep, deep sleep. Like a baby, I'd sleep. And I had the same dream for nights. I wasn't gonna fight it. . . . Every night the angels would come and sing . . . and there would be more and more of them. The power, the intensity . . . it doubled with every new angel. I felt like I was with them singing in a language I've never heard, but knew it was the only language that everybody understood."

John sat quietly as he listened to Natt, thinking he'd never heard his brother speak of any spiritual matters before tonight. It occurred to John that he didn't even know if Natty was in any way religious. Death and the afterlife were subjects his family didn't talk much about. He had no idea how his parents felt either or, for that matter, how he felt. John wasn't even sure if he wanted to be buried or not. After his confirmation the Greco family put all spiritual matters on hold and, as far as he could tell, had no plans for resurrecting them.

"So, it gets to be so loud . . . well, magnificent, that it wakes me up. I felt great, full of energy. I didn't know what to do with myself. So I put on the night light; I'm thinking I might read or something. Then the craziest thing happens. Faye rolls over . . . and, and, and—"

"Yeah?"

"She's so beautiful. Really lovely. . . . It was like I'd never seen her before. I couldn't stay away. I start to kiss her as she's sleeping, and she wakes up—like a completely different woman . . . and we, you know . . . make love—like it was the first time! Y'know?" Natt took a moment to appreciate the moment. John seemed a bit confused.

"So, you think you're crazy for not realizing you have a beautiful wife?" John questioned cautiously.

"No, no! That's just the beginning. After we made love—when we were falling asleep again . . . I heard it."

"What?" John asked with great anticipation.

"Well, that night I wasn't too sure what. I was very drowsy, like I'd been drugged, but I knew I'd heard something. Anyway, the next night, the same thing happens." Natty poured himself a drink and smiled. "By the way, me and Faye are getting along much better lately."

"I'm glad. She's a good woman," said John, earnestly.

"Yeah, she is," said Natty with a softness in his voice. He struggled a bit to gather his thoughts, then continued his story. "Ah . . . oh, yeah. Only this time, this time I know what it is. It's a piano. My piano! Only I didn't know that immediately. A couple notes at first, a few chords . . . I thought it was a neighbor. Now, on the fifth night—"

"The fifth night?"

"The fifth night," he repeated proudly.

"This happened five nights in a row?" sighed John. "Five nights of angels singing and, ah . . . Faye . . . and piano playing?"

"Yeah, five. On the fifth night we make love again. Faye's out like a light, and I'm just about there when all of a sudden the thing goes crazy!"

"The piano?"

"Yes, the piano! Only this time I know it's my piano, your old piano, the one in my basement. I look over at Faye to see if it wakes her, but she's out cold. I even try to wake her up—to listen. She rolls over and mumbles, 'I love you, too, honey' and falls back into a deep sleep; seems she couldn't hear our piano banging away in the basement at all! I can't believe it didn't wake her. Then I think, 'I'm the only one hearing it. I'm going nuts.' So I decide to get up and check it out. On the way down I'm thinking Faye and John and maybe Petey, definitely Tommy . . . they're playing a joke on me, trying to scare the hell out of me. But the closer I get to the basement door the more I know this is no joke. The music! I've never heard anything like it. John, it would've taken six hands. The style—indescribable, fascinating, emotional . . . from a technically perfect player . . . or players . . . sublime! No offense, John, but I knew it wasn't you. Then I think—I *wish* is more like it—maybe, maybe I'm a genius. A composer. A genius composer receiving divine inspiration. Like Mozart! Yes, I think, this must be what it is! How it's done! What it's like. How an ordinary man can somehow tap into God's stream of consciousness! It has to be. What else can it be? I reason. Well, I don't have to tell you, my excitement soon died. When I open the cellar door, the music stops, and I don't feel much like Mozart anymore. I hit the light switch and force myself down the steps. It's very quiet and still, and when I get all the way down the stairs, I can see our piano on the far wall, hidden in a dark shadow. I turn on the rest of the lights and there it is! My basement, the piano . . . just like I remembered it. Nothing. No one . . . no vision . . . no you . . . no ghost, God, or Mozart! If God was trying to communicate with me, he'd just hung up. Then I must've spooked myself . . . y'know what I mean? I stand at the piano, looking, waiting for something to happen, and I get really scared. An icy chill runs through my bones, and then I get angry, really angry—like that time I kicked the shit out of Jack McCann when we were kids. He was big and I was scared to death, but I made it work for me. Same thing. So, I back away from the piano, maybe six feet, and I'm so scared. I can feel this tremendous rage building up inside of me. And I go berserk! Screaming at the top of my lungs, 'I'm here! You got my attention!!! What the Hell do you want!!!!!' Out of the corner of my eye I see something move behind me."

"What?" John blurted out.

"Funny, that's exactly what I said. I do a pivot like a basketball player on a pick-and-roll—ready to attack. I must have looked like a madman. I can feel how red my face is, the veins popping out of my neck, eyes bulging from my head as I shout, 'Whaaaat!!!'"

"And?!"

"Poor Faye . . . I thought she was going to faint—white as chalk—tears streaming down her face. I practically scared her to death, and . . . and at the same time, I knew we were never more alive. I tell her that I thought there was somebody down here. Didn't you hear the piano? I ask her. You know what she said?" John shook his head. "She said, 'Don't you go crazy on me, Natt Greco, not now, not when things could work.' And she meant it. John, I'm in love with my wife, but the piano and the dreams. I know they were real! I'm hearing angels singing . . . and my piano—do you think I'm missing a few screws? A couple buttons?" Natt took his drink from on top of the desk and drank. He wanted an answer to this one.

John considered his question carefully. He didn't want to say something stupid, and the truth was, he thought this was the strangest story he'd ever heard. But . . . very beautiful, too. Before he answered, he looked into his brother's eyes to make sure he wasn't getting his chain pulled. That would be just like Natty. When he was confident that he wasn't the victim of a practical joke, John decided to answer Natt's question with as many questions as he could think of until some sort of reasonable explanation was reached.

"When did it all start?"

"About two weeks ago . . . It ended last Sunday."

"You mean when you yelled at your piano?"

"Yeah . . . the thing with Faye."

"So, the piano doesn't play any—"

Natt cut him off. "No . . . no angels either."

"And Faye?"

"What about Faye?"

"Well, the love . . . do you still—" Once more John was trying to be delicate.

"Never been better . . . didn't even go out last week, stayed home—wanted to," declared Natt, proudly, happily. It was then that he realized how much he'd changed. "Faye wanted to come over tonight. Charlie's got a touch of the flu. John, can you believe it? She really did want to come over. I'm not even lying. I've changed; we've changed. Whatever happened, happened for us. Didn't it?"

"Well . . . " was all John could say. He wasn't sure what his honest answer would've been.

"It's a fucking miracle," proclaimed Natt, an odd but accurate way of looking at it.

John was glad Natt felt that way—for Faye's sake. He thought his brother must be under a lot of pressure and hoped that he was finding some peace within his family. Maybe it was the drinking or the guilt he claimed he didn't have. At any rate Natt seemed pleased with his theory, his realization. So Natt's theory became John's answer: sure, why not a divine marriage counselor. 'If it brings them together, how could it hurt,' John reasoned.

THE NEXT DAY John was drawn into a local church, St. John the Baptist. He had never been inside St. John's before. The renovations had just been completed and this was the first time he saw the church without scaffolding. It was a large church with a beautiful domed apse built over the altar, maybe fifty feet high. John was in the habit of going to church when he felt the need, and the day after Natt's visit, he felt the need. He wanted to pray. It was the one thing he got from his religious training that made him feel better. He prayed for peace, for love, and for his family . . . and he felt better.

8

"WAS NATT ALL right? He seemed a little down toward the end of the night," asked Sharon. John took a sip of his morning coffee and folded back his newspaper. He considered telling her the whole story and then thought better of it.

"I think he's going to be okay," replied John.

"Okay? Is something wrong?"

"No, no. I mean between Natt and Faye." Sharon looked confused. "Well, you know how Natt is," John said, feeling uncomfortable, not wanting to get into Natt's personal affairs.

"You mean his girlfriends?" asked Sharon, knowing full well what he meant. John appreciated her directness, even though it was kind of funny when he was trying to be so discreet. She called a spade a spade, was honest and forthright, and knew her husband could get bogged down in semantic subtleties. 'It was the baseball player in him,' she thought. 'They take things slow and easy; almost an unnatural pace.' It was the way he was brought up, too. The Grecos didn't talk much about their personal problems, especially about sex, any more than they talked about their spiritual beliefs. They were much more open about career and money matters.

"Yes. That's another way of putting it," admitted John. "Did you have a rough time in diplomacy class?" he asked.

She put her coffee cup on the table and gave him a kiss. "What do you think?"

John pulled her onto his lap, put his hand inside her robe, and didn't bother to answer. "No you don't. Not now. I want to hear about Natt," she said coyly.

"Mommy!" cried Maya from the living room.

"Our daughter's calling." She got up from his lap, fixed her robe, and went to get Maya.

"What is it? What is it, honey?" John could hear Sharon saying. "I just fed you. You want to come talk with your mommy and daddy? Daddy is going to tell us all about your Uncle Natt." Maya just wanted to be held by her mother. She was three years old and talking up a storm.

"Daddy, let's walk. Daddy, let's walk," Maya called when she saw her father. She liked to go for walks with her daddy. John gave his daughter a big kiss.

"Bored with the TV? Nothing on? Or did you miss your daddy?" That got a big smile from his daughter as he picked her out of Sharon's arms and gave her a hug.

"Maya has a pretty new dress for Easter," said her mom. "And we're going to walk down Fifth Avenue with our Easter bonnets on!"

"Mommy's so pretty," said the child, running her finger through a dangling curl that hung in front of her eyes. She snuggled into her daddy's lap and soon fell asleep.

"Well?" said Sharon. "Tell me about Natt."

"He's happy."

"He's always happy. What's new about that?"

"No, I mean about Faye. Something's happened to him, to them. They've discovered each other, I guess."

"Ooooh really!" she whispered, trying not to wake Maya. "That's wonderful. What happened?" Sharon could hardly contain her excitement. "I knew it would. She can be so terrific and Natt's—Natt!"

"He said they've been, you know, having a lot more interest lately."

"They're doing it! Oh, that's so nice," she replied with great satisfaction.

"He said Faye wanted to come over last night—for real. But Charlie wasn't feeling well. A touch of the flu. And . . . he sez it's like a new beginning. That they have somehow changed, but he didn't seem to know why."

"He's settling down!" she blurted out. "He hasn't even noticed her in five years and, and now he finally sees this fantastic woman living in his own home. Oh, John! I'm so delighted for them!" Sharon exclaimed. Maya was in a deep sleep; her mother's excitement didn't even stir her.

"Yeah, me, too. About time," uttered John, feeling pretty comfortable about leaving out the piano and angels.

"That's so romantic," she said, drifting, looking kind of dreamy. "It's like the fire when a relationship first begins. Remember how we couldn't get enough of each other?"

"I thought we still couldn't?" he replied, sounding slightly offended.

"Honey, our sex life is wonderful, but we don't feel the need everyday. Nobody does after—" She noticed the distressed look on his face and tried to alter her statement in midthought. "I mean, the relationship moves on. You have to do more than just copulate. Right?" He still didn't look very pleased.

"Yeah, I guess so," he said rather glumly. John reluctantly understood how sexual habits change as the relationship gets older. He knew it was one of the things Natt had been running from all of his life, and he was glad for Natt and Faye. But he also wondered if they had found something nobody else knew about. Or was Natt simply losing his mind to drinking and money and women problems?

"Remember our first time?" Sharon asked, sounding very sexy. John grinned like a teenager, thinking he was about to get lucky. She thought how he looked like a bashful young man, her bashful young man, just like the day he showed up at her parents house overburdened with gifts.

"Do you remember your first time . . . ever? I know it wasn't with me—not the way—"

"Sharon." John cut her off.

"Tell me how you lost your virginity. You never tell me anything about your ex-girlfriends. And I've told you everything—about Danny with the motorcycle, whom my father hated—and David, the guy who mumbled, whom my father, ah, disliked but felt was an improvement over Danny; anyone would have been to him. It's not fair! Just tell me about your first love, and I'll leave you alone." As an afterthought, she added, "Or maybe I won't."

"How come your father disliked Dave and Danny?" asked John, innocently.

"Oh, no you don't. This is how I end up talking about my boyfriends."

"Okay, okay, I'll tell you."

"Not just how it happened. I want the story, the whole setup. I want to know what motivates my husband," she said smugly.

"Alright, let me think," he began slowly. "Well, it had a lot to do with the Mountain Edge Swim Club."

"Uh-huh," she smiled, pleased he was actually going to tell her.

"There was Gail Richardson and Carla Smitcht."

"Two! How old were you?!"

"No, it wasn't like that," he laughed nervously. "They were, well, not best friends, more like rivals. I was sixteen. Gail lived three houses away from me. We went to the prom together but more as friends than a real date. Carla lived on the mountain and was a grade ahead of me, so the only time I really saw her was at the swim club. And Gail wasn't pleased about that . . . not so much because of me, they just didn't like each other. I think Carla gave me attention just to bug Gail. Gail would wear the sexiest swimsuits I'd ever seen. She had an amazing body for a fifteen year old."

"Johnnn," Sharon admonished playfully.

"Well, you said you wanted the whole story." He blushed a bit and continued. "I thought that they both were real, ah, cute. But I didn't get the feeling that they spent much time thinking about me. All the girls liked Karl Page. He was captain of the Mountain Edge football team. Baseball wasn't real big in Mountain Edge at the time. Gail wasn't as good of a swimmer as Carla and, from what I'd heard, not as easy either. It was strange. Gail seemed to want the reputation of being easy, maybe to get Karl's interest. He had a reputation for only going out with girls who, ah, put out. I guess that was where Carla picked up her reputation. Are you following all this?"

"Yes. I had no idea," she giggled, fascinated by the way John had obviously thought long and hard over these matters.

"Uh . . . Carla was very pretty. She had long, dirty-blond hair . . . a good singer, lead roles in all the high school musicals. Her family was German. Her father was an engineer, very practical man. Education was stressed. Carla even spoke German. I thought that was really cool . . . and sexy."

"Sexyyyy," Sharon teased. "I'm sorry. What happened?"

"I'm getting there. Don't rush me. If I have to tell it, I'm telling it right. Okay?"

"Okay."

"So, ah, aaah, the word got around that Carla, well, was the hot package."

Sharon put her hand to her mouth, trying not to laugh. The words sounded so funny coming from her quiet, reserved, shy husband. He didn't seem to notice.

"I guess it got around from Karl Page. But that's what he said about every girl he went out with. So there was a lot of doubt about anything he said. I guess Gail saw me looking at Carla . . . differently. And it made her crazy that I might be attracted to her. You have to remember, I was sixteen, uh, and sixteen-year-old hormones can get pretty nuts over rumors. Besides Carla was . . . nice, especially when she noticed Gail's reaction whenever she paid the slightest attention to me. All of a sudden I was the guy, the focus of their attention for the summer. It wasn't easy."

"Oh, I'll bet," commented Sharon, sarcastically, but very much enjoying every second of his story.

"Well, think about it. They were just trying to get at each other."

"Sounds like they both liked you, silly."

"Well, maybe they did . . . but I'll tell you, it didn't do anything for Karl Page. Those two never let each other out of their sight. If I talked to one, the other would show up within seconds. I could never get anywhere, be alone."

"Oh, poor baby."

"You should be a teenage boy for a day. Anyway, Gail decides I'm paying too much attention to Carla and thinks if she goes out with Karl Page, she'll get back at Carla, because Gail thinks Carla still likes Karl. But she doesn't. Carla actually likes me."

"Uh-huh."

"There was a dangerous side to Karl that I think Gail was attracted to. Gail could do most anything when she set her mind to it, which she rarely did. She was sort of lazy. But real smart. She set her mind to Karl, and in no time they were a couple. I couldn't believe it. Gail always went for guys that she could control. Like me." Sharon laughed so hard she nearly woke up Maya. John didn't see what was so funny. But that's what was so funny. It was all so out of character for him that Sharon couldn't believe what she was hearing.

"If you're gonna laugh—"

"I'm sorry, please," she said with as much politeness as she could muster. He gave her a suspicious glance and continued.

"Well, I guess I was a little jealous, too. Gail and I always liked each other. More than just friends—I thought. And then Karl Page comes along. I was worried about her. But there was nothing I could do and Carla was getting more and more interesting every day."

"What does that mean? Interesting?"

"It means she would spread suntan oil on my back and . . . "

"And?"

"Senior Lifesaving."

"Senior Lifesaving?" Sharon was confused.

"Yeah, I told you she was a good swimmer." Nothing registered. Sharon didn't understand what this had to do with anything. John continued. "Senior Lifesaving is the last course you take to be a qualified lifeguard." Sharon just nodded her head, signalling him to go on. "It's really hard. You have to be a very strong swimmer. The course is three weeks long, three hours a day. It's a lot of swimming, usually carrying somebody else."

"Ooooh, don't tell me. You and Carla were partners. She must have been quite an athlete."

"Well, yes, and yes," John said shyly.

"That's . . . okay, soooo!"

"The swimming instructor, Miss Choy—she was Chinese—was pleased with our work. We worked very hard. We both passed, best in the class."

"Nice try, John. I meant go on with the story."

"Oh, ah, right. Well, uh, the first few days were spent reading about the different lifesaving techniques. Ah . . . holds, approaches, strokes," John swallowed hard before he continued, "and a lot of laps to get in shape. I could feel Gail's eyes on us from the other side of the pool. Boy! She was mad. But she acted like she wasn't, and if I happened to look in her direction, she was always flirting and dancing around Karl Page. It seemed like they were constantly together. I guess that's the way Gail wanted it to seem. Then there was the cross-chest carry."

"The cross-chest carry?" Her interest was peaked.

"Yes, a very effective hold." Sharon was on the edge of her seat. "You carry the drowning person by putting your arm across their chest and balancing their body on your hip. It's a good carry. You can do a real strong sidestroke for quite awhile or a semi-backstroke, uh, by balancing the drowning person on your stomach . . . or groin area."

"Oh, my God."

"That's not proper technique, but it works pretty good."

"For you and Carla."

"Yeah. I thought Gail was gonna explode when she saw us. Carla, she couldn't have been more satisfied. She seemed to enjoy the second technique a lot. Gail was the only one who seemed to notice us. Miss Choy just saw two kids working real hard to become lifeguards. She was very proud of us."

"And was there more going on than just swimming?"

"Yeah."

Sharon took a deep breath. "Go on."

"When Carla carried me, my head rested firmly against her, ah, small breasts."

"And?"

"When I carried her—" John wasn't sure how to phrase this. He paused for a second. "When I carried her, I always got an erection."

"She didn't mind?" Sharon asked, not nearly as surprised as John would have thought.

"She said she really liked it when that happened. What did I know? She was seventeen, an older woman, and this was the highlight of my sporting career." John said, pleading his case. "Whenever I carried Carla, I had to finish our laps way before the others."

"Why?"

"I needed to swim by myself . . . the hard-on. If we finished last, I'd have to get out of the pool with a tent."

"This is too adorable!" Sharon squealed.

John never thought of these moments as adorable. He had only thought of them as amazing. He had been amazed at his own vivid sense of discovery, impressed by what the world had to offer. Johney had learned a secret and wondered if growing up was always going to be this spectacular. And, at the same time, it had worried him—the strength of these feelings and emotions, how they affected not only Carla and him, but other people as well. He had figured that anything that felt this good probably had an equally intense opposite reaction.

"Whenever Carla saw Gail watching us do the cross-chest carry, she would whisper in my ear, 'Johnnn, please slow down. It feels soooo good.'"

"Oh, really? At seventeen? I can't believe that," uttered Sharon in mock astonishment. "Did you slow down?" she asked teasingly.

"A little," he said seriously, not realizing he was being teased.

"So, what did Gail do? She obviously liked you."

"At first she just yelled at me: 'Everyone knows what's going on in that pool. She's making an ass of you.' That kind of stuff, but it seemed to me that I was getting more and more popular. Maybe even more popular than Karl Page, and I think Gail knew it."

"Ewoooo, she was really mad. Sooo?"

"So, twice a summer the swim club had a nighttime pool party for the teenagers . . . big event. I guess after two weeks of me and Carla swimming together Gail had had enough. The night of the party Gail decided to do something about it. I guess she gave Karl a little of what he wanted, and she had every intention of letting it get around, especially to Carla and me. She could depend on Karl Page for that. Karl brought a small bottle of rum to the party to make rum and cokes. I remember him dispensing it in the back of the picnic area, like it was gold."

"You didn't have any?" Sharon asked.

"One . . . to be sociable. Let's see. Where was I? Oh, yeah. The picnic area was the make-out place. A lot of big trees back there, a horseshoe pit and a paddle-ball pole. Very private, especially at night. We called it 'the pit,' because it got so dark at night. By the end of any party, all the couples would end up there."

"Is that where you—"

"No, no, noooo. Don't get ahead of me. We're getting to that."

"Sorry."

"That's where Gail showed Karl her . . . breasts."

"Really!" Sharon was impressed. "That takes nerve. How'd she— without the other kids seeing? Without getting raped?"

"Well, she's pretty smart."

"How do you know all this? Or is it just what you think happened?" Sharon questioned him like a detective, wondering if this was all part of young John's fantasy.

"Gail told me. Besides, I know it's true. I saw the look on Karl's face when he ran from the pit."

"Okay, okay. So, how did it happen? Was it Gail or Carla. I think Gail," reasoned Sharon, speculating on John's first love.

"You wanted the whole story."

"I know, I know. I just can't wait to find out which one it was," she declared excitedly. "Please, continue."

"Alright. Ahhh . . . Gail brings Karl back to the ping-pong tables. Not as far back as the horseshoe pit, but dark enough yet close enough to the others, just in case. They make out for awhile. Karl is all over her, like he's recovering a fumble. I didn't make that up. That was Gail's line." Sharon couldn't keep herself from giggling. It was funny to hear John talk in his very adult gravelly voice like a teenager. 'Almost perverse sounding for such a nice man,' she thought, as she regained her composure and waited for him to continue his story.

"Okay, Gail stops him. He sez stuff like, 'Hey! What's the story? I thought you—' She quiets him with one of her bad girl looks. And she tells him, 'I've got something I want to show you, but you can't touch. Deal?'"

Sharon covered her face with her hands. "I can't believe I'm hearing this," she laughed, enjoying every second of the tale.

"Well, you asked for it."

"I know, I know! I didn't expect it to be this much fun. Please, go on."

"Karl can't believe his good luck. He's speechless. 'Do we have a deal?' Gail asks again. 'Yeah, sure. Deal!' he finally blurts out. Gail slowly steps back from him, maybe three steps. 'You move, I stop.' He nods his head greedily. He understands, probably drooling. He doesn't dare move for fear of Gail changing her mind. He's just another tree in the pit. And that's just how Gail wanted 'im." John was getting into telling his story. Sharon was an excellent audience for him. "One button, two, three, four . . . she let her white cotton blouse hang open, exposing her bra. She has really large breasts."

"It's definitely Gail," Sharon predicted. John ignored her and continued. He enjoyed keeping her in suspense. "How do you know she had large breasts?" she protested.

"I have eyes. Can I continue, or are you gonna keep interrupting?"

Sharon waved her hand like a queen. "Proceed."

"Okay. 'You're not moving?' Gail asked again. She's got him mesmerized like a lion tamer. Karl shook his head 'no.' She undoes her bra, letting her partly suntanned breasts fall out, a look of tremendous pride on her face."

"Oh, right. How do you know that?"

"I know Gail."

"Fine."

"Gail said she let him look while counting to ten. 'Seven . . . eight . . . nine . . . ten. That's enough. Let's get a soda,' she ordered. I remember Karl running by me and Carla and into the men's locker room. The next day Gail's breasts were legendary. I think she liked shedding her prude image, even though she denied Karl's story. 'He's dreaming,' she laughed. But what she was really saying was, 'See what you're missing.' I had to admit just hearing about Gail's . . . well, a teenaged boy can get pretty worked up."

"Even good boys?" Sharon said playfully.

"Yes, especially good boys."

"You think she just wanted your attention?"

"I think we had no idea of what or who we wanted. We just knew what we didn't have. In your teens it seems like the only thing you really know about sexuality is that it's powerful."

Maya woke up. She looked a little grumpy. Sharon took her from John's lap and rocked her a bit. "Maya's had enough of your story, but I'm still waiting for the good part."

"The good part, ah, July 22, 1953?"

"That sounds about right." Sharon sat down at the kitchen table and waited to hear about John's personal holiday, while Maya started a conversation with her dolly.

"I guess the rumor about Gail's breasts left a big impression on all of us, especially Carla."

"Carla? It was Carla," Sharon said. Maya gave her mother a stern look for interrupting her dolly talk.

"That Monday our lifesaving lessons went into the final week. I saw Gail and Carla on Sunday at the pool. Gail was enjoying her new found fame. Carla might have been a little jealous. It was hard to tell. So, Carla suggested that maybe she'd stop by my house before our class. 'We can walk over to the pool together,' she said."

"What did you say? Were you suspicious?"

"I said, 'Okay.'"

"You didn't think anything of it? She never came over before, did she?"

"Well, no. I guess I was just like every other guy at the pool."

"What does that mean?" Sharon asked, truly not understanding what he meant.

"I was still thinking about Gail's breasts."

"Oh."

"At nine o'clock in the morning Carla was at my door. My parents had already left for work. She was wearing a short, blue terry cloth robe and her sexiest black bathing suit underneath. She was even wearing makeup. Then I got suspicious. It didn't feel like an ordinary day. She wanted to hear me play the piano. She liked to sing, so I showed her to the basement where my old Frances Bacon upright was." John hesitated for a moment; that was the same piano Natt now had in his basement. Not that it meant anything. Not that it didn't mean anything. It was just a fact. Sharon thought he paused for dramatic effect.

"John? Honey. What is it?"

"Oh, it's nothing. I was just thinking about that old piano. Got it for free when I was nine years old. Neighbor had it in his garage covered with paint cans. He was moving and wanted to get rid of it. Karl Page helped us—me, Dad, and Natt—move it. I remember how excited I was, how I cleaned it up and got a piano tuner to fix it for next to nothing. He knew I would learn to play. Anyhow, Carla sat on the piano bench and listened. I don't remember what I played. I wasn't very good then. Just some simple melody that I made up on the spot. She was impressed and kissed me when I finished. She said how beautiful the music was and how wonderful it was that I could play an instrument. She asked me if I thought she was beautiful. She was very beautiful. Then she took her robe off and let it drop to the floor. She pushed the straps of her swimsuit off her shoulders and allowed them to fall to her arms. Her breasts were barely covered by the unsupported suit. She blushed a bit and looked kind of shy. She said she liked me a lot, that I was nice. And invited me to hold her. She allowed her bathing suit to fall from her body, an amazing moment for a young man. So hard to believe anything could be so . . . perfect. I understood what Karl Page must have felt when Gail showed him her breasts. An admiration for the pure beauty of a woman's form; the discovery of what I always wanted to know about; an amazement of the moment, a moment I never thought would come soon enough. I felt awe and respect, love of her kindness, and lust for her. I thought I should feel guilty, afraid, but I wasn't. We were young and curious and excited about the feelings we were having. Things seemed much simpler back then. Carla asked if I wanted to lie down with her. We did, on a mat next to the piano."

"Wow."

"Yeah."

"Wow. That sure beats the back seat of a Ford at midnight. What a great first time. I'm glad for you. It sounds sweet and sensual and sexy and in a strange way even innocent, all at the same time. Wonderful," she said. "Thanks for telling me."

"Huh, maybe that's why cars never meant much to me," he said, gazing at Maya. "I've got my father to thank for those summers. He got the neighbors together to build that pool. A hundred dollars apiece, a lot of money back then. He wanted his boys to learn how to swim, and to have some place to go during the dog days of summer. You think he knows we learned about sex and love there?"

"I think he knows. They always know a lot more than they let on."

"Really?"

"He has eyes!" Sharon smiled brightly, stealing one of John's lines. She put her sleeping daughter in the playpen and stared at her husband.

"So do you . . . beautiful eyes," he said. John picked Sharon up and carried her to their bedroom.

9

JOHNEY'S LOVE LIFE wasn't always as simple as the warm summer nights at the Mountain Edge Swim Club. He learned some tough lessons back in his minor league days in those small bush league towns. Folks become much more serious when they get older, and most people work real hard just to make a living and a modest life for their families.

John understood that it was special to be a ballplayer. I'm not talking about the fame or even the money. He realized it was unusual to play a game for a living and that most people sweated bullets in factories and on assembly lines to make ends meet, considering themselves fortunate to have a well-paying job. Even with his years of hard work and long hours he knew that he was blessed, blessed with a talent that most folks would consider heaven on earth. Not that he was making much of a living back when he played with the Toledo Mud Hens, the Highlanders Triple-A farm team.

It became painfully obvious to John that he, and baseball in general, represented a better way of life to many people. To the young boys and girls who looked up to the ballplayers, they were their heroes. To the men and women who built up a community with a baseball team, it was a source of enrichment. To the young ladies who fell for the handsome young ballplayers, they were a way out of their hometowns and a way into a more interesting life. Toledo wasn't a small town, but I suppose all towns are small towns if it's the only town you know.

In 1957, at the age of twenty, John learned more about love and life in

Toledo, Ohio, than it would seem necessary. Trouble was easy to find as a ballplayer. Local guys would pick fights in bars because you blew a play the night before and they lost fifty bucks; boyfriends would became enraged with jealousy because their young girlfriends enjoyed flirting; and most common of all, a ballplayer's girlfriend would grow angry, wanting more from the relationship. John said the first thing his manager told him was, "Keep your pecker in your pants, 'cause things can get messy. You don't want to embarrass the organization." John discovered abstinence was close to impossible. "The only group of fans bigger than nine-year-old boys seemed to be the nineteen-year-old girls," John wrote to Natt, "I can see how this could get complicated. So much opportunity." Natt told him to concentrate on baseball. "There'll be plenty of time for women when you get to New York City," he said, "Promise."

In Toledo, John roomed with a ballplayer named Aaron Frost. Aaron was the quiet, reserved, bitter, and angry type. He didn't talk much, but when he did, it was only in response to a direct question. He was extremely serious. Nobody really knew him. He wasn't very open or friendly for that matter. They always matched Aaron up with a rookie, because nobody liked him much. As it turned out, Aaron and John got along just fine and roomed together for almost two seasons. Neither one of them talked much. They could go for hours without saying a thing to each other, and they both felt perfectly comfortable with this arrangement.

Aaron Frost was a relief pitcher, and like most relief pitchers John assumed that he wanted to get into the starting rotation someday. But Aaron had given up on that idea a long time ago. He'd spent eight years in the minors, was a capable pitcher, but there came a point when he couldn't throw more than two innings, and there always seemed to be some young fire-baller coming up who would go to the show instead of him. His personality probably didn't help either. Anyway, Frosty, as most of the players called him, never was called up, and he knew that he had two or three years left in the league at best. Aaron probably was irritated and a bit sore over the whole situation, but he never told anyone what he was thinking, so nobody really knew for sure.

After rooming with Aaron for the first year the only thing John really knew about him was that he hated the road games. John said he got real moody whenever he had to pack his bags, and even moodier when he had to unpack. That was hard for John to understand. He was so happy just to be there. On a typical night Aaron would drink half a fifth of bourbon and read books on Italian cooking. He liked John because John knew something about cooking and was quiet—or just not around. And when he was around, he spent most of his time writing letters to his parents or Natt.

Natt,

Aaron is acting strange today. We've just lost our third game in a row and it's the first time I've ever seen him smile. That is strange, isn't it? Anyway, we're on our way back to Toledo tonight. I'm writing you on the bus. Sorry for the rough handwriting. Listen, as you know, I'm in a bit of a slump (3 of 23). I'm going back to my old stance tomorrow and I'm not taking batting practice like you told me. I thought I had something going for awhile with that new stance—guess not. I'll write you tomorrow night after the game to let you know how it goes.

Natt would receive a card or letter from Johney almost every day—a page, half a page, nothing long, just enough to let him know what he was thinking about. He sounded somewhat homesick most of the time. Natt always brought John's letters to Tommy's. That's why they all felt like they knew him when he came to the city. Natt never wrote John but he would phone him when the Mud Hens were in Toledo. Those calls were the only thing Aaron didn't like about John. "Do you have'ta talk to your brother every night? What's changed from yesterday?" he would say, giving Johney a dirty look. But the comments and looks ended in late August of 1957.

As it turned out, Aaron Frost had finally made a decision about his life. This would be his last year in the league; he'd had enough. Aaron liked Toledo and planned to open a pizzeria there. Maybe a full-scale restaurant someday. That was part one of his plan. The second decision involved Katie Evans. Katie was a waitress at the local diner. She was in her late twenties, a high school beauty queen who never married. Some say she was always on the look out for the perfect man; and the perfect man was always a ballplayer with great potential. Unfortunately, they always dumped her when they made it to the major leagues. Aaron had dated Katie off and on for the last three years, but then so did many ballplayers. She was a free spirit, not so much by choice but by fate. She had her share of opinions and bad feelings about men. She felt slighted, trapped, and used in Toledo, Ohio, and wanted out more than anything. Only she wanted a man to do it for her. So she dated often, figuring she was increasing her odds. She even went out with John once; she heard he had a real shot at New York City.

Apparently ten years ago, fresh out of high school, Katie was engaged to a Mud Hen. She thought her prayers had been answered until he called her from Los Angeles. He said he'd been traded, that his career was just taking off, so he shouldn't be thinking about marriage right now.

"And then you know what he said?" snipped Katie, as she bitterly told John her story. "He said he'd like to look me up the next time he's in Toledo. You know what I said? I said, 'Why?! So you can give me the clap?'" John never went out with Katie again. She would tell her story to every ballplayer she dated, often before going to bed with them. Sometimes she told it as though it didn't matter, trying to make it sound funny, but anyone could see how hurt she was, if they wanted to.

Katie and Aaron were very much alike. They both felt as if they never got a real shot at what they wanted. In reality, Katie's beauty and Aaron's talent gave them a much better start than most folks. Maybe they never had anybody to point that out. Their lives lacked the drama that they'd expected and craved. Though few people could afford to expect anything from their lives, somehow they did. I know this makes them sound unreasonable, even egotistical, and they were; but they weren't bad people, just misguided, and maybe tired of dealing with life as they saw it, life that grew around them like ivy grows up a wall. Burdened was how they pictured themselves.

"Why are you so happy? We're on a losing streak," asked John. He watched Aaron giddily stumble about their room as though he were drunk. Only John knew he hadn't had a drink all day. Aaron whistled as he put his shirts and socks away, even sang show tunes in the shower. Unusual behavior for a man who used this vocal cords so infrequently that you would think he was being charged by the word.

"Johney, this is it."

"What? This is what?"

"Our last home stand. My last year! I'm out of baseball, retiring. I'm staying here in Toledo, and I'm gonna make pizza for the rest of my life. And I'm not ever gonna leave. No more road trips, Johney boy! I'm even gonna vacation here. I'm leaving baseball to the young hot-shots like you!" He would've patted himself on the back, he was so proud of his decision. "You're a good kid, Johney. Wish me luck." And he smiled for the first time, like he meant it.

"Wow. Good luck. It must be the right thing. I've never seen you so happy. I've never seen you happy," said John, teasing him. They both had a good laugh. Aaron got a couple of glasses and poured his bourbon.

"Have a drink," he said, "to my new life." They raised their glasses and drank. "That's only the beginning, Johney. Let me tell you the best part."

John sat down as he waited to hear the best part. "The best part is . . . I'm gonna ask Katie Evans to marry me. Yeah, I thought we'd have one of those silly baseball weddings. She'd like that," he said confidently.

"Congratulations! That's terrific." John shook Aaron's hand.

"I know she sleeps around a lot, but I can make an honest woman of her. She's always wanted a ballplayer. I could do worse." He went on, convincing himself, until John finally stopped him.

"Frosty, she's a great girl. She just needs to be treated right." That was the first time John ever felt comfortable calling him Frosty, though he was still approaching Aaron cautiously. He knew how sensitive he was, how any little thing could set him off like a firecracker. The first week in the Mud Hen clubhouse Aaron had exploded at John. Johney didn't know any better. He had just caught two innings of perfect relief ball from Aaron in a winning effort over Columbus. Aaron gave up one hit, a double, on what John thought was a crossed sign. He wanted to straighten it out with Aaron so they wouldn't make the same mistake again.

"You gonna tell me how to pitch?! Don't ever tell me how to pitch! You just catch the ball, rookie!" He went on like that and was a bit more expressive with his adjectives for a good ten minutes. The other ballplayers took Johney out and bought him beers all night long to make him feel a little more welcomed. That's where John got filled in on Frosty, how touchy he was.

"Thanks. I'll be good to her," Aaron said. John was relieved that Frosty was in too good of a mood to get defensive. "Yup. I'm going over to the diner to ask her today."

KATIE WASN'T SURPRISED to see Aaron when he strolled into the diner. She owned a baseball schedule. She knew who was coming in every week. What did surprise her was the diamond ring Aaron produced as he plunked himself down at the counter. Aaron had rehearsed the presentation in his mind a thousand times that morning. He was still smelling a bit like bourbon, but his big crescent moon smile told Katie he was serious.

"Aaron! What is this? Oh, it's beautiful," Katie sighed, unable to control her tears.

Aaron just stood there grinning. "Well, uh, will you marry me?"

"Aaron." She was so stunned she couldn't find her voice.

"I know this is sudden. You don't have to give me your answer now. You'll be at the game tonight?"

Katie could barely catch her breath. "Yes, I will. Tonight then."

Aaron was so happy before the game that the whole team noticed and wanted to know if he was on some sort of medication. Aaron couldn't hold it in, but he should have, and before the game he announced that this would be his last season and that he planned to marry Katie Evans.

Frosty got the save that night in a 2 to 1 squeaker over the Clippers. He had more energy than anyone had seen from him in years. And for the most part Aaron had one of his better years, saving twenty five games out of thirty-three with only one loss. His fastball was so hot, it hurt when it hit John's glove. His curve broke as though falling off a cliff. He looked like the best pitcher in the league with ten more years in front of him, but he was just using everything he had left in his seasoned arm. Having a goal seemed to focus Aaron like he'd had never been focused before. The truth about Aaron Frost was that he was one of the few ballplayers who didn't really care all that much about the game. He had some talent. It was easy, but in the end it had nothing to do with his dreams.

Katie was in the stands watching her future husband bewilder batter after batter, and with every pitch her plans seemed more and more achievable. After the game Aaron met Katie in front of home plate. She gave him a big kiss, which made Aaron feel as though he could do no wrong.

"You were great!" Katie shouted in between kisses. "They couldn't get a hit off you if Johney told 'em what was coming!"

"Katie, did you think about my question?"

"Yes. Yes! Aaron Frost. I'll marry you!" she shouted, looking years younger.

"Katie, you've made me the happiest man in Toledo." He picked her up and swung her around the batter's box.

"I'm the second happiest man. I don't have to room with him anymore," joked John as he took off his catching equipment. "Sorry, but I couldn't help overhearing some good news. Congratulations. All the luck in the world."

"Thanks, John," Katie said shyly.

"Yeah, thanks, Johney. Do me a favor. Ask the guys if they'd meet me and Katie at Tyson's. I want to toast my bride. Tell 'em I'm buying."

"Sure. Be glad to," said John.

"You'll be there? I need a best man. Would you do that for me, Johney?"

"You're getting married tonight?"

"No, no." He turned to Katie. "I thought we'd have one of those baseball weddings, twenty-four bat salute, on the field and everything." She smiled her approval. Aaron then turned to John and said, "I want you to be my best man. See, tonight we make the announcement."

BASEBALL & BENEVOLENCE

"Oh, Aaron," said Katie. " I love baseball weddings. They're so silly and fun and romantic all at the same time. I can't believe this is happening. I have to tell Marianne. She'll die. Can I invite my friends to Tyson's, too?"

"Invite 'em all. What'd ya say, Johney?"

"I'd be honored."

So it was settled, nine o'clock at Tyson's for the marriage announcement. Everybody was there: the players, the wives, the girlfriends, Katie's friends, even many of the Columbus Clippers showed up, all having a great time running up Aaron's liquor bill. Aaron didn't mind one bit.

At ten o'clock when Aaron was sure most everybody was there, he raised his mug of beer and said, "Can I have your attention? Can I please have your attention? Alright! Could'ya just shut up for a minute?" He got a few laughs from the crowd. "I'd like to make it official, the way they like things in baseball." Aaron got a few more laughs, which surprised him more than anyone. Nobody ever thought of Aaron as funny, especially Aaron, and he was truly enjoying himself. "Folks, folks! Today Miss Katie Evans has agreed to be my wife." The crowd really started to whoop it up. "Drinks for the house!" Aaron shouted. Streamers and confetti rained down on the exhilarated couple as they accepted congratulations, drank, and generally carried on. Around eleven-thirty Aaron, who was by then smashed out of his mind, wanted to make a toast to his bride-to-be. He tapped his fork on the side of his beer mug, his pinkie raised genteelly in the air. The rowdy crowd came to attention with a roar of approval, inspiring Aaron to make his toast from on top of Tyson's bar. His head missed the slow moving ceiling fan by inches. Before he started to speak, Aaron removed his ball cap and hung it on one of the blades of the fan. The cap slowly orbited around his head, producing one chorus of "Take Me Out to the Ball Game"—for some unknown reason.

"I feel like the sun," Aaron stated in a classic deadpan delivery, producing his biggest laugh of the night. He stared into his audience with a drunken grin, his hair matted to his head from his cap and his face, flushed red. He was very drunk. The colors from the cap seemed to make a circle around Aaron's head; at least that's what John remembered, but he was pretty drunk, too. "I'd like to thank you all for coming on out here tonight helping me run up this bar bill." Shouts of "No problem" and a chant of "Frost-y, Frost-y, Frost-y" came from the crowd. "Congratulate us, guys, gals! Me and Katie are getting married!" he shouted over the din. Katie was surrounded by a group of her girlfriends, standing along the bar. She was beaming, whispering and giggling, her eyes shining up towards her savior.

"As most of you know," Aaron began, "this is my last season of baseball. I'm settling here in Toledo."

Those were the only words Katie heard from Aaron's rather long, drunken, heartfelt toast to his bride. John said Aaron grinned from cheek to cheek the entire time he spoke, completely oblivious to his fiancee's reaction.

As though looking at a thought balloon hanging over Aaron's head, Johney could see Aaron thinking, 'I finally did something right.'

Aaron didn't get it. Not even when he stopped speaking and raised his glass to Katie, did he get it. She looked like a ghost, a deer frozen by headlights, scared to death. She had a choice. She could run or she could say something. I think maybe running would have been the better choice.

"You're what?!!!" Katie shrieked in a blistering falsetto.

Aaron's grand stage on top of the bar became the home of the fool. He looked stunned, then panicked, overwhelmed, and on display with no place to run. Aaron leapt down from the bar, only his cap was left in orbit. A pitcher of beer soaked some unlucky party-goer, as Aaron deliberately kicked it off the bar on his way down. He grabbed Katie by the arm and pulled her out of the restaurant.

Outrage, indignation, contempt, embarrassment, and hatred streaked and stained both their faces. Katie scratched herself free after an exchange of painfully ugly words. Aaron Frost walked down the street after her, but not really. He rejected help from anyone with a resounding and infuriated "Fuck off!" and disappeared into the night just behind Katie Evans.

August 29, 1957

Natt,

I can only imagine the cruel things they must have said. Aaron so desperately wanting the quiet life in Toledo, and Katie pleading to be taken away. It's sad neither one possessed what the other wanted. Aaron didn't come back to our room that night. I went looking for him, but I didn't look in the right place. He was determined to make Toledo, Ohio, his last stop, and he did. We found him the next morning. He had hung himself from the backstop at the park . . . directly over home plate. Nobody has seen Katie since. I guess they both got what they wanted. Aaron never has to step foot outside of Toledo again, and Katie got away. I guess they just broke after coming so close. Aaron's funeral is tomorrow. I wish I could have helped him. He was my friend. I can't believe

things can get this out of control. I guess it wasn't love they were looking for; I suppose it was change they wanted more than anything. They each stayed the same and expected the other to change. I guess that's what happened. I'll write you tomorrow.
Love, Your Brother

10

New York City: November, 1964

"ALMOST READY!" SHARON called from the kitchen in a singsong voice.

"I'll get the kids' table set up, Shar," said Faye with a handful of plates and silverware.

"Wait. Where you going?" asked Natt, playfully. He grabbed his wife from behind as she stepped out of the kitchen. She gave him a coy glance.

"Turkey smells great. I'm starving," Natt whispered in her ear.

"Good. What's everybody else doing?" smiled Faye.

"What they always do. Let's see. The granddads are discussing John's career. This year Mark and Charlie are in on the discussion."

"I'll bet John is happy to hear that. What's he doing?"

"Playing doll house with Maya. Mom Greco and Mom Costa are watching. They're completely charmed by Maya's good manners. I think she's serving pretend tea right now. She likes to do that."

"And you?" Faye flirted, batting her eyelashes.

"Me, I'm just trying to make time with my wife."

"Good boy. But I have work to do. Maybe later." He gave her a wink as she waved the silverware in front of his face.

"Later," Natt said. He strolled over to the tray table bar and poured himself a scotch and soda.

"Does anybody want a drink?" Natt asked.

"Ginger ale!" shouted Mark.

"Me, too," called Charlie, not wanting to be left out.

"How's it going?" asked John. He startled Sharon who was concentrating on creating lump free turkey gravy.

"John! You scared me. Make some noise the next time."

"Sorry. Smells great. Is that my dad's stuffing?" She nodded. He gave her a kiss on the neck.

"Did you put the leaf in the table for me?"

"Yes, ma'am."

Sharon pulled the rolls and chestnuts out of the oven. They filled the kitchen with the smells of Thanksgiving.

"This may sound stupid, but we have plenty to be thankful for," she said.

"It doesn't sound stupid. We do. Not as much as Natt and Faye," he joked. "Should I tell everyone dinner is ready?"

"Tell them five minutes. I think the turkey cooled enough."

"Great. I'm starved."

"Five minutes," John announced as he picked up little Charlie. The boy was delighted by his uncle's attention as he stood listening to his grandfather talk baseball with Mr. Costa. Charlie did his best to fight John off. That was the game they played. He was almost seven and liked roughhousing, football, and baseball. He was a boy.

"Are they still trying to make me a better ballplayer?" John asked Charlie for all to hear.

"Yeah," he said. The kid looked just like Natt. John held the boy in one arm, spun him around, then allowed him to land softly on the living room couch.

"I think they're really onto something," said Natt, rolling his eyes.

"Something my coaches haven't figured?" asked John, knowing this would get a response from his dad and his father-in-law.

"Well, maybe, John—just maybe," said Guy Greco. "I think you'd be much better off catching full-time." He returned his attention to Mr. Costa. "He calls a damn good game. They win more games when Johney catches."

"Now, John, you're a helleva catcher, but don't you think you'd hit better playing second? You don't seem as tired," replied Mike Costa, not so much to John but to Guy. "Son, if you'd play second, I'm sure you'd hit twenty points higher. Guarantee ya the Hall. Wouldn't it, Natt?" The funny thing about these conversations was that the dads never waited for Natt or John to respond.

"He'll make it to the Hall of Fame anyway," insisted Mr. Greco. John wondered how these discussions made Natt feel. They were always talking about him and his career. It had to make Natt feel bad, he reasoned. But if it did, Natt never let on. In fact, he seemed to enjoy their baseball squabbles as much as they did.

"If he played second every day, he'd be more visible, hit better. He should be the lead-off man, too," said Mike Costa, emphatically stating his case.

"You don't get it!" yelled Guy Greco, irritated. "He can do a lot to help the team. That's why he's there. It's a team sport." It was obvious that they'd been going over the same material for the last three hours. The last three years, actually. It was also obvious that they looked forward to going to the ball games and bickering with each other. Guy and Mike had become best friends.

Charlie and Mark were very proud of their Highlander uncle. All of their friends knew who John Greco was. And Charlie was showing signs of becoming a ballplayer himself. All of this made John glad, but a little uncomfortable, too. It was a lot of attention. He didn't deal with the glamour nearly as well as the game itself. Maybe that's why Natt never got jealous. He knew fame made Johney uncomfortable. His brother was simply a great ballplayer. Natt once asked me, "George, how can I be so different from my brother?" The truth was, he wasn't.

"Uhhhh! Excuse me," Natt coughed, pretending to clear his throat, looking for his father and father-in-law's attention. They stopped their argument long enough to hear what Natt had to say.

"I remember John fielding and hitting third base better than any other position," he said confidently. They were speechless and both looked at him with a confounded expression.

"What?!"

"In little league," laughed Natty, mercifully ending their black hole of an argument for at least that Thanksgiving day.

"Charlie, Mark, ball game in the park after dinner?" asked their Uncle John.

"Maybe we can get Mike and Dad to do more than just talk about it," challenged Natt. The kids couldn't wait to get through dinner.

When Mike Costa tried to bring up the St. Louis World Series games again, Sharon was ready for him. "Dad, if John opened his stance, kept his weight back and elbow down, he would have added twenty more points to his Series average regardless of what position he'd played." She was perfect, an actress. No, better, she was fast becoming a knowledgeable baseball fan. And Faye wasn't far behind.

It was hard not to be a baseball fan in New York City. The Highlanders went to the World Series every year from 1960 through 1964, winning it all in '61 and '62. John was a star whether he liked it or not.

Sharon continued with her point, "If he went with the pitch more often, he could spray the ball around the field—keeps the pitchers and defense off balance."

Then Faye piped in, "When John bats from the left side, I think he's trying to pull everything. That short porch in right field can be a little too tempting."

Not only were Faye and Sharon becoming knowledgeable, they were becoming fanatical as well. Of course they had a much better sense of humor about it than Guy and Mike. And they were better at it, the analysis and the actual playing.

The annual family game became a showcase for the Greco women. Faye was the family softball pitcher. Sharon was the catcher, plus she was good with the bat. By the end of their game in Central Park, they would have an audience. Passersby would recognize John and stay to watch. They usually formed pick-up games with anyone who wanted to play. The highlight was watching John kill a softball. It was magnificent, especially when one of the local league players wanted a crack at pitching to the Highlander, John Greco. They'd give John their best stuff. But by major league standards these were very slow pitches, and a softball must have looked like a beach ball to John. Natt really got a kick out of the way Faye and Sharon planned the family softball strategy.

"John, you play the outfield," Sharon would say.

"Which one? Center?" he'd say, playing along.

"All the outfield! We need Natt at third base, Faye pitching, Dad Greco second, Dad Costa shortstop, Mark first base. I'll catch and, oh, Charlie help John out in left field." Sharon was really into managing. She even pretended to have a farm team. "We have a new kid coming up, Maya Greco. I don't want to rush her. She'll play right field when I think she's ready. Right now, she's only three. Until then, John, you'll have to pick up the slack for her," she'd say in her best managerial tone.

John would respond, "Yes, ma'am."

LOOKING BACK ON the '64 season, I can see it was the most involved the Grecos ever were with the games. Sharon and Faye had hopped on the number four train to Ruth Memorial Stadium over twenty times that season, a full third of the Highlander home games. Their attendance was amazing considering just two years earlier Faye was practically a recluse and neither one of them had had any interest in the game. Natt and the boys and the granddads often went with them—just as often they went by themselves.

"They all act like the manager of the team," Natt sighed. "They're all experts, calling for the hit-and-run, double steal, the bunt . . . whatever," he told his brother.

"I know," replied John. "They go over all their moves with me after every game, especially if we lose."

John always would listen politely to his family members, nodding his head along with their suggestions. And when they let him talk, which wasn't often, John would say, "Could work," but only to their most adamant suggestions.

Sharon's passion for baseball grew as she became more aware of the subtlety within the game. She was fascinated by the dirt-kicking managers, barking their impassioned arguments in face to face confrontations with the umpires, even though most arguments were futile. "Their only purpose seems to be to get a future call or just get thrown out of the game," Sharon reasoned. "Sometimes that can really pump up a ball club." She was beginning to sound suspiciously like Phil Rizzuto. For a woman who spent four years at Princeton learning the art of diplomacy, the idea of letting loose was completely foreign and at the same time stimulating to her. "There is an honesty, a frankness, to those confrontations, and an agreed upon line that won't be crossed," Sharon would say. She viewed baseball as confrontational yet civilized, and to Sharon that civility was woven through the heart of the game.

I once asked her what she liked best about baseball, and she said, "I'm addicted to the suspense." Of course, there was one thing that made Sharon irrational: anybody who said anything bad about John. Natt said Sharon was always making things interesting at the ballpark, especially at Fenway Park, in Boston.

It didn't take Sharon long to discover the rivalry between the Highlanders and the Red Sox. At first it surprised her, that these two great intellectual and artistic centers took baseball so seriously. But as she became more involved, she realized that it couldn't be any other way. It was history. Sharon learned that the two teams were in the same division; about the rivalry between Joe DiMaggio and Ted Williams. She was pleased when she learned of the Babe Ruth trade that gave Boston enough money to pay the mortgage on Fenway Park . . . and gave the Highlanders a legend. She learned about the Green Monster Wall in left field at Fenway, the bad blood, and that some of the greatest ball games ever played were between the Highlanders and Red Sox.

Sharon felt it was her moral duty to make at least one pilgrimage a year to Fenway. She loved the little ballpark. Faye and Natt would accompany her because they enjoyed Fenway, too. Besides, somebody had to keep Sharon from getting killed.

John didn't pay much attention to Sharon's fanaticism, especially about Boston. He knew she once dated a diehard Red Sox fan at Princeton. He had broken her heart. John figured her Boston loathing was well-founded, or at least it was based on something more important than just geographical location.

The Highlanders were on fire in late September of 1964. They were going to win the pennant again. Boston was a good ten games back and the only thing they had to look forward to was beating the Highlanders—if they could. Fenway Park was full nevertheless, and the Red Sox fans had much more to look forward to than they thought.

Sharon, Natt, and Faye were coming to town to see the last game of the series. You couldn't miss them at Fenway with their Highlander caps and jackets. Natt carried a silver flask filled with scotch that he drank from during minor altercations between the women, which occurred no matter what section they happened to be in. It was a beautiful September evening at Fenway. John was batting in the lead-off position and playing second base. Mike Costa was very pleased with the line-up card—certain that John had passed on his advice to the Highlander manager, Dillon Southwood.

The Grecos' seats were just nine rows behind the Highlander dugout. John could lean over and talk to them if he wanted, but he never did, not during a game. The threesome got the usual stares and catcalls reserved for flamboyant Highlander fans. John's cheering section didn't disappoint the citizens of Boston, and their exuberance produced many less-than-flattering names from the Red Sox faithful.

John walked to the plate to start the game. Sharon, Faye, and Natt gave him a standing ovation, as though he were royalty. John didn't pay any attention to them. His full concentration was on hitting.

"Sit down!" a Boston fan screamed, which only prolonged John's ovation.

Jack "Doc" Gills was on the mound for Boston. He was having a so-so year with a record of 8 and 8. He'd suffered a few nagging arm and hand injuries but still showed flashes of his past brilliance with a ninety-plus fastball and a great slider. On a good day he could be unhittable.

It was easy to get distracted in the close confines of Fenway Park. John wasn't going to let anybody get into his head, but Jack Gills seemed to have an open channel to anyone who was broadcasting. And those three New Yorkers seemed to have a good clear signal tuned directly into Jack's head. It all started with the first pitch, a ball that was high and outside with not much on it.

"Yes! Yes! Yes!" chanted the New Yorkers into the game from the very first pitch.

Gills glanced up into the crowd as he picked up the rosin bag to dry his sweating palms. 'I shouldn't have drank so much last night,' he thought. 'Who are those morons?' He marched back to the mound and threw John two more balls that weren't even close. John just watched them go by and didn't even notice the chanting, but Doc did. Gills had no concentration, was hung over, and very worried about making his third bad start in a row. He could hear everything, and on the fourth pitch of the game, he was already looking for a little something extra. Doc produced a 93 m.p.h. fastball that had some kind of crazy movement on it. John tried to spin away, but he couldn't, and it nailed him in the back near the spinal cord, dropping him like a tree in the woods. Everybody caught their breath at the same time, and I mean everybody—in Tommy's Bar, at Fenway Park, everybody—especially Natt, Sharon, and Faye. Reality came crashing down, and we were reminded that it was a sport . . . often a dangerous sport.

Jack Gills woke up from his hazy state of mind. The Highlander trainer, Buddy Sophia, came running out of the dugout, but John was already on his feet before Buddy got to home plate. Buddy was pretty fat, so it took him awhile to get there. The injury wasn't as bad as it looked. The ball missed his spine and just hit a muscle. John didn't even rub it. He dusted himself off, put his batting helmet back on, told Buddy he wasn't coming out of the game, and jogged to first base. The Boston fans applauded his courage. As soon as Sharon knew he was okay, she lashed into Jack Gills.

"Get him out of the game! He's dangerous! Ejection! Ejection! Get 'im out before he kills someone!" she shouted at the home plate umpire. The umpire gave Gills a warning and pretended not to hear Sharon's advice. And that was just the first batter of the game.

"He didn't want to hit him. You think he wants to put the lead-off man on base? Nah, he's wild," said Natt.

"Are you kidding? He had nothing— 0 and 3! John was going to walk anyway. Gill's was sending a message," argued Sharon.

Natt thought about it, took a sip from his flask, and said, "You may be right." Faye was still demanding the pitcher's ejection from the game. Natt was beginning to feel slightly claustrophobic, especially after John stole second on Jack's very next pitch. Sharon didn't hold back. Both Greco women could be seen standing and cheering and jumping among a sea of discontented faces. Natt had another drink. It eased the pressure of being hated by hundreds of Boston fans.

"Sit down and shut up!" yelled an unnerved Sox fan, gaining full approval of most everyone in his section. Natt took another sip.

"You shut up! He's my husband!" Sharon yelled back, immediately realizing her mistake. From every direction the Boston fans turned to face her. They were delighted by this interesting piece of information. The Greco women became noticeably less vocal.

After John stole second, Jack Gills began to find his control, and he got the next three batters out to end the top of the first. The game ended up as a pitchers' duel. By the top of the ninth the score was 0-0. Each team had only two hits. Doc Gills had come to his senses after beaming John in the first inning and was throwing his best game of the year. John grounded out to the shortstop his second time up, and the Boston fans were all over him, especially in Sharon's section. Natt had another sip of scotch. Sharon held her tongue which she was dying to wag. Any time she opened her mouth it seemed as though a hundred people would get on John's case. As a result, she sat and waited and prayed for something good to happen, which almost did with John's third at-bat.

"No batter! Nooo batter! Easy out!" called the polite Boston fans.

"He's just waving his limp dick!" and other crude comments came from the not-so-polite fans.

Sharon was reduced to a mere, "Come on, Johney!" Faye resorted to eating hot dogs and Natt, well . . . ordered a beer.

When John came to the plate for his third at-bat, he looked much more comfortable. He dug holes where his feet should be planted and began to push the dirt around with the barrel of his bat before he set himself. This habit of drawing in the dirt was receiving plenty of attention. The pictures were purely subconscious reactions, nothing premeditated. Sometimes he'd draw a star or a crescent moon in the soft, sandy dirt of the batter's box . . . sometimes nothing at all. Some of the Boston fans took to calling him the "Space Cadet," because John seemed to live in his own world once he entered the batter's box, drawing and playing in the dirt like a child, untouched by anyone—not the umpire, not even the thousands of hostile Boston fans. However, anyone who knew John's career also knew that he was most dangerous when he drifted into one of his trance-like at-bats. The New York sportswriters eventually started to report what John drew and charted the symbols in terms of hits. At first it was just a joke from the self-assured New York press. Then after a year of charting, it became something much more as the cryptic pictures began to bear themselves out. By the end of the previous season John had his own box score system written in stars, squares, moons, and triangles.

	Stars	Squares	Moons	Triangles
Singles	63	08	03	03
Doubles	11	21	01	00
Triples	00	02	13	00
Home Runs	00	00	08	25
	74	31	25	28

At Ruth Memorial they even flashed his drawings on the scoreboard to add to the suspense. Folks started to believe in it. The joke was that John only needed to draw more triangles to hit home runs.

When the Boston fans saw him making patterns in the Fenway dirt, they started to chant, "Space Cadet! Space Cadet! Space Cadet!" hoping to disturb his concentration. And, at the same time, they wanted to know what he was drawing. A murmur went through the crowd. "Crescent moon. Moon." They started to get nervous. According to last year's chart, that could mean a triple. It was the craziest thing, but in their heart of hearts they all wanted to believe in the symbols—even the Boston fans. Natt did. He had seen his brother do it all his life. It was almost eerie how quiet it became after John made one of his prehistoric drawings. Even the chanting died, allowing him every opportunity, once again, to prove their validity. Every time he did it, I think it gave folks assurance. He certainly added a whole new dimension to the game. Johney didn't try to make it mysterious, the fans did. When asked about the pictures, he would only say, "I have no idea what I'm doing. I just do it sometimes. I'm not calling my shots if that's what you're asking."

John took the first pitch, ball one. On the second pitch Doc Gills came at him with everything he had left, a high heater just where John liked it. John hit it hard on the sweet part of the bat, a line drive to deep center field. It sounded as though everyone in Fenway Park moaned, "Shit" at the same time. Unfortunately for the Highlanders, T.C. Golden, the Boston center fielder, had him played perfectly. With just a few steps back, a beautiful hit became a 410 foot out. I think T.C. bought into John's chart and decided to play the deep gap. The Boston fans breathed a sigh of relief and toasted the real crescent moon above the park. Sharon was furious with the way the Bostonians gloated over her husband's misfortune.

"Relax!" shouted Faye, sounding even more crazed than Sharon. "It's still tied!" Her face reddened, her hands flying in all directions.

"I know it's tied! That was our chance!" explained Sharon, experiencing a momentary loss of her senses.

"Hello," Natt waved his hands, as though bringing them in for a landing. "It's just a baseball game. Try to enjoy it. Even if they lose, there'll be another game tomorrow," he said, trying his best to pacify them. Natty put his arms around their shoulders and whispered in their ears, "It's baseball. Anything can happen. Be patient."

"Oh, Natt! We had 'em!" cried Faye, passionately, reminding him of how in love he was with her.

"You never have them 'til it's over," he said, as he wrapped his arms around his wife. "Even then, I'm not so sure about it . . . or if it matters," he whispered. Natty always got philosophical after a pint of scotch. He knew better than most that as quickly as one door is closed another opens. For no apparent reason a door had opened between himself and Faye. He couldn't imagine loving another woman more and didn't understand how two people could change as much as they had. But like baseball and his dead arm, it wasn't about understanding. It was about acceptance. Natt watched his formerly reclusive wife cheering for her team and her brother-in-law without a care in the world. He was in love, at the Highlander game, and in Fenway Park. Three places he'd never thought he'd be at the same time.

In the top of the ninth the score was still tied at 0-0. The Highlanders had one out with men on second and third. Boston intentionally walked Freddy Greene, preferring to pitch to John instead. Playing the averages with the open base, it was a good move to try for the double play ball. Sharon took it as a direct insult to her husband's abilities. When the announcer announced John Greco, Faye and Sharon simultaneously broke into a chant of, "John-ney! John-ney! John-ney!"

"Sit down and shut up!" yelled a short, heavy-set man with no shirt on.

"His body resembles a tree stump," Faye whispered to Sharon, and they giggled like school girls.

"Keep your shirt on," called Sharon, giggling all the while.

Natt found his second flask, while Johney made his way to the batter's box. He dug holes for his feet and started to push the dirt around with the barrel of his bat. No discernible shapes or patterns appeared, much to the relief of the Boston fans. He was being pitched with surprising care, considering the bases were loaded. The count ran to 3 and 1. John looked to third base for a sign. He wanted the green light. But the third base coach, Hank Miller, gave him the take sign. Dillon Southwood wanted to walk the run in if he could. The 3-1 pitch came right down the middle for a strike. The count went full. Dillon gave Hank his sign and Hank mercifully gave Johney the green light. John knew the next pitch would be a fastball for a strike. 'What else could Doc do?' he reasoned. John's bat went to the dirt, and a square appeared. "Square" nervously echoed throughout the ballpark.

The pitch came down hard, fast, and fat. Doc made a big mistake. He wanted it over the outside corner, but he laid it right down the middle and up a bit, just like a batting practice fastball. Gills regretted the pitch as soon as the ball left his hand. At first John thought he had a home run, but the ball hit about three inches from the top of the Green Monster in left field and fell in for a double. The Highlanders took the lead 2 to 0.

From second base John could see three of his family members making perfect fools of themselves just above the Highlander dugout. Natt had a finger on top of both the women's heads as they spun around him like tops, chanting, "Yes! Yes! Yes!" completely oblivious to the barrage of insults from the surrounding Boston fans.

The Highlanders won the game 2 to 1, after a bases-loaded threat by Boston in the ninth that didn't quite work out for them. Sharon, Faye, and Natt didn't make any new friends that day. But the Highlanders were in first place, and John Greco was becoming a true Highlander great. Natt and Faye were in love. John and Sharon were in love, and things looked pretty good, just what you would expect when riding a hot streak.

11

Boston: October, 1991

"WE'RE BACK! T.C. Golden here, the voice of the Boston Red Sox. It's the top of the ninth at Fenway and the Sox lead it 11 to 1 over the Toronto Blue Jays. Luckily we have my old buddy, John Greco, in the booth to make it interesting for us. John, you've been out of baseball, oh, what is it? Nine maybe ten weeks? What are you doing here? Don't you have a family?"

"Thanks for the warm welcome, T.C. Yes, I do have a family. I'm taking a vacation I guess. Seeing baseball as a fan, doing some thinking, visiting my old friends, like you T.C., and following the Highlanders a bit."

"Well, folks, what do you think? Has he lost his mind? John, I'm gonna do a test just to see how far gone you are. Do you think the Highlanders are one of the two teams playing in tonight's game?"

John just laughed and replied, "Actually, T.C., the Highlanders have a day off before they play in Baltimore tomorrow, so I thought I'd drop by the booth and allow you the opportunity to do New York City jokes. Maybe help you get through this boring game."

"The pitch, swung at by Coleman, popped up to Betts at second. One away for Toronto in the top of the ninth," announced T.C. "Well, John, that was mighty considerate of you. We did need a little action here."

"Glad to help out."

"Kevin Shan takes a strike on the inside corner, 0 and 1 to Kevin. So, are you looking for a job?"

"Sure. You got one for me? My resume's very short. I know how to play baseball and the piano but, due to my disability, I can't do either. I guess that leaves teaching."

"My, my, that's the longest sentence I've ever heard you make. The pitch, Shan swings. It's hit hard, deep, it's . . . it's . . . caught at the 420 fence, deep in center by Jack McQuillan! Oh, what a catch! He had his body turned the wrong way, but he made the adjustment to make the play! Two down in the top of the ninth for Toronto; the Sox lead it 11 to 1. You know, John, this would have been a much better game if all the scoring hadn't happened in the first inning."

"Humph."

"Thanks for your sparkling analysis. You're really helping me through this game with your insightful commentary. Charlie Weaver takes a ball, down low, 1 and 0."

"You're welcome."

"Weaver takes a strike right down the middle. He's mad at himself. That was his pitch. Charlie Weaver looks as though he were planning a rally, a ten-run rally with two outs in the top of the ninth. Boston's been leading since the first, 11 to 1. Nothing has changed since."

"Sounds like you're tired of this one, T.C."

"Don't say that on the air. We have advertisers," T.C. joked.

"I don't think anybody has been listening since the fifth inning, T.C." They both laughed at how alone they felt. The ballpark was empty except for a handful of diehards and the players.

"The pitch. Swing! It's a grounder to Berry Keating at short . . . the throw to first. Weaver is out! Sox win it by a score of 11 to 1. It's been the same score all day, folks. We'll be back with the post game wrap-up after these brief messages." T.C. sighed as they went off the air, then turned to John. "Hallelujah. Johney, I'll be finished in fifteen minutes. Let's grab a bite to eat, have a few beers. What'd ya say?"

"That's what I'm here for," said John.

T.C. took a long, hard look at John. "Jesus, Johney. What've you been doing on this vacation? You look like hell."

Terry Carmen Golden played center field for the Red Sox when John played his ball back in the sixties. In fact, T.C. was the well-positioned center fielder who caught John's hard hit smash, some twenty-eight years earlier. That was the same day Johney won the game for the Highlanders, and

Sharon, Faye, and Natt made fools of themselves in the Boston stands. T.C. loved to hear John tell the story about that game, especially the part about him being well-positioned. It was the final outcome T.C. didn't appreciate much. T. C. Golden was a fair player at best, a lifetime .241 hitter, pretty good power, maybe 20 homers a year, 50 RBI. He was injury prone and only played three years in the majors. As a result, T.C. repeated any highlight from his career as often as possible. It was a running gag on his broadcast. He'd have Ted Williams in the booth with him, and say, "Ted, what was the greatest play you ever saw me make?" And Ted would go along with him just like everybody else.

"Huh," Ted once grunted. "T.C., that's a tough call. I think it was a blonde in Los Angeles."

John and T.C. became good friends after a minor bench-clearing altercation between the Sox and the Highlanders. They each tried to trade punches but missed and spent the rest of the night in a local bar laughing about it. They were buddies from then on.

Johney was having a pretty good day, despite T.C.'s assessment of his condition. Ever since Chicago, John's unemployment was beginning to agree with him. Now he was even feeling at ease with his nonaccountability. That was probably T.C.'s influence. Terry could put off funeral arrangements until a more convenient date and time. John was beginning to feel a reconnection to the people and places of baseball. As though listening to a favorite song as it rekindled fond feelings, John's vacation was sparking the passion and affection he once felt for the sport.

"C'mon. Let's go. I'm buying," called T.C. He put his arm around his buddy who appeared to be in deep thought. John was picturing the well-positioned T.C. Golden as he made an easy catch of his hard hit drive to center field.

"Okay. You're buying," agreed John. T.C. gave him a light slap on the cheek.

"That's what I like about you, you're so easy," he chuckled. A replay of baseball's greatest hit ran through T.C.'s head, and he thought, 'How can I not buy?'

As they strolled down Yawkey Way in front of Fenway Park, T.C. talked a mile a minute about whatever came to mind. John nodded or shook his head, grunted, sighed, laughed, smiled, giving T.C. whatever he wanted to hear or see.

The traveling must have been getting to John a bit, because he suddenly felt tired. One more game in Baltimore and his trip would be over. He looked forward to seeing Sharon. He missed her a great deal. This was the first time in thirty years of marriage that he had taken a holiday without her. The thought of separate vacations had never occurred to him before, but Sharon knew that John wanted and needed to go. He was scared and wanted to say good-bye to all his old friends, not sure if he would ever see many of them again. He was looking for affirmation of his beliefs and forgiveness for his doubts.

"Anyway, the son-of-a-bitch hits it out of the park, and I gotta eat fried sheep balls!" shouted T.C., practically doubled over by his own anecdote. They stopped walking long enough for T.C. to catch his breath. John hadn't heard a word he'd said. He didn't even pretend out of politeness to have heard T.C.'s story.

"What's the matter? Don't you think that's funny?!" T.C. knew John hadn't been listening. "Spacing out on me," he kidded. "That's okay, Johney. I'll tell you again over dinner. It's a good one."

John stopped dead in his tracks, stunned by a hauntingly familiar face. He still wasn't listening to T.C. as he gazed down the street not believing what he was seeing.

"John. John," nudged T.C., unable to get his attention. "I'm gonna start taking this personally," he said. "What? What are you looking at?!" He was beginning to get worried.

"You know my wife?" asked John.

"Shar? Sure. What?"

"Look."

"Holy—I don't be-lieve—She's coming right towards us. Johney, she's smiling at us." They stood stiffly, watching, waiting, unsure of what to do, both with the same silly expression plastered on their faces, like two boys in love with the same girl.

"It's Sharon. Isn't it?" questioned T.C., while thinking all along, 'What a strange question to ask.'

"Yeah, about twenty-five years younger. That's what she looked like."

"I know."

"I'm not seeing things?"

"Nooo."

The young woman approached them with a warm smile and a kind look. Much the same way you might approach a squirrel in the park, so as not to scare it off. She wore a Boston sweatshirt, blue jeans, and a pair of well-broken-in cowboy boots. Her brown hair was pulled back into a ponytail, and as John watched her stride, he thought he detected a slight limp in her walk.

In her hand was a copy of the 1991 Boston Red Sox program guide and a small radio. T.C. tipped his cap to her when they were close enough to make eye contact. John checked his hands; they were still the same hands filled with wrinkles and sun spots. He wasn't any younger. Not that he thought he would be, but he was beginning to think anything was possible. This road trip had its share of strange moments.

"Excuse me, Mr. Greco," said the young lady. "I heard you on Mr. Golden's broadcast." She acknowledged T.C. with a smile. "I was hoping to meet you. I've been a personal fan of yours all my life." She extended her hand to John. He took it into his own, knowing it would be familiar.

"Well . . . thank you," replied John, hesitantly. He was waiting for something else to happen, for the other shoe to drop, or was this just an amazing coincidence?

"I say personal fan. Well, uh, it's not just the Highlanders I like," she said, self-consciously. She had a lilt to her voice that reminded John of Maya.

"Who could blame you," muttered Terry Carmen. She didn't pay any attention to him and continued with her thought. 'Great. Ignore me, a theme to the day,' thought T.C.

"You did what was right. Many people love you. Do you know that?"

"Well, uh, I'm glad you think so."

"John, don't be so modest," said T.C. "You'll have to excuse him. Half the time he doesn't even know he's doing the right thing. He just does it. Good upbringing, I suppose. A charity here, outstanding moral conviction there—he has no idea what he's doing."

"Thanks, T.C. I didn't know you thought so highly of me."

"Well, he should. You are the Gentleman of Baseball," she smiled.

"The Gentleman of Baseball," repeated T.C. "Hey, that's good! I like that. I'm gonna use it from now on. It fits!"

"Is that a nickname or a title?" asked John.

"Title, like Frank Sinatra: The Chairman of the Board," insisted T.C.

"Uh-huh. That's what the world needs, another P.R. campaign."

"See. See. He's a natural!" declared T.C. "No wonder this young lady is a personal fan of yours. No bull, that's what you get from John Greco!" T.C. was unable to turn off the commentary. Neither John nor the young lady paid much attention to him, continuing with the day's theme. Johney couldn't take his eyes off of her. She looked the same as Sharon did on the day he had met her at the dentist's office.

"Anyway, I just wanted to meet you, to say thank you." She gave him a kiss on the cheek, smiled a regretful smile and walked away.

A pain shot through John's left hand. His brain went numb as he tried to figure out what it all meant. "Did you want my autograph?" John called after her. He wanted to say something, anything. He wanted to spend a few more minutes with her. He felt strangely paternal towards her.

"She didn't ask for one."

"One what?" questioned John.

"An autograph. She didn't ask for one," said T.C., apologetically. "What was that all about, anyway?"

"I don't know. I was a good ballplayer. Well, I was getting good. A lot of people remember my last game. I guess that's what it was about."

"How could she remember. She couldn't have been more than four," said T.C., searching for logic.

"I know. I was just thinking that." John put his hands in his pockets and watched her disappear around the block.

"Why didn't you tell her?"

"Tell her?"

"That she looked like Sharon."

"I think she already knew."

12

New York City: December, 1964

"MAYA, UNCLE NATT needs two trees. Can you pick me out one more?" The child was delighted with her uncle's request, almost as delighted as the Christmas tree salesman.

"You're still doing it," said John, always amazed by his brother's eccentric ritual and Christmas spirit.

"What? Making the perfect tree? Sure. And I'm gonna make us two beautiful wreaths! Remember? Like I always do," Natt said, then turned to Maya, "Honey, we need another blue spruce with the perfect top. Okay?"

John guided his daughter to the spruces. "They all look perfect to me," he said.

"Don't start with me," Natt warned, a bit perturbed. "We have this same conversation every year. You should know by now, this is how I do it. Alright? I need the extra for the wreaths anyway." Natt saw Maya's selection. "Oh! That's it! The perfect top! Thank you, my little bunny," exclaimed Maya's Uncle Natt with an abundance of excitement and a long, deep bow. He picked up his niece and spun her; "airplane ride" was what he called it. She liked it so much that "ride" was one of the first words she learned, so was "Natt."

THE TREE DESIGN took place in the small backyard of Natt and Faye's townhouse. They had the first two floors plus the basement and rented out apartments on the third and fourth floors. Natt had bought it as a fixer upper and did all the work himself. He had rebuilt his house as a fine Italian craftsman would, only the best materials used and the finest furnishings bought. His home looked like something out of a magazine. You couldn't help but get the feeling that this was a man who lived well above his means. Outside, French doors opened onto a small yard where a round, white wrought-iron table sat under a red, green, and orange canopy. The back wall of the yard was made of brick, along which Natt and Faye planted their garden. Natt had laid slate around the perimeter of his small grass yard which he manicured and fertilized to perfection every spring. He was a little obsessed with his grass . . . and perfection. His favorite tool was the garden spade. The only other thing in the yard was an altar-like brick grill. Natt had built it himself. He also built one for John and Sharon. In the summer he would simultaneously char-grill steaks and boil lobsters in a huge twenty gallon pot for all his friends.

Inside the townhouse, Natt had finished his basement, making it into his own private bar and a playroom for Charlie. The place felt like an English pub with its Tiffany lamps, cherry-wood bar, tile floor, paneling, and stained beams that ran the length of the ceiling. Natt had made the paneling himself by staining oak boards and cutting strips of black tar shingles to go in between. He had stripped the master bathroom and remodeled it in pink and white marble with exquisite deco fixtures. They were so ornate that Faye thought they were kind of tacky. Natt loved them so much, though, that she didn't object. The kitchen had all the newest appliances and fixtures and a tile floor that looked as soft as worn brown leather.

Most of the renovations had taken place within the last two years. Altogether, about three years had passed before he was finished, and when he was done, he seemed almost disappointed. I think he enjoyed building it more than anything. But it was more than that. By making their home a showplace, he was trying to make up for all the lost time between himself and Faye. It was his way of proving how much he cared.

"We'll go through the basement. Don't want to get needles all over the living room," said Natt.

Natt opened the two steel sidewalk doors that led to his pub. John and Charlie and Maya helped carry the trees. When they reached the backyard, it had begun to snow.

"Maya!" called her Aunt Faye from the kitchen window. "Lunch!" Maya couldn't decide which was better: being outside in the snow with her dad and uncle or food.

"Come, hon'. Have something to eat with your cousin Charlie. We'll play in the snow later." The food, along with the promise, won her over, and she ran to Aunt Faye's French doors to be let inside.

The snow came down with such intensity that John thought it might turn into a blizzard, but that didn't stop Natt from creating his tree. He sized up Maya's choices, made the perfect cuts, drilled two holes, and assembled the halves with a dowel down the center of the trunks. A little wood glue, a couple C-clamps, and he was finished. John made snowballs and threw them at the brick wall. He didn't want any part of Natt's unnatural tree building.

"I'm all done," Natt said, as he took a step back to admire his handiwork. "Let's get a sandwich and a beer."

"Sounds good." John followed his brother down the steps to the pub. Natt pulled a couple of sandwiches out of the refrigerator, then poured two drafts into chilled mugs. That was unusual, because Natty only used the tap for parties.

"Draft? We having a party?"

"I don't know, maybe."

"Looks like you're all ready. You must have everything," said John, as he inventoried the shelf stock.

"Sit down, sit down. Welcome to Natt's Bar and Grill." They raised their drinks.

"Salute." They clinked their mugs together.

Natt drank his in one gulp and slammed it on the bar. "Aaaaaaah," he sighed. "Go ahead, drink, drink. There's plenty more!" John finished and handed his mug to the bartender. "Hey, what kind of bar do you think I'm running?" admonished Natt. "Fresh beer, fresh glass!" He drew two more beers from the tap, and they did it all over again—and again, and again, and again . . .

"Natty, slow down. If I go home trashed . . . well, you know with the kid and—"

"Johney, I will personally—aaah, c'mon. That's the great thing about the city. No driving! We're gonna make it. You live a block away!"

"Two blocks."

"I've seen you down twenty and nothing!"

John didn't need that much convincing. He didn't have any plans for the rest of the day, but enjoyed hearing Natt's overacted stay-and-drink-with-me speech anyway. From a small ground level window they could see Faye playing in the snow with Charlie and Maya. Natt gazed out the window and smiled.

"I don't know what I was thinking," he said, looking completely bewildered. "Look at her. She's such a good mother . . . and beautiful."

"You weren't thinking."

"That's true. I do that."

"Has the piano given you any more problems?" asked John. He could hear Maya shriek with joy. He instantly thought of angel voices.

"Nah, it didn't give me any to start with. Just opened my eyes. Made me religious again. Huh, I still don't go to church. I mean it made me a better person. I'm not nearly as crazy as I used to be," he frowned. "Nah, crazy, that's not right. I'm not as stupid. Hell, you're the crazy one. Baseball for a living."

"Awww, that was your idea."

"I didn't think you'd go for it! Well, it's a good thing you did. I needed to live vicariously through you. Damn, what happened to my arm? One day I'm throwing heaters in the nineties, the next I'm—hey! Do you think it was all that lawn mowing dad made us do? Or was Sister Margo wrong? Maybe ya don't go blind from whacking. Maybe, jussst maybeeee, your pitching arm dies!"

John laughed so hard and long that his laughter was no longer audible as Natt mimed his limp throwing and whacking arm.

"Know what? Know what? Get this! I should have been ambidextrous— like you!" Natt called, miming two limp and tired arms.

Johney hurt so much he thought he'd never catch his breath if Natt didn't stop his farce. John slid from his bar stool and onto the cool floor, turning red and wheezing.

"C'mon, Johney, get up, get up. You're embarrassing me. Off the floor weee go," coaxed Natt, helping John to his feet. "C'mon, here's your beer." Natt slapped his brother on the back, as though trying to help him breathe, but actually he simply enjoyed giving Johney the playful slaps.

"Enough!" John shouted, pushing his brother away, nearly in wrestle mode.

"I know!" Natt exclaimed, having just received a brilliant idea. "How 'bout we play the piano for old times sake! Say, oh, Chop Sticks?!" And they raced to the piano. They played, and played, and gleefully banged the keys, as though they were kids again, pounding away at the Francis Bacon in Mountain Edge. Within that moment, they had recaptured the vitality of their youth and succeeded in making a connection to their past, to times and places gone by, and more than anything else, to the essence of their souls. They traveled back to their power, to the beginning, the fresh start where all things were equal and anything was possible. Then, as abruptly as their journey began, it came to a jolting conclusion. Natt stared down at his fingers; they surprised him. Heavy as hardened stone atop the keyboard, they suddenly seemed very much out of place. He slid his hand over John's and the childish music ended.

"Johney, I never—ya know, I really love you." Tears formed in Natt's eyes. He didn't try to hold them back.

"Hey, c'mon. I know that, Natty. I love you, too, and Faye and Charlie. You—we have so much."

Natt's eyes swelled even more. "I know. How I know. Listen, Johney, if anything happens to me, you'll take care of them?"

"Yeah, of course. Why?"

"You have to know—" He started to say, then changed his mind. "Remember this, always remember this time. Okay?"

"Yeah, sure." The distressed and foreboding tone of Natt's voice disturbed John a great deal. He told himself it was just the drink. "C'mon, Natty, let's go outside, get some air, play with our kids or something."

Natt smiled; he had another idea. "Let's put up the tree!" he shouted, as he changed gears in a heartbeat.

When the brothers reappeared from Natt's pub, they found a winter wonderland waiting for them. They also found Sharon outside with Faye, playing with the kids. It seemed as if everyone in the Greco family was a little bewitched by snow.

"Our men have returned from the pub," teased Sharon.

"Male bonding, no doubt," replied Faye.

Sharon gave John a kiss, inhaling the scent of stale beer. "Definitely bonding. They're bonded, Faye."

"Enough of this small talk," commanded Natt. "Kids! It's time to put up the tree. Maya, would you help your uncle put up the tree?"

"I think he's going to need it," said Faye, as she put her arm around Natt's waist to steady him.

"Daddy, can I help?!" asked Maya, bounding about.

"Uh-huh. We're all gonna help, honey."

"John, give me a hand," requested Natt. He wanted to shake the snow off the branches. The tree was so perfect even John forgot that it was two halves. They each took a side and picked the tree up vertically, raising it about a foot off the ground, then letting it drop straight down onto the base of its trunk. The kids squealed as the fresh snow fell from the branches, covering them in a shower of powdery ringlets.

"Okay, we'll take it through the kitchen and into the living room," ordered Natt, playfully barking his instructions. "I'll take the front. John, take the back. Faye, open the doors."

The kids were all excited, spinning themselves until dizzy, then allowing their bodies to fall into the soft snowdrifts. Sharon was enjoying all the activity, though the thought had crossed her mind that she wouldn't want that wet tree in her house. She didn't say anything, not wanting to disturb a wonderful moment. The slightly intoxicated men began the Christmas tree procession with two gallant strides toward the house and the French doors where Faye was stationed. On the third stride the tree separated, much like a rocket losing its fuel tank after breaking through the earth's atmosphere. Void of fanfare, it was just a mere separation as the capsule continued on its journey, which was exactly what Natt did. He was holding his half toward the center. He was a man with a mission, to get to his wife. She was his star. He didn't hear, or was too drunk to notice, the bottom half of his tree drop into the foot of cushioning snow. When it happened, John looked stunned, positively dumbfounded as to what to do. While he watched his brother march on without him, he stood motionless, holding the other half of the tree. Sharon dropped into a large snowdrift against the brick wall as if she had been shot, execution style. The kids jumped on her, ready to play. Faye at first appeared confused, but when she realized what had happened, her body wound into a fit of painfully silent, breathless laughter. Natty was alarmed at first; then he noticed his tree. Both Faye and Sharon couldn't regain control of themselves for a solid ten minutes. There was nothing left for Natt and John to do, no way to recapture their self-respect. A snowball fight broke out, and the brothers lost that, too. The fight ended with kissing in the snow and Maya and Charlie doing their best to get in between their parents. They forgot about the tree for the day, instead they gathered around the piano in Natt's pub and sang songs. John sang while his little girl sat on his lap pretending she, too, was playing by holding onto her Daddy's wrists. They all sang, and laughed, and had a blissful time.

Something happened on that snowy day when the tree separated. They were the best people could be, full of forgiveness. The snow and the music had gathered them together and brought with it a profound sense of the present and an appreciation of the moment.

13

New York City: April, 1965

WHEN NATT GOT happy, he also got careless, or maybe the law of averages turned the tables on the luckiest gambler I've ever met. He never saved a penny in his life. What he had left after a minimum of bills were paid was spending money, sometimes a lot of spending money. He earned it in waves. It wasn't unusual for him pull a two-inch wad of bills out of his pocket and give a hundred to somebody who looked down on their luck, like me—no questions asked.

"George, get yourself some new shoes. Please," he'd say as though it would be a personal favor to him if I would just take care of this unpleasant shoe business.

When Natt's luck changed, nobody saw it coming. He just acted the way he always did, except now he was giving his wife much more attention, which made him seem normal, domesticated. Sometimes they would stop by Tommy's after dinner or a show.

Faye wasn't a person who needed lavish gifts, but she knew Natty wanted to give them to her. The way he fixed up their home and bought her beautiful jewelry and clothing really cost him. It cost him more than Natt could ever imagine. When things are going well—or easily—and shaded by the leisure of normalcy and customary habits, you don't expect much to go wrong. When you're sitting on the porch, listening to the birds and sipping ice tea, you just don't expect much of anything else to happen.

"SHARON, IT'S FAYE. I'm sorry to bother you, but I'm really scared." She paused to light a cigarette, then checked the locks on the front door again. Suddenly her home seemed so large with so many ways to get inside.

"What's wrong?"

"Sharrr . . . I'm so scared."

"Honey, it's all right. Tell me what's—" Faye's breathing worried her, almost hyperventilating, Sharon thought. "Faye, try to relax. Is Natt there?" Faye sobbed uncontrollably.

"No . . . oooooh. He's gone. I think he's in trouble. I . . . I . . . think— He left a note," Faye picked up the note from off the hall floor and prepared to read it for the hundredth time, still unable to fully comprehend its meaning.

"Faye? Honey, are you there?"

"Yes."

"Faye, read me Natt's note, okay?" Sharon took a deep breath, afraid of what was about to come. She secretly wished John was home and not down in Ft. Lauderdale for spring training. Her only comfort was that training camp would break in a couple of days, and the season would begin. He would soon be home. How often she had to wait for her baseball player to come home, she thought. The idea might have amused her if the situation had been different. But it wasn't.

> *My darling Faye,*
> *I won't be home for a few days. I have a problem that needs*
> *to be taken care of, a business problem. It's better this*
> *way. Tommy will help if you need anything. I love you and*
> *Charlie very, very much. Everything is gonna be OK.*
> *Love __All__ Ways, Natt.*

"That's it? That's all he wrote?"

"He's not big on writing," cried Faye. "He never writes—not even shopping lists. He must be in trouble, right?" she questioned in a fatal manner. Her voice sounded raspy and raw and had a melancholy tonality. Natt would have called it sexy.

"I don't know what's going on, but I don't think you and Charlie should be alone."

"I don't want to be alone."

"You're coming over here. I could use the company," Sharon insisted.

"Thanks, Shar. I'll pack a bag."

"I'm coming over to get you. You've been through enough. We can call John in Florida. He might know something. Alright?"

"Okay."

When Faye hung up the phone, she felt better. There were people who cared about her. She had a family. Something she never had growing up. By the age of two, Faye had already been in two foster homes. At two and a half, she was adopted by a middle-aged couple in Troy, New York. They thought a child would bring them closer together, maybe even save their marriage. And if one child could bring them love, they figured two children would make them a family, at least that's what Mrs. Roden assumed. So they adopted a four-year-old boy, too. His name was Larry. Larry and Faye quickly became best friends, while Mr. and Mrs. Roden didn't. Things often don't happen as they're planned, and plans this shortsighted and selfish usually don't have much of a chance. By the time Larry was nine and Faye was seven, the fascination with children and the promise that they might make life better for the Roden's was gone. The kids did change their lives, but not the way they had intended.

Mr. Roden was an alcoholic, but unlike Natty, he wasn't any good at it. He was a small, quiet man with a gaunt face and a mustache. He didn't eat much, hardly ever talked, and hated his job at the brewery because it forced him to leave the house, which was something he didn't like to do. He was paranoid and proud of it. Mr. Roden often bragged that he only left the house for a haircut, or work, or to cut the lawn with his John Deere tractor. That tractor was his only pleasure in life. In his own sedate, passive, non-communicative way, he disliked all people, including his own family and especially black people. Faye said living with him was like getting the silent treatment for her entire childhood.

Mrs. Roden viewed herself as somebody very special, although she had no particular talent. Any five minute conversation with her included full details of the modeling career she was once offered in New York City—but turned down to marry Mr. Roden. And as Faye would sadly point out, "Creating one of the most vicious martyrs known to mankind." To say Mrs. Roden was bitter would have been a gross understatement. Maybe that's why Mr. Roden didn't say anything. Divorce was out of the question, not for any religious considerations, but for economic reasons, which to the Rodens was akin to their religion. All their money was tied up in their house. As the market grew stronger, they would sell for a profit and upgrade to a bigger house with a larger lawn for Mr. Roden to cut. Faye's theory was that they wanted as much space between family members as possible.

A good day for Mr. Roden was a day when he didn't have to talk to anyone, particularly the kids. A good day for Mrs. Roden was when Faye and Larry would sit quietly and listen, while she strolled through the memories in her photo albums. The albums were filled with photos of people Faye had never met, because nobody ever came to visit, and they never went visiting. Mrs. Roden blamed this social malfunction on Mr. Roden. Mr. Roden, as usual, didn't respond to the charges. A bad day for the Rodens was any other day, which constituted the vast majority of days.

By the time Faye was fourteen, she was sent away to a state juvenile institution. The Rodens told the state that Faye was impossible to handle, and they could no longer be responsible for her actions. The truth was Mr. and Mrs. Roden practiced a bizarre form of marital misanthropy. They could no longer tolerate the needs and concerns of children, especially teenagers. Larry ran away from home shortly after Faye was sent away. She never saw him again. Faye said it took most of her adult years to regain her mental health, and she knew Larry was probably fighting the same demons. She also said when she accepted the fact that Natt really loved her, she was able to heal. And more than anything, she hoped Larry was able to find somebody like Natt in his life.

Faye went about collecting her things and getting Charlie ready to go to Aunt Sharon's house. The doorbell rang and Faye ran downstairs to let Sharon in.

"Sharon, I'm—" The door flew open, knocking her back and creating a tremendous "BANG!!!" as the cut glass rattled within the door frame.

"Who, who are you!" she screamed, terrified. His face was familiar.

Smithy Lango entered the home with all the presence of a cobra. His skin tan, tight, and tough, like snake skin. She knew this man, had seen him around. She recalled Tommy referring to him as "Shitty" because that's what he was. 'That's right,' she thought. 'His name is Smithy—the man who owes Natt two hundred dollars for betting against John's first big league hit.' The story was famous. We all had laughed about it because the debt kept Smithy Lango away from Tommy's Bar.

"A small price to pay," joked Natt, cracking the place up. But now Smithy was in their home. She was alone. And it was no longer funny.

Smithy was his real name. His parents actually named him Smithy. He worked for Mr. Joseph Jonelli, a local slumlord and bookie with grandiose ideas and plans. Lango's job was primarily to scare elderly people out of their rent stabilized apartments, so Mr. Jonelli could convert them into co-ops or condos or just turn them over at a higher rent. I once heard Smithy Lango brag of balancing a wheelchair-bound woman at the head of her staircase as he politely asked her to vacate her apartment. He considered that to be a very creative idea. Mr. Lango was also part of the collection agency for Mr. Jonelli's bookmaking operation. He worked on commission, fifteen percent of everything he collected. And fifteen percent of Natt's debt would be his largest payday by far. You see, Smithy Lango was motivated, but not just by the money; he also hated the Greco brothers, because they were handsome and popular, and those were two things he thought he should be. *Why* was a mystery to all of us.

As Faye opened the door, she thought to herself, 'Why didn't I use the peephole? I always use the peephole.' But it was too late. Smithy Lango had pushed his way in before their eyes could meet. Faye tried to run up the stairs, but Smithy tackled her from behind, tearing her blouse at the buttons.

"What do you want!!" Faye screamed. "You want money?!"

"MOM!" Charlie wailed at the top of the staircase.

"Charlie, go to your room and lock the door!" The shrill in her voice cut like a knife, and Charlie ran.

"Keep your voice down," said Smithy in a calm, but sleazy, tone. "I don't want to hurt you. I just need to know where Natty is."

"He's—he's not here," replied Faye, scared to death. Lango slapped her hard across the face.

"I know he's not here!" he snarled. "I've been watching this fucking place all day!" His emotions moved from rage to calm in a split second. "Now, tell me where he is. Please. C'mon now, I said the magic word," he hissed, enjoying her fear. Faye folded her arms across her breasts where Lango had ripped her blouse. He towered over her, examining her, running his eyes over her body, implying what would happen next if he received a dissatisfactory answer.

"Hey, you're a mighty fine-looking woman," he grinned, adjusted himself, and waited for her response.

"He's been gone since last night."

"And?"

"That's it. That's all I know." She began to whimper like a little girl. The pain and fear of losing Natt was more than she could bear. She knew Natt would do anything to protect Charlie and her, yet, he wasn't here. She realized she may never see him again. She was crushed and devastated, and even another vicious slap from Smithy couldn't jar her from her despair.

"We're gonna have to do this the hard way." Lango laughed at his own pun as he unbuckled his belt. Faye didn't respond, which infuriated him.

"Son, son, come on down here," he called to Charlie, politely, sadistically. An ugly, insidious smirk crept across his face. Faye uncoiled herself. Her eyes looked through him like lasers. "Me and your mom," he said arrogantly, "are gonna teach you about sex education."

"Nooo!! Please!!" begged Faye.

"Well, love," he explained, "his daddy ain't here to teach him. I feel bad about that. Responsible even. *Now,* are you gonna tell me where Mr. Greco is?"

"He's at Tommy's Bar!"

Smithy slapped her again, knocking her to the floor. "Don't lie to me, bitch. I know he's not at Tommy's!" he growled, practically foaming at the mouth. Then his face took on the inspired look of a man with an idea, a truly evil thought. "Know what? I don't want a woman tonight," he said in a thoughtful manner. "What I'd really like is a little boy."

"Oh, my God . . . oh, oh! God! Help!!" Faye screamed, pleading for God's mercy.

"Maybe you and your god would like to watch me! I'd be glad to put on a show." He slapped her three more times, seemingly unable to restrain himself.

Faye screamed so loud the room began to spin; colors moved as though a kaleidoscope were before her tear soaked eyes. She knew she would have to sacrifice herself to protect her baby. She could feel the adrenaline pouring through her system as she sprang from the floor and attacked him with everything she had. She could remember him laughing, and then . . . nothing, not even a struggle. Lango seemed to go limp in her hands as a damp and sticky flow of blood oozed through her fingers, staining his shirt and matting his greasy hair. He staggered out the front door and into the night. It was only then that Faye recognized Sharon's figure standing before her, holding a bloody object in her hand that turned out to be a lead scallop-shaped paperweight. Faye used it as a doorstop. The women fell into a grasping-for-life hug, like two army buddies after their first combat when the full comprehension of life, death, and war are completely understood and undeniably real.

SHARON MADE MANY phone calls that night. She talked to John who was getting the next plane out of Ft. Lauderdale. She called the police, who came by and took a description of the event and Smithy Lango. The police knew who he was; they said that they would do everything possible to find him and that they would watch both Greco houses. As far as the officers were concerned, Lango got the worst of it anyway. That was of little comfort to

Sharon and Faye. Sharon called Tommy's and a few other of Natt's known hangouts with no luck. She gave Faye a sleeping pill and put her and Charlie to bed. She checked the locks on the doors and windows of their townhouse. It was the first time she felt unsafe in her home.

JOHN WAITED BY the phone in his hotel room praying for Natt to call. He felt helpless. He couldn't get a flight out until morning. He refused to think about what Natt had gotten himself into, because when he did, his imagination ran wild. It was three-thirty-three in the morning when John's phone rang. He had slept only an hour. It was Natt.

"Johney, I can't talk long, so just listen."

"Natt, where are you?" John sounded like some sort of wild animal; his voice laden with sleep.

"It doesn't matter—just listen! I screwed up some bets. I wasn't paying attention."

"Natty, I got money. Let me bail you out."

"You can't bail me out!" shouted Natt. "I'm in too deep."

"Did you hear what happened tonight! Smithy would have raped your wife if Sharon hadn't crack his head open! Natty, let me take care of it!" John yelled, feeling frustrated and powerless. He'd never yelled at this brother in anger before; it was strange, the whole thing was strange. Natt didn't say anything. He knew he had it coming.

"I know what happened. I talked to Tommy. The guys are looking out for them," Natt said, not entirely convinced that would help.

"What about you? What's going on?"

"Johney, I went deep in the count on a few horses."

"What? A few thousand?" Natt was silent. "Ten thousand? Twenty?" pleaded John. He needed to know.

"One hundred and three . . . thousand."

"Holy—Natty. How!? How is that possible?"

"Oh, it's possible. I did it. I did it at the worse possible time. I was beginning to like myself . . . my life. I was growing rather fond of my life," said Natt, mocking himself.

"How can you make jokes now?!" John demanded.

"No joke, kid. All my life I was looking for something, something to make me feel better, that would last, make me feel complete again. The piano plays in the basement. The angels sing golden hymns. Huh, they make me horny and—BAM—it hits me! I'm living with a beautiful woman. I have a wonderful wife, the mother of my child. Maybe I should get to know them.

How do you buy *get to know?* I've tried to buy *get to know* all my life. I was just getting it. I'm all right. There's nothing wrong with me. My family loves me. All I had to do was love them back. Right? Ain't that right, Johney? Like the way we love each other. I'm pretty stupid, huh."

"Natty, we can make a deal. I'll get a second mortgage on the house. I'm gonna make seventy-five thousand dollars this year! We can make payments. It will be okay." He waited for his brother to endorse his plan, but the endorsement never came. His silence was killing Johney. "C'mon! Please, Natty, don't be so stubborn. Dad will help, too. There's a way out!"

"Johney, after I heard what happened tonight, I called in to Jonelli."

"Natty, you're dealing with Jonelli?"

"Just listen, damn it!" The icy chill of reality seized the phone lines. "He's gonna let me run a double or nothing on the Knicks game tomorrow. I got a fifty-fifty chance."

"What? Natty, why? You can't pay the hundred three. Don't do it. This isn't right."

"I gotta do it. It's my only chance. There's no easy payment plans in this business, Johney. You can't trust anybody."

"Why?" asked John, pleading.

"I don't know why. I know I'm staying out in the cold until after I win the Knicks bet. You have lots of friends, Johney; they'll be looking out for you."

"Natt."

"I gotta go, kid. You'll know what to do."

"Natt. Please . . . "

"I'll be looking out for ya, too." Then he whispered, "I'm sorry." And hung up the phone.

WHEN JOHN GOT back to New York, he spent the day trying to reassure Faye that everything was going to be all right. Of course, he had a hard time convincing himself, especially since we spent most of the day moving Faye's things from her home to John and Sharon's. She was afraid to go home without Natt. Secretly John prayed for Natt to call, jumping out of his skin every time the phone rang, and feeling deeply disappointed when it wasn't Natt. I'm sure they all felt that way, but they kept it well disguised.

That night John watched the Knicks game on television, like a man viewing an execution. He realized that he didn't know who he was rooting for—the criminal or the executioner. After all, Natt was a professional gambler first, Knicks fan second, and he was placing the bet of his life. He didn't tell Sharon or Faye about Natt's last bet; there wasn't any point to it. He sat slumped in his chair and waited for the game to end. When it did, the Knicks had defeated the Lakers, 106 to 101. The Knick fans were going crazy while John watched and waited for something to happen, but nothing did, not even a phone call. He didn't see that as a good omen.

"Shar, I'm going over to Tommy's. Maybe he heard something, okay?" He wasn't looking for an answer, and he didn't get one. Faye and Sharon sipped their coffee in the kitchen, not saying much, still numb by the sudden and seemingly ferocious change of fate.

As John left the townhouse, a police car slowed to a stop to check him out. When the policemen saw that it was John Greco himself, they wanted to talk baseball.

"How'z spring training, John?" called the officer behind the wheel.

"They say you're starting catcher this year. Best move they could've made with your bat," said the other officer, cautiously.

"You guys watching my house?"

"Yes, sir, Mr. Greco."

"And Smithy Lango? Anything?"

"Well, he's not in any of his usual hangouts. We'll find him," said the driver, casually.

John made a motion as though he were swinging a bat, mentally putting himself into a game. He took a step closer to the cruiser, put his hands on his knees and looked straight into the eyes of the driver, as though they were in a football huddle and he were the quarterback preparing to call a play. It made the officers uncomfortable. He was invading their space.

"Attempted rape," said John, just stating the facts, nothing more.

"Well, assault for sure. Rape. Attempted rape, that's pretty hard for a young lady to prove," the officer said in his most diplomatic tone, a tone reserved for ballplayers and high-ranking officials, or people who didn't know what they were talking about but to whom he had, or wanted, to be nice.

"Oh, is the same true for seven-year-old boys?" questioned John.

"What?"

"Is it hard for little boys to prove? Attempted rape?"

The question angered the officers, even though there was no malice or sarcasm in John's tone, just concern. Yet to the policemen it was a question only a wise guy or an idiot would ask. Since they couldn't figure out what John's intentions were, they cut the conversation short and drove off quickly, disturbed, bewildered, and agitated by their local hero who had a shot at the Hall of Fame.

"We'll find him!" shouted the driver, a bit disgusted, not knowing how else to respond.

John walked over to Tommy's. Most actions and reactions confused him, so he just accepted them. But there was nothing confusing about the look on Tommy's face when John walked in that night, not even for John. The place was empty, except for us regulars. John took a stool at the end of the bar where Tommy stood washing glasses; he was always washing glasses. You'd think after awhile they'd all be washed.

"He lost. Didn't he, Tommy?" said John.

"Yup."

"Do you know where he is?"

"He wouldn't tell me . . . left you a note. Left it last week—'In case of an emergency,' he said. That asshole," Tommy uttered, brutally drying a mug. "Here." Tommy handed Johney a piece of folded yellow paper.

John was afraid to read it, afraid to look at Tommy, to order a drink, or to walk the streets. He feared everything at that moment. John unfolded the paper and read:

> *Johney,*
> *I don't know if hiding is the best thing. I don't think I have much choice. Please forgive me. I know how bad I've screwed up. Shit, John, it was the first time in my life that I was really happy. Please take care of Charlie and Faye until I can figure something out. I'll be looking out for you.*
> *I love you, kid,*
> *Natty*

John sat in silence while Tommy served him a beer. Tommy knocked on wood and called, "On the house." His words died quickly in the stagnant, stale bar air.

"This is really bad. Isn't it, Tommy?"

"Really bad," Tommy replied. Then he produced a thick envelope from under the bar and handed it to John. "It's money," he said. "About fifteen thousand—for Faye and the kid. He hit pretty big a couple of weeks ago. Can you believe it?"

John took the money and slipped it into his coat pocket as if it were a candy bar he had just purchased. His whole body began to quiver; his hands shook when he tried to raise his beer mug; his facial muscles contracted like an epileptic about to have a fit. Tommy came from around the bar. He wrapped his sizable arms around John, creating a human straitjacket, protecting him from himself.

"George!" Tommy called. "George, take John home." Tommy released Johney from his grip.

"Listen. If anybody can take care of themselves, it's your brother."

"Tommy?"

"Yeah."

"Will they kill him?" Tommy turned his back while reaching for a bottle of very old scotch. He couldn't look John in the eye.

"I don't know, John." That was the most reassuring answer he could give.

"Little George, please, walk him home," requested Tommy.

So I helped John to the door.

"Ja-Ja-John," I said, "you ga-ga-gotta relax. Don't wa-w-w-want the-the ga-ga-girls te-te-to seee you laaaa-like this."

"I know. George? How could Natty . . . " His sentence trailed off when he heard the saddened quality of his own voice.

"He di-di-did it fa-fa-for love, Johney. He-didn't-know any ba-ba-better."

"Love?"

"He m-m-made the r-right choice. It was his la-last chance, John, b-b-but he di-did."

"What choice, George?"

"You'll see . . . John?"

"Yeah."

"You must always f-f-face your fears." John gave me an indulgent nod, and we left.

The walk did him good. The cool spring air drew John out of his funk. He was beginning to regain his composure as the fear in his heart momentarily loosened its hold. But it was to be only a fleeting moment as John was abruptly and viciously attacked.

Wham! Johney was knocked back into the gutter, as Smithy Lango sprang from behind the shadow of a parked van. He stood stiffly, glared intensely, and breathed his sour breath directly into John's face. Johney was stunned by the hit of a blackjack. He wasn't knocked out, but he was dazed. That's how Mr. Lango worked. He liked to ambush his victims. It wasn't for me to stop.

"Ha-ha-help!" I screamed, playing my role. He whacked me in the jaw. I could feel a trickle of blood run down my chin.

"Shut up, you little freak!" He grabbed me by the hair and pulled me close to him. Then he took a piece of paper out of his pocket and shoved it in my mouth.

"You have a meeting, Mr. Highlander. Your invite is in the retard's mouth." Lango, the psychopath, grinned and took off in a waiting car. The whole matter took less than twenty seconds.

"George, you okay?" I nodded and reached over to touch John's head. He caught my wrist and said, "I'm all right, just a bump. Is there any blood?" I shook my head.

"George? George, can I have the paper?" I still had the note in my mouth.

"Ha-ha-here . . . Ja-John," I said, handing him the paper.

"I'm fine, George. Go on back to Tommy's."

When I reached the end of the block, John called out. "Hey, George. Thanks. I'm sorry about dragging you into this." He looked young and proud, which was not easy after being blackjacked. And I thought, how he had so much work ahead of him.

WHEN JOHN GOT home, Sharon was waiting alone for him in the kitchen. Faye had been feeling depressed and exhausted, so Sharon had convinced her to go to bed.

"John! What happened? You're a mess!" The back side of his coat was soaked with gutter water and caked with crud.

"I'm fine," he said unconvincingly and retreated to the refrigerator for ice.

"You're not fine!" protested Sharon.

John wrapped the ice in a paper towel and applied it to the bump on his head, wanting the throbbing pain to go away before the conversation began. Sharon took the ice pack out of his hand, sat him down at the kitchen table, and applied it to his head. For a moment John truly appreciated the rare quiet in the heart of New York City, only to be interrupted by the grating sound of a garbage truck.

"Babe, let's take off your coat," she sighed.

John nodded in agreement. He stood up and emptied his pockets onto the kitchen table. Out came Natt's yellow note, the money envelope, and Smithy's invitation, stained with my blood.

"What is all this?" Sharon gasped.

John didn't reply. He was still trying to figure out the answer himself. He removed his dirty coat, hung it on the hook by the pantry, and sat down at the table again.

'There's still one more note to read,' he thought, as he grabbed the bloodied paper, unfolded it, and read its magazine cut-out letters: 26th & 11th, SW corner, 3:00 a.m., Tonight.

"John?" repeated Sharon, questioning everything. He picked up the yellow piece of paper and handed it to her.

"Read it." And she did.

"I don't understand."

"It means we may never see Natt again because he owes two hundred and six thousand dollars to somebody . . . the Mob, I guess." John grabbed the envelope. "This envelope has fifteen thousand dollars in it. Natt left it with Tommy for Faye and Charlie." He picked up the bloodied note. "This note was delivered by Smithy Lango just . . . just now. He was right here on 10th Street, hit me on the head with something, punched Little George in the mouth and then stuffed the note in. That's why it's wet with blood." John gave her the details as though he were running down the box scores. Sharon sat back in her chair, overwhelmed.

"I can't believe this is happening," she muttered, thinking out loud. "How could he," referring to Natt. "How could he do this! To Faye . . . Charlie— to us?"

"Shar, it just happened."

"It just happened? Our sister-in-law . . . our . . . our nephew was almost raped. Our house needs to be watched by the police. Gangsters want to meet with you at three o'clock in the morning. Your brother is nowhere to be found, and I'm scared to death! And all you can say is 'It just happened!'"

"He didn't want this, Shar. He made a mistake."

"A two-hundred-thousand-dollar mistake. That's not a mistake, John. That's not a mistake! That's a lifetime of work!"

"Honey, it may cost him his life."

From the living room came a yelp, resembling the whimpering of a wounded dog—long sustained tones of nightmarish anguish. They found Faye curled up in a ball on the floor, her face reddened, her eyes distant and bloodshot. She had heard everything that was said. Her most unthinkable thoughts were now confirmed. She was completely shattered.

Sharon held Faye in her arms and said, "I'm sorry, I'm so sorry." She repeated the words a thousand times until she had no voice, no more tears, and no more anger towards her brother-in-law. Sharon was resolved to find a way out, the same resolve John had all along.

John carried Faye to her room and put her to bed. Her body was limp and lifeless and in need of rest. He gently covered her, kissed her on the forehead, and turned off the light. "I'm here for you," he whispered.

That night, before the early morning meeting, Sharon and John agreed to do everything they could to work out the problem, including liquidating all they had—the townhouse, bank accounts, savings bonds, even selling the furniture if it would help.

"We could start with the fifteen thousand Natt left behind," said John. John thought he might be able to get a loan from the Highlanders, against his pay. Altogether they figured they could get their hands on fifty, maybe sixty, thousand dollars fairly quickly. Then they would try to work out monthly payments for Natt. It was starting to sound as though it could work. By two in the morning something similar to, but not quite, optimism set in.

"Why wouldn't they take it," Sharon reasoned. "Twenty-five percent— better than nothing. Right?"

"It's a lot of money," consoled John, trying his best to make it all sound acceptable. At the same time he could picture Tommy, his defeated expression, his broken heart, a man who had just lost his best friend.

What they didn't understand was how far above, or below, reasonable Mr. Joseph Jonelli was. He wasn't content with reasonable. "Reasonable is for the masses," Mr. Jonelli would say. "They have no choice. They lack my vision, my drive, my resources. The worker, the family people, let them enjoy the quiet, reasonable life. Not me!" he often declared, in more ways than one. Mr. Jonelli craved money, fame, and power, but more than anything else he wanted to be remembered, to be part of our history. He desired his notoriety to last long after he was gone, and that he would achieve. Mr. Jonelli secretly mocked the people who believed that compromise was a good deal for everyone. The people who take pride in an honest day's work and loved their families and friends, they were the reasonable; they were his targets, his subjects. He was a true narcissist.

"I'm going with you," stated Sharon. She would have expected an argument from anybody else, but not from John. He was different.

"Good, let's go," John replied in a manner that sounded as casual as suggesting they go to a diner for an early morning breakfast.

Sharon thought it might have been nice to get the argument. John had his fears but lacked a sense of danger, an odd combination that only seemed possible in Johney.

SHARON AND JOHN arrived at the corner of 26th Street and 11th Avenue by taxi. It was exactly three o'clock.

"Sure ya want out here?" asked the cab driver, surveying the dark, deserted gas station.

"This corner is fine," replied John, trying to stay relaxed, blocking his fear. He was thinking, 'What would Natt do in this situation?' And it came to him. "There's an extra twenty in it for you if you pick us up in fifteen minutes."

"Here?" snapped the driver, suspiciously.

"Right here," said John.

"Well, ah, I'll see you in fifteen," said the driver, figuring he could make some easy money. Sharon was noticeably relieved.

As soon as the cab pulled away, a black stretch limo pulled up from behind the station. The symbol of wealth and power rolled into place, intended to intimidate before any human contact is made. It worked. The large black car with its darkened windows gave Sharon a chill, while John didn't seem to notice its dramatic implications. A man got out of the car, adjusted his sports coat and approached them. It was Smithy Lango.

"How nice. You brought a date," he said, his voice dripping with sarcasm. John resisted the urge to attack him. He was here to help Natt.

"This is my wife. Can we get on with this?"

"Why certainly, Mr. Greco. Mr. Jonelli is expecting you," smirked Smithy, motioning to the car, his eyes fixed on Sharon the whole time. He opened the back door of the limo to let John in. Then remembered he had to frisk him first, which he did. Sharon tried to follow her husband into the car, but Lango extended his arm, blocking her path.

"I'll be okay," she said with as much authority as she could muster.

"Good," laughed Smithy Lango, grinning like a comic-strip character as John climbed into the back seat.

"Mr. Jonelli; Mr. John Greco," introduced Smithy Lango, before he closed the door.

"A pleasure, a pleasure to meet you, John! May I call you John?" John nodded his head; this wasn't at all what he had expected. Mr. Jonelli seemed so—pleasant.

"Good. Good. Please, call me Jones. All my friends do. Ah! Ah! And I do have plenty of friends." He sat back in his seat after shaking John's hand, very content with himself, an actor extremely pleased with his last scene. His clear, forthright blue eyes looked straight into John's. Like a good politician, Jonelli believed in a firm handshake and looking a man in the eye. He was heavyset and wore a well-tailored, dark suit. His light brown hair was prematurely gray at the temples. John thought Mr. Jonelli couldn't have been more than forty, but he seemed to enjoy all the trappings of an older, more worldly, and distinguished gentleman. John could easily picture him moving effortlessly through high society social functions, having drinks at the Union Club, delighted by a good Cuban cigar. There was something almost elegant about him. He gave the appearance of a man who was a pillar of the community, exactly the image Mr. Jonelli wanted. In a way, his style resembled Natt's—a wealthier version. John's eyes were drawn to Mr. Jonelli's cane. The stick was burgundy in color and highly polished. 'Maybe cherry wood,' John thought, 'like Natt's bar.' The handle was pure silver, shaped in the form of a single wing. It fit perfectly into his hand.

"The bird that would never fly," he joked, as he held it up for John to admire. He displayed it proudly, in high esteem, almost in awe, as though it were some sort of enchanted divining rod. Etched into one side of the wing was an inverted pyramid, something he called, "The Abracadabra Pyramid," a symbol Mr. Jonelli believed to ward off disaster—the one superstitious indulgence he allowed into his very real and practical world.

```
A B R A C A D A B R A
 A B R A C A D A B R
  A B R A C A D A B
   A B R A C A D A
    A B R A C A D
     A B R A C A
      A B R A C
       A B R A
        A B R
         A B
          A
```

Mr. Jonelli noticed he wasn't getting John's full attention and assumed that he was worried about his wife. Jonelli pushed the button for his electric window and called, "Smithy, check the air in the tires . . . and Smithy, don't finish until I'm finished." The window came back up. Mr. Jonelli turned his attention back to John, forced a smile and said, "It's a good idea to come to these dances alone. Drink?"

"No, thanks. Can we talk about Natt?"

"Well, of course we can. That's why we're here. It's a shame your brother has gotten himself into such an awful mess, though not entirely unexpected. He's been taking my money for years. Ha-ha. I've been patiently waiting for his luck to change. What do they say? 'Lucky in love.' Ha! Ha! I would guess Natt's in love!" he said gleefully. "Ooohoo," he sighed, shifting gears. "I'm a big fan of yours, John. You had a fine season last year. But this year, this season, Mr. Greco, 1965 will be your dream season. The team looks better than ever, and you're destined to be a Highlander great, John. Say, did

I hear you ascertained the catching job all for yourself? About time! Think of the steady at-bats you'll receive. My father, rest his soul, worked on the ground crew when 'The Babe' played. Yes . . . ha! He loved the Highlanders. They still remember the old man at the stadium. I have tickets for life. He willed them to me. Spent all his money on baseball doodads and tickets. Humph." Mr. Jonelli tried to laugh but couldn't quite pull it off. "Still know most of the ground crew. They pass those jobs down from father to son. You know Macky, don't you? Good friend, very good friend of mine."

'It excited him, talking about the Highlanders,' John thought as he patiently listened, thinking things were getting friendlier. Mr. Jonelli paused to take a sip from his drink. John figured it was his turn to talk.

"I'm prepared to pay my brother's—" Mr. Jonelli cut him off.

"Good, good, so you have the two hundred and six thousand?"

"We have twenty thousand, and we'd—" Again Jonelli cut John off, this time with an ever-so-slight wave of the hand as though he were a priest bestowing a blessing.

"Please, Mr. Greco, just answer the question. Do you have the money? All the money?"

"No."

"Do you know where your brother is?"

"No."

Jonelli's voice went icy cold. "I didn't think so."

"I'm willing to sell my home."

"What! And I should wait months for half my money at best. I don't think so. You see, John, you and your lovely wife couldn't possibly be prepared for this. I'm not a bank. That man," pointing to Lango, "is not a teller." Mr. Jonelli paused and looked up as if he were retrieving information from the ceiling of the car.

"Oh, John, John, John," he continued, "it must be nice to think of nothing but shagging fly balls all afternoon." He paused and smiled. "I am an empiric man." John looked lost. "Ah, I believe practical experience is the source of knowledge," he said, playing the part of a wise grandfather. John started to fidget with the cigarette lighter. He didn't know where to take the conversation after telling Mr. Jonelli that he was willing to give up his home. "You have no practical experience," Jonelli went on. "Things have been easy for you. Now your brother, things haven't been quite so easy for him, living and dying on a bet, killing himself to make the money to cover his losses. And to think—all on bets he placed merely to distract himself from his unfortunate baseball career. Not easy at all. I respect Natt, and I respect your talent."

"Mr. Jonelli, wouldn't you rather have fifty thousand dollars than a dead man?" John questioned, completely unaware of Jonelli's motives.

"So now it's fifty? Ha! And who said anything about a dead man, my boy?" He ran his fingers through his hair and fondled his cane, practically gloating over how easily John could be manipulated. "I don't want your money. Truth be known, I don't even want Natt's money. Think. Why would I let a man who didn't have $103,000 bet $206,000! Think! Do you know?"

"I have no idea," John said truthfully.

"John, I want you. I want you to be my partner—for one game." He raised his hand as a boy scout would. "Promise," he said.

John's mind went blank. He couldn't think. He couldn't even get his arms to move. The moment was frozen in time and all he could hear was, 'I want you - I want you - I want you - want you . . .'

"Think of it, Johney. With one game and my connections, I could place wagers throughout the country. We could make millions. I'll give you, oh, five percent." He folded his hands across his belly, reminding John of a Buddha.

"I can't do that. How could I do—"

"You don't understand. Let me help you and your brother. John, let me help your family."

"You want me to throw a game?"

"Ha-ha! I want you to influence a game. After all, this isn't a prizefight!" he joked, and then he became very serious as he shared his ideas. "As the catcher, you are in the most influential position. Even more so than the pitcher." John couldn't believe what he was hearing. He wanted to cover his ears. He wanted to crawl into a ball as Mr. Jonelli's dialogue bombarded all his senses. "There are a variety of ways," Jonelli informed John. "For instance, a passed ball at an appropriate, ha, or inappropriate time, depending on how you look at it. Perhaps a missed tag at the plate, crossed signs with the pitcher, a foul ball you jussst couldn't get to, maybe it was lost in the sun. That happens. A failed throw to second on the steal. Who knows? That throw might even end up in center field, just possibly allowing a run to score. An errant throw to first or third. Maybe you won't get the calls because you're not pulling the glove back into the strike zone. You could have a bad day at the plate, strikeouts, hit into a double play with the bases loaded. Think of it! There are so many things a catcher could do. And the beauty of it is," he put his arm around John and whispered, "the beauty of it is, it will just look as though you've had a bad day. Oh, I know it's not a lock, but it's an edge, a significant edge. You can be subtle. You should be. Just do what needs to be done. I don't want you taken out of the game." Mr. Jonelli took a sip from his drink, smiled, but was disappointed to see John gazing out the window.

Johney longed to be some place else, any place else. Free. He admired Sharon, how she stood her ground, courageously, braving the damp, chilled night air and the presence of people not of this good earth. 'Not of her earth,' he thought. These were people he had only read about or heard about through some other poor soul's misfortune. They were only an abstract idea of somebody else's problems, but now they were Sharon and John's problem and unconscionably real.

"John, you'll do well to pay a bit more attention," said Mr. Jonelli, beginning to sound rattled. "What do you make in a year?" He didn't wait for an answer. "You're a pretty good ballplayer. What? Fifty, maybe up to seventy thousand. Right? So let's see, you're what? Twenty-eight now. You have three to seven years left to play, barring of course injuries, demotions, personal problems which could affect your play. Aaaah! Get you cut altogether! Am I right? Do you hear what I'm saying?" He positively glowed with righteous justification. "I would say your earning potential is somewhere in the neighborhood of, oh, say three hundred thousand. Now, can your family live on that . . . ah, ah . . . figure inflation, taxes, a mortgage, the cost of a college education . . . retirement! I bet you don't even get health insurance when you leave baseball. One hospital stay by anyone in your family, and you're wiped out!" insisted Mr. Jonelli, his voice straining to convey genuine concern. "So, listen to what I'm offering you. I'll clean the slate for Natt. He owes me nothing, free to come and go as he wishes. No accidents. You and your family stand to make two, maybe three hundred thousand on the deal. For one day's work you have a nest egg. I'll tell you something else. You could give your brother a hand with that kind of money. Am I right?" He sat up, adjusted his coat, and looked John square in the eye. "The story around town is Natt would do anything for you," claimed Jonelli in his most sincere tone. "Besides, you shouldn't have to work too hard. Baltimore is going to have a good team this year. I have the money. All I'm looking for is an edge. Your edge. That's a gamble I'm willing to take."

John wiped the steamy window with his hand, relieved to see the cabby pull up, giving Sharon refuge. He thought of writing "help" on the window or drawing a tic-tac-toe board. It was all that came to mind. He didn't understand any of Jonelli's money games: profit—inflation—insurance—nest egg—money, money, money. It didn't matter. The equation was really very simple for John: Game = Natt. He loved them both. How could he chose? One fix was as good as ten, a hundred, a thousand—all the games ever played. Yet, one bullet in Natt's head would make baseball unplayable.

Mr. Jonelli was growing tired of John's seemingly short attention span. "Look at me! Do I look like the son of a grounds keeper?!" he shouted, the smell of booze complemented his now bitter anger. "He wanted me—*me*—to be a ballplayer; if not a player, a grounds keeper! 'It's a good life,' he said. Haaaa! I told him, 'I don't want a good life. I want the best life! Best of everything!' Don't you see? That's what I'm offering you!" He paused to check John's reaction. There wasn't any, but that didn't stop Mr. Jonelli from going on about his father. "He was a bastard, that old man. Talked about Babe Ruth twenty-four hours a day. And grass," Jonelli confessed, more to his glass of scotch than to Johney.

"That's bad?" asked John, feeling the need to say something. Mr. Jonelli considered taking his head off, then reconsidered. He reapplied his phony smile and paternal persona.

"It's late; we'll talk tomorrow. I trust that will be ample time," he said, in a telling way. "John, I'd like to see the Highlanders take the Series if it means anything to you," he said, trying his best to achieve an air of calm. "And, John, don't disappoint me . . . or your brother. Be a rich man." Johney nodded his head in agreement as though he understood, but he understood nothing. Mr. Jonelli raised his cane, a final gesture at a black mass. It was okay for Johney to leave.

John stumbled out of the limo in his rush to get to the cab, brushing his knee against the back bumper. He felt his knee slide off as though the bumper were lubricated. John didn't notice Smithy Lango's gleefully demented happy face or his mock tip of an imaginary cap.

"What happened? I was getting worried," asked Sharon as soon as John got into the cab.

"You okay? Smithy, he didn't—"

"No, no. I'm fine," she said. They fell into each others' arms. "What happened? You have blood on your pants!"

"Nothing, really. I'm not bleeding. I don't know where it came from." He stared at the blood for a moment, confused by its appearance. Then he took Sharon's hand in his own. "Shar, they want me to throw the opener," he whispered, unable to fully comprehend his own words. Tears streamed down her face. She hugged him and held him tight as the yellow taxi drove them home.

14

"YOU LOOK LIKE shit," said Dillon Southwood.

"Didn't sleep well," replied John, doing his best not to think about the night before. He was wishing it would all go away, an elaborate practical joke.

"C'mon! Take a sleeping pill if you have to! You need your rest!" insisted Southwood, figuring the kid was just excited about starting and opening day. "Two days! Come Wednesday, the ride begins." He gave John a good-natured slap on the butt, left the locker room, and walked out onto the field.

It was the first day back in the stadium, a new season, and Dillon Southwood couldn't wait to smell the grass, feel its soul. Ruth Memorial Stadium, Southwood thought, was so peaceful and serene, sitting right there in the middle of the city, in the middle of the South Bronx. 'Like an oasis,' he thought. 'Hummm . . . an oasis for everyone from everything, that's baseball.' Manager Southwood liked his new definition of the game, thought it sounded deep, and considered trying it out on the reporters. Then he thought again, 'No way.' He surveyed the field from the foot of the Highlander dugout. Just he and the ground crew were there, preparing for the day's light workout. Dillon enjoyed his early morning time, before the players and the reporters swarmed the field. He could relax with a cup of coffee without being bothered.

"Macky!" shouted Southwood. "Mac!" Macky didn't hear Southwood at first; he was busy smoothing out the dirt behind second base. "There's a piece of sod sticking up in center," called the manager, meaning: Go fix it.

THE DAY'S PRACTICE was actually more of a press event, which suited John just fine. He had nothing to offer his teammates. He couldn't run, hit, catch, or concentrate. Possessing none of baseball's basic skills, the game seemed like work.

"Kid, go home, get some rest," ordered Southwood. He didn't want John to get down on himself. "What is it? You fighting with Sharon?"

"No."

"Well, go make up anyway."

"Thanks, Woody. I'll be okay tomorrow."

"Yeah-yeah-yeah," muttered Dillon, dismissing him. He watched his prodigy lumber off the field, and he thought, 'Better be okay. This season is screwed without him.'

AS JOHN TRAVELED the subway home, he thought about Natt. He couldn't understand his lack of communication. 'Why didn't he call?' he asked himself. 'Faye needs to know he's okay. Why hasn't he called?'

The train stopped in between stations, just before 125th Street and the Grand Concourse. The lights flickered and went into reserve, creating a dining car effect or a subway hell, all depending on your mood and the mood of your fellow travelers. The train smelled of pizza, and at the foot of a graffitied door lay the rejected half-eaten slice. Somebody had tried to throw it on the tracks, between the narrow space of the train and the station platform; they'd missed. John hadn't noticed the smell before the lights dimmed; he had been busy fighting off sleep. A man tried to read the glass enclosed subway map directly across from him. Then he appeared to have given up in the poor lighting. The train became very quiet as the motors shut down. People folded their papers, closed their books, and waited for the power to return. The motorman made an announcement which nobody understood.

"What?! . . . Que?!" murmured through the entire length of the train. "Shit," "damn it," and a few other choice words, in several languages, could also be heard, but altogether it just sounded like one big grumble.

The train returned to power in less than a minute. The lights, motors, and newspapers were back to their original positions as the subway started to roll again.

The scenario was nothing unusual, except that when the lights returned, the subway map had a message on it that John was certain—well, almost certain—wasn't there before. Painted across the glass in black graffiti letters, was: Don't do it. A line ran through the letters as if to accent the urgency of the words.

"Was that there?" John, slightly panicked, questioned the lady sitting next to him. She put down her book.

"Was what where?" she responded, not pleased by the interruption.

"The map. I mean the 'Don't do it.' Was it there? Before the lights dimmed?"

She looked at him as though he were deranged. "I don't know," she replied with a great deal of attitude and returned to her book, doing her best to block him out.

John was sure it wasn't there before. It was a message for him, about the question he'd been avoiding all day. The thought had occurred to him that he was being superstitious. But none of that mattered; he had finally made a decision. He wasn't going to do it. A burst of energy charged through his system. He felt revitalized, in control. John realized there wasn't any other choice for him or for his brother. Natt's soul, he reasoned, was better off in the hands of fate and not Mr. Jonelli.

WHEN JOHN ARRIVED home, he was greeted at the door by Maya. She ran from playing doll house with her Aunt Faye, as soon as she heard the key in the lock.

"Daddy, Daddy's hoooome," squealed the little girl, as she jumped into his open arms. He spun her around and kissed her while she giggled the whole time. Maya pretended not to like the coarseness of her Daddy's beard as she ran her hand down his scruffy cheek, something she learned from her mom.

"How's my girl?" asked John in a jolly, honey-coated tone. She was a darling child. Her hair was starting to get very dark, like her mother's. She was pretty, well-behaved, and at only four years old, loved baseball. Well, at least, she liked to see her daddy in his baseball uniform. Maya got very excited when he wore it. John was her superhero.

"Daddy, I'm playing doll house with Aunt Faye," she said. Faye appeared behind the little girl and gave her a kiss on the head.

"John, would you like to join us?" she asked in a very ladylike manner.

"Yes, Daddy! Pleaseeee."

"I'd love to," replied John, as he carried his daughter into the living room.

"You look much better today. How are you feeling?" he asked his sister-in-law. She shrugged her shoulders and nodded her head in a manner that said both that she wasn't sure and, yet, better.

"I'm fine, exhausted, but okay I guess. Maya's helped me. You know how I love kids."

"Yeah, they can make a lot of things right." He rearranged some furniture in the doll house. "Where's Sharon?"

"Food shopping. Charlie's at school."

"Faye?"

"Yeah?"

"You know you can stay here as long as you want."

"I know."

"We have plenty of room." He was trying to think of all the things he wanted to say about Natt, but he just kept talking obvious nonsense. "Don't worry about money. It would be good for Charlie and Maya to play together, you know, like brother and sister. Sharon could put in more time at the mayor's office; she likes her work, and—"

Faye put a finger to John's lips to quiet him. She was beginning to feel uncomfortable, knowing how John didn't often string more than two sentences together. 'He's trying so hard,' she thought. "I know this is difficult for you. We love him a lot," she said sadly, wondering why he hadn't called.

"Faye, I can't do what they want."

"What, the game?" she questioned.

"You know?"

"Sharon told me." John frowned. "Well, what else were we going to talk about? The weather?"

"I, I—"

"John, *don't do it.* Natt would die if he found out you compromised yourself. And he will find out. What's the matter? You look like you just saw a ghost." John told her about his subway ride home. She thought his mind obviously had been working overtime. "Well, the subway's right, too," she agreed.

Faye set a miniature table while Maya watched. Maya could barely keep her eyes open. She smiled at her Aunt Faye and moved her miniature baby into its bedroom. "We've been playing all morning," Faye offered.

John took Maya's little hand into his own. 'She's a miracle,' he thought.

"So then, you wouldn't hate me?" asked John, referring to the fix.

"I'd hate you if you did. You're doing the only thing you can do. You're not capable of anything else. Don't you see? Natt would never forgive himself if you let them change the part of you he loves most."

BASEBALL & BENEVOLENCE

Honesty—that was the quality in John that Natt adored . . . a childlike honesty. But to Natty, John was more of a man than anyone he'd ever met. His brother was bound by his principles, a reasoned, natural order of work ethics, sportsmanship, and dedication. Yet, there were people who saw him as weak, a person who could be taken advantage of because of those very convictions. John never seemed to notice those people, and somehow, maybe through his beliefs, his decency, things seemed to work themselves out. Natt had always marveled at his brother's strength and good fortune.

That afternoon John fell asleep with his arms wrapped around his daughter on the living room floor. Faye covered them up with a quilted blanket. 'They look so sweet,' she thought. She couldn't decide if he was the strongest or weakest, most foolish or most brilliant man she had ever met. It didn't matter. What did matter was that John was part her family, her long lost brother, reincarnated into everything she always dreamed he'd be.

"Sleep, angels. I don't feel so alone, anymore," Faye uttered in a hushed voice. She got on her hands and knees and kissed Maya on the forehead. She wished them sweet dreams, then retired to her room to rest.

15

"BABE, BABE," SHARON cooed into John's ear. Even the smell of dinner cooking didn't wake him. It usually did. Maya pushed on his shoulder playfully.

"Daddy, Mommy wants you," she called in a singsong voice.

John was trying to fight his way out of a dream. He could hear their voices. He wanted to get to them, but the sleep enveloped him like a multilayered bubble, each layer able to flex and expand as he tried to reach them. John came out of his dream world as if he'd been ejected from a jet fighter. "Wha-huh!"

He startled Sharon. "It's okay," she soothed. She ran her hand through his hair to calm him and, at the same time, smoothed out his matted hair which was making him look pretty silly. Maya giggled and ran her tiny hand through his hair, too. She wanted to do everything her mother did.

"It's o-tay, Daddy," she said, as she patted his head.

"Tommy's on the phone," Sharon said. "Want to call him back?"

"No, no," he mumbled. The room was spinning; he was still groggy. John staggered to the kitchen to get the phone.

"Hell-o?"

"Jesus, you sound like a bullfrog. Listen, you got a meeting. Y'know what I mean? My back room, ten o'clock tonight. Ya'wanna tell me about it?" asked Tommy, like a father questioning his son's car accident.

"It's about Natt."

"I know that!"

"Have you heard from him, Tommy?"

"Not a peep. Something's not right. Isn't like 'im."

"Yeah, I know."

"Soooo, what's going on?!" he demanded.

John told him everything that had happened since the night before, including the subway and how he couldn't go through with Jonelli's plan. Tommy didn't interrupt, and when John finished, there was a long moment of silence.

"You see," he said, "I can't do it." John paused, waiting for Tommy's reaction.

"Shit," groaned Tommy.

"What do you think?"

Tommy put the receiver on the bar, poured himself a shot of whiskey and downed it, then picked up the receiver again. "Honestly? I don't know about Jonelli," meaning that he didn't know how dangerous he was. "Besides the book biz, he's legit—real estate, owns lots of buildings. I wouldn't think he'd try anything this big. He's not Mafia." Tommy was thinking out loud, more than conversing. "Boy-oh-boy, that's a crazy-assed sounding bet he wants to make. Must have a screw loose, or he's a true-blue gambler. He's supposed to be real smart. Covers himself well. I'm surprised he's coming to the bar. Well, I gotta let him in the back way."

"Tommy, will they kill Natt?" John didn't mince words.

"You've asked me that before. I still don't know," said Tommy, irritated and frustrated that the truth wouldn't provide a better answer. He wiped the bar while he talked, then wiped his brow with the same rag. "Listen, kid. We'll be here, right up front if you need us. And kid, you don't want to be seen with these people. Ya know?"

JOHN ARRIVED AT Tommy's just before ten. Tommy ushered him into the back room and gave him a club soda. It was Monday night and slow. There were seven people in the whole bar, including me, Tommy, and Two Face Pete. A long-haired kid was sipping beers by himself and playing the juke box, probably killing time waiting for a bus. Janet and her boyfriend, Benny, seemed to be getting along fine. And there was a young girl with long blonde hair, love beads, headband, blue jeans, and a tie-dyed blouse; she was a hippie. She sat at the end of the bar, drank white wine and didn't attempt to have a conversation with anyone. The hippies were good kids. Sometimes they'd ask Tommy to update his juke box, and he'd say, "Nope." That would be the end of it; they never pushed Tommy any harder. The musical history of Tommy's juke box ended with Elvis, Jackie Wilson, Sam Cooke, and Billie Holiday. The majority of space went to Sinatra, Patsy Cline, Satchmo, Duke Ellington, Glenn Miller, and Woody Guthrie—in that order, and it was never going to change. That was the music that Tommy loved; it catered to all of his emotional and musical needs.

John hummed along to "This Land is Your Land" while he waited. The hippies often played that one. Every thirty seconds Tommy would pop his head into the back room to see if he was all right—if Mr. Jonelli had arrived. It struck John as funny how Tommy's bald head would appear through a ten inch door opening, accompanied by a blast of music. 'Like a human jack-in-the-box,' he thought. Then just as quickly, Tommy would disappear after a brief exchange.

"Okay?"

"Okay." Tommy felt personally responsible for John, now that Natt wasn't around. He was playing the juke box exceptionally loud that night. I suppose so nobody could think or hear, maybe even to discourage business. That wouldn't be unlike Tommy. Not that it mattered to this crowd; they were just getting drunk. The music felt good. John was on the second verse of Nat King Cole's "Unforgettable" when the pounding on the door shook his seat.

Bam! Bam! Bam!—a battering-ram to the castle gate. The abrupt pounding jarred and startled Johney from the comfort and peace of mind that the music had offered. He opened the first of three locks on Tommy's door. Bam!

"Okay, okay. I'm here. Give me a second," called John, over Mr. Cole, finally getting all the locks to open. The ever-grinning Smithy Lango was followed by the dapper Mr. Jonelli.

"Nice place," said Mr. Lango with oozing sarcasm, certain he had just delivered the cutting quip of the year. Mr. Jonelli paid no attention to Smithy's remarks; he was strictly tolerated.

"Ah! John, you're looking well," said Jonelli, extending his hand. They shook hands, while Lango took his position at the door, out of sight.

"Mr. Jonelli," greeted John.

Both men took a seat at the table, a poker table appropriately enough. It was surrounded by shelves of bar supplies, a refrigerator, and a dilapidated stove that didn't work. The room was lit by three bare bulbs, two in wall sockets and one that hung from a cord in the middle of the room. The light made everyone look yellowish and sickly. A blast of "Take the A Train" flooded the room when Tommy popped his head in again. Smithy's hand moved for his breast pocket, then retreated when he saw it was Tommy.

"Oh," Tommy said. "You okay?"

"Okay," said John, politely. Tommy closed the door slowly, as the sound of the "A Train" faded into the distance.

"Shall we get down to business," Mr. Jonelli suggested graciously.

Johney looked Jonelli straight in the eye, wanting to appear serious and confident. "Yah, I can't do it," said John. He received the exact opposite reaction he desired from his adversary. Jonelli acted as though John were making a joke. Johney laughed with him, not knowing what else to do.

John noticed something different about Mr. Jonelli tonight, but couldn't immediately put his finger on it. Jonelli wore an impeccable dark brown Peterborough Row suit with a perfectly pressed white linen shirt and a red and blue striped tie, tied in a Windsor knot. 'Very presidential,' John thought. But that wasn't what was different. He walked with a cane, even though he didn't seem to have any trouble walking. 'That's it, the cane,' John thought. It wasn't the silver wing with the abracadabra pyramid, the cane that had made such a big impression the night before. It was just an ordinary black hook cane. John thought of asking him about it, but then reconsidered. Mr. Jonelli didn't look too happy after he finished laughing.

"John, I don't think you quite understand. We have a deal."

"I want to help my brother, but what you want," he lowered his head as if to ask Natt for forgiveness, "is impossible."

Jonelli tapped his cane on the floor, biding his time, methodically considering his next move. "Well, John, I'm afraid we have a problem . . . our problem. You see, the bets . . . our bets, excuse me—ha ha—are already in. Spent most of the day making them. So you see this isn't about your brother anymore, John." His cane tapped time.

"I never agreed to this. Call your bets off."

"Mr. Greco, it's a done deal. Now, if it's the money, say you need a bigger cut, sayyy—ten percent? Maybe we can work something out. That would be about a half a million dollars." He heavily emphasized "half a million." "Would that do?" questioned Jonelli, looking for his opponent's breaking point. John's dumbfounded expression read as a poker face. Jonelli continued to sweeten the pot. He went on and on, one unethical proposition after another. Mr. Jonelli really wanted this sale.

'Maybe he did place the bets,' John wondered. In a quiet form of self-defense, John's thoughts drifted with every persistent word out of Mr. Jonelli's mouth. John's apparent disinterest angered and fanned Jonelli's flames, creating, quite accidentally for John, the deal of a lifetime—not that Mr. Jonelli was actually going to give Johney a million dollars. Funny thing was, John being John, he probably would've believed Jonelli. But John refused to listen, not that the money would have influenced John's decision. He felt like he was viewing Mr. Jonelli from above, watching his lips move, hands gesture, eyes gleam with greed. The only detail that really made an impression on John was how uncomfortable Mr. Jonelli was with his new cane. He tapped and tapped and tapped, and switched it from hand to hand, then back again, as if it hurt to hold for too long. Once, while he was speaking, Jonelli looked down at it in total disgust. 'A very harsh reaction to a cane,' John thought.

"Well, my boy?" asked Mr. Jonelli, certain he had his sale. "Deal?"

"Oh, ahhh, I can't," said John. "Please cancel your bets. I'll get you Natt's money. It will just take some time."

Jonelli got up from his chair, allowing the cane to fall. A twisted smile appeared on his face when it slapped the cement floor. He leaned over the poker table, hands on the green felt island, and spoke within inches of John's face. His tone was no longer friendly.

"I'm afraid all bets will stand . . . and you'll do your job. In time, you will realize that it's for the best, for your family." The word "family" was poisoned with implication.

"There is no deal," responded John.

"Our business, let's see," Mr. Jonelli said, ignoring the ballplayer's reply, "will conclude in two days time, Wednesday to be exact, when the Highlanders lose by two, and I'm certain you've done all that is necessary to provide me with my edge. Not until then."

"You heard me," stated John, determined to hold his ground. He wanted there to be no doubt, knowing they had both played their hands to the limit. Now something had to give. He was certain that Jonelli knew he would never cheat. Yet, he didn't understand why Mr. Jonelli thought he could still persuade him. If not for his brother and not for the money, why? Was his own life at stake now? 'Maybe,' John thought.

Mr. Jonelli picked up his insubordinate cane. Smithy opened the back door for him. They were about to leave, but Jonelli just had to have the last word.

"John, no matter what, you will play on Wednesday."

"Right," replied John. "No matter what." They finally agreed on something.

"Good night, Mr. Greco."

16

"FIFTH PRECINCT."

"I want to report a missing person."

"How long has the person been missing?"

"Since Saturday, ah, almost four days."

"Please hold."

It was Tuesday morning. Nobody had heard from Natt since John had, late Sunday night in Florida. Faye knew her husband was in hiding, but feared much worse. Obviously, the lack of communication worried her most of all. There wasn't any reason for him not to make contact, except for the most horrid of reasons.

"Detective Kerrins speaking. How can I help you?" Kerrins sat behind a steel gray metal desk, littered with styrofoam coffee cups, empty take-out cartons, packages of salt and pepper and mustard and ketchup, various plastic utensils, and several volumes of cumbersome photo albums filled with unattractive pictures of every known criminal in the city.

Detective Brian Kerrins was in his midthirties, kept himself in reasonably good shape for a bachelor who ate nothing but junk food and didn't mind taking a drink every now and then. Kerrins was a smart cop whose life was his work. He came from a long line of policemen, but he was unusual for a fifteen-year veteran. He wasn't nearly as cynical as would be expected and not as down on the city as most people, though he had his moments. He saw New York as a place yet to be born. "If we can make it, the world can make it," was his philosophy. Detective Kerrins in essence was a true romantic, a cop on a mission, on par with a slightly saner Don Quixote, but as his young partner, Detective Weinman, was fond of saying, "Crustier."

Max Weinman was more of a realist. His immaculate desk faced Kerrins' in a clashing confrontation between dirty and clean. Detective Weinman enjoyed playing with Detective Kerrins' optimism by contributing to his philosophy.

"And if we can't make it, we're fucked," he'd say with a good-natured, wide-angle smirk. His eyes would twinkle with the knowledge of how easy it was to get under Kerrins' skin. 'Always joking,' Kerrins would think, a bit annoyed. They balanced each other well.

"I'd like to report a missing person."

"Uh-huh."

"He's my husband."

"Okay, ma'am. What's your name, your husband's name, and how long has he been missing?" Kerrins took a sip of coffee in between questions. He drank a lot of coffee.

"Mrs. Natt Greco . . . Faye. My husband is Natt Greco. He's been missing since Saturday."

"Greco. Are you related to John Greco, the ballplayer?"

"Yes. He's Natt's younger brother. I'm his sister-in-law."

"Wow." Kerrins covered the phone with his hand. "Hey, Max, John Greco, the Highlander—"

"Yeah?"

"His brother is missing. This is the wife," he said, pointing to the phone with his free hand.

"John's wife?"

"Nooo, the brother's wife!" said Kerrins, annoyed. He often looked annoyed with Weinman. 'He's a detective? Doesn't follow my conversation half the time. Aah, just enjoys breaking my balls . . . Asshole,' thought Kerrins. He was actually very fond of Weinman, he just had a gruff way of expressing himself, or not expressing himself. Most of the time he only yelled at Max in his head, and Max knew it.

"Detective Kerrins? Detective Kerrins, are you still there?"

"Yes, I'm here. Now, if I can have your address."

"Well, my home address is 2 East 12th Street, but I'm not there."

"You've moved? Or you're not there right—"

"I'm staying with John and Sharon. My brother and sister-in-law."

"Okay, address?"

"Twenty-four East 10th Street."

"Apartment?"

"It's a townhouse. They own it."

"Uh-huh. Mrs. Greco, wasn't there a problem at your place on Saturday night?"

"Yes, a man tried to . . . We had an intruder."

"Uh-huh. Were you hurt, loss of property, anybody else hurt?"

"No." Faye wasn't sure if the truth was the best answer or if this whole thing was a bad idea. It occurred to her that press in a matter such as this could hurt John's career.

"Mrs. Greco, do you have any idea why your husband might be missing?"

"No," said Faye, hesitantly; she was a bad liar.

"Uh-huh," replied Detective Kerrins, suspiciously. "Okay, let's get a description, and I'll put out a bulletin."

"He looks like a young Walt Disney."

Kerrins covered the phone again with his hand. "Max, she sez her husband looks like a young Walt Disney." Detective Weinman's eyes widened, obviously amused. "Sooo, that would be a white male—"

"Yes, yes. Six foot three, two hundred pounds, thirty-three, brown eyes, brown hair, a little gray at the temples, thin mustache, handsome, likes to wear nice suits, elegant, charming. He looks like Walt Disney!" said Faye, again, getting a bit frustrated.

"Uh-huh. Well, we'll get the bulletin out right away. I'd like to stop by today, get a photo, ah, interview the family."

"Oh. Okay. But John won't be home 'til two, maybe three o'clock."

"That'll be fine. Around three then."

"Okay."

"Oh, Mrs. Greco."

"Yes?"

"If you need anything or should he turn up, give me a call. Detective Brian Kerrins, Fifth Precinct."

"Yes. I will. Thank you, Detective Kerrins."

Faye felt relieved that the police were on the case, though she wasn't sure how John was going to take it or if Natt would appreciate their investigation. She just knew that she felt much better about things, and she thought Detective Kerrins was nice in an odd sort of way.

"WELL?" SAID WEINMAN.

"I think there's something going on."

"Yeah, the guy is missing. That's what's going on. Could be anything. I heard the guy was a real womanizer and gambler."

"Max, she was the woman with the intruder Saturday night. She was the attempted rape. There's a warrant out for that piece of shit Smithy Lango. They didn't pick him up yet?!" He wasn't looking for a response. He knew finding Smithy Lango wasn't a priority for the department because nothing serious went down, meaning nobody was hurt except Lango.

"I know," said Max, "when they ID'ed Lango, Natt Greco was the connection. Only she didn't say anything about him missing on Saturday."

"We gotta pick Lango up. He's the problem here or part of it. Works for Mr. Jonelli. Geez! There's a sleazeball," muttered Kerrins. "Just once I'd like to get my hands on him and not one of his flunkies."

"You think John Greco's got something—"

"Shit, I hope not. If that guy is into something, well, baseball is screwed," insisted Kerrins. He waved his hand in a dramatic gesture, knocked over his coffee, and continued with his thought as he stood up to avoid the spill. Weinman was impressed. "C'mon, Max, you're a Highlander fan. He's a great ballplayer. Ever see him interviewed? The guy still doesn't know the 'one-game-at-a-time speech.' Max, he thinks ya have to answer all the questions honestly." Kerrins grabbed a stack of coffee soaked papers and waved them around emphatically. "This guy's a piece of work. He thinks America is mom and apple pie and freedom with equal rights for all; but most of all, he thinks America is working."

"Sounds just like you," said Weinman, not sure if he should be getting on him. Kerrins just ignored him and continued his thought.

"Only I'm not naive, just hopeful. This guy, this guy . . . he isn't a Holy-Roller, a con artist. Max, even you must see that! He's for real. Even New Yorkers see it; the people love him. If, if he's corrupt, then, aaaaah, what's the point?"

Max toyed with the idea of egging him on but the despair in Kerrins' eyes silenced him. 'He's really worked up,' Weinman thought, 'even for Kerrins.' After all, fifteen years on the NYPD wasn't able to tame his optimism. But this . . . this to Kerrins, the baseball believer, was unthinkable. If John Greco was an act, a fake, it would break his hopeful back.

"And?"

"Then . . . it's just like ya say, Max. The world is screwed. We're fucked."

17

WHEN JOHN REACHED the stadium for the pre-opening day workout, he stopped at the ticket window.

"Good morning, Anne."

"Oh. Hello, John. How are ya?"

"Pretty good. Think I can get twenty-five tickets for the opener?"

"Sh-ure, John," said Anne in a thick Brooklyn accent. "You's know ya have to pay after ten, don'tcha?"

"I know. Would you deduct it from my paycheck?" Anne smiled her approval. "And, Anne, could you leave two tickets at the advanced ticket window for my brother, Natt Greco." Natt never missed opening day. John was certain his brother would be there, just as always.

"Sh-ure." replied Anne. She liked John. 'Always so polite, not full of himself like some of the other players. If I was thirty years younger,' she thought.

"BRRRRRR. HONEY, IT'S chilly out. We'd better get your gloves on. Okay, sweetie?"

"Aunt Faye, can-I-go-on-the-slide?" asked Maya.

"Yes, the slide, the swings, in the sandbox. What else do they have in the park?"

"Jun-gle-gym-see-saw-Deb-by-Bil-ly-and-Jane . . . " She made a song of all her friends' names. Maya enjoyed talking as much as her mother did and singing like her father. She talked while her Aunt Faye bundled her up for play time. 'It's a lovely crisp, clear day out,' Faye thought. She was glad to be able to help out baby-sitting. It did her good and allowed Sharon the time to take a meeting at the mayor's office. 'John seemed much more at ease today,' she thought. Faye felt much better after speaking with Detective Kerrins, relieved that he was coming over in the afternoon. 'The police needed to be involved,' she reasoned as she prepared for the park.

Smithy Lango sat slumped behind the wheel of a black '61 Ford Galaxy, impatiently waiting for Faye to come out of the townhouse. He had a job to do. Lango was uncomfortable working in broad daylight. Normally he wouldn't even be out of bed yet. But he had a message to deliver and wouldn't mind "whacking the bitch;" his head still throbbed from the other night.

I suppose the idea was to get Faye in the leg or something, *something* meaning: to really scare the heck out of them. Lango's job was to penetrate John Greco's hazy attention span and what Mr. Jonelli deemed to be his moral high ground. Of course, it didn't work out that way. Smithy Lango was a psycho, but that didn't make him especially good at his work. Truth was, he was totally incompetent. Smithy wasn't very accomplished with a gun . . . or knife . . . or, for that matter, any technical skill involving weaponry. His only two qualifications were his body-builder strength and his demented mind, which made him intimidating and, at the same time, easy for Jonelli to manipulate. I found it surprising that a seemingly smart man like Mr. Jonelli would have anything to do with him. Though in the end Smithy Lango did serve his purpose, proving in fact that Jonelli was much smarter than anybody thought. Smithy became Mr. Jonelli's fall guy, and he never saw it coming, providing a third quality Jonelli appreciated about him: he was stupid. Buried within Smithy Lango was the knowledge of some very gruesome crimes, and he was the last witness to them.

Faye opened one of the two large oak doors and stepped outside to see how cold it really was. The townhouse was of the brick federal style with columns that framed the front double doorway and seven steps leading down to street level. The oak doors contained large full-length panes that were covered by crisscrossed wrought-iron bars, making them especially hard to see into.

When Smithy saw Faye, he reached for his gun—a Browning semi-automatic pistol, his pride and joy—and was about to saw Faye's feet off when she went back inside.

"Shit! She saw me!" Lango panicked as he pounded the steering wheel.

"Jesus fucking Christ, I missed the bitch!! I fucking hate daylight. Everybody on the block must know I'm here! The police gotta be here any second!"

"Sweetie, your aunt needs a scarf," said Faye, as she returned into the house. Smithy Lango could see her moving behind the darkened glass.

"There she is. Get this fucking job done!!!" he screamed at himself.

At that peak moment of paranoia, Smithy Lango jumped out of the Galaxy and pumped five shots into what he thought were Faye's legs. Of course with the glare, the sunshine, the nakedness he felt, all he was really shooting at was a dark, ghostly form.

The little girl was dead. She died instantly. Some would say mercifully. Two shots hit: one to the leg, one to the heart. The other three shots sprayed large shards of broken glass, cutting her tiny body like ribbon. She was unrecognizable. Smithy ran to the corner of 10th Street and commandeered a taxi, physically pulling the cabby out of his driver's seat and throwing him into the middle of University Avenue, right in front of Tommy's Bar. The Galaxy wasn't his after all, just a space to bide time.

Faye's scream was heard around the world. The media made sure of that. She wasn't touched by bullets or glass; her torture was psychological. She was found by the police picking pieces of glass from Maya's lifeless body, crying tears that wouldn't end, and she was as vicious as a rabid alley cat to anyone who tried to help her. It wasn't until the arrival of Detectives Kerrins and Weinman, that any sense of order began to return.

"She won't let us near the body. It's bad. She's covered with blood," said the reporting officer to the detectives.

When Kerrins started up the steps, he could hear her barely audible, low pitched wailing. "Oh-my-God-oh-my-God-oh-my-God . . . " over and over again.

"Faye?" said Kerrins in a strong but mindful tone. "Faye. It's Detective Kerrins. We spoke this morning." She didn't respond. Kerrins made his way to the top of the stoop and looked though the bars at Faye and the dead child. He crossed himself as Faye stared at him vacantly.

"How can God let this happen?" she said in anguish and bitter grief. He opened the door and extended his hand to her.

"I don't know. I honestly don't know. Let her go, Faye. Let her go. You don't want her parents to see her like this." Faye trembled and sobbed and then, in a final act of surrender, she carefully placed the body where she sat and slipped her hand into his. He pulled her to her feet. The child's blood stained and dripped from her dress. "I'll take care of you, Faye," whispered the detective as he led her down the steps.

"They don't know—Sharon and John—they don't know. My baby . . . Charlie. He's coming home from school soon."

"I'll take care of everything." He steadied her with a firm grip on her arm and a saneness in his gaze. They stood facing each other. "Listen, you gotta be strong for the parents—for your family. I want to send you to the hospital, St. Vincent's, right down the street. You need to be treated so you can get strong. Okay? I'll take care of things . . . alright?" She nodded her head and climbed into the back of a waiting ambulance. The rest of the emergency crews were already down to business when Faye's ambulance drove off. Detective Weinman had the street blocked off to everyone but residents. Patrolmen searched for the weapon and witnesses, though Detective Kerrins had a pretty fair idea who was behind this.

"Do you believe this shit," said Weinman as they removed the child's body. "They're shooting children. This world is—"

Kerrins stopped him in midsentence. He put his hand over his own mouth, a gesture that read as a kind way to say, "Shut up."

"Don't say it. I don't wanna hear it," he whispered.

18

SHARON SAT ON the living room couch in a zombie-like state, her eyes as red as hot coals, her body limp and heavily drugged by a sedative. She listened to John tell the detectives about Natt, the gambling, the money, the fix, the non-deal, the blackmail, the assault, the attempted rape, Smithy Lango, and Mr. Jonelli.

Mr. and Mrs. Costa and John's parents sat quietly in the kitchen, smoking cigarette after cigarette, trying their best to hold themselves together. One by one they would break down and be comforted by the others. Little Charlie, only seven, had cried himself out and had fallen asleep listening to the hushed voices coming from the living room. His grandfather carried him to his bed. Later they would take him to the hospital to see his mom, and then back to Mountain Edge, New Jersey, until some sort of normalcy was restored. Sharon would go back to Queens with her parents. They would handle the funeral arrangements and take care of their daughter. John's reaction appeared cold, distant, reserved. He didn't want anybody's comforting or sympathies. He wasn't going anywhere with anyone. The only thing he wanted to do was stay in his house. He wanted to feel the pain and the guilt and accept the responsibility for a horror he felt he could have easily prevented. He wanted to be in the rooms where the spirit of his daughter would be, where maybe he could feel her presence one more time. John gave the detectives all the information he had. His tone was somber. He looked at the floor while speaking, unable to face his wife. He wasn't sure if she blamed him, or Natt, or anyone for that matter. He questioned and requestioned himself for the role he had played and the decisions he had made. He gave answers to the detectives as if reading from the phone book. He couldn't wait for them all to leave, all of them. He wanted to be alone.

By seven o'clock they were gone, and John had his wish. Yellow police tape sealed the front of the house with him left inside. He wandered through the home as if he were a stranger looking for something of value. In the kitchen he splashed warm water on his face; maybe he was trying to create the tears that wouldn't come or replenish the youth he felt rapidly evaporating from his dry, taut skin. In the living room he played a single chord on the piano, but all he could hear was the dissonance between the augmented tones. This house was his, but everything in it seemed foreign, somehow different from the day before. In the master bedroom he smelled the familiar perfume and thought of Sharon. He ran his hand across her silk nightgown. He could see her in it—beautiful, sexy. With his left hand he picked up an amethyst earring off their dresser. The earrings were a birthday gift he had given her; amethyst was her birthstone. Forming a fist, he pressed the stone into the palm of his hand and released it, leaving a deep impression, so deep it took some time before it disappeared. John considered going into Maya's room. In fact he wanted to, but instead he stood at her doorway and gazed into the darkness, afraid the darkness was all that was left for her. 'How could a just God take her like this?' he thought. 'How could the same maker create people who would do this?' He wouldn't allow himself passage into her room, so he sat on the floor in the hall, just outside her doorway. The only light came from the master bedroom. It streamed out from the open door and onto the staircase below, leaving John in dim brownish yellow light, staring at long shadows that reflected off the staircase spindles. He was very much alone. It was what he wanted—to think, but to think about what? To ask questions of God that people have asked since the beginning of human time? He always smiled knowingly at folks who asked such unanswerable questions. Faith . . . faith had always been the answer. Didn't they know that? Isn't that what he always believed? Not so easy to believe it now. 'Not so easy to believe,' he thought.

"Why?!" he shouted. "How could you? Is this a test?! Well! Let's turn on the radio." He said in a deranged voice. "BEEEEEEEEEEEP . . . Oh. It is a test." He mocked himself as he spoke in a sickly, weakened voice. 'An actual emergency,' he thought. "So, where do I report?" He wasn't sure if it was a question or not. John wrapped his arms tightly around his legs, put his head to his knees, and allowed a violent flow of tears. "My God, Natty, what did we do?!"

John pounded his fist onto the floorboards, feeling as though his world had been taken away from him, feeling that he had been left with nothing, fighting the compulsion to kill. 'Have to be strong. If I'm not strong, I have nothing.' And nothingness, John began to see, was the end result of pure evil, the end of faith and love. He began to understand that holding onto goodness and the hope it generated was one of the most difficult accomplishments of life, but paramount to it.

John realized how desperately he needed to surround himself with infinite goodness. He needed to go where the people are brought together. Appropriate or not, he would play ball the next day. He needed the game, the fans, the other players in order to control his rage. He had to allow himself to believe in the strength he found there. For Johney, baseball encompassed what all loving parents want for their children. It was what John wanted for Maya. He had to believe. He prayed to God that she was with him, and he prayed for strength. Because he knew he'd need it.

19

New York City: April 15, 1965

"CHRIST!" SHOUTED BILL Singer, popping out of his chair like bread from a toaster, as he spotted John Greco through the window of Manager Southwood's office. "What the hell is he doing here?!"

"Coming to work," said Southwood, stone faced.

"We don't need this, Dillon. Shouldn't he be home with his wife, his family?! Wouldn't that make more sense!" Singer paced the small office trying to think how this would play with the public. That was his job. Bill Singer Jr. was in charge of the New York Highlanders' public relations department. The public's perception was his business, and he didn't like the way this opening day was shaping up. 'What . . . with the murder and all, why it's plain old bad business,' Singer thought. "Shhhh-oot, Dillon! Everybody and their brother is in town for this one!" moaned Singer. "They're expecting the greatest Highlander season ever! And now this whole damn messy business!"

Dillon was always amazed and impressed by Billyboy Singer's lack of compassion and communication skills. *Billyboy* was how Southwood referred to Mr. Singer in a less than affectionate manner. In fifteen years time Bill Singer Jr. would return to his roots in the South to become a moderately successful televangelist, dedicating his life to God, Reaganomics, and making a great deal more money than even he dreamed possible by preaching the gospel, developing a sizable following, and glorifying the miracle he personally witnessed in Ruth Memorial Stadium on that very day in April of 1965. Of course, he neglected to inform his viewers that if he had had his say, the whole thing would've never happened.

"You're not gonna let him play? Are you?"

"Maybe," said Manager Southwood. He kind of enjoyed Billyboy getting all worked up. 'Never did like him,' Dillon thought.

"Listen to me. Dillon, listen to me!" demanded Singer. Southwood begrudgingly lifted his head in Singer's direction. He was growing very tired of him.

"We don't know where this boy has been, what he's up to. The whole town is talking! Now I don't have to spell it out for you," but he did anyway. "I-T-A-L-I-A-N. Get it, man?" Singer plopped himself down in his seat, satisfied he had made his point. He was fond of ending his sentences with "man." It made him feel hip, with-it, on the pulse, where a good P.R. man should be, although he didn't get much of a reaction from Southwood. That didn't surprise him; he never did. But he felt this was an important point, so he pressed on. "If it was a nigger—"

"That's enough!" shouted the manager. When Southwood said *that's enough,* every Highlander knew it was. But somehow Bill Singer never caught on.

"Dillonnnnn . . . why aren't you listening to me, mannn?" he whined, completely unaware of how his high-pitched, sparrow-like tone nauseated Southwood.

"Because you're a prejudiced little prick. Now get your butt out of my office! Mannn!!!" Singer was shocked, taken aback, and scared to death all at the same time. He prided himself on his people skills. He thought for sure Dillon Southwood was a good-old-boy, that he wouldn't mind, that they would relate on the subject matter.

"But, but, but—what do I tell the press? About Greco?" He stood in the doorway ready to make a quick exit. Southwood gave him a stern look from behind his desk.

"Tell them he's here. He plays if he wants. He sits on the bench if he wants. Either way the Highlanders extend their deepest sympathies and regrets to John and his family." Singer gave a disappointed nod of the head and was about to do the hundred yard dash. "Oh, and Billyboy." Singer froze in his tracks. "Tell them we're glad he's here and that there will be a moment of silence before the game." Singer was about to respond, but Southwood's raised brow prevented his comment. "Now, go do whatever it is you do," suggested Manager Southwood. Billyboy was dismissed.

"MR., AHHH, JOSEPH Jonelli or is it Jones nowadays?" asked Detective Weinman, looking at a scrap of paper. "Do you know why you're here?"

Jonelli turned to his lawyer, Ira Gottlieb, as if to say, "Do I?" Gottlieb nodded his head in some sort of coded yes and no; he resembled an infant with a weak neck.

"No," said Jonelli. He sat stiffly, uncomfortable in his padded, gray metal chair. The chair had strips of gaffer's tape that ran across the seat and stuck to his trousers.

"We called you down because you and a Mr. Smithy Lango—Brian, is Smithy really his first name?"

"Yup," said Kerrins as he chain smoked cigarettes behind his garbage dump desk. He could tell Mr. Jonelli couldn't stand the smoke.

Jonelli grew impatient. 'They know damn well who I am. Nothing but childish games,' he thought. And he was right. Mr. Jonelli's bookmaking operation had been shut down by Kerrins a few times, though he never went to jail himself. Dedicated employees, such as Smithy Lango, didn't mind taking a six month vacation every few years, if the price was right. And it always was. Besides, Mr. Jonelli was a respectable businessman. Every politician in the city knew that, especially around campaign time. It seemed as though he became more respectable every year, more public—more charitable—more charming—more untouchable. Detectives Kerrins and Weinman knew him well. To them, he was an extremely dangerous and slippery "piece of shit." The smoke, the uncertainty of Mr. Jonelli's name, the obviously stupid questions, they were just games. The detectives wanted to send him a message.

"You and a Mr. Lango are suspected of racketeering and the murder of one Maya Anne Greco; possibly the murder of Natt Greco."

"This is absurd!" shouted Jonelli, completely outraged.

"C'mon, Joey. You don't have to act for us. We're old buddies," said Kerrins, calmly.

"I don't think that's necessary," said Ira Gottlieb. Ira was smart to say something before Mr. Jonelli did. It was apparent Jonelli and Kerrins had developed a deep-seated hatred over the years. The cat and mouse game had become tiring for Jonelli. To Jonelli's way of thinking, Detective Kerrins was a fool who refused to play ball. He didn't understand the city, how things worked, and young Weinman was equally as naive. If they would ask the right questions, they'd receive the proper response. A few simple questions would make their lives fuller, richer; and all of their lives much easier.

Instead, they insisted on inconveniencing him and making a nuisance of themselves. Mr. Jonelli had a warped, but to date, effective rationale of the world he lived in.

To Kerrins' way of thinking, Jonelli was the worst kind of criminal: smart, rich, and without a conscience—a social deviant of the highest order. His crimes had nothing to do with survival. They were motivated by greed and power and a perverse sense of superiority. He was the sort of man who could kill a little girl and still sleep nights.

"Is my client under arrest?"

"No, but he will be as soon as we find Lango," said Weinman. He circled around Jonelli's chair and in a fake whisper said, "He's not gonna take a murder rap for you."

"Lango is a loose cannon. He, he painted apartments for me. Nothing more!" insisted Jonelli, indignantly.

"Doesn't he kill little girls for you, too?" Kerrins questioned him with all the innocence of a boy asking which way to the zoo.

Gottlieb gave Mr. Jonelli a silencing glance and whispered, "Don't even think about responding." He cleared his throat and, turning to the detectives, said, "Well, gentlemen. If my client isn't under arrest, I think he's been more than kind."

"Not so fast, Ira. The ball game is coming on, opening day. Aren't you interested, Joey?" asked Kerrins.

"No," said Mr. Jonelli. He stood up to leave, leaning all of his weight on his cane.

"Really. I heard you were a big Baltimore fan?" jabbed Weinman.

"Bet your father is rolling in his grave," said Kerrins, and as an after-thought, he added, "Grounds keeper, wasn't he?"

Ira Gottlieb, Esquire, took Mr. Jonelli by the arm in an effort to lead him to safety. The detectives were on sensitive ground, and the lawyer knew it.

"Go," whispered Gottlieb to Jonelli.

"Joe," called Weinman. "You had him figured all wrong. John Greco. You should have known better." Mr. Jonelli turned slowly. His expression disturbed the detectives a great deal. His face came to life with shining patronizing eyes and a slight smile which he didn't try to repress, as though he was just reminded of what went right today. Jonelli said nothing as he was guided out of the precinct by Gottlieb. But the detectives had no trouble reading his thought balloon. The word "idiot" hung in the air.

"CAN'T SAY I expected you, kid," said the manager. Dillon Southwood put his size thirteen foot on the bench right next to where John sat in front of his locker. He leaned over and put his forearms on his raised knee, arms crossed.

John stared into his locker as though he were waiting for it to change into something else. His teammates were dressed and on the field. Batting practice was over. The game would begin in less than ten minutes, right after Robert Merrill sang "The Star Spangled Banner, " and a senator threw out the first ball.

"Marianne . . . my wife, my high school sweetheart," said Dillon, reflectively. "Perfect health, we thought. Had a headache on a Saturday night. Humph. Now that was unusual. Uh, so we didn't go to our Christmas party. I was disappointed—really looking forward to that party. All our friends would be there. She died the next morning—aneurysm; thirty-five bleeping years old. God, I loved that woman. Never did remarry. I'm a widower, you know. Got drunk every night for two straight years. And you know what?" John looked up from the void of his locker. Southwood was trying to keep his eyes from misting up.

"What?" asked John.

"It didn't help, nothing helped. I could still feel the pain like it was that very morning all over again. Every morning without her was just like the day she died." Dillon sat down on the bench next to John. It was the same space Ruth and DiMaggio once occupied, where Lou Gehrig contemplated his last game when he told the folks, "I consider myself the luckiest man on the face of the earth," even though he knew he was dying.

"How did you . . . " John's voice faded, unsure of what he wanted to ask, or maybe just afraid to ask.

"One day . . . one day I'm dead drunk in some dive bar in Florida. I can't remember the name, but I'll never forget the name of the town. Indiantown. Indiantown, Florida. Made an impression on me. Don't know why, looked like a thousand other towns. I was there trying to resurrect my baseball career. Spring training, I guess. Can't remember if I was crying in my beer or what. I thought I was just thinking to myself when out of the blue the bartender sez to me, 'You still love her.' And I say, 'Yeah.' He sez, 'That's okay. She still loves you, too. Accept it, and move on.' Accept it, and move on. Can you beat that? And I saw he was right. My fear was of the dark. You know—that's it. All she wrote. Over." Southwood took John's glove out of his locker, put it on, and made a pocket with his fist.

"She still loves me. I feel it. Her soul lives. It really does. And so does your little girl's."

BASEBALL & BENEVOLENCE

From outside on the playing field they could hear the drums and brass of the pregame marching band. The day was gray and on the cool side, but that wouldn't dampen the spirits of the sixty-thousand baseball fans, out from their winter hibernation, eager to live again.

John's jersey hung open, unbuttoned, revealing his dark blue T-shirt with the white NY, printed on it Highlander style. It was easily the most respected logo in sports. Yet, there were men, such as Mr. Jonelli, who would trivialize its association with pride and sportsmanship for their own greed, damage the very fabric of the nation's psyche—its love for itself.

Johney still couldn't believe how much he had lost by acting on his instincts. "She never had a chance." John rubbed his eyes.

"Yeah, I know," said Southwood. "That's the hard part of acceptance. Ya have'ta accept that she's not yours anymore. You won't see her grow. You can only believe that she will grow." Southwood removed John's glove from his hand and placed it on the bench next to him. He stood up tall with his silver hair falling out from under his cap. He arched his back to stretch it out a bit, then ran his hand around the nape of his neck and added pressure to make it crack.

"There's been a lot of talk, a lot of . . . speculation, John."

Johney stood up, took his cap out of his locker, buttoned his jersey. He was afraid of what would come next. He looked for something to do, any action to busy himself as he tied and retied his cleats.

Southwood continued, "Well, well, ah . . . I don't believe a bleeping word of it! You're in my line-up, batting fifth, unless you tell me otherwise! And, and—" Southwood's face turned red with anger. "Don't let that dickbrain Bill Singer rattle ya! Any problems, you come to me. Okay?"

John felt a wave a relief rush through his system, and he smiled. Something he didn't think he'd be able to do for a long time. The manager's eyes swelled up when he saw it, but he didn't feel embarrassed by it. Southwood headed for the field, then realized he'd forgotten something very important.

"Johney . . . "

"Yeah?"

"I'm sorry about your little angel."

There was an awkward moment of silence between them before Johney said anything.

"Hey, Woody?"

"Yeah?"

John wanted to thank him for being a good friend, for his help, his trust, his wisdom. He wanted to say that he loved him, but he didn't say it. Love was the right word, thanking him was just being polite, but it was the best he could do at the time.

"Thanks."

"You're welcome. Now, would you get your butt on the field."

"HOLY COW!" SHOUTED Phil "the Scooter" Rizzuto, the Highlander broadcaster. His voice rang through a cheap Japanese transistor radio that sat on top of Jason Wheeler's slightly burnt dresser. The dresser had been pulled out of a fire on 162nd Street and left for garbage. Only one side was actually scorched. Jason pushed the bad side against the wall, so it couldn't be seen. It took a little time for the smell of burnt wood, lacquer, and water damage to dissipate, but it did. And Jason Wheeler had himself a dresser, something his mom couldn't afford to buy him.

"Unbelievable! John Greco is on the field. We haven't seen him until just now! What? Three minutes before game time. He's in the starting line-up! And it looks like he's gonna play! Holy cow! I don't believe it! That kid's got some kind of grit, I'll tell you that! Of course our hearts go out to John and his family, his lovely wife Sharon ... the whole Greco family. What a tragedy! But it looks like John's here to play some ball! Could be the best thing for 'im."

"Alright!" Jason clapped his hands in broken time as he emptied his shoe box filled with baseball cards. He was searching for John Greco's rookie year. "Here!" he said out loud. Jason held the card above his head as he laid in bed. He stared at a picture of John in his batting stance and read the vital statistics as though he had a friend in the room with him, which he didn't. It was the information, John's life, that was so important to Jason. It had been ever since his mother read the back of John's card to him. "Jo-hn Gre-co. Born 4/21/37, Na-Ne-wark ... Newark, Ne-New Jer-sey." He sounded out each word, even though he knew the information by heart.

John Greco was Jason's favorite baseball player. Opening day at the stadium rivaled the excitement of Christmas Eve. To Jason's way of thinking, John and Jason had much in common. The day John made the Highlanders was the most amazing day of Jason's life. You see, Jason Wheeler was born on April 21, 1950, in Newark, New Jersey, exactly thirteen years after John. To most this would be an interesting fact at best. To Jason Wheeler, a reclusive Down's syndrome teenager, life in the South Bronx was more or less confined to the three room apartment he shared with his mother and a two block area that extended to the stadium on 161st Street. To Jason this fact of birth and baseball was life itself—his life, his only life. Luckily he had Phil Rizzuto, a nice man, to deliver it directly into his bedroom, where it was safe, free from the hatred and prejudice that seemed to engulf his world, and anger and cruelty he couldn't comprehend. After Jason's father died, his mom decided to move out of Newark and back to the old neighborhood.

'It's cheaper and Jason's so excited about living next to that big old ballpark,' she reasoned. But the hate seemed to follow them everywhere. Angela Wheeler's son wasn't a good-looking boy. His head was deformed and swollen, his eyes crossed, and his skin and features were either too light or too dark for the majority of folks. But the boy had a heart of gold, and any act of kindness was returned tenfold. "Cause that's the way he is. He's God's child," Angela Wheeler often said as proud as can be.

Baseball to Jason was infinite, would always be there, unlike his father who one day was gone. Jason was sure that he was right about baseball, even though he'd never actually been to a game. He was afraid. Jason saw the game and John Greco as living in the Bronx with him. He never felt lonely as long as Mr. Rizzuto was there to tell him all about the Highlanders.

His mom tried to warn him. She knew how he looked forward to this day. "Jason, honey, John Greco probably won't play, because of his little girl." But he did, and as Jason would later say, "And how!"

"YOU'VE GOT THIS crowd nervous, John," said Hank Miller, the third base coach, trying his best to lighten things up after the moment of silence. John put on his chest protector and pulled out a piece of Bazooka bubble gum from his pocket.

"You want half, Hank?" asked John.

"Nah. You know I'm a tobacco man." Hank spit out a big wad while he tried to act normal. John put on his shin guards. "They're all wondering why you're here today," Hank said as he stepped out of the dugout to have a look at the huge crowd. His own words surprised him. He wasn't acting naturally.

"Same reason I'm always here." John stepped out of the dugout to get in line with the umpires at home plate; the national anthem was about to be sung.

"Ladies and Gentlemen," boomed the aristocratic voice of Bob Sheppard, the stadium announcer. **"Please rise for our national anthem, performed by the Barringer High School Marching Band of Newark, New Jersey, and Mr. Robert Merrill of the New York City Metropolitan Opera."**

"DO YA SEE him, George?" questioned Two Face Pete, as he scanned the park with his binoculars.

"Na-na-na . . . No, Pa-Paa . . . Pete," I said.

"Hey! You's guys think ya could keep it down? A little respect!" said the construction worker who sat in front of us. He was very patriotic and didn't appreciate our talking during the anthem. So we waited until the end of the song; Merrill did a nice job. The crowd roared; the construction worker belched his approval. We were free to search for Natt again.

"LEON, PUT THE ball game on," requested Mr. Jonelli, speaking into the phone to his chauffeur as they traveled from the police station to his summer home in East Hampton. Jonelli made himself a scotch and soda and settled back into his thoughts as a red-headed hooker unzipped his pants. He was feeling good about himself. Kerrins and Weinman couldn't touch him; he was sure of that.

"... AND IT'S AAAAAA ... base hit!" shouted Phil Rizzuto. **"He'sss in there for a double down the third base line! That drives in two! Oh, I'll tell ya, Greco really turned on that pitch. Just out of reach of Charlie Krug's glove! And it was a rocket—got out there so fast I wasn't sure if John was gonna make it to second or not. And just like that, the Highlanders lead it in the bottom of the first 2 to 0 with two outs and John Greco on second base! Boy, that kid is something! He stepped out of the box, drew a square in the dirt, and hit the very first pitch he saw!"** Phil took a breather while they ran a beer commercial. He swiveled around and leaned his head back over his chair, looking at nothing but the pitted ceiling of the broadcasting booth, and said to anyone listening, "Boy, I hope that's gonna put these ugly rumors to rest. I hope."

The local papers weren't kind in reporting the Greco story. The articles were filled with speculation and suspicion, especially concerning Natt Greco and his alleged Mafia connections.

"AHH-HA-HA-HA! That-a-boy, Johney. Show me up," laughed Mr. Jonelli, talking to himself, full of unbalanced self-satisfaction. He sighed as the hooker did her job.

"JESUS, JOHNEY, YOU'D think ya just hit a grand slammer," cried Jimmy Boyle, the Baltimore second baseman, reacting to the intensity of the crowd noise. John asked for time. The second base umpire signaled time out as the stadium continued to rock, rejoicing in John's double as though it proved his innocence. Maybe it was the excitement of opening day, or maybe it was a profound sense of relief they felt, knowing John Greco was still theirs.

DETECTIVE KERRINS FELT it as he listened to the game in his shabby, rather depressing office. After the hit, he was confident enough to turn off the radio and get back to work, although working was what he'd been doing. For the first time in his life listening to a ball game could qualify as work.

JOHN STRETCHED HIS legs. He was a little stiff from not doing his warm-ups before the game. He walked to the edge of the dirt directly behind second, brushed himself off, and stretched his legs some more. The crowd still cheered so the umpire didn't rush him. The intoxicating smell of freshly cut grass enticed him into taking a knee.

"What are ya doing? We got a game to play here!" shouted the umpire.

'Natt's here,' John thought. 'He's in the ballpark.'

"Wha-wha-what's . . . he da-da-doing?" I asked, feeling his pain.

"I don't know, George. Don't know," said Two Face Pete with one of his better faces on.

Manager Southwood hustled out and onto the field, afraid John might be hurt. "You okay, son?"

"I think so."

"Nothin' wrong?"

John shook his head.

"But . . . "

"But what?"

"Nothing," said John. "I'm seeing the ball better than I ever have," trying to reassure his manager.

"Good . . . good. Hey, if you're tired—"

"No, no. I'm not. I wanna play," he insisted.

"Okay then. Let's play." Southwood helped him up, gave him a pat on the behind, and returned to the dugout.

"He okay, Woody?" called Hank Miller from his third base box which he never really stood inside.

"Yeah, he wants to play," replied Southwood, shrugging his shoulders.

The inning ended with the next batter when Cliff Oakes smashed a long fly ball 400 feet to center field. Everybody in the stadium thought it was gone. Unfortunately, Jody Reed, the Baltimore center fielder, was playing deep and caught it off the top of the fence. He practically danced back to the dugout. A long sad "Ahhhaaa . . . " registered the crowd's disappointment.

John returned to the edge of the infield where the dirt met the grass behind second, and he felt his brother's presence once again. It was still there, an energy field, a curtain between the infield and the outfield. He stepped between the dirt and grass a couple of times while Southwood watched from the top step of the dugout.

"What the hell is he doing?" he muttered, more concerned than angry.

"Miller! Would'ya—" Dillon waved his hand in a circular motion meaning, 'Get him off the field.'

"Hey, I think he sees us," shouted Pete, waving his hands like a crazed man. We both waved from our seats just behind the first base line. The man in front of us was about to tell Pete to shut up again, but his jaw dropped when he saw John coming off the field and heading in our direction.

"Seen my brother?" John called to us from the short fence separating the public from the field. The entire section turned to see who he was questioning.

"Na-na-na-no, Ja-John-y," sputtered out of my mouth. "Na-na-not yet." Then they all turned back to John to get his response.

"Keep an eye out. Alright? I think he's here." Hank Miller stood behind John, listening, waiting to guide him back to the dugout.

"Johney, thanks for the tickets!" Pete called immodestly, as John retreated.

"You know him?" asked the bewildered construction worker.

"Good friends," replied Pete, proudly. The man left us alone the rest of the game, even bought us a beer.

Nothing much happened in the second inning, unless you count the pigeon that got nailed in the head by a foul ball. John was catching a solid game, but in the third, Hughie Doolan, the Highlander pitcher, got a little wild. John made some nice scoops out of the dirt and with his chest, blocked a pitch that was three feet out of the strike zone. The fans were thankful for his efforts, renewing their confidence all the more. But that didn't keep Doolan from walking a couple of batters anyway. With men on first and second and two outs, it appeared as though Doolan would get out of his rocky inning after all. But he began to tighten and started to aim the ball instead of pitch it. Clay Allen, the designated hitter, knew Doolan was in trouble. His delivery looked as stiff as an ironing board or as Southwood was fond of saying, "A scarecrow with a big stick up his butt." John went out to the mound with the ball to try to calm Doolan down.

"High, tight fastballs, Hughie. He can't hit 'em, and he can't lay off 'em," said John, handing him the ball.

"Yeah-yeah-yeah, I know! I read the scouting reports, too," snipped Doolan, irritated by the visit. "I don't know what's wrong with me. I'm spooked or somethin'," confessed the pitcher.

John raised a brow and said, "I know what'ya mean."

The count went full and just when everybody thought Hughie Doolan would make it out of the inning, he laid a pitch right through the heart of the plate. Clay Allen could hardly believe his eyes and promptly deposited Hughie's offering fifteen rows deep into the right field upper deck. Mercifully, the side was retired when the next batter, center fielder Jody Reed, popped out. Baltimore was up 3 to 2. Hughie Doolan pulled a hangnail from his right thumb and sauntered back to the dugout, showered in a chorus of expressive catcalls.

"Fuck! Three fucking runs!!!" screamed Doolan as he threw his glove at the near empty water cooler. The glass bottle spun off the cooler and was about to fall just as John caught it.

"Now, cool down, son. We've got a lotta game left to play," consoled Southwood in his best fatherly voice. He always tried that before he got mad.

"Yeah! Well, why don't you try talking to your catcher!" Doolan shouted in frustration, acting as if Johney gave him some bad information. Hughie could be obnoxious. I realize he was scared about blowing the opener, but on this day he outdid himself. Southwood gave his catcher a look to make sure he wasn't about to attack Mr. Doolan, but John simply removed his catching gear. There wasn't a thing Hughie could say to provoke him, or so he thought. John was up third in the inning; that and the strange vibrations in the outfield occupied his thoughts.

"Did he tell you to throw it right down the middle with nothing on it!" bellowed Southwood. The entire bench tipped their caps over their eyes. They knew Southwood would go on a rampage if he noticed any smirks. Doolan wanted to yell back, but thought better of it. It was only the third inning, and if he kept talking, Southwood would pull him from the game with no chance for the win.

In the third, Freddy "Mr. Clean" Greene, the Highlander designated hitter, walked on four straight Tim Clarke pitches. Freddy had a career year last season, batting .318 with 33 homers and 123 RBI. He was still feeling pretty good about it, as he should, after nine years in the league.

"You afraid of me, Timmy?" called Freddy, with a good-natured laugh as he trotted to first.

Tim took off his cap, wiped his brow, and said, "Not when you're on base, Freddy. You can hit, but you can't run." Freddy gave Tim a sly smile and took a good healthy lead off first base. Tim threw over a few times, nothing serious. They wanted the double-play ball.

Muddy Ames, the Highlander third baseman, batted clean-up, fourth. He either hit them out of the park or struck out. Muddy never bunted. He struck out, which brought John up to bat with one out and a man on first. Freddy really wanted to steal a base, but everyone in the park knew he wasn't going anywhere unless John moved him. Tim Clarke was right. Freddy couldn't run.

"Johney!" called Doolan as John was about to step up to the plate. John knew the voice, he didn't turn around. "Johney, hit one for me. Will'ya?" That was as close to an apology as Hughie could get. And John accepted it by giving him a slight glance. Southwood was pleased by what he saw. He had handled the problem well. 'Now we might even win,' he thought.

The crowd gave John a huge ovation when Bob Sheppard made his plate announcement. There wasn't any doubt; John was on their side. I know that many of the people felt a bit guilty for thinking otherwise. Maybe that's why the applause seemed somewhat exaggerated.

"Strike one! I'll tell you, that was one good curve Clarke just threw past Greco. All he could do was watch it fall off the table! 1 and 0 to John Greco. Clarke checks Greene at first—the wind-up. The pitch! Another curve ball! And it was a dandy! 2 and 0," exclaimed Rizzuto.

The fact was, John was experiencing something Phil Rizzuto could never call or know. The baseball looked as hittable as a beach ball, which obviously surprised him. John could see that Clarke was making quality pitches, which surprised him even more and left him frozen at the plate viewing baseball as it might be played on the moon in zero gravity. 'What's going on?' John wondered. To Rizzuto and the rest of the world, it looked and sounded as if Clarke had found his great stuff, that John was destined to strikeout. 'I'm the only one who's seeing this,' he realized as he set himself for the next pitch. Everything appeared to be in slow motion, as though he were a hummingbird and everybody else stayed human. The next two junk pitches seemed to take forever to get to home plate, and they were both fastballs. Clarke was trying to get him to swing at a bad pitch, but John wasn't biting and the knowledge he possessed made him smile. Clarke was furious, angered by what he thought was Greco's lack of respect for the challenge he posed. The crowd noise accelerated into a whirlwind of high-pitched overtones and then disappeared, leaving only quiet, and the painful sounds only a dog could hear, as though the voices had sounded so long ago they were no longer there. And then it happened.

BASEBALL & BENEVOLENCE

"I love you, John," said a lone voice, full of sadness. It was Natt. John spun in the batter's box as though stung by a bee. The ball whizzed by his head; full count. Johney desperately searched the seats behind home plate for his brother, but all he found were a thousand pairs of curious eyes, mouths moving but saying nothing, at least not to him. Natt wasn't there and at the same time he was.

"Time out!" yelled the umpire, waving his hands and vacating his position from behind the catcher. John stood with his back to the game, staring into the stands. His bat fell to the ground with a simple release as if he'd forgotten to hold onto it. A single tear rolled down his cheek. He knew Natt was dead. Yet he was everywhere; John could feel him, within him. Natt wanted love and forgiveness. He wanted to be with his brother one last time, to show him the importance of his life, especially at a time when life itself must have seemed so cheap, so disposable.

"What the . . . " uttered Southwood, jumping out of his hole and onto the field. The crowd grew quiet as the Highlander manager marched to his batter.

John stood like a statue glorifying the human spirit. His strength and courage . . . his passion for life emerged. Within a single motion, grace presented itself through John for all who cared to see. He opened his arms in a gesture that welcomed his brother and at the same time pleaded with the humanity that surrounded him. "Reveal your decency," John muttered. Collectively they became a part of him, felt his pain, his pride, his guilt and outrage, but most of all his love. For a solitary moment they glimpsed the universe binding and entwining us all. Johney was no stranger to them. He was a good man, a family man, and for that alone he should be respected.

"Son, I'm gonna have to take you out," said Dillon Southwood in the calmest tone he could find.

"I need to play," said John. He picked up his bat and walked slowly to the batter's box. Dillon Southwood carefully considered his reply, then decided to say just what he was thinking.

"Son, I'm afraid you're in for some kind of a breakdown."

"Yeah." John thought about it for a second. "It's not gonna happen today. Let me play, Woody." Southwood took his cap off and scratched his head. He felt the crowd's compassion.

"Can we play some ball? Please!" hollered Steve Schneider, the home plate umpire.

"Go ahead," Dillon said, pointing his finger at John. "But we play baseball for the rest of the day. Right?"

"Right."

Johney reestablished his position in the box and began an inner dialogue with his brother. 'Natty, it's your first at-bat in the big leagues.' They stepped up to the plate, then pulled back, while the bat drew a crescent moon in the soft earth.

"Well . . . okay it looks like we're ready to play. My heart goes out to that young man. He's had a tough time of it lately. Now John doubled his first time up to score the Highlanders only two runs of the ball game. The count is full, one out, and Freddy Greene on first. Baltimore leads it in the bottom of the third! 3 to 2! The pitch. Swing! It's a hit! It's gone! No, no . . . it's deep into the left center gap! The wind held it up! And Tony Petralli bobbles it!! Easy standup triple for John Greco!! And the score is tied at three! With one out and a man on third, the Highlanders are looking for the go-ahead run! And listen to that crowd!" called Phil, gushing with youthful enthusiasm.

The Highlanders didn't go ahead that inning; center fielder Cliff Oakes and first baseman Mike Kirkpatrick both struck out. Seems Tim Clarke really did have his good stuff that day. But despite that, Natt got his first hit and RBI, while John felt the joy of seeing a favorite place through his brother's eyes. Of course, the possibility that he was actually going crazy had occurred to him, but it all felt too good to matter. Like a painkilling drug, he gladly accepted it.

In the fourth inning both Hughie Doolan and Tim Clarke settled down enough to get their sides out—one, two, three. In the fifth, Doolan had gained command of all of his pitches. John didn't have to work as hard, just provide a solid target. Hughie's curve ball began to break hard and sharp, much like Clarke's. His fastball heated up to around 92 m.p.h., and if that wasn't enough, even his trick lollipop pitch started to fall in for strikes. Doolan struck out the side in the fifth, retiring six straight batters, producing a much needed attitude adjustment. Hughie became positively giddy. On the last strike the crowd exploded into a huge roar as Hughie ran from the mound full of energy, and himself. His ritual was to touch the caps of each of his infielders after blanking a side. It had to be done or his luck would run out, leaving him to face the next inning with only his ability, and no pitcher ever thought that was enough. Doolan also had some taboos that needed to be avoided in order not to break the spell. He didn't like to see a ball tossed in the dugout while he was on the bench or have anyone touch his left arm, his pitching arm. His reasoning was that as long as it was perfectly in tune with the game, it was perfect. And anything, especially a touch, could disrupt this infinite balance he craved. That's why whenever Hughie was on a streak you could always find him in some far corner of the dugout. His left arm would be by the wall so nobody could accidentally bump, rub, or touch it. Of course, there was one other peculiar rule he had to follow. He couldn't tell anybody not to touch his arm. He figured that would be tampering with the universal order of things to happen.

"Hits! We need some hits!" chanted Hank Miller, as he paced back and fourth clapping his hands, offering encouragement to anybody who'd make eye contact with him. So Hughie closed his eyes and pretended to meditate while Miller passed him by. Doolan stayed clear of the overtly enthusiastic after he finished his touch-the-cap ritual. He had to be very careful, now that the crowd was really starting to get into the game. Spirits were running high.

"Goldstein, Greene, Ames . . . Greco on deck," Southwood commanded.

John grabbed his bat, put a doughnut on the end, and took a few light, easy swings to loosen himself up. He could get real tight after kneeling in the catcher's crouch.

"You gonna get me some runs, Johney?" said Hughie, trying to sound as friendly as possible as he hid in the corner of the dugout.

"That's my job," said John with a tone of finality. He wasn't trying to be rude, just trying to stay focused.

"Okay, bottom of the fifth. The score is tied 3 to 3, and Bob Goldstein will lead off the inning for the Highlanders! Bobby is 0 and 2 on the day. He's flied out to left and grounded out to the shortstop. Bob's looking for his first hit of the season!"

"C'mon, Bob-eeee!" shouted the ever-smiling Freddy Greene.

"The pitch. Ball! High and outside fastball. And Bob wasn't buying! He's got a good eye; he'll get his walks. That's for sure. Batted .275 last year. Not a lot of power, just puts it in play. Good speed on the base paths. The wind-up . . . Pitch. Ball two! High inside fastball, and Goldstein laid off it! 0 and 2 to Bobby. I'll tell you one thing, Clarke had better start to get that fastball down. He doesn't have enough stuff to put it up there! I don't know why he doesn't stick with that good curve ball and slider of his. He's gonna get into trouble if he doesn't watch it. The pitch. And he jammed 'im!! But it falls in! A little looper behind third base!!! And the Highlanders have the lead-off man on in the fifth!" announced Scooter Rizzuto. Rizzuto was certain Southwood would try to bunt the man over, but it didn't happen.

Freddy Greene saw a rising fastball coming his way, and he took his cut. Unfortunately, he got under it a bit, an easy fly ball for the Baltimore left fielder, Tony Petralli.

"Oooohhhh!" Phil was disappointed.

Southwood actually had the hit-and-run on. He didn't use the bunt much.

Muddy Ames had another tough at-bat. He went down on three swinging strikes, none of which were in the strike zone. He didn't even get a piece of the ball. On the third strike Goldstein stole second, and what looked like a promising inning quickly became not-so-promising. The Highlanders had two outs and a man on second. Either Clarke was getting tougher or Ames should have reported to training camp sooner. Doolan was starting to get jumpy, stuck in the corner protecting his perfect arm. You wouldn't say he was a gracious man.

"Shit! Ooooh. C'mon Ames!" Hughie whined in protest, after the strikeout.

"Doolan!"

"Yeah!?"

"Shut up," said Southwood. "John, green light," called the manager.

". . . And that brings John Greco to the plate! The crowd gives him a nice hand. They love him here in the Bronx. John's 2 for 2 on the day, batting one thousand percent for the season! But that'll go down . . . hah-ha! Maybe! John has all of the Highlander RBI's for the game. Three! Has all the Highlanders RBI's for the year!"

John knocked the doughnut off his bat and took a few strong cuts before entering the box. The crowd noise whirred with intensity, much as it did his last time up. The bat boy approached him with great trepidation, not sure if he should grab the doughnut now or wait until after John's at-bat. He was a young black kid, twelve or thirteen. 'Younger than usual,' John thought. 'Scared to death of making a mistake.' James Darwin didn't want to get in anybody's way. His only concern was to do everything just right, and he looked extremely uncomfortable as he tried to figure out what "just right" was. John took his last practice swing, then picked the doughnut off the ground and handed it to the nearly paralyzed boy.

"First game, son?" The kid nodded his head and swallowed hard. The whole day was a dream come true, though overwhelming. John was one of his heroes, and it took a great deal of courage for the boy just to speak to him.

"James Darwin m'name, sir."

"John Greco." He checked his bat for fractures. "Touch my bat for luck?" Darwin's eyes lit up as a smile blossomed, a smile that could mend a broken heart. He touched the bat tentatively as if it were an ancient artifact possessing great power.

"Thanks," said John and started for home plate.

"Batter up!" yelled the umpire, trying to hurry him along.

"Mr. Greco?" called James Darwin. John turned to face the boy. "My parents, they cried for you and your family." Johney nodded a silent thank you.

"Take care of them, son," said John, and he entered the box.

John waited as Clarke's curve ball missed, low and inside. He could see the umpire motion that it was, in fact, a ball. He could see the vendors working the stands, the people imploring him to hit, and the airplane flying overhead. But once again he heard nothing, only absolute quiet, as if sound had imploded, sucked into a vacuum somewhere in the heavens. The tranquility somehow enhanced all of his other senses, including a sixth sense that allowed John to relax while Tim Clarke threw him balls. He was being pitched very carefully. John felt he could see everything—from Charlie Krug guarding the line at third to Muddy Ames swinging an imaginary bat in the Highlander dugout. He could feel Dillon Southwood's concern, not just for the game but for him personally. He saw the cloud of dust when Jake Snyder punched his glove at first base and the way he was balanced to move in any direction, ready to play the ball. John could smell the earth beneath his feet, its bitter-sweet odor of all things, its life and death and life again. He sensed the unbridled joy of Jason Wheeler and the good people who sent John and his family their prayers. He knew them. They were why he had to come to the ballpark. But he also understood how quickly things could change, how different today could be from yesterday.

"Ball twooo," called the umpire. "Ball threeee." John stepped out of the batter's box while Clarke thought about his next pitch. The words *send a message* intruded on John's lucid stillness and wouldn't leave. He had no idea what message or how to send it.

'Oh boy,' thought Southwood. 'What now?' "Hank!" Southwood shouted, tapping his forehead and pointing to John, signaling Miller to go see what was happening. Hank jogged down the third base line to where John was pounding dirt out of his spikes and home plate umpire Steve Schneider was breathing down his back to keep the game moving.

"So, aaah, everything all right?" asked Hank, trying to keep it casual. John nodded. Though he had no idea what Hank actually said, John knew what Hank was thinking—essentially, 'Why aren't you batting?'

"So . . . you're gonna finish your at-bat?" Hank always started sentences with "so" when he felt awkward.

"What kinda bullshit is dis!" shouted Schneider. Hank looked at John, leaving the question open for him to answer. John walked back to the box, pushed the dirt around with his bat, and drew a triangle. Schneider was satisfied with John's silent reply. The crowd buzzed—that was *the* symbol.

"The pitch! Swing! It's, it's going . . . going! It's waaay outta here!!! A monster shot deep into the left center field bleachers. Holy cowwwwww!!! That scores two, and John Greco puts the Highlanders up in the bottom of the fifth, five to three!!! Tim Clarke made a mistake on that pitch— up in the strike zone with not much on it. It's gotta be a 500 footer!! Maybe! Holy cow!!! Unbelievable!!!"

Even as John rounded the bases in a glorious home run trot, he knew that this wasn't the message. It was a magnificent homer. Some kid even gloved it thirty rows deep in the bleachers. 'What optimists kids can be,' he thought. 'To bring a glove to a once-in-a-lifetime seat.' And that's what it was—a once-in-a-lifetime shot. But it wasn't the message.

The cheering seemed as though it would never stop. Sound came back to John like a blast from a cannon. He made a curtain call, tipping his cap to the crowd. James Darwin felt like the luckiest kid on earth; after all, he was sure his touch had something to do with it. Hughie Doolan was positive he had the opening day win, but still sat in the corner guarding his arm. The construction worker bought another round of beers for me and Two Face Pete. Jason Wheeler jumped on his bed swimming in a sea of contentment. Joe Jonelli laughed and poured himself another drink as he patted himself on the back for being such an excellent student of human nature. Natt, well, Natt had to be smiling, somewhere, maybe inside his brother's heart. The possession that seemed so real an hour ago could easily be rationalized as pure delirium—not that John was rationalizing. Time had a way of creating doubt, even one short hour later. John was human; faith and belief only had their moments. But, there was one thing he was absolutely sure of: This was not the message.

Dillon Southwood congratulated John with a handshake and watched his players celebrate as though it were the seventh game of the World Series. A reality check reminded him that it was still the fifth inning . . . of the first game . . . with a hundred and sixty-one more to go, not including the play-offs. The phone rang in the dugout. One of the coaches picked it up as the celebration continued.

"Woody! It's Bill Singer," said the coach, rolling his eyes. Dillon grabbed the phone from his hand. The call didn't please him.

"Yeah!?"

"Woody, I know you're busy. Just wanted to tell ya—playing Greco was genius! The head honcho . . . uuh, Mr. Harrington is very pleased! Listen, help me out here! Could ya make sure he's available for interviews after the game? We don't want him rushing home or anything—if ya know what I mean!"

"Bill . . . "

"Yeah, Wood?"

"Don't ever call me here." And Dillon hung up the phone.

"Listen up, listen up!" shouted Southwood, clapping his hands. All festivities stopped. One more Southwood "listen up" and the crowd buzz might have halted, too. "Let's not get too confident. We still got four more innings to play and we're only up by two. Stay focused! This is a good team. They can beat'cha if ya don't!"

The crowd let out a huge sigh as Cliff Oakes got under a fastball that popped straight up. Walt Rose, the Baltimore catcher, caught it behind home plate. Out three, the fifth was history.

In the top of the sixth, Hughie Doolan had another strong inning, which he firmly attributed to his maintaining a virgin arm. True, he did strike out Tony Petralli in three pitches, but he also walked Charlie Krug in four. If it wasn't for Mike Kirkpatrick's diving stab of a hard hit drive off first base which he then turned into a brilliant double play, they probably would've been out there much longer. Doolan's stuff was getting weak.

In the bottom of the sixth, Kirkpatrick muscled Timmy Clarke's first pitch into the right center field gap. Jody Reed misplayed the ball coming off the wall, allowing Mike a standup triple. That prompted a visit by Matt Connelly, the Baltimore manager. His slow, steady, deliberate walk to the mound bought time for his bullpen to warm up. He was very careful not to step on any of the white chalk lines. Connelly considered it bad luck. He had a laid-back style of managing, coupled with an extremely dry sense of humor.

"Nice day," said Connelly when he finally got out to the mound.

"Yeah, Matt. It's a nice day if you like gray, cold, and damp," replied Clarke. Translation: "Leave me alone."

Connelly rubbed his beer belly and waited for his catcher Walt Rose to get to the mound, an orchestrated maneuver to buy even more time for the pen. Walt, all six foot seven inches of him, lumbered on up as though he was gonna get himself a soft drink.

"Walt, I get the feeling Tim still wants to pitch. What'd ya think? Does he have anything left?" Clarke didn't even look at him. He knew Walt would only answer what he felt was the truth. That's why Connelly asked.

"Yeah. He's still got somethin'," said Walt, perusing the confines of the majestic ballpark.

"Alright then . . . oh, ah . . . Walt, stick with the breaking stuff on the kids." Connelly left the mound just as slowly and deliberately as he had arrived, careful not to step on the lines.

Clarke, in his third year on the team, had to laugh at the way Connelly and Rose never talked to him, just about him, while he was standing right there. They still considered Timmy a kid, and that was that.

Kirkpatrick took a big lead off third. 'Too big,' Clarke thought for a man who didn't run all that well. The crowd started pounding their feet and clapping their hands to the rhythm of the rally music, played on the grand old organ. Orlando Melendez, the rookie just up from Toledo, was at-bat.

"Blazing speed, excellent fielder!" declared Mr. Rizzuto. **"Got some pop in his bat, too! Seventeen homers in the minors; .272 average with 69 RBI's last year. He's gonna help this team."**

Maybe Mr. Melendez would, but he didn't help on this particular at-bat. Orlando tried to bunt, but Clarke caught it in the air about six feet in front of the mound and fired it back to Charlie Krug at third. The suicide squeeze was on. Kirkpatrick was caught in a run-down and tried to run it right down Walt Rose's throat. He soon regretted this decision. Walt was like running into a brick wall with a lot of attitude; not only did Mike hit it, it hit back. The inning ended when Dave Di Marco, the Highlander shortstop, lofted a fly ball deep into center—deep but very playable. It was a hit the Italians would refer to as *bella,* because they sincerely enjoyed the flight of a long, lazy fly ball. It would be appropriate to say that Manager Southwood wasn't pleased with his team's execution of basic baseball skills in the sixth. And he said so in some very direct language.

"Shit! Shit!—Shit! Shit! Shit! . . . Shhhhhit!!!" Southwood screamed at everyone and no one.

Hughie Doolan ran on the field like a dedicated athlete showing a little extra hustle in the late innings. In actuality Hughie just wanted the sanctuary of the mound to avoid getting his arm touched. Bob Sheppard announced the seventh inning stretch and two choruses of "Take Me Out to the Ball Game." The organ played as John caught Hughie's warm-up pitches.

Johney wished for a better day. Even with all the excitement, the heavy-hearted grayness of the weather seemed unfair. Then he thought, 'Could be worse. Could be raining.' The rain was nature's umpire. It decided whether or not the ceremony of leisure would be performed and to what degree it would be enjoyed by players and fans alike. The raindrops were the tears of God, providing life in the face of death and a cleansing of the earth. In any case, it was lousy baseball weather. It rained often in 1965.

BASEBALL & BENEVOLENCE

We finally saw action in the seventh. Walt Rose tomahawked Doolan's second offering for a single into right. Nobody was out. Hughie thought he had thrown a good pitch. 'Rose,' he figured, 'just got lucky.' His arm was still untouched. Hughie was starting to believe in his chaste arm a little too much and was getting lazy. John went to the mound before Boyle's at-bat.

"You had nothing on that last pitch."

"Bullshiiiiit," squealed Hughie. John shoved the ball into Doolan's glove and walked back to home, confident he had at least gotten his attention. It was just as John suspected. Doolan came out of his funk and had Jimmy Boyle talking to himself all the way back to the Oriole dugout. Terry Cues swung at Hughie's first two pitches and watched the third sail by for a called strike, two outs. Hughie stood on the mound, scratching his crotch and grinning at Johney. His self-congratulatory expression read like a billboard while a surge of adrenaline flooded his system, clouded his judgment, and caused a total breakdown of concentration.

Ruben Blair, the Baltimore right fielder, took Doolan's next offering, a 77 m.p.h. fastball and stuck it in the left field seats. Ruben's home run tied the score 5 to 5, two outs. The only sound to be heard in the stadium after a disappointed sigh, came from two wired Oriole fans doing bird calls in the bleachers. Clay Allen came within inches of putting the Orioles ahead on the very next pitch. But Cliff Oakes made a spectacular leaping grab over the center field fence for the third out. Unfortunately, Cliff landed badly on his right foot and broke his ankle. Doolan was no longer smiling as he took a long, slow walk back to the dugout. He was in no hurry to get another "hotdoggingit" lecture from Southwood.

"You could mix'em up more," Hughie said to John in an unnaturally loud voice, considering he was only standing three feet away. Obviously, Hughie wanted his teammates to hear his statement. He felt the need to delegate some responsibility for the inconsistent inning, to make it sound as if it wasn't all his fault, which it was. John just ignored him, not feeling particularly threatened by Hughie's accusations. John figured his teammates knew the story. Hughie, as usual, was just making a fool of himself. Not getting the reaction he'd aimed for, Doolan thought he'd try again.

"Greco! Can you—" he started to say, but was interrupted by what appeared to be spasms of hideously frightful pain, as though he was about to have a heart attack. Doolan turned his head ever so slowly, every inch a sacrifice, as he cast his eyes down at the small black hand wrapped around his pure pitching arm.

"Good luck. Mr. Doolan, I . . . I got good luck," said James Darwin, nodding his head up and down, trying to maintain his smile in the face of rage. He was losing his battle to convince Hughie Doolan of his value.

"Get your nigger hand off me!" Doolan exploded.

"But but but," the kid whimpered and started to cry. He was afraid Doolan was about to hurt him. John picked Hughie up by his jersey and threw him with superhuman strength into the bat racks. Hughie thought about fighting back, but was scared by John's intensity. Nobody had ever seen John Greco mad and certainly had never seen him get physical with anybody. It just wasn't part of his character. I suppose John wasn't about to let another kid get abused, not that the whole team didn't want to kill Doolan by now.

"Alright! Alright!! That's enough!!!" shouted Southwood. "Hank! Get Compton and Waits up and throwing. You're finished, Hughie!"

"You're pulling me out!?! I got good stuff! I can still win it!" Doolan shouted back defiantly.

"Either bench it and shut up, or hit the showers!"

"But, Wood, it's my game to win," Hughie pleaded. "This is how you treat your best pitcher? On opening dayyy?"

Southwood got up and into Doolan's face, his blood pressure rising. Southwood was feeling bitter and resentful, and he was too young for that.

"You crossed the line. Now get out before you divide this whole team!" Southwood's veins popped out of his neck like a knotted tree stump. It was all he could do to keep from strangling his young star.

"Moran, Goldstein, Greene—Muddy on deck!" called Hank, breaking the tension.

Hughie grabbed his glove and headed for the locker room. He didn't want anything more to do with this game. "There's never a good excuse for being touched by a nigger," Hughie muttered to himself, "or a wop." That's what his daddy had taught him.

"Come here, son," called Dillon to his bat boy. Southwood took a seat on the bench and patted the open space next to him. The poor kid was still shaking and afraid of what might happen next. He looked toward John for approval of Southwood's request. John nodded in Woody's direction with a faint smile.

"I'm sorry, Manager Southwood. I didn't—"

"No, no, son. I'm sorry any of us had to listen to that ignorant son-of-a-bitch. It's not right." He took off his cap and ran his hand through his prematurely silver-gray hair, rubbed his chin, and closed his eyes. 'I'm tired by the young season already,' he thought, and then remembered he had a game to manage. "How 'bout you shake my hand for managerial luck. I can use some." Dillon looked to the sky as if in prayer and extended his hand to the kid. James Darwin laughed the laugh of a boy who still had time to grow up—time all kids should have, though it seemed it was harder and harder for them to get.

In the bottom of the seventh, Timmy Clarke still had his good stuff and, in fact, appeared to be getting stronger. Willie Moran battled Clarke hard but wasn't able to get around on much. With a full count, Willie did the unexpected; he laid down a perfect bunt straight up the third base line. Third baseman Charlie Krug got on his hands and knees trying to blow the ball over the foul line. It didn't work, and the Highlanders had their lead-off man on base. Next, Bob Goldstein hit a frozen rope into right, but Ruben Blair had him played perfectly. With one step to the left, the line drive was his. One out, man on first. Freddy Greene hit a long foul ball into the right field upper deck. A fan made a nice catch, but after that Freddy went down swinging for the second out. Willie was still on first. That brought up Muddy Ames who hadn't hit a lick all day. He walked up to the batter's box talking to his bat and dug himself an extra deep hole for his right foot. Mr. Ames was prepared to take his cuts. Clarke had him 0 and 2, but on the next pitch Muddy golfed a low and inside fastball out of the dirt for a double up the third base line. The count was still two outs with men on second and third, and John Greco coming to bat. Walt Rose lumbered back out to the mound.

"We walk him, right?" said Walt, wondering why Connelly wasn't coming out to change pitchers. There was action in the Baltimore bullpen.

"No. I want him," said Clark with a vicious look in his eye.

"You want him. Ya want him?! Oh, that's beautiful," declared Rose, sarcastically. "Let me help you. Ya got an open base! We walk him and pitch to—who?! Oakes is out of the game!"

"Nick Balsamo," stated Clarke, flatly.

"Right! Pitch to Balsamo. Greco's been hammering ya all day." Clarke gave him a strange look. "What?!" Walt sensed that he wasn't getting through.

"I want 'im," said Clarke, squeezing the ball with both hands like he was trying to mold it.

"Dis guy's made chopped meat of you," muttered Rose. He looked toward the bench. "They want us to put him on!"

"Oh, I'm gonna put him on, Walt." A light went on in the catcher's head. It didn't happen often, but Walt Rose understood the nasty side of baseball, and he was beginning to see Timmy through different, more appreciative, eyes. Rose actually felt a twinge of respect for the very young Mr. Clarke.

"Okay! Bottom of the seventh, Ames on second, Goldstein on third, two outs! John Greco coming to bat! John doubled in the first, tripled in the third, and homered in the fifth! He's responsible for all five Highlander runs. And what a hand he's getting from the crowd! The house that Ruth built has come alive in the seventh!" announced Phil.

When John entered the batter's box in the seventh, it wasn't like any of his other three at-bats; it was normal—no supervision, no possessions, no soundlessness, no enriched senses of any kind. He was just a ballplayer, who was about to get a message.

"A base hit will put the Highlanders in the lead!" explained Rizzuto, doing his best to keep the transistorized crowd pumped.

Tim Clarke wasn't about to show any remorse for a hard luck ballplayer like John. This was business to him. 'Nothing personal,' he told himself. Truth was, it was very personal. If not for Greco, he'd be taking home the win. Now, after Muddy Ames' at-bat, Clark knew he was out of gas and that infuriated him. If he was leaving the game, so was Greco, and he wasn't about to let John beat him again.

"Pretty good day, huh, John?" said Rose. His voice sounded muffled and distant from behind the catcher's mask.

"Yeah," mumbled John, setting himself for the pitch.

"Looks like you're getting first," said Walt, as he jumped out of his crouch and extended his mitt as far outside of home plate as his arm would allow.

"They're gonna intentionally walk 'im. Can't say I blame 'em—with the open base and all. John's had Clarke's number all day."

The crowd booed the Orioles' strategy. John relaxed his muscles, as he waited out the four pitches before he could take his base. To everyone's disbelief, Tim Clarke reared back and fired one directly at John's head. John saw it coming, but couldn't believe it. 'He's throwing at me,' he thought as he stood frozen at the plate. In an instant the crowd stopped booing and everyone stood up, breathlessly watching as if witnessing a crime.

"I, I . . . can't believe it! I can't believe it!!" shouted Rizzuto, voicing his outrage for everybody in the park. **"He could be killed! In all my years in baseball I've never seen a man thrown at while being intentionally walked! Never!! There's something wrong with that kid Clarke!"**

John could see the seams of the ball as it screamed for his head. All he could do in the brief amount of time was tuck his chin to his chest. With his legs planted as rigid as poles into the earth, he waited to be crucified. The ball struck the back of his batting helmet and ricocheted into the Baltimore dugout. John hit the ground.

"You're outta here!!!" shouted Schneider, the home plate umpire, wasting no time, waving his arms and pointing his gnarled finger at Tim Clarke. The irate benches and bullpens emptied, debris was thrown on the field with indignation, while John laid dazed in the dust of home plate. For a moment it seemed as though the whole world had cracked.

"John, don't move," called Buddy Sophia, the Highlander trainer.

"I'm okay, Bud. He didn't have much on it." The sight of the ball coming at his head shook him up more than the hit itself.

"It looked worse than it was," John claimed, as anarchy erupted around them. Dillon Southwood stood close by, guarding his injured player and listening intently to his conversation with the trainer. "Honest, Buddy. It just grazed me," John insisted.

John pulled himself up in time to witness the brawl. He saw a man jump out of the stands and attack a Baltimore player. The entire sight sickened him. He didn't want this done for him. "Jesus, I don't want it," he cried. He grabbed a handful of dirt and flung it above home. Through a silhouette of particles John viewed a shameful outline of the human race. The fear of brazen injustice turned the crowd inside out. Players and fans alike performed flagrant indiscretions with viciousness. Their prejudices were released on what should have been hallowed grounds. The callous pride of the middle class, the unpardonable arrogance of the rich, and criminal resentment of the poor—they were all here, ready to join this reprehensible transgression. Good people degenerated into a collective fall from grace. 'Is this our true nature?' John questioned. He found himself at the center of a breeding ground for hate. The thought had occurred to me that Mr. Jonelli was probably enjoying this portion of today's game.

"My God! It's a ball game!" he screamed. "Have we forgotten why we come here?" Southwood viewed the scene and listened to John's words like some sort of bizarre voiceover. He considered them carefully and decided it was a damn good question.

Where was Tim Clarke's compassion? Hughie Doolan's heart? Walt Rose's mind? How could their thoughts be so self-centered? Couldn't they see how their arrogance destroyed? How it reinforced the fear we all live with, the fear of each other? John wanted to tell them how easy it was to lose and never win; how simple it was to barricade the doors and never come out; how quickly a baby's breath could disappear; and how the importance of life itself could degenerate to nothingness. 'It's a ball game,' he repeated to himself. 'In the greatest park of them all. Don't teach your children this. Teach them how to live and love. . . . That's the message.'

"Huh, bump's not too bad," said Buddy, astonished. He hardly felt a bump at all. "You should come out of the game though, could have a concussion."

"No, I can't. Miracle in the ninth," said John, as he surveyed the damage, then brushed himself off and jogged to first base.

"We're not pulling 'im, Bud?" questioned Southwood, dumbfounded.

"Nah, it didn't get much of 'im." Buddy shook his head, but he couldn't suppress a slight smile, although he knew this was no time to be smiling.

"What?" Dillon asked curiously, knowing Buddy to be a serious man.

"Says he's got a miracle in the ninth," the trainer laughed nervously.

Dillon ran both hands through his hair, scanned the bleakness of the day and arched his back to stretched it out a bit. "I wouldn't doubt it," he replied.

When order was finally restored, the ballpark had been defiled. Only Tim Clarke was thrown out. Warnings were issued to both sides while security guards surrounded the field. It was then, and only then, that it occurred to Walt Rose that this had not been such a good idea after all. A twenty minute game delay was necessary for the ground crew to complete field maintenance.

Big Joe Hagan, a right-handed reliever, replaced Timmy Clarke on the mound for the Orioles. Big Joe was six feet four inches tall, 275 pounds. He had one pitch, an alarming rising fastball that he threw for strikes, just daring any batter to hit it. Nick Balsamo batted for the injured Cliff Oakes in the bottom of the seventh with two outs and the bases loaded. Big Joe struck him out with three pitches. Nick swung behind every one of them. It wasn't pretty.

In the eighth, Southwood called on his ace right-handed reliever, Luke Waits. Luke wasn't a big man, five feet ten inches and 175 pounds—wasn't small either. But it was astounding to see the kind of heat that came from his arm. Whereas in a man like Big Joe, you half expected it. Luke had an outstanding heater and a wicked curve that a hitter would swear was coming right down Broadway and then would go someplace else. John liked Luke. He was a good man, carried himself with dignity and never had a bad word to say about anyone. John was glad Luke could get the win. It was a nice way to start off the season for a reliever.

Luke began the eighth with some control problems. The count went full on Jody Reed after spraying the stands with foul balls. Jody found ball four and walked to first. Luke wanted to kick himself for allowing the lead-off man on. Now he had to dig himself out of a hole.

"Maybe he just needs to get loose," Southwood mumbled, pacing the dugout. Tony Petralli made Luke and Dillon feel much better. He got under the first pitch and popped out to Muddy Ames in front of the Oriole dugout. The top of the eighth ended abruptly when Charlie Krug grounded to Dave Di Marco at short. Dave turned the double play.

Things were much simpler for Baltimore in the eighth. Big Joe Hagan struck out Mike Kirkpatrick, Orlando Melendez, and Dave Di Marco. Inning over: score still 5 to 5.

A commercial jet circled the stadium waiting to land at Kennedy or, more likely, LaGuardia. Dillon Southwood thought about flying for a moment as he recalled a dream he had the night before. He was in fact flying but without a plane and without any trouble at all. Like the jet overhead, he was also circling the stadium, the latifundium of the Bronx. It was a beautiful day with a bright blue sky. The park was filled to capacity, and the players were on the field. But they weren't playing. Instead they watched as he flew above them. As most people would do, Southwood reasoned, if they saw a man flying. He remembered how the act of flying was overshadowed by the simple emotional content of the dream. He felt immense joy, and he knew that everyone in the ballpark shared his happiness, even the opposing team— because these feelings weren't derived from winning. They were something much, much more. The wise manager chased the dream away but not the good spirits it left behind. He settled himself to face the ninth and remembered what Buddy had said . . . about the miracle and all. Dillon made himself laugh when he thought, 'All ninth innings are miracles.'

In the top of the ninth, Luke got it going pretty good. Jake Snyder hit a weak grounder to second for the first out. That brought Walt Rose to the plate, and Luke promptly ran the first two high heaters around 95 m.p.h. up and in, right under Walt's chin, scaring the heck out of him. Walt tried to act like they didn't, but they did. Luke was warned by Schneider.

"One more and you're outta here!" Schneider wasn't about to lose control again.

Luke threw three perfect strikes. The third one caught Walt looking. He was so embarrassed, he argued the call with Schneider, but the umpire wasn't hearing any of it and gave Mr. Rose a threatening glance. Walt Rose stopped his charade and sulked his way back to the Oriole bench.

Two outs. Nobody on base. Jimmy Boyle tried to bunt his way on, not having a hit all day and little, or no mentionable, power. The bunt attempt might have worked if Schneider didn't call Boyle out for leaving the batter's box before the bunt. Manager Connelly hustled out to home plate for one of those classic nose to nose shouting matches with Schneider. He knew he couldn't win but was trying to get the next call to go his way. Connelly reasoned his team would do well in extra innings. He felt he had the better pitching. A call coming his way in the late innings could mean the difference between winning and losing. All he wanted was to battle enough to make a point but not get himself thrown out, which he was able to accomplish through years of practice. On the way back to the bench, Connelly wanted to kick himself for not pinch-hitting some power for Boyle.

In the bottom of the ninth, Dillon Southwood had the best part of his order coming up, and he planned to stay with them . . . maybe. After Willie Moran struck out for the first out, Southwood wasn't so sure. It was the right setup for the odds—righty pitcher, lefty batter—but that didn't make much difference the way Big Joe was throwing. Not only did he retire the last five Highlander batters, he struck them out. Southwood had to shake things up, so he pulled the right-handed hitting Goldstein to pinch-hit Doug Hansen. Hansen provided left-handed power. He was a slugger who could easily put it in the short right field porch, an excellent fastball hitter. Southwood figured it would be a good contest between Hansen and Big Joe. One swing of the bat and the Highlanders could win it. Hansen took two tremendous cuts at Hagan's fastballs.

"Strike twooo!!" shouted Schneider, as he made a fist and pulled back his right arm as though shooting an arrow.

Hansen stepped out of the box to regain his concentration and was greeted by a smattering of boos. Five strikeouts in a row had made the fans skittish or plain old mean from Doug Hansen's point of view. Doug stepped back into the box and used the boos as motivation. 'There's no way I'm gonna be the pinch-hitting goat,' he told himself.

"The pitch! Base hit! Right over second base and Jimmy Boyle's head!" called Rizzuto. The organ blared rally music while the fans clapped and stomped and yelled, trying their best to make as much noise as possible. **"One out, Hansen on first."**

Connelly was starting to get nervous. 'Was Big Joe getting tired?' The Baltimore manager slowly walked out to the mound, ever so careful not to step on any lines. Walt Rose made the trip, too. The fans booed.

"Nice day," said Connelly.

"I'm not tired," declared Big Joe. Connelly just smiled.

"Well, Walt, what do you think?"

"Don't play this bull with me. I'm no rookie," demanded Joe.

"When it comes to pitching you're not honest either!" barked Connelly. "Now don't get down, Joe. You pitched us out of some deep shit, but the idea is to play as a team and win this thing. Now, I ask you again, Walt, does he have anything?" Joe glared at Walt while waiting for his answer.

"Maybe . . . one more batter," Rose said cautiously. He gave Big Joe an apologetic look. Connelly didn't hesitate and waved his left arm in the direction of the bullpen. He wanted his left-hander, Bob Cushing. Joe handed Connelly the ball and walked off the field, careful to step on every white line he could find between the mound and the bench.

Bob Cushing was a square-jawed man with a husky build. You could easily imagine him wearing a flannel shirt and jeans, chopping wood, and eating blood rare steaks somewhere in Alaska. He was actually from central Jersey, not far from where John grew up. They even played basketball against each other in high school. He wasn't much of a basketball player, though he thought he was. You see, Bob Cushing was endowed with the greatest trait a pitcher could have, self-confidence. He had a quick delivery, deceptive speed on his fastball, and an outstanding off speed change-up. Most players weren't happy to see him enter the game.

The first batter Cushing faced was Freddy Greene, the Highlander designated hitter. He pitched Greene so very carefully that he walked him. Maybe the pressure of the first game was the cause or the fact that one swing could end the game; or perhaps the size and intensity of the crowd or what he ate for breakfast that morning was the cause. Whatever it was, Cushing's confidence looked mighty conservative.

"One out! Greene on first. Hansen on second!"

Walt Rose jogged out to the mound and brought with him another huge chorus of boos. "Cush, what's the matter, man? Throw strikes." Cushing pounded the ball into his mitt, tilted his head back, and spit in the direction of second base.

"This place is so close to home," said Cushing, bowing his head in submission as though giving a confession. Walt gave him an anxious look. He didn't know what to say or how to react, and he glanced over to the bench for some help. That was his natural reaction when he didn't know what to do. Sometimes he regretted it. Connelly raised an eyebrow as if to say, 'What?!' Walt wasn't sure how to react to that either, so he didn't. Rose decided to do the ballplayer thing; he slapped Cush on the behind and said, "C'mon, you've pitched here. Strikes!" And he walked back to home, taking an even louder chorus of boos with him.

The cavalry call played on the organ and the massive crowd yelled, "Charge!!!" Then it happened five more times, drowning out the calls for beer and hot dogs. The scoreboard flashed the score of the Boston-Cleveland game. Boston was losing in the eighth, and the crowd went crazy. Rally music and hand-clapping, foot-stomping, heart-pounding madness erupted, all to perpetuate the unhinging of Baltimore pitcher Bob Cushing.

Muddy Ames stepped into the batter's box, knowing a single could win it for his team. He was a strong, strapping black Southerner, built like a bull with soft hands and, while protecting third, the speed of a cat. But everything else he did was real slow and deliberate. Muddy rarely swung at the first pitch, so Cushing was spotted a strike if he could put the ball over the plate.

"That-a-boy, Cush!" shouted Rose after Schneider called a strike.

The crowd noise intensified, and Cushing threw two borderline balls that would have been excellent strikes if Schneider gave him a call. But he didn't. Schneider's strike zone was small but consistent and therefore inarguable. The count went to 2 and 1 on Muddy. Cushing caught his breath and threw a beautiful change-up that painted the outside corner of the plate.

"Strike two!" That quieted the crowd for a moment, but they were right back in it as soon as Cushing started his wind-up.

"Another change-up!" cried Scooter.

Ames was completely fooled. He started to swing, then pulled his bat back, trying to change his mind. The ball hit Muddy's bat anyway. It was a little looper that looked as if Terry Cues might get to between short and right center field. The runners were frozen, not sure if he could make the catch. Cues made a diving attempt for the ball, only to have it hit off the palm of his glove and roll into the outfield. Everybody was safe with the bases loaded, one out, tied score, and John Greco coming to bat in the ninth. Everyone was feeling very safe. John walked to the batter's box. It was time to deliver the message.

Muddy's hit was pure luck and Cushing knew it, which infuriated him to no end. "I found my good stuff. Greco won't be a problem," he said to himself. The new attitude showed in his body language. Cushing raised his large square jaw and in an act of vain defiance spat a wad of tobacco in the direction of home plate. He rolled up the sleeves on his jersey, determined to strike out John Greco.

"I need some luck," John said, as he extended the barrel of his bat for James Darwin to touch. The bat boy ran his hand across the wood. Then nodded his head reassuringly and smiled. The kid's smile reminded John of what he had to do. He thought to himself, 'If they need a miracle to remember why they come together, I can give it to them.'

"Well, alright! We got a barn burner here at Ruth Memorial Stadium! John Greco steps up to the plate! Let's see . . . double in the

first, triple in the third, homer in the fifth, hit by a Tim Clarke pitch in the seventh! Oh boy! That was scary! He has all the Highlander RBI's and he's back in the bottom of the ninth facing the tough left-hander, Bob Cushing. Muddy on first, Freddy Greene on second, and Douglas Hansen on third. Bases loaded! One out! John's a switch hitter, sooo he'll be batting from the right side! It's all tied up at five!" announced Phil Rizzuto.

The crowd was on its feet, clapping, hollering, rejoicing in their preferable odds at achieving victory. Only a sacrifice fly was needed for the win.

"The pitch! . . . Holy cow! That had some kind'da heat on it! What was that?" questioned Rizzuto.

"Ninety-four," an assistant called out.

"Yeah?! Wow! Ninety-four miles per hour, ladies and gentlemen. All he could do was look at it!"

Cushing was feeling real good, loose. He knew he had another notch he could turn it up to. John stepped out of the box. It was time. His bat drew a triangle in the dirt, and the place erupted.

"I don't have to tell you what a Greco triangle means, but I will anyway! He's telling Bob Cushing that he's gonna hit the big one! And the way he's going today, I wouldn't doubt it! The pitch! Strike two! Wow! That was, that had to be? Help me."

"Ninety-nine," his assistant called out.

"Holy cow! Ninety-nine miles per hour! You're kidding me! 0 and 2 to Mr. Greco!" called Rizzuto, amazed by the velocity of Cushing's pitches.

John stepped out of the box again, which irritated Cushing.

"C'mon, John. I got a plane to catch!" yelled Schneider.

Johney filled his lungs with air, not paying any attention to Schneider's comment. He moved back into the box, his bat drawn to the dirt as though it were a divining rod. He wrote in large block letters: L O V E. Then he heard the cheering subside to a trickle. He heard their thoughts, their snickers, the snide laughter, and finally the all-out ridicule for a man who dared to send a message.

"He's crazy!"

"Baseball! Just play baseball!"

"What'da fuck ya doing!!" shouted an angry fan.

Walt Rose slipped off his mask, grinned at his buddies on the bench, and kicked the dirt from his cleats. Mr. Rose was certain John Greco had lost his mind. "What are you? Some kinda born-again bullshit," Rose remarked.

John took a couple of practice swings and acted as if he didn't hear. Walt shook his head in disbelief and pulled his mask back on.

The day was growing dark; the lights went on at three in the afternoon. You'd think there were an eclipse. The crowd was getting antsy, unnerved by John's behavior and the foreboding weather. The wind began to gust as the black clouds overhead threatened to burst.

"This the miracle?" Buddy Sophia asked Dillon, getting his medicine box ready, thinking he had better be prepared. Buddy's hands trembled as he replayed Greco's words in his head; he felt the tension of the day and recalled the seriousness of John's tone and expression.

"I guess we'll know it when we see it," said Southwood, matter-of-factly. He kept staring into the sky as though expecting a flying saucer.

"Well, I don't know what's going on with John Greco. This probably isn't the time to be preaching, but I do think the fans are giving him an awful tough time of it. You gotta remember this young man has been through a lot lately, and he's played an outstanding game. The Highlanders wouldn't even be in it if it wasn't for Johney. I think the fans are being a little unfair to Mr. Greco," said Rizzuto, while thinking all along, 'That poor kid's gonna get himself killed if he doesn't score the run.'

"C'mon, Babe! Play ball!" shouted a fan, sarcastically. The people around the fan laughed.

John stepped into the box and set himself. The crowd quickly forgot about LOVE and the foreboding skies and began to chant and clap in time, "We wanna hit! We wanna hit! We wanna hit! . . . " Cushing wanted nothing more than to end the inning. He felt claustrophobic, as if the walls and grandstands were sneaking up on him while his skin itched and tingled from head to toe. He felt a drop of rain on his hand when he started his wind-up; the water seemed to pump his adrenaline without disrupting his delivery. It was the best pitch he had ever made, a rising fastball, 101 m.p.h., unhittable.

"The pitch!"

Frrrraaaawaaaccckkkk!! The sound echoed with the shock and suddenness of a gigantic screen door slamming. Frightened pigeons and gulls flocked from their roosts in the lighting towers. If not for the birds, the moment would have appeared frozen in time. Everything stopped as the people caught their breath, sensing the implications of this event. They didn't need to act or react; it was simply there to experience, to absorb. The message had been sent.

"Oh . . . my . . . God," muttered Dillon Southwood. He stood at the top of the dugout steps with all the rest of his players and marveled at the flight of the ball from the most magnificent hit ever. The Baltimore center fielder, Jody Reed, never moved from his spot. He simply watched as the ball flew a hundred feet over his head, then hit the uppermost point of the white gable facade that surrounded Ruth Memorial Stadium. When the ball hit, it bounded straight up, and then, as if a gust of wind had pushed it, the ball flew out of the stadium and into the heart of the Bronx . . . and the country. John watched from home plate, then slowly circled the base paths. The sun broke through a wall of ominous clouds to cast a beam of light on the house that Ruth built. The people stood and watched in silent awe. Jake Snyder removed his cap as a sign of respect when John rounded first. Jimmy Boyle and Terry Cues at second and short followed suit, then Charlie Krug at third. None of the Baltimore players left their positions until well after John touched home.

Southwood tipped his cap as John trotted to home plate. There were tears in the eyes of the people. Collectively they had witnessed something that would change their lives forever. Then the applause came; thunderous oceans of applause, waves of relief . . . they were not alone. Many shook hands with the folks around them, even introduced themselves or simply exchanged a warm smile. When the game ended, the Highlanders' 9 to 5 win seemed inconsequential. Dillon Southwood remembered his dream and wondered how many other folks had a similar one. He knew he was not alone.

ANGELA WHEELER DROPPED her bags to rest her strained arms and tired feet. She had two more blocks to go when she reached the River Avenue side of Ruth Stadium where the subway ran overhead. Baseball made her think of her son; then again, almost everything made her think of Jason. He was all she had and vice versa. Vendors with carts full of pennants, T-shirts, pins, buttons, baseballs, and miniature bats waited for the big crowd about to leave the game. A sign hung over a blue entrance door that read: Bleachers. The four train clanked and banged overhead. Angela was surprised. 'Usually folks are leaving the stadium by now,' she thought.

Whhaaackkk!!! 'What was that?!' Angela's natural reaction was to duck. 'Gun fire? Large caliber—shotgun maybe?' It all sounded so familiar, yet foreign.

The huge crowd gasped. "Haaaah!!" 'What happened? Somebody killed? Maybe.' Angela had lived in the neighborhood most of her life and never heard anything quite like this. It was as though all the right tones were there but in the wrong sequence and emotional order, especially the eerie silence that followed. Duncccck!!!! The sound came from above, but it wasn't the train. Her attention was drawn to the top of the stadium. A ball shot into the air and then fell not twenty feet from where she was standing. It took two bounces and landed in one of her shopping bags, right next to a can of peas. She pulled the ball out from her canned goods and examined it. The ball had a large splinter embedded from where it had hit the white facade.

One of the vendors who had witnessed the whole scenario began to yell, "Hey, Lady! Hey! Lady!! Hey! Hey! Hundred bucks!!!" He was fanning the money in front of his face as though trying to cool himself. "Hundred bucks for the ball!" he shouted. Angela gave him no response. "Two hundred!!" he pleaded.

Angela Wheeler ignored the vendor, dropped the ball back into her groceries, picked up her bags, and walked home.

"DID YOU HEAR? The whole street is buzzing!" exclaimed Max Weinman, as he climbed into the passenger seat of an unmarked cruiser.

"What?" said Detective Kerrins, sounding disinterested. He was still nursing a hangover.

"Black with sugar." Weinman handed Kerrins his coffee.

"What? What buzz!" demanded the more interested but grumpy Kerrins.

"The Highlander game." Max took a sip of coffee.

"Yeah . . . and?"

"Well, they won the game, 9 to 5."

"The streets are buzzing because the 'Landers won a ball game." Kerrins gave him a derisive look.

"Let me finish."

"I'm listening."

"John Greco."

"Yeah?"

"He hits a grand slam in the ninth!"

"Wow."

"Yeah wow, but that's not the best part. The ball doesn't just go out of the park—"

"You're telling me he hit an inside the park slammer? That's impossible," Kerrins said, dismissing him.

"No-no-no-no, you don't get it. Be patient. Listen to me, now," insisted Weinman, half choking after swallowing coffee down the wrong tube.

"Please, enlighten me."

"Uu-huh-huh." He cleared a space in his throat for air to pass through. "Impossible—impossible? You haven't heard impossible!" Max's face turned red as the pitch of his voice went up an octave. "I'm telling you, the guy hit it out of the park! Out of the stadium! It's on the number four train coming into Manhattan as we speak!" cried Weinman with all the exuberance of a lunatic spouting the gospel.

"Nah, you're shitting me."

"No shit, man. The guy really did it. Heard Rizzuto on the radio in the coffee shop. He was joking about how he would've bunted in the situation. The guy really did it! There were people in that shop I know could give two shits about baseball with their ears glued to the radio. It was weird; people crying over it! Like it means something?"

"Huh. Something good, right?"

"Yeah, I guess so," Max thought about it. "I guess."

"Hey, let's not get too carried away. I mean with the perfect pitch—what was the pitch?"

"Cush-ing, fast-ball, one-hun-dred-one miles per hour," Weinman said, accenting every syllable.

"Christ! This is bullshit! You're trying to see what kind of asshole I am! Nobody throws that fast!" the detective declared adamantly. Kerrins noticed a group of people leaving the coffee shop, most of them were smiling, a few were wiping away tears. 'Like they just got laid,' thought Kerrins. He pulled himself up in his seat. "Okay, okay. He hits this pitch with the best wood possible, like he's got a micrometer on it or somethin'. A good stiff wind. It could go out. There was a guy—What was his name? . . . Ah, ah, Josh— yeah—Josh Gibson. That's it! The old Negro League. They say he hit one out during an exhibition game. Right field, I think," said Kerrins, content with his reasonable hypothesis. "What field did Greco hit it out of?" Kerrins asked, confident it would be the short porch.

"Left center," grinned Weinman.

Kerrins rubbed his forehead. He knew his theory was in trouble. "We're talking 550, 650 feet."

"Yeah, somewhere around there," said Max, setting him up the whole way.

"It could happen," Kerrins muttered with an indifferent attitude, as his hangover cramped his optimism.

"There is one other thing," said the young rookie detective, calmly.

Kerrins sipped his coffee and noticed something odd. The people—they were strange. With so many happy faces on the street, he found it hard to believe he was still in New York.

"What's that, Max?"

Weinman got the feeling Kerrins didn't want to hear anymore, which made telling him all the better. "Well, after the first strike he steps out of the box and draws a triangle in the dirt. Ya know, like Ruth calling his shot!"

"That's nothing. Everybody knows he's always drawing in the dirt! All that junk was made up by the press to sell papers."

"Wait a minute. Listen to me."

"I'm listening."

"He let strike two go right pass 'im. Doesn't even think about swinging. Then steps out again."

"What! Two triangles!? Give me a break!"

"Nooo. Get this," Weinman lowered his voice. "He writes L-O-V-E in the dirt, steps up and—wham—out she goes! Bingo!" Weinman was bursting at the seams. He was delighted to get the story before Kerrins did. Then he added, "They say the sound of the bat hitting the ball . . . was . . . was . . . not of this world." Max grinned with satisfaction, as he went right for Kerrins' Irish Catholic jugular.

But that was the story and after Max told it, it got him thinking. Kerrins swallowed hard and said, "If you're shitting me—"

"Ask anybody! This guy's world news."

Neither one spoke. This bizarre event had actually happened, and now it was sinking in—not only for them, but for the entire country. "First the little girl . . . and now this," was heard all over town.

"You know Smithy Lango is not in the city," Kerrins hissed.

"I know. Jonelli's got him hidden good. Aaah! He's a dumb shit; he'll make a mistake."

"Yeah. That's what I'm afraid of," replied Kerrins, looking at his watch. "McCarthy's? On 14th Street?"

"Yeah, cheap drafts. They've got a TV. Maybe we can catch something about the game on the news."

"JOHN! JOHN! JUST a few questions for the press," Bill Singer called from across the clubhouse. Singer extended his hand to John. They shook hands, and Bill put his arm around him as though they were best buddies. "Magic moment out there, John. I felt something . . . here." He patted his heart with an aggrandized gesture. "Now, I believe you're gonna get everything you want out of this business . . ." He continued to give John his spiel while a crowd of reporters gathered around his locker.

"John, do you . . ."

"John, can you tell us . . ."

"Is there a reason why Dillon . . . "

"The connection between your brother . . . "

"How did you know the ball was . . . "

"Has your daughter's death . . . "

"What's it like to . . . "

"Why love?"

The questions came and came, and John could see how badly they wanted, needed the answers. The crowd grew with not only reporters, but teammates, security and maintenance people, grounds people, even management. Anybody who could get into the locker room gravitated around John's space, waiting, wanting something more from him as if he possessed another degree of knowledge. All the while Bill Singer stood right next to him, smiling like a personal manager and getting so close, so very close, it was an invasion of privacy. Singer wanted to tap into his energy, bathe in his essence, be a part of him. John changed into his street clothes as they continued to fire question after question at him, begging, pleading for something, anything more he could possibly offer them. When John finished dressing, he sat on the bench in front of his locker, not sure if there was anything more to tell. It was apparent that his play had answered as many questions as it had created. Maybe they were better questions. He had to think about that. He had to get home to Sharon and what was left of his family.

"C'mon, John! Just a statement about the game!" Some invisible person called out.

"John, please just—" Bill Singer started to say, but Johney cut him off.

"I'm taking the next few days off to be with my family." The locker room became very quiet. He was speaking softly and more to the tile floor than any person. "I'll rejoin the team next week in Cleveland. Ah . . . it was important to me that I played the opener. I don't want to talk about why. This is a difficult time for me. This game should've been one of the happiest moments in my life . . . but . . . well, ah . . . maybe it is a happy moment, in the saddest part of me." John brought his hand to his mouth and squeezed his lips vertically, as though trying to force the words out, trying his best to give them a reasonable answer, to explain what had happened to him. "I had an opportunity to send a message, to answer your questions as a baseball player. I'm not much at talking." Uneasy laughter escaped from the crowd. "But, uh, it killed all of us a little . . . when—" He noticed his hands starting to shake, he could feel his own grief. "And my little girl, she was gunned down—" He was close to tears. "Well, I had this opportunity and that's what

I wanted to say. Love. That's what I wanted to say. We should have classes . . . learn to love. It'd be a good thing." He started to make his way through the crowd.

"John, what do you mean when you say 'had an opportunity?'"

"Are you aware that some people are calling this a miracle?"

"John, was this a miracle?"

"The interview is over, gentlemen," bellowed Southwood. He emerged from the pack. "I'm sure you can all understand Mr. Greco's situation." Dillon took John by the elbow and ushered him out of the locker room to a back exit of the stadium. A car stood waiting for him.

"John, don't take the subway tonight. Okay? The car and driver are yours for the week. Mr. Harrington insists," said Dillon, as he opened the door. John just nodded his head as he slipped into the back seat.

"He'll take you wherever you want to go. Alright?"

"Yeah." Southwood pushed the door closed, and the car pulled away. The sign over the stadium exit read: Emergency Vehicles Only. Dillon put his hands in his pockets. It was starting to get dark, there was a chill in the air. Something unusual caught his eye, a shimmer of light, a reflection off the back bumper when the car made its turn out of the stadium. Then he saw the people following the path of the automobile with flickering candles in hand. 'Must be twenty-five, maybe thirty of 'em,' Dillon thought as he walked to the gate to get a better look. He couldn't believe what he saw. Dillon opened the gate, letting himself out. Encircling the entire ballpark, were thousands of people, all unable to release the moment. Most were sitting quietly, some were singing, many were praying. 'They really believe it's a miracle,' he thought. 'Like one of those crying icons or the shadow of Christ on somebody's oak tree.' The papers later called the view "The Halo Over Manhattan." They had an aerial shot taken by a helicopter, and that's just what it looked like, a halo. Southwood looked out into the sea of cars on the Major Deegan. 'All kinds of people just trying to get home from work. Just trying to get by,' he thought. Then he thought of John, and he said aloud, "Bless you, son."

"HELLO, FRANKIE. . . . YES, Joe Jonelli here. . . . Yes . . . Ha-ha! Well, it was a miracle for me anyway! Listen, I'll send my driver Leon around tomorrow to pick up the money. . . . I'm sure he can handle it! Better luck next time, Frankie . . . Don't worry. I'll have him bring a wheelbarrow! Yes. . . . Yes. . . . Thank you. Good-bye. . . . Hello, Tony. Joe Jonelli. . . . I know I covered the spread. You could call it that. Listen, I want to send . . . "

20

"DAD, IT'S JOHN. I'm at the house. Thanks. Yeah, it was something. Listen, I dropped a set of keys off at Tommy's . . . Yeah . . . No, my friend George. He's gonna fix the door. Uh-huh, and the glass, too. Dad, let me talk to Sharon. Yeah? . . . Uh-huh. Dad, I'll be over in an hour. We'll talk then. Okay."

"John?"

"Shar, how are you, honey?"

"I'm okay, sedated on something. Faye is too. Sorry about my dad. Your home run is on all the news reports. He's all excited. We watched the game. I don't know how you did it." John wasn't sure if she was talking about the hit or just playing ball in general, probably both.

"Shar, I got the week off."

"Oh. . . . That's good."

"Honey, I'm at the house. Do you need anything?"

"Oh . . . ah?"

"I'll be over soon. I got a car for the week."

"Ah. My makeup bag . . . and . . . my black pumps for the service, I think." Her voice faded. She was sobbing and trying to be strong at the same time by pretending she wasn't crying.

"John," she said in a weak voice.

"Shar, I'll be—"

"John, the funeral is tomorrow morning."

"I know . . . "

"No wake. I can't do it—not-with-out-see-ing-her," she wept. John knew the child couldn't be viewed. Their daughter was hideously disfigured, killed by men with no pity, no conscience.

"I love you, Shar. I'll be right there. Okay?"

"I love you, too." She hung up the phone.

THE FUNERAL WAS just for immediate family and close friends. Only a couple of aggressive reporters needed to be escorted out. Father McPherson performed the Catholic high mass at St. Mary's. It sounded beautiful, forgiving, and sometimes even enlightening. But to John, on this day, it just sounded like the Latin it was. The church pipe organ and a single French horn played Mozart, while a woman with an angelic voice sang from above the pews. A baby softly cried intermittently during the service. The host, or consecrated wafer, was received by those who had confessed their sins. Neither John, Sharon, nor Faye took part. They felt the tragic guilt of parents who had lost their child. Yet, they didn't know how to confess it or even if they could. The small white casket tied them to their seats. Grief, shame and outrage paralyzed them as they waited to bury their little girl under the shade of an elm tree in Woodlawn Cemetery.

DURING THE WEEK that followed, Sharon remained with her parents, under doctors' supervision. Without drugs she would work herself into such a frenzy, the doctors thought she might have a complete nervous breakdown. John was so exhausted that all he could do was wrap his arms around his wife and sleep the time away.

Faye found amazing inner strength and inspiration as she read about John's opening day miracle. There were stories in all the papers and on the television news broadcast every day since it had happened. The *New York Times* ran a profile piece on John, complete with Ruth Stadium diagrams that marked the flight of the ball as it left the stadium. The headline read: Greco's Miracle Hit, but Where's the Ball? No longer fogged in by large doses of drugs, Faye realized that John had changed things for the better, maybe not a lot nor for long. 'Only time will tell,' she reasoned as she attempted to nurse Sharon and John back to health.

'Natt would be proud of me,' she thought, as she also bravely accepted the loss of her husband.

21

'WHY?' THOUGHT JOHN, still groggy with sleep. 'Why are these same pictures in Detroit and Cleveland?' He rolled over in his Cleveland, Ohio, hotel room bed, opened the one eye that wasn't caked shut, and found himself staring at an all too familiar tropical sunrise print, practically insinuating that these cities had nothing more to offer than thoughts of some place else. He grabbed a pillow, pulled it over his head, and went back to sleep.

He had arrived early in Cleveland. The Highlanders were still traveling from Boston, riding a five game winning streak, and still answering questions about John Greco and opening day. The writers were camped out in the lobby waiting for John's arrival, and they would be there when he left. He locked his door, slept, and waited for his teammates. 'Maybe they could distract some of these guys,' he thought.

John slept for another hour or so. It was Friday night. The next game wasn't until Saturday night. He wasn't feeling hungry, or thirsty, or sociable, or alive for that matter. It didn't feel much like Friday night to him. Sharon wasn't well when he had left for the airport, and for all his sleeping, he still felt exhausted. John continued to doze off and on. The desk lamp light burned just below the tropical sunrise. As it stung his bloodshot eyes, he tried to recall turning it on.

"What!" yelled John. He was startled by a dark figure blocking the sun. His heart palpitated while his mind raced through a collage of ugly scenarios.

He reached for the bat that rested under the covers. "Who are you?" he demanded at the top of his lungs, while swinging his directionless bat as a blind man would.

"Jimmy Jackson! Your roommate!"

"My roommate is Cliff Oakes!" John stood on the bed towering over Jackson with his bat cocked and ready to strike.

"Uh, Oakes broke his ankle. Remember? Opening day. You made history. Remember, brother? Little tense, ain't yah?" Jackson was a young powerful-looking kid supposedly just called up from Toledo. His arms and shoulders were massive, his legs as solid as tree trunks. He was the blackest black person John had ever seen.

"Yes, sir, I'm patrolling center field at Ruth Stadium and rooming with a saint who's about to become a legend," Jackson said proudly, with just a hint of humor. His delivery almost made John laugh.

"John Greco," said John, extending his bat free hand.

"Like I'd don't know! Hah-ha."

'Friendly,' John thought. Jackson offered John his hand.

"Very pleased to meet ya, sir," said Jimmy, flashing the whitest teeth on the planet.

"Same here," replied John, not quite sure what to make of this unusually happy person.

"Uh, you won't need this." Jackson removed the bat from John's hand. "I don't even snore. Promise."

"Hey! I saw the pack of reporters downstairs. Brought you and me hamburgers and fries. Thought ya might be trapped." He started to unravel his white deli bags.

"Thanks, I am hungry. How come I didn't see you at camp, spring training?"

"Just traded from the Dodgers. I'm the player to be named later. You want mustard?" He didn't wait for a reply. "Mannn, I love mustard and ketchup on my burgers! Hey, I'm real sorry—about your little girl. She's in a good place. Don't you worry. She's in a real fine place. You dig? Now, the way I see it, you got the power." Jackson talked in between bites of food for twenty straight minutes. John had no idea what he was talking about most of the time, but he liked him. Jimmy Jackson was refreshing. The kid never stopped talking, and he wasn't looking for any answers. John listened, ate his dinner, and drank beer. He was beginning to feel relaxed. The time was flying by, and John realized that he, too, had been talking incessantly—talking over things he didn't even want to remember.

"So, ahh, I'm laying in bed all week. My wife, she's not well. And I'm thinking, 'What am I doing?' I wrote this message because, well, because I felt so much hate . . . in them, in me. I felt it everywhere. Not just in the stadium, I mean everywhere. It scared the heck out of me, like I was catching baseballs along with everything else. So, on the one hand I'm thinking, if I can send a message, 'What would do the most good?' And ah, ah, on the other hand, my stomach acid is eating me up inside. I know who killed my daughter and probably my brother. If I was a man, I'd get a gun. Right? I'd go after them. Right? The hate I felt made me want to do it all the more, made me feel guilty for not doing it. But I couldn't live with myself if I was a killer. Boyyy, I can't believe I'm telling you this." He took a long, hard pull from his beer.

"Mr. Greco."

"C'mon. John."

"Mr. Greco," Jackson repeated with a smile. "I don't think you know how important that one hit has become to folks. It renewed a lot of faith. And your family's tragedy, well, it broke your heart, but it didn't break your spirit. That gun you're talking about . . . that . . . that would break you," said Jimmy Jackson, waving his long neck beer bottle.

"I'll tell you one thing! Folks are gonna remember 'love' written in the dirt one heck of a lot longer than another murder," stated Jackson firmly.

"Cheers," said John, glad for Jackson's company. He felt much better. Their bottles clanked together. It was official—they were buddies. "I gotta sneak out a here. Get some air. Been in this room all day."

"I know, smells like it! Ha-ha hah!"

"Hey, how many of those beers you have?"

"Four."

"Well, no more. How many games you play in?"

"Four. These questions are too easy. Hah-ha ha!"

"All right, all right. I got one! What's your major league average?"

Jackson puffed out his chest. "Five fifty-nine," he declared.

"That's nothing." John puffed out his chest. "One game. One thousand percent. Huh-huh?!" They laughed like drunken teenagers. Everything sounded as if it was the funniest thing they had ever heard.

"You know what Rizzuto said, don'tcha, John?"

"No, what? About my average?"

"Yeah. He said . . . ah-ha ha." Jackson paused to catch his breath. "He said, 'It was bound to go down!' Ha-ha!"

"You don't really believe that? Do ya?!" joked Johney, doing his best

Southwood impersonation by running his hands through his hair, arching his back, and speaking in a gruff voice.

"It doesn't matter what I believe. Do you believe?" Jackson had a way of turning a conversation into a roller coaster ride. The smile disappeared from his face and was replaced by a look of genuine concern.

"What? Hit a thousand? C'mon?" John knew that wasn't what he meant. "What are you talking about? Believe what?" Jimmy Jackson rested his beer on the night table. He didn't reply, just waited. "I'll admit, I've changed my thinking on a few subjects," said John, as he opened the sliding door a crack, breathed in the fresh air, and gazed out into the city of Cleveland.

"Like what?" asked Jimmy.

"Well . . . fear. I guess."

"Yeah, that's a biggy."

John suddenly recalled a conversation he had had with his father some twenty years ago. It was about being bullied by a bigger, stronger neighborhood kid. His dad told him, "If you believe in the cause, fight. If you don't, run. But don't be afraid to do one or the other." John never saw the wisdom in such advice. 'How do you win?' he thought. It wasn't until recently that he realized his father was telling him that sometimes it was okay to lose. It was a fact of life. But the fear he felt when his daughter was murdered became both embarrassing and selfish to him. 'Dad's rule never had a chance,' he figured. Fear was much easier to deal with head-on, alone, when it was only yourself involved. The selfishness, he thought, was his daughter's sacrifice to give him life. The embarrassment was his own acceptance of it and his virtual relief that it wasn't his own death.

"After Maya's death, I sat in my house . . . by myself and considered suicide as a way out of the fear. I was ready to do it. Until . . . until the absurdity—" John paced the room, amazed by his own stupidity, amused by his own ridiculous simple-mindedness. He paused in front of Jackson who was sitting up in his bed. He wanted to make a point, something he rarely did. "Well, I was gonna kill myself because I feared death."

"Drastic," commented Jackson, after taking a sip of beer.

"The worst thing in life is death. When I accepted it, I wasn't as afraid anymore."

"Cool," said Jackson as if filling in the blanks. "And your daughter?"

"I loved her. I love her more than myself. I always did," stated John, reflectively. Jimmy rolled himself off the bed and grabbed another beer out of the small refrigerator.

"Is that why you wrote 'love' in the dirt?" He opened a bottle by snapping its cap on the edge of the window sill. The suds foamed around the top, and he slurped them off.

"Yeah, that. But more than that. They needed to hear it, see it. And, and, ah . . . I wasn't afraid to lose." John became lost in his confession, completely unaware of his young confessor's percipient, yet rogue-like, behavior.

"You want another beer?"

"Naah."

"I think you should," said Jackson. "Better yet, I think we should go on down to the bar and do some shots. Back 'em up with a few more beers. Whaddaya say? We'll get through this night. C'mon!"

"No, I had enough. I'm gonna take that walk. Maybe next night off."

"You want company? On the walk—I could use a walk. You don't have to go alone."

"Thanks, but I like to wander by myself; helps me think." John slipped on his jacket. "I'll see ya later," he said. Jimmy Jackson didn't reply. He nodded his head "yes," which slowly turned to "no" after John left the room.

John ducked out a side entrance of the hotel. The few writers who were left were in the bar waiting for their story to come to them, mostly single men with no families and nothing better to do. They weren't ambitious enough to man all the exits. John walked a few blocks. There wasn't much to see. Most of the businesses were closed for the night. The temperature dropped as the wind blew in off Lake Erie. John looked for a place to get warm. Down the block he saw the neon lights of a place called Marty's Topless Review and Bar. He turned up his collar and followed the blinking red glow.

The place was painted black. Everything in it was black: the bar, tables, chairs—everything . . . except for the bartender, Marty; he was white as a ghost. The only color came from light gels aimed onto a circular stage at the end of the bar. The stage was maybe ten feet wide, surrounded by a heavy black velvet curtain. It reminded John of a huge impractical shower stall. The place was still, in limbo—no dancers, no music, no activity, just a blue light on the stall. John figured they were in between shows, or maybe it was still too early or too late. He'd completely lost track of the time. About ten guys sat around the bar waiting for something to happen. Marty was fussing with some kind of electrical equipment and not servicing the bar. One of the guys kept calling his name in a futile effort to get a drink.

"Heeeeyyy! Waa I gotta du ta gitta drink!" shouted one of Marty's better customers.

"I'll be right with ya! Fucking thing," screamed Marty. "Just let me get this damn thing going!" Marty slammed a black door and pounded his fist into it. The Four Seasons began to sing "Sherry Baby" in the middle of the chorus. The tubes in the equipment needed to warm up, and Frankie Valley went from a low octave to his piercing falsetto in one Sher-ry ba-aa-by! The velvet shower stall opened automatically, revealing a blonde, wearing bright orange lipstick and a bikini. She sat on a stool. The lights went to red, and she got up off the stool and started go-go stripping. Marty looked relieved. Sherry took off her top to reveal the largest breasts John had ever seen. The men started to hoot and holler and wave dollars at Sherry's crotch. Marty smiled. John walked out. Sherry was making him uncomfortable.

When he exited Marty's Topless Review, John noticed a dark Gothic, but somehow modest, church right across the street. The stone of the church was blackened from age and city dirt and soot . . . and living across the street from Marty's. The wrought-iron gate was open. John decided to go in. 'Maybe light a candle,' he thought. By the looks of things, this was a very poor parish. No one was inside, at least no one he could see. On a blackboard in the vestibule was a sign written in chalk. It read: Welcome to St. Jude's.

The windows of St. Jude's were stained glass, nothing elaborate, no pictures of the apostles or biblical scenes of any sort, just colored squares of glass framed by large wooden shutters. The shutters could be closed to seal off the recessed windows from light. 'Why,' John wondered, 'would they want to do that?' The altar was a single slab of marble supported by two pedestals. A fresco of Jesus Christ was above the altar, his outstretched arms promising forgiveness and comfort. 'Inviting,' John thought. 'In a not-of-this-world sort of way.'

John dipped his hand into the stoup and blessed himself with its holy water, making the stations of the cross—an old Catholic habit. He lit a candle and said a prayer for Maya and Natt. Most churches he thought had a warmth and peacefulness about them; St. Jude's was that, but it also had the aura of an intensely holy space. Of course, after Marty's . . .

John settled into a pew close to the altar. The smell of frankincense drifted in the air. He closed his eyes and drifted along with it, allowing himself to meditate. He felt the quiet, the perfect order, and stillness of absolute peace. He felt safe and content, as though he were a child again. John remembered the first time he experienced such self-fulfilling joy. He was five years old, sitting on the front porch with his friend, Fran Ward. She was also five. It was snowing and so quiet that they could hear the snow hit the ground and kiss their faces. "Saaaaaaah," hissed the flakes as they melted on their skin. John's mother must have thought there was something wrong. Not hearing the sounds of child's play, she came to the door wearing her apron, looking for her boy, expecting a snowball fight or at the very least snow man construction.

"There you are!" called Betty Greco, her tone filled with the excitement only a mother could produce for her babies. "What are you two doing? You're so quiet," she asked, her love shined down through the snowstorm.

"We're getting snowflake kisses, Mommy," said little Johney.

"Yes," agreed Fran, very seriously. "If you're very quiet, you can hear the snowflakes kiss your cheeks," she said in her small singsong voice.

"Oooooh, snowflake kisses," said Mom, as though she knew all about them. Betty Greco stepped out onto the porch with her arms crossed at the waist. She tried to keep warm as she lifted her head to the sky, and stood very still while the flakes landed and went "saaaaaah" on her skin.

"John, Fran, you're right! They're like angel kisses from heaven, your snowflake kisses!" She gave them each a big hug as they gathered in the magic of the snow. In the distance Betty spotted Mr. Gooding, walking his old dog, Hunter, through the snowy streets.

"I hope he's all right," said Betty as she faced the cold.

Some twenty years ago, Mr. and Mrs. Gooding had moved into the neighborhood. Retired and in their golden years, they enjoyed the vitality of the younger people in the community, especially the children. The Goodings would take walks around the block, holding hands, greeting their neighbors with genuine warmth, while their ever-lovable dog, Hunter, attracted the attention of the kids who just had to pet him. Hunter's sizable, wet Springer Spaniel tongue would lick them from cheek to cheek. He was well-known as the friendliest dog on the block and loved to run and play and tussle with all the kids. While in their seventies and obviously still very much in love, Mr. and Mrs. Gooding had been an inspiration to many folks around town. That was the Gooding legacy.

"And they're such lovely people," Betty Greco always said.

As a kid, Natt used to cut the Goodings' lawn. It was a unique lawn. The front yard was half yellow and half dark green grass, not mixed, but divided, like two foreign countries on a map. Mr. Gooding said it was diseased. There was nothing he could do about it, and he'd tried everything, including digging up all the yellow grass and replanting. But it still came up yellow.

"I'm glad it's the grass that's diseased and not me or Mrs. Gooding," he'd tell Natt, as though the grass in some way offered them protection by assuming an illness.

Whenever folks saw the Goodings, they'd say, "Hope we're like them when we get older."

A tear ran down Betty Greco's face as she watched Mr. Gooding walk alone with Hunter. Eve Gooding had recently passed away, leaving him heartbroken in the white house with the yellow and green lawn. Ever since then he just wasn't himself. He was even down right mean, yelling at the kids to get off his yard, often slamming the door behind him after reprimanding the offenders. Natt got yelled at frequently by Mr. Gooding. His yard was a shortcut to school that Natty dared to take.

Unfortunately, Mr. Gooding had become reclusive. He rarely walked Hunter. He'd just let the dog run free to go where he pleased, which was on the Greco lawn most of the time as John's dad pointed out. Betty Greco would say it didn't matter and clean up after Hunter. The whole situation made her sad. Maybe that's why the sight of Mr. Gooding walking the dog again, made such a big impression on her.

"I'll be right back," said Betty. She had an idea, went inside the house to get her coat, scarf, and gloves, and returned. "C'mon, kids. Let's go see Mr. Gooding and Hunter. " She took their little hands and marched into the snowstorm as though she were on some kind of a mission. At first Mr. Gooding put his head down, pretending to brave the cold wind. But there wasn't any wind, and he soon realized that he couldn't avoid the meeting. Betty Greco was determined to intercept his path. He forced a smile as Hunter strained at the leash, begging to run and play and greet the new arrivals.

"Good afternoon, Mr. Gooding. Isn't the snow beautiful!" called Betty. She studied her surroundings and inhaled a deep breath of fresh air. The weight of the snow on the evergreens gave them an enchanted quality, she thought. The kids jumped into a drift a full two feet taller than themselves. Hunter begged for freedom.

"Hum, ayyyyy, yes, beautiful," replied the frail, uninspired man.

Betty Greco took him by the arm and said, "Please come over to dinner. We'd love to have you, say . . . Saturday?"

"Well, ayyyyyy, thanks but—"

"No buts! Mr. Gooding, you've got to get out of that house." She smiled the most disarming smile imaginable. "I'm making lasagna."

"Lasagna . . . well, that's another story." He was completely charmed and offered her a sincere smile. "I'd be glad to join you and your family for dinner."

"Good." They walked a little bit, enjoying the beauty of the day and feeling good about the rebirth of their friendship.

"Oh, and Mr. Gooding . . . "

"Yes, Betty."

"If you yell at my boy Natt one more time, I'm gonna come over and give you a good swift kick!" Again, the disarming smile.

"Whaaat!! . . . Haaaa-hah haaa-ha ha-haaaaa!!!" Mr. Gooding laughed so hard his eyes watered. Betty laughed, too. Hunter's leash fell from his hand.

"Here, Hunter. Here, boy!" cried the children. The dog ran as fast as he could to join Fran and John. The three of them rolled and played in the snow the way dogs and kids and even adults should. Betty Greco gave Mr. Gooding a hug and called the kids over to show him how to get snowflake kisses.

"You should see this. It's really cute," she giggled. With a nod of his head, Mr. Gooding seemed like his former self again.

John's mom could have just as easily stood on that front porch with her arms folded and done nothing but feel sorry for her neighbor. She could have said it was too cold, or she needed to get dinner started, but she didn't. Even at the age of five, John knew his mother had made an important difference in this man's life. He had changed before their very eyes. He remembered Mr. Gooding's laugh, a laugh that his mom had brought back to life. 'Just like a magic trick,' he thought.

As John meditated in Cleveland's St. Jude's Church, he traveled back in time, recalling the many events of his life from snowflake kisses to an unlikely home run at Ruth Memorial Stadium. He realized events happened to all degrees within a grand spectrum of emotional and philosophical shades. Some of his were sad, even regrettable, but most were valuable and positive experiences. We all have the ability to create, he reasoned. Only indifference creates nothing, making a void in the heart, stagnation of the soul, and an opportunity for the corrupt. Some events might influence a neighborhood and improve the community, like Betty Greco's, while others might influence a city and improve the world. The operative word was improve, he reasoned, which could so easily be substituted with deteriorate.

A gunshot shattered the silence. Small pieces of wood and plaster fluttered down and around Smithy Lango, where he stood sweating, grinning, and breathing heavily. This would be his main event. The peace was splintered into a million pieces, sending shock waves through John's system as if he were in an electric chair.

"Hey, Johney-boy, how ya doing! Ya don't have'ta get on your knees to me! Me!!!" declared Lango. He poked himself in the chest with his gun as if "me" needed to be emphasized a little more to make his point. "Ya know

I'm not here to show mercy." He laughed in a raw, hoarse voice as if he'd been hollering at the moon most of the night. John tried to rise from the pew.

"Don't get up!" ordered Lango. He unzipped his pants, exposed himself, and peed down the center aisle that led to John and the altar. He shook himself and said, "Don't wanna stain my trousers. Right, Johney?!" He laughed so hard at his own amusement that John could see he was actually enjoying himself. 'Was he this grotesque when he killed my daughter?' The thought sent a chill down John's spine, followed by a surge of energy unlike anything he had ever felt before.

"Aaaaah, you big shot ballplayers—what! Think ya can fuck around with my payday! Assholes. All of you's!" Lango stamped his foot in the man-made puddle, pleased by the distance of his splash. He grinned. "Man, that brother of yours. What a jerk. Could've lived easy for the rest of his life. But . . . he's dead," he said matter-of-factly. "Wouldn't even try to talk sense into his dumb-shit Highlander brother. Maaan. Can you believe that?! He wouldn't even talk to you, Johney." His tone squealed higher as he waved his gun like a flag.

"Oh. Hey, man, huh—really sorry about the little girl." John wasn't sure but Lango sounded as though he was actually asking for forgiveness. His tone had changed so dramatically, but he was just setting Johney up. "I would'da liked'ta fucked her first. Tah-ha. Tah-ha. Tah-ha!" he laughed, completely out of control. The vileness turned John's stomach inside out. His rage turned to courage, the courage to power. John stood up, which surprised the monster, and spoke in a deliberate tone of voice without a hint of fear.

"You destroy my family, this holy place. And for what?! Money?!!" John's eyes remained fixed on Smithy as he walked slowly down the aisle.

"Don't get any closer!" demanded Smithy Lango, his voice filled with outrage. After all, he was the man with the gun, with the power. 'How dare you not respect it,' he thought. His eyes narrowed. Lango began to scan the area around him from floor to ceiling. "Don't get any closer!" His eyes darted from right to left. "Get any closer!"—left to right. He spun, as if somebody had just tapped him on the shoulder.

"Doooon't—Don't! Don't! Don't! Don't! God damn it!!" He stamped his feet like a little boy insisting on his way. His ashen face dripped with sweat, his sneakers stained and damp. Smithy appeared to be getting violently ill, as though the church itself were closing in on him, suffocating him, burning him up with fever. He reacted to the unseeable, shooting his gun at unknown targets, but not at John as he continued to approach. Lango's marksmanship became even more random as pews splintered and stained glass shattered. A bullet whistled past John's head and demolished the hand of Christ. Then suddenly, there was silence. Smithy was out of bullets. Once again, he had failed another job. His eyes couldn't focus. John stood directly in front of him, separated by a puddle of urine. Lango's head and body lunged in every direction. He was unable to fix his sights on any one given point, seeing things that could actually make his demented soul cringe with repugnance and horror.

John realized that Lango wasn't shooting at him and looked about the church to find his target. He saw nothing. Smithy allowed his cherished gun to fall onto the soiled church tile, then pulled a sizable switchblade from his coat pocket. He frantically stabbed into the empty air about him, as if being viciously attacked on all fronts. After fighting himself into exhaustion, it appeared to John that Smithy wanted nothing more than to leave the church and abort his ill-fated plan, though he seemed unable to evacuate his puddle and, instead, ended up on his knees.

"Help me. Help me!" he pleaded to John, moaning like an animal caught in a trap. He raised his arms over his head in an act of surrender, but it didn't look quite right because he refused to drop his knife. "Forgive meee!!! Forgive mee!!! I'm not ready to die!!! I repent! I repent, I said!!! C'mon, I repent—"

Suddenly all was quiet, even Smithy. Silence. John waited to see what the mad dog would do next. Lango, still on his knees, looked around with a bewildered expression on his already demented face, checking the waters. "The acid," he scoffed, he blamed, and considered the possibilities. He concluded that he was free from whatever it was. John watched with great trepidation. He imagined Smithy Lango was given a final choice.

"Aaaaaaaaaaaaaah." Lango jumped to his feet, wiping the urine from his hands onto his pants.

All fear left John. It was replaced by an acceptance of what will be, will be. The decision wasn't his to make. "Well?" asked John in a flat, dead, emotionless tone of voice. Lightning struck nearby and thunder sounded, a pouring rain pelted St. Jude's. Water dripped from a bullet hole in the ceiling, adding to the already existing puddle between John and Smithy, a line drawn in the sand. 'He's gonna walk. This murderer's gonna walk!' John thought, as he faced Smithy head on. Every second seemed more like an hour. 'How much longer will I have to wait for him to make this simple choice. Why doesn't he go?' Thunder sounded again as Smithy began to wade through the puddle toward him. John had an uneasy feeling. He felt odd, almost relieved.

"I'm gonna show you mercy." Lango flashed his shiny blade in front of him. It caught and reflected the candlelight, and for a moment John thought he saw something, one brief and glorious frame of angels. "I'm not gonna kill ya." He raised his hands into the air as though attending some kind of mock revival meeting, shaking and shimmying them back and forth as his arms descended. "After all we've been through, Johney-boy. Misteeer Miracle!!!" he announced, Vegas emcee style. "It's the least I could do." He backed John down the aisle, all the way to the marble altar, sadistically flailing the knife in front of him. John positioned himself behind the altar, and picked up a brass candlestick holder to defend himself.

"Look at me! Ha-ha. I'm a priest!" Smithy shouted, as he grabbed a stole off a hanger and draped it around his neck, then tied it into a knot as if it were a winter scarf. A loud clap of thunder exploded nearby. Smithy didn't seem to notice.

John waited, on his toes, playing defense under the apse of the Church. Waiting. Ready. Waiting for the play to come his way.

"Ahhhaaaaaaaa!!!" roared Lango. He reared back into a wind-up and pitched the switchblade like a fastball, directly at John's heart.

Johney reacted as a catcher would, shielding his body with his glove hand, only he didn't have a glove. The blade punctured his left hand, blood spurting, the knife suspended by flesh, like some kind of gruesome Halloween prop. John fell to his knees in agonizing pain.

Lango put his hands on the edge of the altar and his body into a push-up position. He did three quick ones. On the last push-up he clapped his hands as a Marine would do, pumping himself up. "Ahhhhhh." Smithy took a deep breath of air, refreshed himself with holy water, and leaned over the altar to watch the bloody show. He smiled. "Helleva catch, John. I can see why the Highlanders signed ya." Needless to say, he laughed.

John waited. The smell of urine and rank body odor permeated the air, overpowering even the frankincense. After a while Lango recovered from what he thought was an outstanding joke. He had an idea, yet another way to torment.

"Ya know," Smithy sneered, "I'm not even sure your brother—Natty. Okay, okay! I'm sure." He paused, thinking, considering the very best way to phrase his cruel thought, his next punishment. He pointed his finger in the air, a professor giving a lecture. "No, I'm sure. He definitely wasn't dead when we buried 'im. Tah-ha. Tah-ha. Tah-ha. Tah-ha, ha-ha."

"God damn you."

"God damn me? God damn me? Is that all ya got to say?! Believe me man, if God could damn me, he would've! That little problem I had . . . that wasn't your God. LSD! LSD! LSD—Belladonna, man!! Ya know! I'm tripping! You want something real, I'll give ya real, man!"

"Where did you bury him?"

"Ta-ha! Right." He picked his nose and thought of another idea. "I've changed my mind. I am gonna kill ya. So you can ask 'im yourself." Smithy said in a calm voice as though it were the only civilized thing to do. Then he planted his grimy hands on the altar, braced himself, and with everything he had, pushed the five hundred pounds of marble off its pedestal. A gold chalice hit the floor, followed by the Bible.

John scrambled to get away, and almost did, but he slipped on his own blood as the weight of the stone came crushing down on his already damaged hand. He was trapped. Smithy Lango could hardly contain himself.

"No more baseball for you, Johney. Now you're just like me," he said proudly. He picked up an iron cross. "Of course, after I beat you over the head with this a few dozen times, we'll be different again. You'll be dead."

Lango was right about one thing: John's career as a ballplayer was over. No one would ever see his encore. His arm was broken in three places, the hand crushed, rendering it almost totally paralyzed with only limited movement in his thumb. John didn't whine or beg for his life. He accepted his forthcoming death with courage. That, more than anything, disturbed and enraged Smithy Lango as he slowly approached John with seething contempt. And then it happened.

Ba-baaang!!! Every shutter over every window slammed closed in the blink of an eye. Smithy froze in his tracks and started sweating profusely once again. Thunder sounded in the distance.

"Did you see that?" Lango wanted to scream his question but didn't have the voice. He knew it was real. John didn't answer as Lango sprinted down the center aisle in an effort to get out. He slipped and fell in his urine, immediately got up and ran to the large oak doors. They wouldn't open. He tried all the doors. They wouldn't open. He tried prying them open with the iron cross. They still wouldn't open. The shutters. Locked tight. Prying. Wouldn't open. Prying. Completely secured. Prying, prying, prying, prying. "Fuuuuuuuucckk," screamed Lango.

"That's right, scream," said John in a calm, steady voice. The pain was no longer a factor. His system was shutting down. He was about to pass out.

"Hey! You got a real nice voice. How's about I cut those chords," Lango said like the devil himself.

"Go ahead if you think it's gonna get you out of here," John smiled weakly. The pain was making him faint. He wouldn't have to witness Smithy Lango's blasphemy much longer.

"I'll kill you!!!"

"Fine."

"Tell them to let me out! Tell them! Greco! Tell them!! Or I'll kill you! You tell them, God damn it! Tell 'em! Tell 'em! Taaaaalk!!" He ran through St. Jude's ramming his body against doors and walls and shuttered windows, beating himself to a pulp. Every once in a while he'd beg John, "Tell them, pleaseeee, tell them." He'd say it the way a small child might. Just as quickly his tone was turned inside out. "It's hot . . . it's so hot in here . . . so fucking hot!" Burning with fever, Lango, took off his clothes. Then started to babble: I repent-I repent-I repent-I repent-I repent-I repent-I repent-I repent-I repent-I repent-I repent-I repent-I repent-I repent-I repent-I repent-I repent-I repent-I repent—" but he didn't mean it.

John passed out from the pain. Thunder clapped close by, so close, in fact, lightning might have hit across the street.

SMITHY LANGO DIED that night, beating his head against St. Jude's. He was found the next morning lying in the puddle of water and urine, wearing only a soiled pair of briefs. John was taken to the hospital, forever batting a thousand.

PART II: THE RECOVERY

22

New York City: May, 1965

"AAAAAAH!"

"It's alright. It's okay, baby. I'm here, I'm here . . . Hush, baby. Hush," cooed Sharon in an angelic tone, as she wiped the sweat from her husband's brow. John sat up in their bed breathing heavily, trying his best to shake off the dreams. His arm still throbbed with pain as the doctors said it would. Now the cast was beginning to itch, making his dreams that much more uncomfortable—and relentless.

This was the third week of the dreams and the third week of teams of Highlander doctors who did their best to save John's crushed hand, but I knew it wasn't going to happen. The damage was too extensive—too many hours had passed before surgery, too little blood to keep the nerves alive. One doctor recommended an amputation, but Sharon wouldn't hear of it. The Highlander management wasn't too happy with the idea either. I was relieved to hear that. John said nothing about the discussions. It wasn't until the third week that he even spoke. When he did, all he talked about were the dreams. Sharon would sit on the edge of the bed and listen, sometimes feeding him Faye's chicken soup, but most of the time just stroking his head, asking questions, and praying for their recovery.

"Bad dream?" she said softly.

"Not bad. Disturbing, I guess," he said as he sipped his tea. "Ray Chapman . . . I don't even know what he looks like, but there he was."

John drifted, remembering, feeling the dream.

"Who's Ray Chapman?" she asked.

"Uh, oh, Chapman. Shortstop for Cleveland in 1920," John said. Sharon gave him a puzzled look. "Funny, that date . . . August 16th, 1920 . . . Polo Grounds. I always remember that date and place. The year after the whole White Sox scandal went down." He added as an afterthought.

Sharon pretended to understand. She was glad to hear him talking again. "That's why you remember the date?" she asked, not sure where he was going with his story.

"No." He sounded slightly surprised. The painkillers had him drifting everywhere. Sometimes Sharon wasn't even sure if he knew who she was. He was easily confused with all the friends and family and ballplayers coming by to visit. His first week home he had no idea why fans, police and reporters camped outside the house. Sharon was positive John didn't know who he was talking to most of the time, but he always smiled and extended a warm greeting. He was glad that they had come. "Good to see ya," he'd say, though he wasn't quite sure why or how his arm and hand had gotten into such a state. He did seem to be genuinely happy to be alive and for the first month of his recovery, remembered little or nothing of his life and St. Jude's Church. When all the Highlanders began to show up at his bedside, Sharon had to inform him that he was a ballplayer, which seemed to please him a great deal.

"So, what about the date?" she asked, enticing him to speak with her pretty eyes. Johney was also pleased to find out Sharon was his wife. He later admitted to me that he had no idea who his beautiful nurse was, but was delighted to be married to her just the same. Sharon was almost thankful for his loss of memory. 'It was merciful, very merciful,' she thought. The doctors were confident he'd soon regain his thoughts and history.

"Shock," they said, "just shock from a traumatic experience." In his fifth week he was able to remember again, with the exception of most of the events that happened at St. Jude's. He knew he was injured there and that Smithy Lango died there, but he couldn't recall how.

"John, honey, the date? Ray Chapman?" she asked, reeling in his attention.

"Oh, yeah." He was fighting to regain his train of thought. "Sorry. Ah, well . . . like I said, 1920. The year Babe Ruth was traded from the Red Sox to the Highlanders." Sharon smiled, urging him to continue. "Uh, there was a pitcher named Carl Mays. He came with Ruth in the same trade. Boston was broke; they needed the cash. Can you imagine giving up Babe Ruth for money? And, and this guy Mays, he was a good pitcher, too. Won 26 games that year.”

‘This is so unlike John,’ she thought. He wasn’t big on statistics and history; it sounded as though Natt were speaking.

“So, uh, in my dream it’s August 16th, 1920, and I’m playing in the game, catching for Carl Mays. Babe in right field. It’s a hot muggy day; the temperature on the diamond is close to a hundred. This guy Mays has a reputation for being tough, real tough. He doesn’t like the way Chapman is crowding the plate.”

“Ray Chapman?”

“Uh-huh.”

“Cleveland?”

“Yeah. The count goes full, two outs. I call for an inside fastball. Figure we strike ’im out or jam ’im, but Karl gets this crazy look in his eyes; he’s madder than heck. Rather walk the guy, than give ’im the plate. It’s too late. Here it comes . . . high and hard. Pure heat. The ball gets away from ’im. Karl wanted chin music, ended up skulling ’im. Ray dropped to the lime. Died the next day. I watched the whole thing, Shar . . . it was as though I were there.”

“Honey, it was a dream. He didn’t really die. Nobody dies for baseball. It’s just a game. Right?”

“No, Shar. It’s true. Ray Chapman really did die at the Polo Grounds.”

“Oh,” she said in a surprised hush. “That’s disconcerting.”

“Ya know how dreams are always flip-flopping things around?” She nodded, trying to quell his overly excited tone. “You’re in a clear, clean swimming pool and the next thing ya know—bang—it’s filled with mud!”

‘He’s really getting worked up,’ she thought and, again, it was out of character for him. Sharon hadn’t seen him get this agitated since he told her about Mrs. Kauffman, his fourth grade teacher, the one who put him in the slowest reading group. John knew he wasn’t a good reader. What he detested was the color-coded books from blue to red to green to yellow. “Yellow meant you were slow,” he would say, the humiliation registering in his soft-spoken voice.

“Where was I?” he asked, shyly.

“Flip-flopping,” she whispered into his ear.

“Right . . . ah. Yeah, well, that’s what happened.”

“What happened?”

“When the ball hit Ray Chapman, it was me. I became him.” Sharon searched for something to say. It was easy enough to see the parallel between the two innocent men, the fragile balance they both had faced between life and death and hopefully rebirth. Yet, she couldn't be sure what exactly he was trying to say. Did he even know? There wasn't the slightest bit of anger in his voice, though sometimes she wished there would be. His lack of angst often made her feel foolish for her own temper. She, the diplomat, felt out of control compared to him. Yet she loved and admired him for it. His gift of calm didn't come from suppression or weakness or any form of superiority or guilt. He told his dream with only a sense of fascination and wonder, knowing fully the consequences of his accident and the condition of his life.

23

New York City: Spring, 1967

"I'LL GET IT!" called Faye from the kitchen. Charlie had just left for school. She was about to do the breakfast dishes, then maybe have another cup of coffee and read her book.

'Things have become a bit more sane in the past year,' she thought. The idea gave her great comfort as she ran to answer the front door. This was Faye's morning routine, ever since she sold the house on 12th Street and moved in with John and Sharon. She peeked through the curtain. There was Detective Kerrins, looking not as self-confident as she had remembered him. He gave her an awkward smile and didn't seem to know what to do with his hands. Faye opened the door.

"Hi . . . ah, Mrs. Greco." He tipped his hat.

"Detective Kerrins?" She was surprised to see him again. When the Grand Jury decided not to indict, she figured that would be the end of it. 'It's been well over a year,' she thought.

"Do you need to speak to John?"

"No." 'What am I doing here?' he asked himself. "Oh, we're still keeping an eye on Jonelli. I know he's guilty. But—"

"Yes."

"Well, I was wondering if I could have a word with you? It's not business. No. Nothing like that . . . it's just—"

"Would you like some coffee? I just made it."

"Sure, that'd be great," said Kerrins. He stood on the stoop, nodding his head up and down while shuffling his hands in and out of his pockets.

"Come in," she said, flipping her long reddish-brown mane of hair off her face. He entered. Faye knew what he wanted. He could barely keep his eyes off her throughout the hearing. Kerrins followed her through the entry hall, past the living room, the main staircase, and into the kitchen. He watched her bottom sway from side to side in a pair of threadbare blue-jeans.

"Please, have a seat."

Kerrins sat down at the small round wooden table. 'Nice table,' he thought, did a little woodworking himself. 'Solid oak, king's crown molding inlaid around the width, beautiful finish, same color as her hair.'

"Sugar?"

"Nah, I like it." He patted his belly. "Trying to lose some weight." Faye smiled and served the coffee. Then she sat down across from him. He took a quick sip while he tried to figure out just what he was doing there. Detective Kerrins was far from a ladies' man. He wasn't what he considered to be a charmer. 'Chitchat. Hate it.' Kerrins saw himself as average, normal, and decent in mind and body. As he put it, "a ten on a scale of one to twenty." He thought most women found him boring, but the truth was, Kerrins had buried himself in his work for years. Now he was thirty-seven, lonely, and inspired by Faye Greco's beauty, passion, bravery, and beauty. 'She made a damn good witness,' he thought.

"Me, too," said Faye. Kerrins looked confused. "Weight. I need to—"

"What?! You're perfect," he interrupted. She blushed. Kerrins realized that he might be coming on a little strong. "Well. I mean, ya look great!" He wasn't sure if that was any better.

"Thanks," she replied, still blushing.

"Hey, this is a veeery nice table." He ran his hand across it and thought how stupid "veeery nice" must have sounded to her. He could see it in her eyes. "I do a little woodworking." 'Brilliant,' he thought. 'Every time I open my mouth I step in it.' Detective Kerrins tended to be hard on himself when it came to his romantic interest.

"Yes. Natt made it for me." 'I can't believe I just said that!' she scolded herself.

"Oh." 'Oh!? Good comeback, Kerrins.' "Hey, maybe this isn't a good time," he said.

"No!" She wanted to die. 'I sound so desperate!' "I mean—" She turned the radio on, attempting to ease the tension. . . . *The Beatles: I Wanna Hold Your Hand* . . . She spun the dial. 'Too obvious.' . . . *Percy Sledge: When a Man Loves a Woman* . . . 'Waaay too obvious.' She spun it again. . . . *Ottis Redding: Sitting on the Dock of the Bay* . . . 'Good. Love this song.'

"I mean— I was hoping . . . you would call or or drop by." She sipped her coffee.

"Yeah? Huh." He leaned across the table. "Can I be straight with you?"

"I wish you would."

"Good. I'm not much good at small talk. That's why I didn't call. I'm real bad on the phone." He put his hands in his pockets. "Listen. I thought maybe we might go out. Aaaah, you know, dinner or something," he said, snapping his hands out of his pockets as though something had bit him. "If you're not interested . . . or," he whispered, "it's too soon. I'll understand, no hard feelings."

She smiled, "That would be nice, Detective Kerrins."

"Brian. You can call me Brian." He was so happy he wanted to jump out of his seat. He couldn't wait to tell Detective Weinman.

"Brian. Please, call me Faye."

"Faye, I thought—well, not really knowing about Mr. Greco—"

"Brian, my husband has been dead for over two years." The detective in him started to come out. He couldn't help it. He wanted to start clean.

"Faye, there's always a possibility. No body was ever found—"

"John said he was dead." She crossed her arms and began to tear up.

'Great! You're gonna blow the whole thing! Asshole!' He wanted to kick himself, but he couldn't stop being a detective. "On the word of Smithy Lango?"

"Look, it's more than that! Do you want to go out with me or not?"

"Yes, I'm sorry. Really! Ah, ah, that's what I'm here for. I want to go out with you. I just didn't want to rush ya. That's all."

"Faye . . . Faye? . . . I thought I heard voices. Oh, Detective Kerrins," said Sharon, surprised to see Kerrins, then pleasantly surprised to see them together.

"Mrs. Greco," the detective said politely, as he rose from his chair.

"Oh, don't mind me. Just getting some more coffee." She poured herself a cup, lifted the milk off the table, poured it, put it back, smiled at Faye and said, "Bye."

"I guess John's gonna hear all about this." He surprised himself by speaking his thoughts.

"He likes you. Thought you and Detective Weinman did—"

"Hey, I don't know why, Lango—"

"Lango had the backing to get lost. We all knew that . . . just couldn't prove it. Besides, he's dead." Kerrins knew she was right, but he couldn't help feeling guilty.

"I'm not here to get you upset. Maybe this is a crazy idea, being so close to this case and everything." He regretted saying those words the instant they came out of his mouth. Mr. Kerrins opted for damage control. Before she could respond, he hit himself on the head with the palm of his hand and blurted out, "What am I doing?! I better get out of here before I screw everything up." She laughed. 'Thank God she laughed!' Faye brushed her hand over his. He couldn't tell if it was an accident or not.

"Don't go. Finish your coffee."

"I should maybe keep my month shut. I've been thinking, ya know . . . when it might be a good time . . . to approach you, but I just couldn't figure it. 'Til today. I'm driving by—there's a parking space right in front of your house. Boy, haven't seen that in awhile. And somethin's telling me, 'Now . . . now is the time.'" She smiled again. 'Damn.' He liked seeing her smile. He'd never really seen it before today, never heard her laugh either. 'She's magical, enchanting even,' he gushed.

"Well, I'm glad you did," she said, flattered. Kerrins drank his coffee slowly. He didn't want to leave. "I thought—" She shook her head from side to side, trying to think of the best way to phrase her interest. "I thought—"

"Yes?" He knew this was going to be good, remembering the feeling of receiving a note in fifth grade. Who's it from? What's it say? His heart was pounding. It could be intercepted. Will the teacher read it? 'Christ! Has it been that long?! I'm a friggin' detective for God's sake!' "You thought what?" he asked calmly with an air of sophistication, as he tried his best to mask his childlike excitement.

"I thought there might be an attraction," said Faye.

'Yesssss,' he thought, holding on the "s" like a trophy. He was beginning to enjoy this game. "Can I ask you a personal question?" he said. A funny sensation hit him. The flirtation was becoming fun.

"Maybe . . . maybe not," she answered, pleased by the dance. He looked deep into her eyes.

"Do you really like baseball?" He was serious. She laughed and laughed and so did he, but when they regained their composure, she could see that he was waiting for his answer. She took a deep breath, he noticed how her breasts rose to the occasion.

"Brian, I love baseball." And she was serious.

He repressed his elation and said, "I thought so."

"Yourself? Baseball?" She could feel the intensity of his gaze. His eyes walked all over her as if he couldn't decide which was the best part. Her eyes darted about the kitchen. She could feel it coming again. She was about to blush.

"I've been looking all my life for a woman who loves baseball." 'Too much! Way too much. You don't even know her!' Yet, he felt as though he did.

"There are plenty of women who love baseball, Detective Kerrins," she replied coyly.

"Yeah? I never meet 'em."

"You just did. More coffee?"

"Thanks." Faye brought the steaming pot to the table and poured for him. The smell of coffee sobered Kerrins, breaking his schoolboy mood. He could view the front door from where he sat and couldn't help but become a detective again.

"Faye? What does he do?" Faye knew instantly who *he* was.

"Are you sure you're not playing detective today?" she asked. But then that was the question most asked of her by everyone. The better question would be, "What do they do?" The doorbell rang. She was relieved to get a break in the action.

"Excuse me," she said to Kerrins. "I'll get it!" Faye called up the stairs. She returned a minute later carrying three bundles of letters.

'Must be two hundred letters there,' thought Kerrins. "Wow," he said, "you get that kind of mail every day?"

"Except Monday, we get a small bag on Monday. Look." She fanned the letters in front of him, then covered the entire table with them. "From all over the country. Look at these." As she pulled from the pile, "Canada, Italy, Brazil, Cuba, Venezuela, Japan—"

"Here's one from Greenland. Holy shh-cow, Algeria!"

Faye watched as he dipped into the letters with the same joy she had when they'd first started to arrive. 'It was nice to share them with him,' she thought.

"This is unbelievable! Every day? What are they? You must have—"

"Close to two hundred thousand. At the beginning, mostly sympathy and get well cards. Then requests for autographed pictures. We don't do them anymore. The Highlanders handle it now. They come over once a month with the photos. He spends an entire day signing them. They mail them out. The autograph mail goes directly to the stadium. This," she ran her hand through the letters, "this is personal."

"His friends?"

"No. Well, sort of. They're people who want to tell him their story. They feel compelled to write him. You wouldn't believe the amount of letters and cards that start, 'I've never written a letter in my life, but I had to write to you.'"

"No kidding."

"Yes. No kidding."

"What kind of stuff?" He was fascinated.

"Well, mostly stories about their families—children, parents, friends; that sort of thing. Some are about sickness and miraculous recoveries . . . ummm, spirits, premonitions, God. Those can be very strange. Some are just funny stories. I suppose most are about their dreams, and how John inspired them to believe in them again."

"Boy-oh-boy, that's too much—really something. Tell me one. The first one to pop into your head."

"Okay, aaah. Okay. A woman wrote John about her sister and brother-in-law. Uhhhhh. They had a large family, lots of kids. The brother-in-law was a hard worker. But with the size of their family and all, it was all he could do to make ends meet. Anyway, the guy dies of a heart attack; he's only in his early forties. Everybody's grieving, 'He's so young.' 'What's gonna happen to the family?' 'All the bills.' So on and so on. Sooo, it turns out that the brother-in-law actually had a written will."

"This is where it gets good. Right?"

"Right. The will says pretty much what you'd expect. The wife gets everything."

"But?" Kerrins chimed in.

"But a beautifully framed family portrait that hung in the living room."

"Uh-huh."

"He wants to be buried with it."

"Uh-huh."

"So, they all think, 'Isn't that sweet' . . . the kind, loving provider, good husband and father wants to be buried with a picture of his family over his heart. On the day of his wake they open the casket and hang the portrait above him. The whole family is there. The widow is heartbroken. So many people come to the wake, an uncle tries to make room by rearranging the flowers around the casket."

"It's always the uncles that cause all the trouble," said Kerrins, facetiously.

"Listen to this!" Faye patted Kerrins' hand, demanding his full attention. She received it. "The uncle bumps the casket while trying to make room. The portrait drops off its hook, hits the deceased on the chest, falls to the floor, breaks the frame and out spills twenty-nine thousand dollars in hundred dollar bills for all to see!!"

"Noooo! He wanted to be buried with it?! That's rich!" laughed Kerrins.

"Yes! Thought he might need it, I suppose! Wait, wait! There's more!" Faye grabbed his arm. They had one of those awkward, but meaningful, moments, which I'm sure they both enjoyed.

"Well . . . uh." Faye continued slowly. "The widow puts two and two together, runs up to the casket, and starts beating him on the chest, yelling, 'You bastard! You bastard, you!'" Kerrins and Faye laughed as though they were best friends swapping secrets. "Then, then to top it off, she's on her hands and knees gathering the money. The funeral director is trying to get her up, to instill some decorum back into the proceedings. She shouts at him, 'This wake is over! Make sure he gets his picture!'"

"Oh, that's good! Really good!" Kerrins laughed.

"Yeah, one of my favorites," said Faye, trying to catch her breath.

"I can't remember the last time I laughed that hard." Their eyes met for just a moment. Kerrins cleared his throat, adjusted his collar. "So, why?"

"Why?"

"Yeah, why did this woman send John the story?"

"Oh, I think a couple of reasons." Faye's mood changed from joyous, tearful laughter to a reflective, almost melancholy, sobriety. "I think she knew how tragic and, maybe after some time, how funny it was. And I think she thinks it's a miracle. I don't think it was her sister-in-law either; I think it was her. That's an easy one. Some cards come in with only a single thought or word printed. We get thousands of cards that just say, 'LOVE .' They're nice; people sending love through the mail. I like that. A card came in the other day; all it said was, 'You'll get your chance.'" She made a silly face. "Now, whats that mean?" Faye brought the empty cups to the sink, while Kerrins considered her question. "A card came in the first week from a young mother in North Carolina. She had lost her only son in a car accident. She writes John twice a year—on Christmas and on the anniversary of her boy's death. The woman thanks him for giving her the will to live," said Faye, as the tap water flowed over her hands.

"Boy, that's a lot of responsibility."

"People have a feeling about John. There's a lot going on out there. I know that." Kerrins could have easily agreed with her, but he didn't want to interrupt; he wanted to hear her speak. "You asked me what they do. That's what they do," she said, pointing to the mail. "They answer the cards and letters. Well, most of the time. They do charity work, too. But mostly we're just together, healing ourselves." She gazed out the kitchen window. A squirrel climbed the red maple out back. She knew Kerrins was looking at her. It made her feel good.

"Faye . . . I was thinking maybe we could have dinner. Tomorrow night?"

She turned to face him, smiled, and said, "Yes, tomorrow would be nice, Brian."

"Good," said the detective.

24

April 9, 1967

Dear Mr. Greco,
My name is Angela Wheeler. I live just a block away from
Ruth Stadium in the Bronx with my boy Jason. I'm writing
you to request an autograph, but I would have to meet with
you to do it. The autograph is for Jason on his seventeenth
birthday in two weeks. I have the ball you hit outside of the
stadium and would like for you to sign it. It would mean so
much to him! I hope you and your family are well. If this
is possible, please call me, 455-9835. If you don't call, I
will understand and will not bother you again. Thank you.

Sincerely,
Angela Wheeler

P.S. Call after 9:30 pm. Jason will be asleep. It's a surprise!

"You think she really has it?" asked Sharon, after reading Angela Wheeler's request.

"Yeah, I think so. This letter isn't like the others." John read it and reread it. He couldn't help but feel there was something more than just these few simple lines. It made him feel curious and excited at the same time. 'She has the ball!' he thought, anxious to see it. The funny thing was, finding the ball never concerned John before, not even when he had received other letters from people who claimed to have it in their possession.

"Are you gonna call?" asked Sharon.

"I think so. Tomorrow all right with you?"

"To call?"

"No. I'm calling tonight. To have her over, I mean."

"Sure," Sharon said mechanically, as she sorted the responses by zip code. "By the way, I think there's something happening in our kitchen," she whispered in a mischievous, sexy tone of voice. John immediately filed Angela Wheeler's letter in the today pile on top of his desk, then looked toward Sharon with great interest. He hadn't seen that romantic glint in her eyes in quite some time. It was a welcomed sight.

"Oh, yeah. . . . What?" His arm wrapped around her waist, pulling her closer.

"Know what?" she murmured with an air of intrigue. "Now don't embarrass her, but Faye and Detective Kerrins are having coffee in the kitchen." She raised her brow knowingly.

"No kidding. And they're . . . uuhhhhh . . . happy," he smiled.

"Looked more like—"

"Very happy?" he interrupted. She kissed him on the neck and allowed her head to rest on his shoulder.

"More like . . . in lust."

"Oh? Well, sometimes lust can be—" She put her finger to his lips, slid her arms around his waist, and guided him to their bed. End of conversation.

ANGELA WHEELER APPROACHED the front steps of the Greco house with great caution as though having to cross a rickety bridge over a hundred-foot drop. She rang the bell and pressed her husband's St. Anthony medal to her lips. 'This was the doorway,' she thought. It was the doorway she had read about in all the papers where the little girl was killed. 'How could they pass through it every day?' she wondered. Then she noticed the shutters. A small heart was cut into the center of each panel. She felt better. Sharon answered the door.

"Hello, Mrs. Greco?" Angela Wheeler asked politely.

Angela was a dark skinned black woman in her midthirties. Her hair was pushed back in a bun. She wore a pink cardigan, a light blue maid's uniform, and carried a large carpetbagger's bag. Angela Wheeler wasn't particularly attractive, too many hard years, long hours, and sleepless nights. Her husband, a white man, died in the Korean War some fourteen years ago. She loved him very much, but had to admit an integrated marriage in 1949 was "progressive and taxing." That was as tough as she got on the subject or any other subject. "Taxing," was what she'd say, often followed by a burst of laughter. Angela found that the word so understated most situations, it amused her and made her feel better almost immediately. She'd been using it ever since the day she heard Betty Davis say it in a movie. Betty was in some sort of crisis situation that she found "taxing." It made Angela laugh, always did. Mrs. Wheeler refused to dwell on anything, feel sorry for herself, or victimized—only taxed. Besides, Jason was the one who was really burdened, she reasoned. He was taxed by black and white, the strong, weak, and so called normal. "He has'ta pay dues and taxes to everybody, just to breathe," she'd say. "They're just not ready for us. We's way ahead of our time. Taxed to the max!" Angela would proclaim, and a smile would rise from the depths of her soul. Her love was not about to let herself or her boy down. They had a role to play: the middle-aged black woman and her half white Down's syndrome son. "We are the teachers," she'd say. "Teaching love and respect—or die trying. Otherwise you just die." I had to admire her strength in the face of such overwhelming odds.

"Mrs. Wheeler?" asked Sharon.

"Yes-yes, my Lord! Call me Angela! I always get nervous when folks call me Mrs. Wheeler. They either want money or got bad news," she joked. Sharon liked her.

"Fine," she laughed. "I'm Sharon. Please, come in."

"Oh, Sharon, what a lovely home you and Mr. Greco have," declared Angela, as she took a seat on the living room couch.

"John," corrected Sharon. They laughed. "He should be down in just a second."

"I don't wanna take much of your time. I'm on my lunch break so I haven't got much anyway." She fumbled through her rather large bag as she looked for the ball. "This is so nice of you to have me over," she smiled, then resumed her search. John could be heard coming down the steps. Angela's search intensified. Her bag was obviously very full.

"Angela Wheeler. This is my husband, John Greco." They exchanged greetings. Sharon served coffee.

"Well, I won't pretend to know anything about baseball," Angela said, raising her right hand as if she were about to take an oath. "But my boy, Jason. He's just crazy for it! And . . . Mr. Greco—"

"John."

"John, you're by far his favorite player," Angela complimented. He smiled politely. "Yes, indeed," she continued, "Jason loves the Highlanders. I think because when he was little I'd tell him how I was born in the Bronx right next to that big old ballpark. I'd tell 'im how ya could hear the people applauding from my apartment window. He always liked that idea. He was so excited when he got your baseball card. Ya know why?!"

"No. Why?" asked Sharon. John kept smiling. 'Angela Wheeler has plenty of personality,' he thought.

"Because Jason and John were both born on April 21st in Newark, New Jersey." Angela spooned three sugars into her black coffee, seemingly content just to pass this information along.

"Really, wow. How old is he?" asked John, ready to show some enthusiasm.

"Seventeen, in a week."

"Teenager. I'll bet he's a handful," said Sharon.

"Oh, no! He's a good boy," Angela said, as she accidentally brushed John's crippled hand in her overly excited state. She often became excitable when she spoke of Jason. Tears clouded her vision. "Please, John, may I see?" she said, referring to his hand. Drawing attention to it took John by surprise. 'Nobody had ever been that direct about it,' he thought. 'Nobody who wasn't a doctor.' People avoided looking at it and, especially, talking about it. In a way her openness made him feel more at ease. Even his friends and teammates couldn't handle the subject, except Dillon Southwood. John extended his hand to her. Angela took it between her own hands and pressed them together. "I understand why he cried for weeks," she whispered. "Jason. Jason understands, feels things, more than most. Don't you worry, John. There's still life in this hand." She let go. He wasn't sure what to do. 'Thank her?' he wondered.

"What school does he go to?" asked John, changing the subject.

"Oh, John, he don't go to school. Jason needs special education. He has a tutor." She started to dig through her bag again.

"Here it is! Jason calls it 'the miracle baseball.' My goodness, you don't know what I had to go through to get this out of the apartment!" She handed the ball to John. The moment he touched it he felt a slight electrical shock.

"Shocked ya, didn't it! Right?" exclaimed Angela, laughing.

"Yeah, how did you know?!" He looked over to Sharon, confirming that it did in fact shock him.

"I rubbed it on my nylons. Love doing that! Really gets folks going," she joked, then proceeded to tell the story of how she got the ball. " . . . And one of those vendor men he kept yelling, 'Two hundred! I'll give you three hundred!!!!' I was tempted. Three hundred and fifty dollars for a baseball! But I couldn't do it. I knew how much Jason would love it. 'The best gift ever!' That's what he always sez. The best gift ever," she murmured, shaking her head slowly in momentary amazement. "'Where did you get it?' he shouted. I thought he was gonna faint! 'The stadium, where else,' I said."

"Does he go to a lot of games?" asked Sharon.

"Oh, no. Never been to one. I can't get 'im to go. He's afraid; the other kids they taunt and tease 'im. That's why he don't go to school no more. No." She shook her head. "Won't go. . . . But he loves Phil Rizzuto. That's how he heard about the ball you hit, John. He was so excited. The boy was practically bouncing off the walls when I got home, yelling 'Hoooooly cow!' over and over again. You'd think we'd just won the numbers! Haa-ha! He listens on the radio in his bedroom." Angela leaned over the coffee table as if she were about to tell a secret. "He wants a TV," she whispered. "Well, let me tell you when I showed him the ball he forgot all about that TV. I said there's a man at the stadium who'll give us four hundred dollars for it. You can have the TV. Your decision. You know what he said? He said, 'No way! This is better than a thousand televisions.'"

"He sounds very smart. Is he a genius?" asked John, seriously.

"Ooooh, ha-ha! No, John. My boy is retarded. But he has flashes of brilliance. Ha-haa! I'll never forget giving him that ball. I was about to pull that big white splinter out of it. Well! I thought he was gonna die. 'Mom! What are ya doing!' You'd think I was hurting him or somethin'. First time I ever saw him completely white. My husband, he was a white man. Died in Korea—land mine. Private Jason Wheeler Sr., a good man," she said without missing a beat. "Do you know what Jason . . . my boy, said?" she asked, full of motherly pride. Then she sipped her coffee while she waited for their response.

"No?" they said simultaneously, completely mesmerized.

"He said, 'That's how they'll know.' I said, 'Know what?' He said, 'They'll know it's *the* ball.' Imagine that! Wood from Ruth Stadium. Proof! I never knew my boy could understand anything like 'proof.' Oh, he understands other things, but proof! It was all I could do to teach him a few times tables. Proof?!" she marveled. "I was so proud. I knew I had to bring that ball home. No two ways about it. No, uh, five hundred dollars neither!" she laughed. "Nobody ever gives him enough credit. Not even me. Ya know? They tell ya he's retarded, and they're amazed if he can walk," she said, shaking her head at the unjust shame of it all. "Ya know what he sez about you, John?" John could only shake his head; her love for her child made him think of Maya, of what could have been. Sharon looked sad. She was feeling it, too. "He sez, you're running the bases that come after home. Now, I don't know what that means exactly, but—I don't know—sounds right. Doesn't it? He's got something. Right?"

"He may be onto something, Angela. I don't know," replied John, as he looked intensely at the ball. 'Looks new,' he thought, 'with only the dirt they use to rough 'em up.' Probably the only hit on this ball was his own.

"Can I see it?" asked Sharon, meaning the ball.

"Sure." He handed it to her.

"I know what this looks like!" Sharon said. She held it up to the window where the afternoon sunshine streamed in, casting a long shadow on the floor. "Hah, it looks like the baseball version of the sword in the stone—Excalibur."

"Good thing I didn't pull it out," stated Angela. "I would have been Queen of Baseball." They laughed. "I don't think I could deal with that, honey! I got me a kid to raise!" Angela glanced at her watch. "Oh, boy-o-boy, I'm late. Gotta work a double, too." She stood up to get going. "I almost forgot what I come for. The ball."

"Would you—" Sharon handed the ball to Angela who handed it to John.

"I've got an idea. Bring Jason over on our birthday. We'll have a party. I'll sign it then. That'd be a good surprise. Right?" The idea of having a party suddenly sounded appealing. He thought of Natt. Natt and party were synonymous to John. It would be their first, a coming out party of sorts. Then he thought maybe Sharon wouldn't approve. Next week was the second anniversary of Maya's death.

"Yes, please, Angela. We'd love to meet Jason," she said, putting his worries to rest.

"I didn't come here to put you good people out. Besides, we always go to Chinatown on our birthdays, but maybe we could stop by after dinner. Say, eight o'clock?" asked Angela, knowing how much it would mean to her boy.

"It's settled then," said John. He felt good knowing how pleased the boy would be. But it wasn't just for Jason. The idea of bringing their friends together for a party seemed to give both Sharon and Johney a new lease on life.

"God bless you both," praised Angela, and for a moment it looked as though she might cry, but she was too overjoyed for that. She had made something happen. 'When things are getting you down, you gotta go out and make something good happen,' she remembered her man advocating. He was right. Angela thanked him for their son and missed him deeply.

"Like the hearts in your shutters!" called Angela from the sidewalk.

'Shutters.' The image struck John in a powerful way. The word opened a door to an empty room that gave Johney an unsettling, vague feeling.

Sharon and John waved good-bye, framed in the very doorway where their daughter's life had been taken. Angela thought, 'It seems somehow right and brave of them to want to be within it—forgiving.'

25

"WAITER, WE NEED another bottle of wine. This one's empty," said Kerrins, as he handed the drained bottle to the waiter.

"So, that was a very sad childhood you had," he said, not in a mean way—nor sincere, nor pitying, nor compassionate, nor condescending—not in any way. That's why it sounded so hysterically funny. Faye couldn't stop laughing, which made Kerrins laugh. It didn't matter that they were making fools of themselves. Nobody would notice at Mario's restaurant.

Mario's had all the classic elements of romance: music, candlelight, wood floors, checkered tablecloths, rich Northern Italian food. Something ineffable about Mario's changed people's perceptions. A lawlessness hung in the air, as though it weren't a restaurant at all but its own country. 'Must be in the food,' Kerrins figured. The "normal" became loud and silly and Italian at Mario's. Mario himself wanted a sweet, quiet place, but then he opted to have fun and be rich. It wasn't a hard choice for Mario. He believed in destiny and was willing to follow what he perceived to be his life's path.

Kerrins told Faye the story of how he once saw a man at Mario's get on top of and walk down a long table of twenty, wielding a whip, kicking over glasses, and acting as if he were a cowboy.

"It was the end of the night. The guy was real drunk. The management hardly noticed. Like it happened all the time! What a mess!" Faye giggled and squeezed his hand, creating one of many awkward, but pleasant, moments that passed between them. The waiter brought more wine.

"Think we can survive another date?" asked Kerrins.

"Why wouldn't we?" she replied with concern. Kerrins held up the bottle of wine and poured.

"Oh, just talking. We've been out every night for over a week now. I keep asking myself when is it gonna end. Uh, not that I want it to! I guess I just expect it to. Ya know, I'm having a really good time. Best time I've ever had."

She smiled and took his hand. "Me, too," she said softly.

Kerrins patted her hand in a fatherly way, an act he instantly regretted. 'Moron!' That's what Max would've said. Kerrins could just picture Weinman badgering him. 'Kiss her!' Max would have shouted. 'Kiss her! She wants to be kissed!' Kerrins tried to block the thought; he reached for a bread stick . . . then another. They both felt uncomfortably close to talking about sex, a topic each had avoided for their own reasons. Kerrins was afraid to rush her. He didn't want to embarrass himself. He was also afraid of the "big nonperformance," as he put it. She was driving him crazy: her hair, the perfume, the sexy black dress with the spaghetti straps . . . the shoulders, beautiful bare shoulders that led down to perfect breasts, the size of baseballs. 'Baseball breasts,' he thought. 'Strong. Firm. Just enough. Baseball breasts,' he kept thinking, completely overstimulated. That asinine phrase floated in his head, and he couldn't get rid of it. He could easily picture the obsessed grin that was growing across his face. It very much concerned him. 'Semen poisoning! Baseball breasts! Prematureeee—One, two, three. You're out!'

'The first date was tough,' thought Faye. Her words seemed to have had a seven second delay, in case they needed editing. Her conversation had been stiff, way too cautious. Ten years had past since her last official date. And now, even after five dates with Brian, she still worried if her dress was right, her hair, her attitude . . . her shoes! Was it all too much? Too little? Too sexy? Not sexy enough? By the end of their third date she had begun to wonder why he hadn't kissed her yet. 'Will he ever kiss me? It's the dress. He doesn't like my dress, my perfume, my lipstick,' at least that's what she thought. But her seven second delay continued to keep her upbeat.

The power of Mario's was beginning to get the best of him. Kerrins had an incredible urge to clear the table with one swing of his arm and make love to her right then and there. Instead, he changed the subject before there was any talk of it.

"Season starts soon," he said. She looked at him as if he were speaking a foreign language. He tried not to stare at her breasts and found himself not looking at her at all. She thought maybe he didn't find her attractive. They sat in awkward silence, looking mighty suspicious in Mario's.

Faye's tongue slowly licked her upper lip, a nervous habit. She tried desperately to remember some of the tips in that article about feeling beautiful and sexy. 'Feel good about yourself, the way a woman should.' That was the only "damn" line she could remember. Again, her tongue wandered across her lips from one side to the other and then back again. Kerrins fought off an erection by recalling the excruciating pain of something he referred to as "blueballs."

'He looks so uncomfortable,' she thought. 'It's me. I'm turning him off. Damn it! I don't remember how to date!' "Can't do worse than last year," she replied, still talking baseball.

Kerrins nodded his head and tried to adjust his trousers at the same time. "Sixth place. Who would have believed it? They need John," he stated as though he cared, and he did, but at the time he didn't.

She slipped off her heels and, throwing caution to the wind, hooked her foot around his calf. Touchy-feelie began. Kerrins acted as though nothing were happening, while he thought about a PBS special on brain surgery. Discreetly, he took her hand. "They need more pitching," he said. Breathlessly, she agreed.

"Lowest finish since 1925," she said seductively. 'What's wrong with me?!' She squirmed in her seat. 'Oh, no. My nipples are hard.' Kerrins tried not to stare at them. Faye casually slid her body down the chair, pretending to get comfortable, wondering if he noticed how excited she had become.

'Baseball breast nipples,' he thought.

She sipped from her wine glass and rubbed his calf with her foot in an effort to distract him. Kerrins found her touch wonderfully painful. Faye's slide only succeeded in hiking her cocktail dress up to midthigh level, revealing a lovely pair of legs. Detective Kerrins was better off without a good view; he had enough battles to fight.

"More wine?" he asked.

"Yes, please."

"Best Chianti in the city!" he proclaimed. She smiled. "To love," he toasted, laying all his cards on the table.

"To love," she replied. They both turned a bit red.

"Faye?"

"Yes?"

"I've been thinking."

"Yes."

"Dessert . . . at my place?"

"Let's go," she said with a sense of urgency. Her chair practically kicked out from under her.

The detective threw a wad of bills on the table, adjusted his trousers, and happily followed her out.

Several regular patrons applauded.

26

"LET HIM PLAY? I couldn't believe he'd show up! Didn't let on though." Southwood took a big gulp of scotch, sucked in some air, and puffed out his chest. Detective Kerrins knew he was going to get the scoop now. He lit another cigarette and waited for the details.

"We got this public relations guy, Bill Singer. Sleazeball. He goes nuts when he sees John walk into the locker room. Ya know, thinks it's bad for business. Well, I love jamming a stick up his butt." Kerrins nodded accordingly. "He sez, 'You're not gonna play him!?' Like I'm some kind of idiot if I do— Hi, Marla. Yes, good to see you, too," Southwood called. Marla blew him a kiss. "Cliff Oakes' wife. Real looker! Ain't she?"

Kerrins caught Faye's eye. She was talking with Bob and Rachel Goldstein and Muddy Ames. 'Damn, they're all here,' he thought, as he gave Faye a wink.

"I saw that. Heard the rumors about you two," joked Southwood with a note of approval.

"Yeah, I'm pretty lucky. So, you weren't gonna play him?" questioned Kerrins, picking up their conversation, trying to pump Southwood for his perspective of *the* game. Kerrins was amazed to be talking one-on-one with the skipper himself and determined to make the best of it. In a room full of people, he didn't have to be a detective to know that this situation wasn't going to last long. He took a drag from his cigarette and prepared to listen attentively.

"I didn't say anything. I wasn't sure what I would do. But I liked pushing Singer's buttons, so I let him believe whatever he wanted."

"What made ya go with him?"

"Hey, he was one of my best players. And he really wanted to play. I didn't believe any of those bullshit rumors floating around. I know this man! Hell, if he wasn't playing well, I could've taken 'im out. No big deal. Hello, Judy!" Judy Kirkpatrick kissed Dillon on the cheek. They exchanged pleasantries, and she drifted to another group of players and wives. "Fine gal! Judy. Mike Kirkpatrick's wife."

Kerrins didn't have to start Southwood up again. He launched right back into the point of his story, the part about managing, the part he felt strongly about, really believed in, lived his life by. He was getting very nostalgic and quite drunk. "Ya want people who really wanna play. Oh, everyone sez they wanna play. But half the time they're thinking 'bout something else! Especially the rookies. Ya know, most these kids never had two pennies to rub together in their lives. They're thinking, constantly thinking. They think about hitting, houses, fielding, family, RBI's, girlfriends, dancing, dinner, homers, press, babies, bats, strikes, balls, and the best of 'em are thinking the pitch, the pitch! What's the pitch!? Every damn thing under the sun! See what I mean?!"

"Uh-huh," replied Kerrins. 'What a character,' he thought.

"John Greco, he wasn't thinking. How could he be thinking? Impossible! On automatic, had something to prove, and he did. Didn't he? Huh? But it was more than that. I saw a man who needed to play, as though his life depended on it!"

"Yeah, but you must've considered pulling 'im? I heard he was doing some real strange stuff. I don't mean the writing. I heard he was talking to himself—a lot—hanging around second and talking to himself, even talking to people in the stands. Didn't you think he was losing it?" Kerrins was having fun. This was a boyhood dream, talking baseball with the manager of the New York Highlanders. He wished his dad were here. He wished his dad were alive. He wished Weinman could see this, and he washed his wishes down with a large gulp of beer.

"If managers benched guys for talking to themselves, baseball would be out of business," Southwood laughed. "The people in the stands . . . See those three guys by the buffet table?" He pointed to Tommy, Pete, and me, then waved when he caught my eye. "How's it going, George?" called the manager. I smiled politely as Tommy and Pete grinned, impressed by Dillon's recognition of me.

"Yeah. Tommy, the bar owner, he testified for the grand jury," said Kerrins.

"Yeah, and Little George and Pete, his brother's best friends. John was looking for his brother. Natt always came on Opening Day." Dillon finished his drink and crunched on a scotch flavored ice cube. "I'm nct so sure he wasn't there."

"What?"

"Oh, it's nothing."

"C'mon. I heard what you said. What do ya mean?" Kerrins asked, trying not to sound too pushy. Southwood was a master at evading tough questions when he wanted. Kerrins' only advantage was that Dillon had had a few. He could be very talkative after several scotches . . . and a loss.

The '67 season was only a week old, and the Highlanders already had lost three straight, including today's game, a real heartbreaker on a beautiful Saturday afternoon. They lost to Washington in the ninth: 3 to 2.

'Good weather for John's birthday cookout though,' thought Kerrins. Most of the guys, like Dillon, came over right after the game. Kerrins figured Southwood to be on his fourth or fifth scotch by now. His nose was turning red.

"Sometimes you have to check your sanity meter," Southwood said, as he stared off. "I'd be lying if I told you that I didn't check it every day since that game."

Kerrins gave him a funny look and thought, 'What the hell does that mean?'

But Southwood kept talking, "People may forget, but I replay it every day. It still gives me a chill. Wasn't like any other day I've ever spent on this planet." Southwood sighed, put his hands in his pockets, considered another drink, and smiled a "hello" in Janet Greene's direction.

"C'mon. It was just a game. Right?"

"Most of the time."

"What are you saying?"

"You tell me. For the last nine years, I've managed the greatest club in baseball history. Nobody at this party has gotten over that game yet. And nobody would trade the experience either. I used to go to parties, and guys like you would want to talk about the World Series. Now, it's just the game, the Love Game."

'The score: nine to five, nine to five, nine to five,' ran through the detective's head like a subway moving people back and forth to work. 'Was it a miracle? Or was it a glimpse of something we shouldn't have seen? A mistake,' he thought. Then he thought again. 'I should slap myself.' Southwood smiled and chuckled as though reading his mind.

"Got ya thinking, don't I? Just like all my players," Southwood uttered thoughtfully. He laughed, shaking it off. Kerrins tried to laugh with him. But he wasn't that good of an actor.

"What about Greco?"

"What about 'im?"

"He seems okay. I mean for a guy . . . ya know. This party—" Kerrins couldn't bring himself to say what he was thinking.

Southwood leaned over and whispered in his ear, "Who's been screwed?"

"Yeah." They thought a lot alike.

"He hasn't been out of the house all year." Southwood paused to compose his thoughts. "I'll grant'cha, he is different. I don't know about well."

"You know why he's having this party?" asked Kerrins, as he prepared to give Southwood the evening's scoop.

"For his birthday."

"Yeah, but not just that. You're gonna like this. It's really for the kid who owns the ball. He's coming over a little later with his mom."

"*The* ball?" questioned Southwood. Kerrins had his undivided attention. Somehow Dillon Southwood instinctively knew what Kerrins was talking about; it was Kerrins' reverent tone that provided him with all the information he needed.

"Yeah. But that's just the half of it." He was beginning to feel like Weinman. "The kid's birthday is today, too. And get this, born in Newark, New Jersey, just like John."

Southwood smiled. "There's more, isn't there?"

"He has Down's syndrome. Lost his dad. Father died in Korea."

"Uh-huh. Mmmm. Makes sense. John doesn't have parties for himself. Of course, he always had Natt for that," said Dillon, thinking aloud.

'Natt's a hard man to get away from,' thought Kerrins.

Southwood took Kerrins by the arm as if he were sending him in to pinch hit and whispered, "Is it really *the ball*," as though discussing an exceptional archaeological discovery. "Everybody and their brother claims to have it."

"John's convinced. Says it has a piece of stadium wood stuck in it."

Southwood smiled. "Haa haaaa . . . perfect. I shouldn't have expected a normal night at the Grecos." He crunched on another cube.

"Is he pumping you for information, Woody? That's what he does. Don't you, Detective Kerrins?" said Faye, looking radiant. She wore a long floral print dress with a rose sweater. The night air was getting a bit cool.

BASEBALL & BENEVOLENCE

Dillon glanced over to John who was enjoying making one-handed barbecue. The manager drew a deep breath and took in the festive atmosphere. John and Sharon had set up the picnic tables around their soon-to-be garden. Strings of hot pepper lights outlined the small walled-in backyard. Sharon had added balloons, streamers, and pin-the-tail-on-the-donkey, which Charlie played all afternoon. Sam Cooke sang "We're Having a Party" about nineteen times from the living room hi-fi. Everybody sang along. The get-together had become a warm celebration, sad only when they thought about who wasn't there. So they tried not to—in an effort to appreciate who and what they did have.

Sharon was staying close to John. She needed to feel his strength, and she knew he needed her help.

"It feels good. Doesn't it, John?" said Sharon, meaning the party, friends, fun in general. She wrapped her arms around him. He flipped a burger, but it fell into the coals.

"Oh, well," he said and gave her a kiss. "It feels real good."

"Seems as if we've been inside forever," she said.

John stared into the sky; the stars were out. Clear, crisp, clean air filled his lungs. The smell of the fire reminded him of so many other blissful, carefree spring nights and that summer was just around the corner. He watched his father swing an imaginary bat, while Doug Hansen helped correct his stance. His mom and Faye laughed as Detective Kerrins acted out a story. John knew Natt would have approved. 'Kerrins is a good guy. He makes Faye happy,' he thought.

"Close your eyes," said Sharon. Hers were already shut. He obliged her. The sounds of Duke Ellington played in the background. Conversation, many conversations sang like bees. Laughter rose and fell in tides. Charcoal scent lingered and drifted on a light breeze. Children screamed and squealed with unbridled excitement. Bright colors exploded like fireworks under their closed eyelids. The feel of Sharon's body next to his own gave him a sense of timelessness, where everything existed at once. Had anything really changed? He couldn't tell. Everything could be found dancing in the air, or so it seemed.

"Hamburger, please, Mr. Greco." It was Cliff Oakes' little girl, Kate, followed by the Kirkpatrick boys, Billy and Danny. Danny was older and played the guitar; he wanted to be a Beatle.

Then came Charlie piping, "Hot dog, Uncle John!"

"Me, too! Me, too!" shouted the Kirkpatrick boys.

A couple of Charlie's friends from the neighborhood followed close behind, shouting, "Corn on the cob!! Hamburgers! Hot dogs! Hot dogs!! Hot dogs!!!" making a game out of who could ask for them the fastest and loudest.

"C'mon, Shar. We've got some business."

"They look very hungry," she noted with a smile.

"Now wait a minute," said John in a playful voice. He pulled Charlie out of the crowd of kids. "Charlie, all these kids are your friends?" Charlie nodded his head. He looked a little embarrassed after Johney gave him a big hug. Mary Clarke was in the crowd of friends. Charlie liked her. They all laughed and giggled and pushed and shoved, until every last one of them was served. Then they disappeared to some secret corner of the house.

"Any ballplayers in that crowd?" asked Dillon Southwood. He gave Sharon a peck on the cheek and moved cautiously, a man well aware of how much he'd had to drink.

"Charlie's real good," said Sharon. She took Southwood's arm to steady him.

"Yeah, hit for the cycle last year in the Little League All-Star game. You want something to eat, Woody?" John flipped a burger; this time successfully.

"No thanks. So, ah . . . happy birthday. Here, I gotcha a little something." He pressed his hand to his breast pocket as though looking for a pen, and pulled out a small bottle from the inner pocket of his sports jacket. "I wasn't sure if I wanted to give you this . . . it means a lot to me." The bottle was corked, and inside there was nothing but sandy dirt. The label read: April 15th, 1965.

"I figured ya'd like it or think I'm some kinda nut case," Southwood explained. John was about to thank him, but Southwood gave him a sign, waved him off. "There's a speech that goes with it," he said. John accepted the sign. Sharon could feel Dillon tense up a bit. What he wanted to say was obviously important and not easy for him.

"Hmmm . . . it's the dirt from home plate. The dirt that made your letters, John. Scooped it up with my hands and put it in my back pocket. Felt like a dammed fool!

"It's been sitting on the desk in my den. Sometimes I just stare at it for hours. I think how hard it is just to say the word out loud, by myself, alone in my own damn den! It doesn't feel right saying it. Doesn't feel strong or powerful or in control. Just feels like an excuse for weakness. An apology, like, like begging for forgiveness when ya did nothing wrong. Well, that's what I thought, for a long time anyhow. It still don't come easy, but I'm thinking, and thinking, and looking at, and through, and upside-down at this little bottle of earth.

"How scared—Nah! Not scared, wrong word. How 'bothered' I was by what you did. Sure, at first it was easy to dismiss. I was just like the fickle fans at the stadium. Go ahead! Go right ahead! Draw all the stars and moons and geometry you want. Get hits. Get lucky!" he smiled knowingly at the thought. "But, but you crossed the line. Made 'em all think. Made 'em look up from their scorecards and deal wid'cha as a person. Not only you! But the guy next to 'im and the woman next to him! I'll bet it bothered a lot of people. We didn't like it, never mind appreciate it. We were embarrassed, shamed! Haa-ha! Think about what didn't get done because of those feelings?!"

"Dillon," said John, trying to break in. Southwood appeared extremely agitated. 'And to what end?' thought Johney. But his manager waved him off again. He had to finish what he'd started.

"I'm fine. Really, I'm okay!" He held up the bottle. "This . . . dust." He shook his head, amused by its universal joke, funny to few, because it took a long time to get. For all practical purposes Dillon appeared to be having a really good time.

Hank Miller watched the exchange while his wife Cathy chatted with Rachel Goldstein and the trainer, Buddy Sophia. He was tempted to wander on over, see what all the fun was about. But Cathy had a firm grip on his arm and wasn't letting him go anywhere. That was the rule, their code. Hank smiled accordingly and waited for his sign as any good third base coach would. 'What's gotten into Woody? Was there a play on or not?' he wondered. Hank watched Dillon's animated hand and body language. 'He was jazzed,' Hank thought.

"Other folks—we're not taught about that," Dillon sighed. "We are a country of heroes. Singulars. Ha-haa! Singulars! Is that possible!?" He looked toward Sharon figuring she'd know, but not really looking for an answer. She shrugged her shoulders. Not that it mattered, because no one noticed. Southwood was on his horse again. "Damn lucky to be a Highlander. Right, John? That's the dream. The expectation. Wow! Damn luck!" He scratched his head, rubbed his belly. The play was on. "We could have been busting our butts, like most folks. I've been thinking hard, real hard about this thing." He picked up a stick and wrote L-O-V-E in the rich dark earth of the garden. "You've let them in. Everybody. Gave 'em respect. Equality. Hope." He handed John the bottle. "Your playing days are over because of it, shattered into a trillion pieces. That's a few of 'em." His hand gripped John's. The bottle entwined between them. "I love you, son. Don't ever forget that or the good you did." Southwood spoke the words free of shame with determination and conviction. He meant what he said. He needed to say them.

Hank Miller saw the play develop. Sharon and John gave the manager a hug. They were all safe. The kids ran through the party in a long snaking train, laughing, shouting, having the best time. And then, just as quickly, they disappeared around the bend.

"What's this I hear about a special guest," inquired Southwood, shaking the moment. John didn't see the change-up coming. He drew a blank. Sharon made the call.

"John . . . Angela and Jason."

"Oh." He glanced at his watch. "They should be here any minute. Woody, the kid Jason has the ball!" said John, genuinely excited. "Angela, Jason's mother, said it bounced right into her shopping bag. She was resting outside the stadium before walking home."

"Can you believe it," Sharon added.

"Sounds about right," said Dillon, philosophically. "Hey, I know all about the kid." He pointed in the direction of Detective Kerrins. Kerrins was in the middle of doing a Chuck Berry duck walk; he had them all going. Faye was laughing so hard both hands covered her face as she wiped away the tears. "Sweet Little Sixteen" played on the hi-fi.

"He was always such a tough, serious man. What happened?" Sharon giggled.

"I know about the boy's, ah, condition. Could rattle him. Don't you think? All these people. Party—" questioned Southwood, trying to be diplomatic.

"I don't know. He'll be with Angela. His mother is a strong woman," said John.

"I think he'll be fine. You're his only friends. The Highlanders, I mean," said Sharon. "He knows all of you. It will be a great birthday for him. Did you know it was his birthday, too?"

Dillon nodded and motioned in Kerrins' direction. "Everything," he said. The front doorbell rang. "Probably them now," said Southwood.

"John, let's get it before the kids scare the heck out of him. Dillon, you'd better stay here. You can scare the heck out of anybody," Sharon kidded. Southwood smiled at John. John handed him the spatula.

"Howdy, John, Shar!" Much to their disappointment, it was only Hughie Doolan. He wore a Stetson, cowboy boots, and a white three-quarter-cut leather jacket with fringe hanging from the arms and across the chest. A silver star was studded over his right breast pocket. He looked like a desperate country western singer, nowhere near the class of Hank Williams. However, it was an improvement over the flashy suits he usually wore. Everyone at the party said so. Hughie shoved a bag of beers into John's good arm, said, "Happy birthday, Johney," and sauntered to the back patio. You could tell he felt good about the new image. Sharon took the beer from John who stood on the stoop and looked out into the night. He took a deep breath and was about to follow Sharon back to the party when he heard:

"John Greco! John Greco! Mom! That's John Greco!" The boy was so excited he could have been jumping rope.

"I know, Jason. I know, honey. Mr. and Mrs. Greco are expecting us." Her smile lit up the night. Sharon returned to join John on the stoop.

"This-this-this is my surprise!" shouted Jason. Angela nodded her head. He wrapped his arms around her. "The best mom. Best mom," he repeated.

"Hi, John, Sharon," called Angela while being hugged by her boy. "He's really thrilled. Jason. Now, now let me introduce you." He didn't want to let go, holding onto his mother to sustain the moment.

"C'mon now, Jason," she consoled with all the patience of a saint. He released her and Angela ushered him to the Greco's front steps. He kept his head bowed the whole time, afraid to look, maybe afraid they would disappear or, much worst, not like him. John and Sharon ascended the steps and met them halfway. "Jason Wheeler, meet John and Sharon Greco. Sharon's John's wife," Angela said lovingly. Her tone expressed a reasoned care and sensitivity. The poor kid swallowed hard. When he lifted his head, his face was stained with tears of joy.

"I—I'm . . . pleased . . . to meet you." The boy struggled with his words. His degree of Down's syndrome appeared to be moderate. The shape and size of his head was only slightly out of proportion with the rest of his body. Even with his flattened skull and slanting eyes, he gave the impression of being much more aware than most. He seemed to experience the present with intensity and immediacy. Jason was easily overwhelmed, gratified, and focused during each moment. Society's emotional labyrinth of stop and go signals had no effect on him. Jason was a straight, innocent line, very much a child—a super child.

"Hey, like your jacket," said John. It was a navy blue and white Highlander satin.

"Oh, he don't go nowhere without that jacket come spring time," Angela said, beaming.

"Well, I can see why. He looks very handsome," complimented Sharon.

"Please, come in. We have two birthdays to celebrate now! Let's see. We have ice cream and cake and most of the Highlanders inside."

"Nooo!! Really!" Jason exclaimed.

"Really. Happy birthday, Jason," said John, as he gave him an affectionate pat on the shoulder.

"John, it's your birthday, too. Right?" He seemed very pleased to know this information.

"Same day, same town. You and me." John took Jason's hand and led him into the house. Sharon and Angela followed close behind.

"He's so happy! Thank you, Sharon."

"No. Thank you, Angela. We needed this. We really did." Angela smiled her appreciation and said a silent pray as she walked through the threshold of the house.

"Well, who's this? A future prospect?" called Southwood from the grill. He smiled at Jason and chuckled as he filled a large order of hot dogs for the Kirkpatrick boys. Dillon got a kick out of being the cookout chef. He enjoyed being in charge, kept him from drinking so much.

"Manager Southwood," said Jason, under his breath, tightening his grip on John's hand. "I saw his picture in the paper!"

"Yeah, he gets his picture taken a lot," said John.

'He's jolly,' Jason thought of Southwood. That surprised him. 'Is this how men act?' He didn't know; there were no men in his world.

"Freddy Greene! Muddy Ames!" Jason exclaimed, unable to contain himself.

Freddy flashed his big silver and gold grin and said, "Hey, kiddo." Ames waved. That was as friendly as Muddy got. Jason felt as though he had landed in the middle of a wonderful dream, where his baseball cards came to life everywhere he looked, and his favorite player was there to guide him.

"You want something to eat?" asked John.

"Hot dog, please."

"Boys! They can eat," remarked Angela, shaking her head. "He just had Chinese."

John introduced him to Southwood.

"Manager Southwood, best manager ever. I know you are," greeted Jason. And he meant it.

"Well, thanks. Maybe I can manage that hot dog now." He handed Jason his dog. "You wanted mustard?" Jason nodded as he scanned the crowd for cards. He spotted Dave Di Marco.

"Dave Di Marco. Highlander shortstop. Rookie year: 1963, batted .265,

43 RBI's, and 5 home runs. Called to the majors in May as a utility infielder. Born in Bay Village, Ohio, 1941. Has trouble with the breaking ball, but making steady progress," Jason rattled off.

"Has he been reading my scouting reports?" demanded Southwood, playfully.

"Haaaa! Isn't that great?" said Angela, enthusiastically. "His tutor, Miss Palmer, she said he wouldn't be able to read. I said, 'You got to get 'im interested! Teach him to read the backs of those baseball cards he's always looking at. I know he wants to understand 'em!' Well! She thought I was crazy. 'Too many numbers,' she'd say. 'Just confuse the boy to no end,' she'd say. I said, 'Listen girl, you want a job? Teach him the cards.' That was four years ago. Now he's reading the sports pages. Three papers a day during baseball season." Her voice cracked with pride.

"Takes me all day," confessed Jason, drawing kind laughter.

"Oh, I wouldn't worry about that, son. Hughie Doolan over there still can't read or dress himself," explained Southwood, "and he's practically a millionaire!" A huge laugh erupted from the group. Hughie Doolan thought he heard his name mentioned, but didn't care. He was busy trying to pick up the model Willie Moran brought to the party.

From out of the darkened house appeared Sharon, awash in the glow of candlelight and sparklers, surrounded by children, carrying a beautiful cake—devil's food chocolate with vanilla frosting and strawberries on top. They sang "Happy Birthday" to John and Jason. Even Hughie Doolan joined in. The kids grabbed the sparklers before they died out. Little Charlie whirled his around, a make-believe wind-up from a hard-throwing under-handed pitcher.

"I don't know how we're gonna top this next year," Angela Wheeler declared as her eyes became a bit misty.

"We'll think of something," said John, cutting the cake.

Sharon and Faye served vanilla, chocolate, and strawberry ice cream. Jason was quite content as he ate his cake and ice cream, his mom by his side, a healthy smile on his face, relishing each moment.

The manager barked orders from the children. "Cake for Danny! Ice cream for Kate! Strawberry! Soda for Charlie and Mark! Seven-up!" The kids loved him. He got results.

"Angela, have the ball?" asked John.

She patted her rather large bag. "I'm always prepared." Angela watched Jason who was busy gathering autographs for his new autograph book. The book was Angela's birthday present to her son. She never dreamt it would be this successful. 'The players are real good . . . real nice to the boy,' she thought.

"Does he know?" asked John, meaning Jason.

She rolled her eyes. "It's a surprise. Remember?"

"Right. Listen, do me a favor. Dillon Southwood wants to see the ball. When you show him, do the shock trick. Okay?" asked Johney as he planned his first practical joke. Angela's eyes darted in Dillon's direction. Then she turned to find Jason talking baseball with Luke Waits back by the house. She'd never seen her boy so comfortable. He hardly ever left her side when they went out, and there he was, talking with one of his heroes. 'The Lord works in mysterious ways,' Angela mused. She pulled the ball from her bag. "Better be dry enough." She rubbed it on the bag.

John touched it. "Works."

Angela gave him a devilish grin. "Let's do it now," she whispered.

"Okay, but build it up a bit. You know, before ya show 'im, tell him strange things happen around the ball. Make something up. Okay?" Angela was with him all the way. There was nothing that pleased her more than a good joke played on somebody else. They approached their victim. "Make sure it's got a good charge."

"Uh-huh."

"Woody, wanna see the famous ball?" asked John, feigning innocence. John thought Angela carried her bag as though she were guarding her virginity, already overacting.

"Are you kidding? I've been waiting." He lifted little Kate Oakes off his knee. "Go play with the other kids, sweetie. Alright? Kiss for Papa Woody." Kate gave him a peck on the cheek and ran to her parents. Angela and John took a seat on either side of Dillon on the picnic bench, backs against the table, facing the decorated side wall. A five-and-dime happy birthday sign hung just in front of them.

"I gotta warn ya, Mr. Southwood," began Angela in a grave tone, "Strange, I'm talking strange things happen around this ball. Almost didn't bring it." She looked serious, scared.

'Convincing,' thought John. Her acting was improving.

"C'mon! It's a baseball." It was hard to tell if he wasn't buying it, or if he was just acting tough, rational, manly.

"Oh no. Mr. Southwood—"

"Woody. Please."

"Oh no. Wood—"

Ba-Bang! Slammed the screen door. One of the kids had kicked out the doorstop by accident. "Gotta fix that door," said John, appreciating the timing. He thought he saw Dillon jump.

"That's just it . . . it's not just a baseball. You look at it long enough, I swear," she said turning her chin skyward, "it'll tell ya secrets. Why, why just the other day. The ball told me to write to Mr. Greco."

'She's losing him. He thinks she's crazy,' thought John as both he and Southwood listened intently to Angela with frozen happy-face expressions.

"Well, let's see," said Dillon, politely.

"Oh! I hope you're a good man, Mr. Southwood. The ball doesn't take ta nothin' else. Why the last man to see this ball took me out on a fine date. Had 'im up for coffee afterwards, showed him the ball. He was a perfect gentleman 'til then. Then—then! Well! All over me. Ya know what I'm talking 'bout?" she said confidentially. "I threw 'im out! That night—the very same night! His dry cleaning store burnt to the ground!"

'Ooooh, brother,' thought John. 'She's funny.' He tried to repress his laughter. He was afraid he might spoil the joke.

"I, I . . . felt bad at first. 'Til I read it in the papers!" Angela's eyes widened like a spooked cat. "He was married! Married with a capital 'M.' Married with a wife and four children! No! Five children. Five babies! I'm telling ya, Mr. Southwood, it—was—the—ball!"

Dillon glanced over at John who held onto his mask for dear life. Southwood smiled at Angela, cautiously. He didn't want to upset her, wasn't sure if she was all there. 'Poor woman,' he thought, but he wanted to see it . . . had to see the ball. Angela, still caught up in the heat of her performance and much to John's amazement, moaned.

"Married. He was married . . . five kids."

Southwood adjusted himself on the bench as if he were about to pull the pitcher. "Well, Mrs. Wheeler—" He caught himself and tried a friendlier approach, "Angela. I don't own any dry cleaning stores. I just wanna look at it."

"I'm just warning ya, Mr. Southwood."

"And I appreciate that," said Dillon, as he gave John a concerned glance. Angela dipped into her bag, grabbed the ball, and gave it a few good strokes before pulling it out. She handed it to Dillon.

"Well I'll be—" exclaimed Southwood, reaching, grabbing, shocked.

Ba-bang! Slammed the screen door again. Ba-bang! Slammed the memory, slammed the shutters of St. Jude's. Like an avalanche, John could see Smithy Lango. Instantly he recalled the smell and blood and horror—the shutters. "Aaaaaaaah," he moaned. A freezing cold shiver ran down his spine. The missing piece of memory pounded his mask like a fouled-off fast-ball. 'The shutters slammed.' He remembered how the shutters slammed. He heard Detective Kerrins ask the question that baffled the police most. 'Why? Why did Smithy Lango kill himself?' The answer was simple. He didn't. John had been protected, but not to play baseball.

"Haha! Ha-haaa," laughed Southwood. "I think it scared John more than me!"

"Oh, he's just acting, too!" laughed Angela. "You're a real good actor, John! Had me going!"

"You made all that stuff up! The dry cleaners! Married!! And, and, John, get this!" Southwood mimicked Angela, "Four. No. Five kids! Ha-haaa ha-ha!" He slapped his knee.

John's act had just begun. He pretended nothing was wrong, tried to simulate the role of birthday boy and conspirator. 'The ball. Jason and his mom received it for a purpose.' John was convinced. 'They were the true inspiration behind this party. Part of the healing,' John surmised as the fragments of St. Jude's displayed a world beyond his comprehension. *"You destroy everything that is decent. For what?! Money!"* John's own words flowed through his veins like ice water. He only thought he had remembered St. Jude's. Now, two years later, he really did.

A crowd had gathered to investigate the commotion, the joke, and the ball.

"Damn, that's it! Gotta be. Look at that splinter," declared Southwood. "I remember how it shot straight up in the air after it hit. Hank!" shouted Dillon.

Hank materialized immediately. "Yeah, Woody."

Southwood held the ball up to the moonlight. "Look at that!" he said admiringly. "Have the building people check out the facade. Ya know, uh, uh, the Irish guy—"

"I'll take care of it," said Hank, anxious to get a better look.

Jason and Luke Waits found Angela and Dillon at the center of all the activity. His ball was being passed around as if it were an exceptional show and tell item. Angela drew the boy into the group. He quietly sat himself next to her. This wasn't how she had planned her surprise. Jason's eyes never left the flight of the ball. He watched as the players handled it ever so carefully with respect and awe.

"You don't mind, do you? Thought John could sign it for us," said Angela to Jason. He hugged his mother. "Best mom," he said. "Best mom."

"How did ya git it?!" called Hughie Doolan from somewhere in the crowd.

The intensity behind the question alarmed Jason. "They're not gonna take it!?" he cried.

"No! Let them try," said the protective Mrs. Wheeler, provoking a round of applause.

"So, how did you get the ball?" asked Southwood, in a much less threatening manner.

Angela told her story right down to the canned vegetables and the vendor who had offered her six hundred dollars on the spot, a slight inflationary exaggeration . . . another round of applause.

"You okay?" Sharon asked John. He didn't look well.

"Oh, yeah, yeah, fine." He gave her the little boy look. "Too much cake," he said. "It was too good." Sharon accepted his explanation. She'd made the cake. 'It was good,' she thought.

"Want me to get you some seltzer?"

"No, I'll be fine in a minute."

"Don't suffer unnecessarily," she said with a twinkle in her eye.

"No. I wouldn't do that." He was positive his suffering was for something necessary.

" . . . Well, he was so excited. I thought the boy had gone mad on me, hollering, 'I got it! I got it!'" explained Angela as she entertained the crowd.

The screen door slammed once again with yet another harsh ba-bang startling most everyone.

"Will somebody fix that damn door!" shouted John, vehemently. The buzz of the party hushed in amazement. The sound of The Capitols singing "Cool Jerk" filled in the audio space, lending a degree of absurdity to the event. Nobody at any time had ever heard John Greco raise his voice in anger before, not even his own parents, not in a ball game, not while drinking, not even after his own daughter's death . . . not until St. Jude's. The only person to ever hear such a tone from John Greco's mouth was Smithy Lango, and he was dead. John came to his senses, realized that he had effectively killed the party spirit and did his best to salvage what had otherwise been a wonderful day. "Ah, ah, everybody. I'm . . . really sorry. Guess that door gave me a slight headache. Shar, could I have a beer? Maybe we can get this thing going again?" he said, still feeling edgy, until Muddy Ames broke the stilted silence.

"Three sentences in a row from John Greco? I must be dreaming," said Muddy, in his flat, deadpan Louisiana accent, to a roar of relieved laughter.

Angela watched as her son retrieved his ball from Hank Miller. She knew exactly what he'd do next. 'How could they not love that boy?' she marveled.

She thought briefly of her in-laws and couldn't understand how they could reject their grandson, not to mention their own son. Jason was a great deal like his dad, kind and generous. Jason's father was truly a good man, a war hero, who had given his life for his country. Yet his parents wouldn't even come to his funeral, not if Angela and *the boy* were attending. Jason was never referred to as Jason by the in-laws, only as *the boy.* "They're not well people, very bitter," Angela would say of the Wheelers, implying nothing, just stating the facts. She had tried to show them that she was a good wife and mother. As it turned out, the birth of Jason Jr. just confirmed and reinforced their beliefs and prejudices. "Mulatto babies, retardation—that's what happens when ya mix the races," said Jason's grandfather to his son. 'He would have said niggers, if I wasn't in the room,' thought Angela. She was sure of it! 'His idea of being diplomatic,' she figured. From that day on Jason Sr. never spoke to his family again. He loved his wife and son too much for that. "We've got enough pain," he reasoned. "They can't even contain their hatred," said Jason Sr. For that he was never able to forgive them, though Angela wished he'd at least try to make them understand. None of it meant anything now. Her man was gone. She watched as Jason approached John Greco with the ball. She knew what Jason would do; she knew what his father, a decent man, would have done.

"I, I, I want you to have this," said Jason, offering John the ball, thinking that was why he had become upset. John took it from him. He rolled it under his nose as though to smell or kiss it, but more likely he was just trying to think of what to do. He was surprised by Jason's smile; the kid seemed genuinely happy to give away his most prized possession. This was not a hollow gesture at all, only a sincere act of good will. The baseball seemed to make them both feel better, closer somehow. John knew what to do. He slipped it into the pocket of Jason's blue and white Highlander satin jacket.

"It will always be my ball. That's history, but I want you to hold onto it, take care of it for me. I'll be checking up on you. Alright?" Jason nodded his head, taking the instructions very seriously, a squire given a task. He pulled it out of his pocket, held it up, and it became the moon.

"I'll take good care of it, John. Won't lose it. Never ever, ever sell it."

"Good. It's a deal," said John.

Angela came over to find out how it all turned out. "What's going on?" she asked, concerned by the seriousness of Jason's expression.

"This is important!" Jason insisted with a steady grip on the ball. "It's the whole world . . . what keeps it good!" he declared.

"I know. I know, honey. That's why Mr. Greco wants you to protect it," agreed Angela. Jason was satisfied. "He's got some strange ideas about that ball, John," whispered Angela.

"Kid, how'z 'bout a look-see?" yelped Hughie Doolan in his version of country talk as he meandered on over. Jason handed Hughie the baseball and his autograph book, while Willie Moran said good night and thanked his hosts as he left the party. The lovely model was firmly attached to his arm.

Sharon handed John a beer and gave him a kiss. "She's beautiful, isn't she?" quizzed Sharon. John knew the answer to this question. It was the only test he'd never failed. It was the truth.

"Yeah, but I like my women beautiful and bright," he said, flashing his smile. For that he received another kiss.

"Aaaah, that's nice. That's right," said Angela, approvingly. A devoted couple always did her heart good. The sight rekindled her own loving memories.

"Angela, what did Jason mean by 'keeps the world good?'" Sharon asked, as though she'd been thinking about it the entire time.

"Oh, that. Huh. How can I explain it? Well, it's not so crazy. Jason thinks folks were better, kinder after John hit that home run. Thinks it changed people . . . in a good way. He wouldn't go out of the apartment before it. Now, he's even making us some extra money, sweeping storefronts. I think he's right." Angela looked toward the heavens. "I also think it's wearing off," she said, half joking.

"John! John, sign it. Okay?!" cried Jason, all excited.

"That's it! Once he gets an idea in his head, the world stops 'til it gets done," laughed Angela. Jason tried to hand John a pen and the ball.

"Now, now, hold on," directed John. "I've only got one hand." He handed his beer to Sharon and took the pen from Jason. "You'll have to hold it for me. Maybe we should go inside, find a table and light. I don't want to mess this up."

They all moved into the kitchen. John sat at the table. "Put it on the table and hold it real steady," instructed John. Sharon and Angela watched over them as if John was about to sign an important document. John's crippled hand swayed at his side unable to assist in the simple task.

"Aaaaah!! Oh! I'm sorry. Oh! Oh!! I'm so so so so soo . . . sorry," cried Jason from out of nowhere. Tears streamed down his face. He was devastated.

Angela gathered the boy up in her arms. "It's okay, baby. It's all right. Tell me what's the matter," she said, over and over again in a calm reassuring tone. She ran her hand through his hair and wiped his tears all the while.

Jason seemed unable to regain control; he was in complete surrender to his emotions.

"Sometimes this happens," Angela said quietly, giving Sharon and John her reassurance. Sharon handed Angela tissues while John got the boy a glass of water. Both were just trying to be helpful, but feeling helpless all the same. "It has to run its course," she said.

"What's wrong. Tell your mama what's wrong, child," Angela said softly, getting him to stop his shaking long enough to drink some water. It helped.

"Just takes some time and patience. He'll recover," said Angela in a hushed tone, as she pressed the boy's head against her shoulder, not allowing him to feel alone.

"What happened?" asked Sharon, bewildered. John leaned his chest over the kitchen table with both of his arms folded in front of him. He wanted Jason to know he was there for him, too, but wasn't sure if he was succeeding.

"Oh, it could be anything," said Angela. "He's very sensitive. Thoughts, memories, understanding an idea can overwhelm him sometimes," she explained. "Last week it was death. Goldfish died. He'd started to get it. Ya know what I mean?" The more she spoke the calmer Jason became. "Like the whole thing about the ball making the world better. I don't know about anybody else in this world, but it made our world better. He understood what you did, John Greco. You made it simple. You reminded people to care. Folks maybe were a bit more forgiving. 'Cause of that old ball, my boy gathered the courage to leave his bedroom. You got to understand, this child's been dumped on his entire life by blacks, whites, schools, and, and, ah, everybody in between, even his own family. He's not a bright boy, but eventually he gets to understanding the hate." Tears swelled up in her eyes, too. She placed her hand on John's arm. "You gotta know, that ball, that game—you, Mr. Greco—got him understanding the love. To think, I damn near sold it for a television." Jason stopped his shaking. He was feeling better.

"We get mail. People tell us similar stories," said Sharon, cutting herself off, unsure of how she wanted to make her point.

"They've helped you. Right?" said Angela, leading her.

"Yes."

"They helped you, you helped them," Angela smiled knowingly. "It's the second part you good people have trouble with. Been in so much pain, don't even know ya helped folks. That's fine, but tell me one thing, John Greco. You must know something. Not a man alive can do what you did. I'm no baseball expert, but I ain't no fool neither. Drive a ball that far and splinter wood on top of it? That's not power. That's Power! With a capital 'G.' You must know somethin', John Greco." Angela grabbed a tissue and wiped her boy's face. John picked up the pen.

"Think you can hold the ball for me?" he asked Jason, willing to accept no for an answer. John thought maybe somehow he had scared the kid before. He watched Jason for a moment, remembering a story Natt told him the first week he had moved to New York City. It wasn't really a story, just a Nattism. "You think you've stepped in all the shit that can be stepped in, had all the bad breaks. Then you turn around, and there's somebody ten times worse off—and they're happy, 'cause this was a good day for them. Happens all the time in this city," he'd say. Then he'd smile, and John would smile back. 'Sounded kind of depressing,' John thought. 'Until now.' Natt's tale of Voltairian tragedy and the human spirit never got much of a laugh at Tommy's Bar. But Natty wasn't playing this one for laughs; it was too close to home, too near the heart of New York City. I guess he just wanted John to know where he was living, to realize the strength of its tough, hardened, and intensely aware people.

Jason steadied the ball carefully while his hero wrote under the splinter: John Greco 4/15/65. On the opposite side, John wrote in block letters: REMEMBER. Jason was pleased. He kept turning it back and forth, reading and rereading it, over and over again.

"What do you say?" questioned Angela, sternly.

"Thanks, John."

"And?"

"Thanks, Sharon," he said, eyes shining as he gave each of them a hug.

"So? What do you know, John Greco?" asked Angela directly. Sharon seemed pleased by her matter-of-factness. John tapped the pen on the table trying to think of a reasonable answer. Angela cleared her throat as if to say, "I'm waiting."

"That game was the only moment in my life that I felt sure of the future. I knew I could do it. I knew I should do it. And I had a choice. That's all I know," said John. He considered adjusting himself, had the urge to spit, but thought better of it—old nervous habits.

"Well! Isn't that enough?" Angela grinned like a trial lawyer who had just won her case.

"Well, I guess."

"What do you do with that kind of knowledge?" said Sharon, more thinking aloud than asking an actual question.

"As far as I'm concerned, he already did it. Go wherever it takes ya, both of you." They appreciated the optimistic advice, but it still scared them.

"Hey, Jason. What made you so upset?" asked Sharon, sweetly.

"John's hurt hand. He can't play."

"Oh, baby, you knew that. You told me. Right?" said Angela.

"I know," he agreed. "Now I see how it hurts."

"GREAT PARTY, JOHNEY. Had a lot of fun. . . . That Angela is a pip. . . . So, we gonna see you at the ballpark any time soon?" asked Southwood on his way out the door.

"Maybe," replied John.

"Don't stay away much longer. Do us good to have you back. Still need a good scout. Job's yours anytime."

"I'm thinking about it," said John. Southwood nodded his approval.

"Hey, Woody?" John called after him.

"Yeah."

"What happened to Jimmy Jackson, the center fielder? Traded?"

"Jackson? Uh . . . oh, yeah. Don'tcha remember? Shame. Promising rookie. Helleva bat. Died in a car accident in Cleveland. Ten years ago—1957. I'll never forget that year. He took the Giants and Dodgers with 'im," Southwood laughed, enjoying his sad joke and alcohol haze.

"Yeah. That's right."

27

Bronx, New York: 1969

"JASON. YOU'RE LATE, honey. What took you so long?" called Angela, the moment he stepped foot in the apartment.

"Only ten minutes. C'mon, Mom!"

"Twenty minutes, Jason." She was mad. "You know how I worry. Please don't make me worry like that. Did Mr. Lopez try to get you to work late again? Because I already told him no. N-O! He just doesn't wanna listen. I want you in this house by nine p.m. Does he understand that? He can bag them groceries himself!"

"He didn't ask me to work late." Angela gave him the look.

"I met a man."

"You what?!"

"He was a nice man."

"What?!" shouted his mother, her eyes bulging from her head.

"Mom!"

"Don't you Mom me! You tell me everything he said and done. You hear? You think because you can read and write and work a bit that you got this whole world figured? Well, ya don't! Believe you me."

"He wanted to know about the ball."

"What about the ball?"

"Said he heard I had it. Wanted to give me seven hundred and fifty dollars for it."

"And?"

"Told him it wasn't mine, that it's John Greco's, but he let's me keep it."

"What'd he say?"

"He said, fifteen hundred bucks! But-but-but I told 'im—it's not for sale at any price, even if I did own it. He said I must be good friends with John Greco to turn down his offer. I told 'im how John takes me to the games on opening day, and on our birthday, and the playoffs when we get in."

"Oh, child. Why ya tell a perfect stranger so much? You don't know what they want."

"Mom, I can tell the good and the bad people. He was a nice man. Said the Highlanders are going through a hard time. He said they need John. I think he's right. I told 'im John was gonna start scouting next season. He liked that."

"Oh, I remember a few years back. Couldn't get a word out of ya, now can't shut yah up!" She smiled and gave him a quick peck on the cheek. "I'm still mad, though," she said unconvincingly, thinking how far her boy had come. 'He's becoming a man. He even got us a TV.' Their new General Electric television flickered and murmured in the background. Jason had bought it with his own hard earned money.

"**The Mayhouse Manor! New York's newest and most exceptional four star hotel,**" said the announcer. "**Come! Experience what most can only dream about,**" said an impeccably dressed gentleman standing in the center of a magnificent lobby while holding a fancy cane. Angela gave the television a dirty look and shut "the thing" off.

"So? Then what? He didn't follow ya or anything. Did he?"

"No, Mom. I said, 'Not for any price.' And he said, 'Good.' And he walked away."

"Did he say 'good' like he meant it or was he being mean? Ya know, like making fun?"

"Oh, no. Good good! He was happy for me. He was nice. He looked like the man we like on TV! Uuhhhh . . . Walt Disney."

28

"MAN, THAT SONOFABITCH. I thought I was giving up the ghost today," sighed Detective Kerrins. He downed his double shot of Four Roses and chased it with one of McCarthy's twenty-five cent drafts. Weinman did the same.

"Martin, set us up!" ordered Max. He wiped his brow and the back of his neck with a cocktail napkin, soaked. "The humidity," said Max.

Kerrins wasn't paying any attention to him. His eyes were focused on the grizzly bartender as he leisurely worked his way down the length of the thirty-foot bar. Martin was the only bartender, and that's how he did it, one customer at a time, in order—wiping—serving—making change. Every once in awhile he'd knock three times on the bar, a free drink, after every third drink, unless he didn't like you. No amount of customers changed his pace. No amount of yelling or complaining got you a drink ahead of anybody else. It just got you unliked. Those were Martin's rules at McCarthy's. If you didn't like them, leave. If you didn't leave, Martin would yell obscenities in an incomprehensible Welsh accent until you did. Kerrins and Weinman got a kick out of Martin's sense of order. Besides, the drinks were cheap.

As Max Weinman continued his discourse on the weather, the Highlander's were playing on the silenced television. The box score flashed across the screen. They were losing to Baltimore: 7 to 1. Southwood looked upset. Nobody in the stands looked happy either, and neither did anybody at McCarthy's. Of course, nobody there ever did; for all practical purposes it was a bum bar. Kerrins counted the guys getting a drink before him. 'Five, no, six before us!' He knew the rules. 'Maybe Martin would make an exception for a guy who almost got his head blown off. Nah, probably not,' he figured.

"Martin!" shouted Weinman again. The bartender gave him a look of complete indifference. The next step would be the verbal assault and then out. Three strikes.

"Would you shut up! You know how it works," yelled an irritable Kerrins.

"What?"

"What nothing. You know how it works. That's all."

"Hey, you still pissed off about tonight?"

"You mean the gun to my head? Oh, no-no-no! Should I be?" Kerrins chuckled sarcastically.

"I got there."

"A little late, partner."

"Hey, I saved your life!"

"If you were a tad earlier, ya wouldn't of had to do that, asshole," Kerrins argued. Martin stood in front of them waiting for their order. "Again," Kerrins demanded. Martin pretended not to notice his tone of voice.

"You're being unreasonable!" blasted Weinman. "You should have given me more time to get around back. But nooo! You bust in—you're surprised a murdering junk dealer has a lot of junkie friends? What?! What happened? You couldn't wait another minute? Have an appointment? You're the asshole!" Martin delivered the drinks and rapped on the bar three times. "This ain't the fucking movies. You're acting like a kid. A forty-year-old rookie! I don't know you lately. What's the matter with you? You got a death wish?" questioned Weinman, angrily, but with an undercurrent of concern.

"Aaaaah." Kerrins waved him off, downed his double, and lit a cigarette. Baltimore scored another run: 8 to 1.

"C'mon, you taught me. Remember? You would've kicked my ass if I pulled that hot-shot shit. As a matter of fact you did, once," said Weinman.

"Twice," corrected Kerrins.

Max downed his whiskey. "Maybe. But I was young and dumb. What's your excuse? Senility?"

"Ha-haa," Kerrins forced a laugh. "Senility." The television caught Kerrins' eye. His skin flushed from a burning rage. He jumped behind the bar to turn up the sound. Martin gave him a look and continued serving drinks. There *he* was, squeezed in between Highlander innings "of all places." Right there along with the beer and car commercials was Mr. Jonelli, now known as "J.J." to the public. Kerrins hadn't put it together before. J.J. Estates was Jonelli's new company. 'He's big,' thought Kerrins. 'All over town, lots of buildings, good buildings, owned luxury condo's and fancy office towers on Fifth Avenue. And now this, the guy was really going public, making his own commercials.'

"The Mayhouse Manor! Come experience what most can only dream about!" Jonelli, or J.J. the pitch man, sizzled with charm and an image that said: Money.

"He's J.J.? This is a really bad day," said Kerrins, as he killed his beer.

"Damn. He owns the new Mayhouse Manor. Central Park South, right?" said Max, filled with disdain and a bit of awe. "I knew he was doing well, but this—"

"Looks like he owns a good chunk of the city," said Kerrins, wishing Martin would get his "ass" down the line.

"Get the feeling we're chasing the wrong guys?" asked Max. Kerrins counted three guys before his next drink.

"He's been sanitized, Max. That's the trick. Make the dirty money at any cost. Then hire a public relations firm to clean up your image. Perception is what's important in America. The average guy is gonna think he's a a a blue blood in a year or two. They're gonna want to stay at his hotel and be just like him. Looks like Jonelli is a criminal success story, and you and me and the Grecos and maybe a handful of other people will be the only ones to know or care."

"What happened to you, Brian? You used to be so optimistic. C'mon! We can still do all those cop things to make his life, uuuhhhh, irritating. Buck up, little camper!" Kerrins scowled at Max, which kept him from laughing. 'Weinman's been getting away with too much shit lately,' he thought.

"Ah, Martin. Glad you're here," Max schmoozed. Martin gave Max the stone face. Max didn't care. "My friend here, Detective Kerrins, has had a very bad day. Seems he just about got his head blown off, and I had to save his life." Martin resembled Mount Rushmore. "And to top it off, one of New York's worst citizens is now one of its richest and well on his way to being one of its most respected citizens. Bad day, right, Martin?" Martin's expression didn't change, not even a little bit.

"Double us up, Martin," said Kerrins, watching the screen. The Highlander's got a run: 8 to 2, and Phil Rizzuto shouted, **"Holy cow! It's gone!"** Martin went to work. Max thought he saw a slight smile from him as he wiped down the bar, but he decided not to press the issue when the drinks arrived.

"C'mon, Brian!" Max only called him Brian when they were drunk. It sounded silly to him any other time. He was just "Kerrins." Max kept trying, "You're alive! Let's celebrate! I didn't have to kill the kid! Let's celebrate!"

No reaction came from Kerrins. Even worse, Kerrins began sipping his shot, not at all like him. Max downed his, trying to set an example. Kerrins still wasn't paying Max any attention. He was, as the hippies would say, "spaced out."

"It's something else, isn't it? You have even more problems on those broad shoulders of yours. I can feel it," mocked the young detective. "What? Money? Need a loan?" No reaction. "Wait, wait! I know. Don't tell me." Kerrins tried to ignore his energetic associate. "Uuuuh, midlife crisis! Huh? Nah, that doesn't make any sense. You should be past that. I know. I know! It's so obvious. You're gay! Right? You wanna be a dancer? Go to cooking school? Paris! You want to paint! That's okay. Doesn't bother me. I got plenty of—"

"Would you shut up. I can't even get into a little self-pity around you," Kerrins said as he pulled a strand of long reddish hair off his jacket. "I feel like I've spent my entire life waiting for something horrible to happen and today it almost did." Kerrins snubbed out his cigarette and watched the smoke linger as it slowly rose up to McCarthy's dingy tin ceiling.

"Hey, you wanna be like these guys?" asked Max, as he made a hand motion around McCarthy's depressing bar. "We're happy drunks," proclaimed Weinman, full of glee. "First thing you taught me. Say, why do we come here anyway? C'mon, c'mon. Why do we come here?"

"It's cheap."

"And?"

"That makes us happy." Kerrins wanted to say something else but declined.

"And?"

"And what damn it?!" Kerrins downed the remainder of his shot. "Faye's working a shift tonight over at Tommy's."

"Uh-huh."

"We had a fight. I don't like her tending bar. Ya know, guys hitting on her. It can get rough. She likes it."

"Guys hitting on her?" asked Max, pulling his chain.

"No! Bartending. I don't like that she likes it!"

"Oooooooh."

"She's an attractive woman, ya know!!" Kerrins blurted out. Every head in the bar turned to look for her. The detectives downed their drafts to chase the whiskey.

"I said, 'I don't like it.' You know what she said?"

"No what?"

"She said she needed the money. Money! I didn't know what to say back. Sounded like a pretty good excuse. She said she needed to save for Charlie's education. College in three, four years . . . somethin' like that."

"Unreasonable!" declared Weinman, sincerely trashed. "What are you gonna do? Why don't you marry her!? . . . Hey, maybe she'd give us free drinks."

29

"I'M NOT CATCHING you at a bad time, am I?"

"No way! Are you kidding?" cried Jason, as he greeted John at the door of his Bronx apartment. He had been eagerly awaiting John since his call from the stadium to ask if he could visit.

"Please, sit down. I'm making stew for dinner. Wanna stay? Mom will be home in an hour."

"No, I gotta get home." John gazed out of one of the Wheeler's living room windows. It overlooked a congested courtyard of fire escapes, clothes lines, and debris.

"Just started my scouting job," he called to Jason who had disappeared into the kitchen, "was in the neighborhood and thought I'd drop by. See how you're doing."

The apartment had a homey, lived-in warmth about it, very clean and organized, uncluttered. Two basic tenement windows provided a small amount of natural light in the living room. They were the kind of windows the City painted flower pots or drapes on when abandoned, the kind of windows children drew—simple. A thin red and green rug with a swirling, paisley-like pattern covered the living room floor. Half the rug was taken up by a small Formica dinning table and two metal chairs with red seat cushions. A slightly battered colonial chair and couch took up the other half. The brand new television sat on its skeleton stand in between the windows, where it could be viewed from any angle.

Jason handed John a bottle of coke and seemed quite content just to watch him drink it. He considered John's visit to be a phenomenon, and it was happening right here in his home.

"You always come over to my place, so I thought I'd visit you for a change."

"Want to see the rest of it?" Jason asked proudly, meaning the apartment. "Sure."

He took John's hand and guided him into Angela's room—chest of drawers, single bed, makeup table. Everything was very functional with the exception of a majestic oval standing mirror with a lovely mahogany frame. It appeared to be an antique. The beautifully polished finish lit up the mirror and the room.

"I bought that last Christmas with the money I make."

"You have very good taste," complimented John. "It's beautiful."

"Yeah," said Jason. "I like looking in it. I look better in it. Mom couldn't believe it! She sez it makes her feel like a princess," he laughed. There was a wedding picture on Angela's dressing table. Jason noticed John looking at it. "That's my mom and dad."

"Handsome couple," said John. And they were. 'Tragedy,' he thought. 'They looked so in love.' Jason took John by the hand again, always the crippled one, the hand most everybody avoided. In a way, John appreciated Jason's fearlessness. 'Made the limb good for something.'

"Now my room," stated Jason, continuing the tour, delighted John would see it.

Jason's room was half the size of Angela's. He had one small window that looked directly out onto a brick wall, maybe six feet away. The room was painted white with a black ceiling. White speckles of paint dotted the black. A poster of Martin Luther King hung on the back of Jason's door. The room had an earthy smell about it that John wasn't able to place, until Jason told him about the dresser and the fire. His bed and dresser took up most of the available space. Two shelves of untreated, warping pine protruded from the walls, one over the bed, the other over the dresser directly in front of the bed. The dresser shelf and all other available space held books, amazing books. Piles of books were lined and balanced in every nook and corner. His closet was crammed beyond capacity with hundreds of books and very few articles of clothing. 'Camus, Cervantes . . . Dante, Dickens, Dostoevsky . . . Kafka, Tolstoy, Twain,' read John.

"You read these?" asked John.

"I try to. They were my father's. Sometimes I read the same line over a lot. An hour sometimes. Sometimes I understand. My dad liked to read," he sighed. "I'm a lot better reader now. My favorite book is *Tom Sawyer*. Mom reads it with me. Miss Palmer, my tutor, she's teaching me the dictionary, so I understand more."

John smiled approvingly, then stared at the oddly painted ceiling with a perplexed glance. Jason was ready to explain its meaning.

"That's my galaxy!" Jason proclaimed. "It makes me feel safe. Mom did it when I was little."

"That's good, real nice," said John, sincerely. The limitations of Jason's world surrounded him in the tiny room. 'Everything in it speaks of wonderment and shows curiosity,' he thought. Jason had mistaken the sadness in John's eyes for disapproval and immediately began to apologize.

"I know I'm not smart," he said, looking for forgiveness as if the very idea of him reading was some sort of crime.

"Aaah, you're plenty smart . . . and brave, too." John understood what Jason was thinking. It made John feel awful. "I think it's great," he said, a bit ashamed of his own inability to articulate how that kind of prejudice made him feel.

"Hey, the ball. That's a good place." He was glad to move on, past the misunderstanding; he never felt particularly smart himself. Jason seemed pleased that John had noticed his perfect placement of the ball. On the shelf above the bed was a clay candlestick holder, on it rested the ball. 'A powerful place—the right place—in the Jason's galaxy—his heavens,' thought John. As Jason reached for it, it slipped off the holder, hitting the floor with a thud.

Ba-bang! The shutters slammed tight on the stained glass windows of St. Jude's, and John remembered more than he wanted. He couldn't shake the image of the Cleveland church. Johney possessed information he couldn't repeat and didn't know how to use. What he did know made him nervous. What he didn't, even more so. And somehow Jason, he felt, unknowingly had something to do with it.

'Why me? Why the hit? The shutters?' John wondered, drifting through Jason's galaxy. He didn't consider himself an especially religious person; he told me that he'd never felt any kind of calling. But what he didn't understand was that people can be reached in many different ways. 'Have I been chosen for something?' he asked himself, then decided he couldn't rule out insanity. 'Could an insane world seem this real?' he questioned. It was a mystery to him. 'Why did this happen?' he asked again and again and again, but the answer never came. He thought if he prayed, then maybe . . . So, he'd taken to praying recently, something he hadn't done much of since he was a teenager. In his darker moments John wondered if his family had somehow been sacrificed. I found that idea to be a very troubling confession. Maybe that's what kept him at a distance from his own faith.

'The ball, a ball.' As John stared at the baseball while Jason held his crippled hand, another idea occurred to him. It ran through him like electricity. A split second passed when John thought he could feel Jason's hand in his own.   For the first time in five years, he began to see it all so clearly, to understand the event . . . a fleeting moment when millions opened their hearts and eased his loss, if only briefly. It was as if a door had opened providing a window of opportunity, a glimpse of what could be if only the people would come together. His faith was beginning to return.

"I can't think of a better place for it," said John.

They sat on the bed and finished their cokes, admiring Jason's universe. Jason thought of a funny story that John might like, and told him about the Baseball Man, the man who looked like Walt Disney.

30

"OH, IT'S SUCH a beautiful night. Let's just walk," said Faye. It was a comfortable late August evening. The sky was clear, growing glossy black, speckled with shimmering stars. A light breeze blew from the east, just in time to cool off the day.

"Sure," said Kerrins. He left a few extra dollars on the table. 'The waiter was excellent,' he thought. Kerrins appreciated a waiter's honest answer when asked, "What's good tonight?"

Kerrins took Faye's hand and they strolled down Fifth Avenue from 69th Street. Tonight everything was new—each building, each light. They stopped and sat down on a bench at Grand Army Plaza where the sound of the fountain in front of the Plaza Hotel seemed to calm the nervousness of the city. The smell of hot pretzels drifted by as they contentedly gazed into the wide open expanse of Central Park. The lights of a thousand buildings shone over them, for them, the part of the city everyone owned. A hansom cab pulled up beside their bench with a not-so-handsome horse. The young couple in the cab didn't seem to mind as the driver called out the famous sights and smoked his cigar. Laughter came in waves from a crowd of men and women dressed in formal attire. They kissed each other good-bye as limousines came and went in an endless train under the awning of the Plaza. The doorman at the hotel was the engineer; he provided their whistle. Across the street, the fall fashions were brightly displayed at Bergdorf Goodman; people window-shopped, whispering, shouting, or simply stating their opinions of the new line. Faye and Kerrins watched as new scenes with fresh actors and props played themselves out every few minutes.

"I could watch people all day," said Faye, sounding dreamy.

"You should be a detective," said Kerrins.

"Oh, stop." She waited a few beats, then said teasingly, "I know why you said that."

"Really, why?" Kerrins asked in the same teasing tone. Not much was going to bother him tonight. He was feeling too good, the best he'd felt in weeks, and he had no idea why.

"You don't like me bartending," she smiled at him as if she'd just given away his secret.

"Oh?" He decided to play dumb.

"C'mon? Admit it. You don't."

"Okay. I don't," he said with as little emotion as possible. "Wanna get a drink at Trader Vic's?" he asked casually, trying to change the subject. A moment passed before he realized that going to a bar probably wasn't the best way to avoid the subject. Faye laughed. He looked so uncomfortable.

"Let's just talk about it," she said, as she nuzzled in close to him. "Do you not like it because you think women shouldn't work or because it's a bar?"

"Because it's bar," he stated flatly.

"Good. This is good. Answer number one would have been a problem." Kerrins just shook his head, completely charmed.

"Okay, you don't like Tommy's because—"

"Hey, Tommy's is fine. He runs a good bar. Nice crowd there. It's just . . . just that it makes me jealous. Ya know other guys flirting with ya—that kinda stuff. I'm not saying that's your fault. Ah, you're a good-looking woman. Uh . . . hey, it's part of the job. Right? Not your problem, it's mine." Faye gave him a kiss on the cheek.

"Thanks for telling me. You don't have to worry. You and Charlie are my only men. You're all I need . . . all I can handle . . . all I want. Okay?"

"Okay." They kissed.

"How do you think I feel?" Faye gave him a little shove in the ribs.

"What? Feel about what?" asked Kerrins, confused.

"I read all those stories about police officers in the papers. I pray every night for you to come home safe. You think it doesn't upset me? It does. I've seen too much, Brian. I really think I have." She stared vacantly at the window-shoppers.

"I know you have," said Kerrins. He held her especially tight and whispered in her ear. "I love you, Faye." Then he pulled her to her feet and into a deep embrace, creating yet another drama at Grand Army Plaza—just the kind of drama I like to see.

"C'mon, let's walk. Let's walk straight down Fifth Avenue!" he said passionately. And they did.

When they got to Fifth Avenue and 42nd Street, right in front of the New York Public Library, Detective Brian Kerrins asked Faye Greco to marry him. And they were both ecstatic when Faye said, "Yes."

31

IN MAY OF 1971 Faye and Brian married. They had a small service performed by a Unitarian minister named Susan Oliver in John and Sharon's backyard. John and his dad built a pergola by the garden. Delicate white strips of wooden trelliswork framed the elated couple as they took their vows. The weather was perfect and all the spring flowers were in bloom. Sharon had planted tulips, daffodils, crocuses, and snapdragons for the ceremony. Even the forsythia blossomed in time. Faye would have liked a church wedding, but the Catholic Church wouldn't grant her the necessary annulment from Natt. Kerrins didn't mind as long as he was marrying Faye. Max Weinman was the best man; Sharon, the matron-of-honor.

After a honeymoon in Martha's Vineyard, the Kerrins' with Charlie moved around the corner to 29 East 11th Street, where they rented a two bedroom apartment on the top floors of a townhouse. Faye didn't want to be far from Sharon and John. Kerrins was just glad to get out of his tiny studio apartment.

IN 1976 CHARLIE Greco was accepted to, and attended, Columbia University in upper Manhattan. He majored in social sciences and played baseball for the same school as Lou Gehrig. He was a catcher, like his uncle, and was developing into a fine prospect. Natt would have been proud. Charlie Greco graduated in 1980 from Columbia with honors and decided to give baseball a try. His Uncle John signed him to a minor league contract that sent him to the Carolina league, A ball at Prince William; a year later, AA ball in Albany, New York, where he hit .279 with 15 homers and 59 RBI. Within three years Charlie was playing AAA in Columbus, Ohio, and during his second year he had made the shuttle from Columbus to Ruth Stadium twice. When he did, the whole family turned out for him, the same way they used to for John. Kerrins was thrilled when the kid got his first Highlander base hit. He was proud as could be when they retrieved the ball for Charlie, a memento of the occasion. On July 23, 1985, Charlie hit his first home run at the big ballpark. Ruth Stadium erupted with excitement, followed by what could only be described as an eerie silence. Phil Rizzuto said it was out of respect for Charlie's Uncle John. The game was against the very same Baltimore Orioles, twenty years between Greco homers at the stadium. Phil said that Charlie Greco was there to stay. He summed up the feelings of the Highlander faithful when he said, "The fans love 'im."

KERRINS RETIRED FROM the police force in 1975, much to Faye's relief. That same year Faye and Kerrins bought into Tommy's bar as partners. Tommy wanted to take it easier, but he wasn't ready to throw in the towel just yet.

Two Face Pete died in 1979 of lung cancer. He was only fifty-three and had never smoked a cigarette in his life. His time had come. We had a wonderful Irish funeral. Pete loved it. Natt was there, in spirit.

The bar had changed a bit by 1982. Tommy was strictly part-time. Faye and Kerrins added a kitchen and served pub food. It was a good time for them; they were together. I still swept up, kept an eye out, and lived upstairs for the same rent. My work went on.

ANGELA AND JASON continued their long-standing friendship with John and Sharon. Not much had changed for them. Life did get a little easier as Jason gained more confidence in himself and his abilities.

"It all started with that ball," Angela would say. The truth was it started long before the ball. It started with her. Her love gave Jason a life. Her love sustained it. Now he had friends, good friends in Sharon and John, and a much better job. He worked at the B&E supermarket. Jason progressed from bagger to stock boy, to cashier, to assistant manager by 1976. Achieving management was a proud day for a kid who fought all the odds. He would bend over backwards to help a customer. He even founded an Assist-the-Elderly program. They could call in their orders, and the store would shop and deliver for them. It helped the old folks and increased the store's profits by eight percent. Jason was self-proficient, something Angela secretly thought she would never see.

"My boy even has health insurance," she declared with all the enthusiasm of a lottery winner. Not that everything was perfect—far from it. The neighborhood had gotten tougher and tougher. Drugs had crippled the South Bronx, as they did most everywhere, especially in big cities. Drugs and violence went hand in hand.

"Money-money-money. That's all people seem to care about," complained Angela. She was right. Drugs were destroying their world, followed by AIDS and crack and predators of all ethnic and social backgrounds, people who had no conscience and plenty of apathy. But through it all Jason became stronger. He had found himself, his cause. Jason wanted to help the dispirited, even if that only meant taking underprivileged kids to a ball game. Often they would laugh at him, but he always overcame their juvenile cruelty.

"Remember John's game," he'd say to Angela. "Remember!" he'd say when she was down.

IN 1975 DILLON Southwood "retired" as the New York Highlanders' manager. He moved to a quiet fishing village in Maine, where he ate fresh lobster often, and washed it down with ice cold beer. In his farewell speech Dillon said that his life had been blessed, and with the exception of missing his beloved wife, he couldn't imagine it going any better if he had planned it. When asked for the most memorable moment in his career, he answered without hesitation, "April 15th, 1965—The Love Game." Not the pennants or even winning the World Series could surpass that experience. "My life was changed by that one game," said Southwood. When asked if he would expand on his answer, he said he would, but he'd have to go away and think about it for a few years. That was Dillon's last big laugh from the New York media. He'd given them many wonderful quotes and many great baseball moments. They would miss him. He tipped his cap, said thank you, and retreated to the solitude of Maine.

THE OTHER SIGNIFICANT Highlander event of 1975 was the sale of the team from Mr. Harrington to Mr. Jack Brenner. Mr. Brenner, a Texas oil man from Houston, made many promises. He guaranteed New York a baseball winner and the Texas establishment a strong economy. In 1975 he started his plan for a pennant victory by replacing Dillon Southwood with Sam Evers. Sam was replaced by Norm Perry in '76. Norm was replaced by

Earl Gutteridge in '77. Earl was replaced by Hank Miller in '78. Hank was replaced by Aaron "Doc" Adams in '80. Aaron was replaced by Billy Baker in '81, and Billy was replaced once again by John's friend, Hank Miller, in 1982. The Texas economy didn't fare so well either.

IN 1978 MARK Costa married Debbie Hall in Boulder, Colorado. They met during Mark's last year at the University of Colorado and in a whirlwind love affair tied the knot three months later at City Hall. The news took the whole family by surprise. John and Sharon, along with Sharon's parents, made the trip out to Boulder to welcome Mark's new bride into the family.

After college Mark and Debbie moved to Golden, Colorado, where they both taught grade school. In 1979 Thomas Costa was born, and in 1981 Karen Costa. The grandparents were delighted, though they wished the new family lived closer.

When Mr. Costa retired from the fire department in 1970, he and Sharon's mom stayed in Astoria, Queens. After buying a brand new Ford LTD, Mike and Joan became interested in planning and taking day or weekend trips to nearby locations. He loved driving that car.

IN 1977 GUY Greco retired from tool and dye making, while Mom Greco continued working for Sears. She enjoyed it. In 1980 they moved out of the old Greco house in Mountain Edge and into a new two bedroom condo twenty minutes away. It was much easier for them to handle with many less rooms to clean and no yard to maintain. The move was a new beginning for them.

In '81 the family had a scare when Dad Greco was found to have colon cancer. Luckily the cancer was benign. The polyps were removed. He had to have some radiation therapy. He's fine now, still likes to play the horses, and argue baseball with Mike Costa.

THROUGHOUT THE SEVENTIES Mr. Jonelli continued to build and expand his now vast empire. By 1979 J.J., or J. Jones, Enterprises became a Fortune 500 company, making Mr. Jonelli one of the ten richest men in the world. It seemed as though he was into something new almost every year. In 1973 his real estate company went national, then international in '76. The Mayhouse Manor Hotel wasn't just a grand New York City hotel on Central Park South, it was now a chain of hotels in every major city in the country.

By the end of 1979, Mr. Jonelli had gained notoriety as one of America's greatest businessmen and entrepreneurs. His sophisticated image seemed to delight the public. Mr. Jonelli, now known simply as "J.J." to his employees, colleagues, and many fans, became the darling of Wall Street. His disarming charm, sharp wit, intelligence, and perceived wisdom represented to many what most Americans considered the ideal elder statesman. He was thought to be rich, kind, and tough as nails—a strong grandfather figure. Some admirers saw him as the new and improved Uncle Sam. The J.J. blitz was all just as his powerful public relations people had planned. The public's perception of Jonelli was reinforced night after night when they saw him on the evening news, either opening up some posh new business or giving away one of those oversized checks to one charity or another. In a way, "J.J." personified everything Americans wanted throughout the eighties. He was too rich to care about those oversized checks and wealthy enough to have good friends in significant positions, including whatever administration happened to be in office.

By 1982 reality was beginning to close in on Mr. Jonelli's wildest dreams. His picture appeared on the cover of many prominent magazines, and America was coming out of its recession, just as the President and "J.J." said it would. Jonelli celebrated the upcoming decade of prosperity by dangerously over-leveraging himself. He created The J.J. Health and Racket Club, The J.J. Spa and Resorts International, and J.J. International Men's Wear. Many Americans followed his example by dangerously over-leveraging themselves to buy into his sense of lifestyle. Mr. Jonelli's abracadabra cane became his trademark, making the walking stick a must for every well-dressed man. "Things are good," Jonelli would say. "Very good." And he would smile for the cameras.

LIFE FOR SHARON and John wasn't nearly as eventful through the seventies and into the eighties, which was fine with them. The quiet life felt pretty good for a change, though they found Mr. Jonelli's emergence as an American folk hero mortifying.

By 1975 the cards and letters still came in, but only a trickle each month and mostly from folks who had maintained a correspondence with the Grecos over the years. For the most part the meaning of "The Love Game" had been all but forgotten by the time the eighties rolled around, relegated to an excellent piece of American trivia. It seemed that a great deal of important history had become trivia. Maybe the rapid pace of life had a way of trivializing most everything and everybody. Maybe folks needed to learn how to take a break from the isolationism of technology, to talk to each other again, to revitalize the search for the core of human existence.

John's entire career became trivia, just like so many ballplayers who didn't possess Hall of Fame numbers. Some fifteen years after the fact, the question was: Who was the only person to hit a ball completely out of Ruth Memorial Stadium? Most people knew the answer, but didn't find it meaningful. Only the dreamers could remember what it all meant by the end of 1989.

John and Sharon spent many nights in their living room just talking. He would sit at the piano and softly voice chords with his good hand, background music for his rich voice. On those nights he told Sharon all of his secrets, about the late Jimmy Jackson and his visit in the Cleveland hotel room, about the shutters of St. Jude's, and, of course, Jason's Baseball Man, the man who looked liked Walt Disney. She was the only person who knew his secrets, though others, especially Kerrins, had suspected that there was much more to John's story. Dillon Southwood and Faye also had their suspicions, but in their own ways accepted what they didn't know. Hard to say if they were content with the knowledge they possessed or if they just didn't want to know anymore. Maybe that's why John never told Faye about the Baseball Man. He often questioned his own judgment regarding the matter. Faye knew Natt would come back to her and the family if he could.

"She's so happy with Brian. Let her be happy, John," Sharon insisted. "She doesn't need to know. Besides lots of men could look like Walt Disney." But in their hearts they knew it was Natt. John asked Jason to let him know if he ever saw the Baseball Man again. He told Jason that he wanted to meet him. That crucial meeting wouldn't come until years later.

Throughout the seventies and all of Mr. Brenner's managerial changes, John remained a Highlander scout. He was good at his job and found many exceptional young athletes with plenty of talent, but also with the spirit to be a Highlander. That was the most important qualification to Johney. He was famous for signing people other scouts wouldn't even consider, only to have them go on to outstanding major league careers. Strength, heart, and conviction to the game and the people of this great country were the qualities John sought. He didn't want ballplayers who only looked for the big salaries. He wanted those who understood that playing ball was an honor. John wouldn't sign anyone who didn't see it that way. Sometimes his idealism got him in trouble with the main office, but through the years his gut feelings had many folks in baseball circles calling him a genius, a title he wasn't comfortable wearing, but appreciated all the same. To John it was important for the prospect to understand the gift of his talent and to take responsibility for it. John was also driven to find the first female ballplayer; often scouting women's high school and college teams for talented athletes, an endeavor most of baseball considered to be a waste of time. John took a lot of kidding about it, but he was sure we'd have the first female player by the year 2000, and he wanted her to be a Highlander. Of course, this idea pleased many ballplayers who had young daughters.

Sharon continued her work as an advisor to Mayor Washington in the early seventies and was asked to manage the election and re-election campaigns of Mayor Weldon starting in the mideighties. Her political work, inspired by mounting urban decay, transformed Sharon Greco into a tireless social activist. Drug prevention, environmental concerns, and homelessness were among the many concerns that filled Sharon's agenda for many years. Trips to Washington, D.C., happened most every month. Sharon, as an activist, lobbied passionately for many causes that affected the quality of all lives. Why so much political resistance existed was at once obvious to her and yet inconceivable. Men like Mr. Jonelli seemed to gum up the system for their own personal gain. Politicians needed their money to be re-elected. Most of these men and women didn't possess the heart and soul of her husband, she thought. But there were a few, so Sharon made the trips because there was hope, the one thing Americans could depend on, the one thing that filled every card and letter John and Sharon had received during their recovery.

By 1975 Sharon and John had given up on the idea of having another baby. It just wasn't to be. They still mourned the loss of their daughter, felt the pain as would any responsible parent, and, at the same time, dreamed of what could have been for their family if only tragedy had passed them by.

IN 1982 FAYE'S brother Larry died in New York City of AIDS; he was among the first victims. She received a call from the Rodens some six months after the fact. It was the first contact she had had with them in over twenty-seven years, and all they had to say was that Larry was dead, nothing more. They never spoke again. There was a cruel irony in Faye and Larry living only ten blocks away from each other for some twenty years.

BY 1982 THEY still hadn't found Natt . . . or his body.

PART III: THE DISCOVERY

32

Bronx, New York: February, 1982

ANGELA'S DEATH CAME as no surprise to anyone. Jason was prepared as best as possible by Angela herself. The cancer in her breast couldn't be stopped. It was just a matter of time, a little under two years to be exact. The poor woman went through months of radiation and various other treatments before her doctors decided it wasn't doing her any good. Angela came home to the Bronx to spend the last three weeks of her life with her son. She was in a lot of pain, but not physical pain—she had drugs for that. Angela worried about Jason. Night after night he'd come home from work and say to himself, 'I have to be strong, so Mom won't worry.' Some nights he was, but most of the time he was only human. When she got really bad during her last week, Sharon and John sat with Angela and Jason until her time came. I wouldn't have expected anything less from a relationship that had grown so loving over the years. They spoke softly about the goodness of their friendship and how it had changed their lives. I felt proud about bringing them together. These were sad days, but somehow Angela managed to end each one of them on an optimistic note. She was determined to prove to Jason that life goes on, for him and for her, and they would be together again some day. Sharon and John promised Angela that they'd always look after Jason. That made her feel much better about leaving him, for now.

"John?" said Jason, snapping a long silence.

John seemed startled by the voice. His thoughts were miles away on a Jersey beach, Asbury Park, with his brother Natt. 'Everything was so simple then,' he thought. Jason's red swollen eyes pleaded to be let in. They also wanted to see the simplicity. John leaned forward on the worn colonial couch, his elbows on his knees. He gave Jason his complete attention.

"Do you remember the first game you took me to?" asked Jason. John nodded his head and cupped his hand under his chin, listening.

"You told everybody I was your friend."

"Well, you are my friend," replied John.

"You and Sharon were my first friends . . . and my mom. I want to thank you for that, and, and I want you to know I have lots of friends now. At the store, in the neighborhood, me and Mom have lots of friends," repeated Jason in an effort to make a point that eluded John.

"Jason, I know you and your mom have friends." He eyed a table full of food brought over by the neighbors. Get well cards outlined every inch of the apartment.

"I, I just wanted to thank you. I was so afraid before."

"Before?"

"When I was alone, when Phil Rizzuto was my only friend."

"Hey, I was scared before I met you, too," John confided. Jason placed his hand over John's hand. "You're welcome," said John, trying to keep it simple. "Hey, I got to introduce you to Phil. Next game, okay?"

"Really? Wow! That'd be great!" exclaimed Jason, momentarily forgetting all of his troubles.

"Jason," called Angela from her bed. Her voice quivered.

Sharon appeared at the door, trying to keep herself together. "Jason, go see your mother. Alright?" Her arms were folded at the waist. A February wind whistled from outside releasing an involuntary shiver from Jason, the time had come, the pending news awaited him. Jason, now a thirty-two-year-old man knew what was going to happen next. He was as ready as any other man, just as Angela had always prayed he'd be when her time came.

"Oh, I am so proud of you. Come. Give your mama a kiss."

"Ma."

"Don't you 'Ma' me! It's my turn to do the talking. You sit down. Listen," she said, her voice weakening with every word. Jason sat on the edge of her bed, a single teardrop rolled down his cheek. "You cry if you want to, son. Later, you'll feel the calm," she said, nodding her head slowly. She tried to smile. "You know I'll always love you. I'll be watching out for ya. You can't hide your secret from me. You know it all better than anyone.

Don'tcha?" Jason's tears stopped. They had an understanding, an idea about what worked, and they talked about it often. "John and Sharon . . . they're your family now. Mr. Lopez, Mrs. Flahe downstairs, all the folks at the store, Tony and Jerry across the hall, they're all your family now. What did I teach you?"

"Treat people with respect . . . "

"That's right. Treat folks with respect and sometimes you'll get it back. Sometimes you'll get love, like Sharon and John. That's how to make the world your family. Ya keep trying, cause that's how a life worth living feels good. The way you made me and your father feel, you know that?" Jason nodded his head. Angela took her son's hand in her own and said her last words. "Don't mourn too long. Go. Be happy. . . . It's okay. . . . "

"I love you, Angela," Jason said quietly, as though he didn't want to wake her. The clock on the wall sounded the hour, twelve midnight, February 18, 1982. She was fifty years old.

ANGELA WHEELER WAS buried two days later. Those who knew her truly did love her. Her long-time friends from the Grand Concourse Hotel, shopkeepers, neighbors, even the mailman came; many with their families. Even Jason's friends from the B&E came. John and Sharon arrived with Dillon Southwood, who was in town visiting. He never forgot the one evening he spent with Angela at John and Jason's birthday party. "Four! No! Five kids!" Dillon got a laugh every time he thought of her feeding him the bull. As it turned out, Angela and Jason had a very large family. That was their secret. Well over two hundred people attended Angela Wheeler's funeral; none of them related.

John and Sharon asked Jason to come live with them, if he wanted to. He didn't. But he accepted a standing invitation to visit whenever he was feeling down or lonely. He felt secure with the knowledge that he would always have a place to go if he needed people to care for him. Jason was comfortable with his life. He valued his job and his friends, could afford the rent, and he felt closer to Angela living in the Bronx in the shadow of the grand old ballpark. So, he stayed.

33

"HEY, JASON, HOW ya doing?"

Jason wasn't sure how he was doing. The funeral was over, his mother had been buried, and now he was alone. Everyone, including himself, had to get back to the business of living their lives. But it just felt as though he were taking one more step away from Angela, and Jason was afraid to leave her behind.

The day was warm for February. The sun was out. Its rays made him feel better, calmer. He supposed this was the calm Angela spoke of as he sat on a bench just outside the stadium. Jason had spent the better part of an hour breathing in the fresh winter air and staring at the baseball bat monument, a large vertical bat some thirty feet high with its barrel to the ground. It was kind of silly looking, he thought, but it made him feel a bit more settled just knowing it was there. He was trying his best to work through his emotions and get on with things, but without much success, at least not until the Baseball Man asked him how he was doing.

The man's eyes sparkled with kindness as he extended his arms to each side as if to drink in the day.

"Do you mind if I sit down," he said affably.

Jason was so surprised to see him that he had a hard time finding his voice.

'It's been ten maybe twelve years,' he thought. John still asked if he'd seen the Baseball Man whenever they talked. Jason didn't know why, but he knew this man was important to John.

"No," said Jason, meaning he didn't mind. The man unbuttoned his chestnut brown overcoat before he sat down, revealing a conservative dark gray suit, a red and blue striped tie, and a perfectly pressed white button-down cotton shirt. Jason thought it was odd how the man hadn't changed since the last time he'd seen him, not his clothes, not his appearance. 'The Baseball Man didn't age,' he thought.

"So, you ready to sell me the ball?" he said, smiling.

"No," replied Jason.

"Good, that's good. You hold onto it!" he said as he patted Jason's knee a couple times, like a grandfather giving advice, only he didn't look that old.

"Do you know John Greco? He always asks about you."

"Well, who doesn't know him. He's the man who hit the home run. I'll bet you know him pretty good."

"Yeah, he's my best friend."

"Yeah?"

"I'm like part of his family. John and Sharon say I can come over anytime I want. Spend the night if I want to. They have a bed for me," Jason said proudly. It was his most comforting thought in days, and he decided right then and there that he would visit John and Sharon that night. "John wants to meet you."

"All in good time, all in good time. Say, maybe you could do me a favor." The man pressed his hands against his coat pockets, found what he was looking for, and handed it to Jason—a Highlander baseball card of a player Jason had never heard of; his name was Ben Johnson.

"Would you give this card to John for me," requested the Baseball Man.

Jason handled the card at its edges. It was in perfect condition. "I'm gonna see him tonight," he said, but looked confused. He wasn't sure of how to phrase the question he had been wanting to ask all along. So he blurted out, "Who are you?"

"I'm a good friend. What is it you call me? The Baseball Man? No! Walt Disney. Just tell him that. He'll understand. Will you do that for me?"

'He's a nice man,' Jason thought. 'Why not?'

"Okay, but who's Ben Johnson?" Jason asked.

"Ben Johnson, ah . . . Ben Johnson was a great center fielder."

"Oh," said Jason, figuring that was a good enough reason.

"Yes, sir. Ben Johnson was a great one. He could run like the wind and jump like a cat. Stole many a homer off that deep center field wall. Made sure-fire singles die as outs with his speed. A great one!"

"Wow! John should know about him," cried Jason, getting all excited.

"Ha-ah! You're right, absolutely right. John should know about him." He gave a good-natured laugh and stood to rebutton his overcoat.

"You're going?" Jason didn't want him to leave. He was enjoying his company, glad to just sit outside the stadium talking baseball with Walt. This was the best he felt in quite awhile, 'like watching a ball game,' he thought.

"Yeah, gotta go. Running out of time," he seemed a bit sad about it. Then he stood completely still for just an instant, as if he were considering staying, but more as though he were listening to something. He smiled, turned to Jason, and said, "Real sorry to hear about your mom, son. Don't worry about her. She's in a good place." Hundreds of people had said the exact same words to him, but for some reason this time they worked. He believed them.

That same day Jason spent the night with the Grecos. He told them about his meeting with the Baseball Man, gave John the Ben Johnson card, and slept like a baby for the first time since his mother's illness.

"THINK I'VE FOUND something." John flipped through scouting reports in a file cabinet marked, Scouting Reports 1933. Ben Johnson's card said that he had played only one year for the Highlanders—1936, his rookie year. John figured that he would have been scouted a few years before then.

"What, what did you find?" asked Sharon, intrigued by the detective work.

"Mr. Dean Halloway, Highlander scout, found him playing ball for a minor league club in Hoboken, New Jersey," said John, half reading from a yellowed record.

"And?"

"Huh . . . well, he liked 'im." Sharon gave him a questioning glance. "A lot. Let's see. Humph, batted .310 in the minors. Ah, had some power, not much. Mainly a go-with-the-pitch-slap-it-to-all-fields type hitter. Excellent eye. Walked often. Very few strikeouts. Lead-off hitter. He signed 'im."

"That's it?"

"Uh . . . he was a very fast runner. Halloway said he played the shallowest center field he'd ever seen. 'His ability to backpedal and run down the ball is nothing short of astounding,'" John read from Halloway's report.

"Is this telling you anything?" asked Sharon.

"No," said John. "Well, I would've liked to have seen him play," he added as an afterthought.

"Why doesn't he just tell us what he wants us to know," she said irritably.

"I don't know. Maybe he doesn't know the questions or knows the questions but doesn't know the answers."

"Yeah. And maybe Ben Johnson is just a new friend Natt pals around with."

"That's possible. Is he dead?" asked John, missing Sharon's joke.

"Is that you, Mr. Greco?" asked Darryl, the security guard, as he poked his head into the archive room.

"Yeah, Darryl. It's me and Sharon."

"Oh, Mrs. Greco. Well, it's certainly good to see you again. Been too long, too long! Still as beautiful as ever!" he smiled sincerely.

"Oooh, thank you, Darryl. You look real good, too. It has been a long time," she sighed, suddenly feeling very sentimental. The last time she had seen him they were both much younger. Darryl and John started their jobs at the ballpark in the same year, 1959.

"Hey, Darryl, do you remember a player named Ben Johnson?" asked John.

"Played in 1936," said Sharon.

"Well! I'm not that old," cried Darryl, delighted by their request for his assistance. "But I am a bit of a baseball nut and, ah, I did meet the man once or twice," said Darryl, trying not to sound as if he were bragging. "I think I got all these records in my head," he said, glancing over the file cabinets. "I was ten in 1936. Me and my dad went to the games all the time that year. He was unemployed," Darryl shared. "Best times I ever had with my dad was when he wasn't working. Never saw him when he was." He shook his head. "Yeah, I remember Ben Johnson. Like lightning, he was." Darryl seemed to be replaying the moments in his head, as if they were family movies he hadn't seen in decades. A slight smile crossed his lips. His eyes began to shine. "Back then center field was a monster . . . oh, over 460 feet. Somethin' like that. The kid always looked like he was playing way out of position, played it shallow. He wasn't very big. Looked awful small in that field. But damn! He didn't look human, the way he could run. Like, like . . . he was fast! But, he seemed to know, ya know? Like a sixth sense! He knew where the ball was going. The batter would barely finish his swing, and he'd be off and running. Just brilliant! He was. My daddy just loved him. Gotta big kick out of 'im," Darryl said nostalgically. "He could hit some, too! And just as graceful as could be." His expression went from elation to pity. "What a shame," sighed Darryl, turning Ben Johnson's brilliant year inside out.

"What's a shame?!" they said simultaneously.

"The collision."

"The collision?"

"Oh, yeah, tragedy really. Just before the Series with the Giants. Him and, aah, the left fielder. What was his name? . . . Roy. Roy Collins, that's it. It was Johnson's ball. Ya know how that stuff happens. Nobody's fault really, just fate. Johnson was running full out! They collided, Ben and Roy. Ben got the worst of it. Shattered the kid's knee to pieces. I think he was only twenty-two. Never played again. Yes, sir, a knee injury back then, it's over. Shame. He looked like a great one—like you, John. Makes ya wonder how many of the great ones got away. The guys that never had a chance."

Darryl never tired of talking baseball, even if the story had a sad ending. That was Darryl's talent; he was a true historian in his own right, a living archive, possessing a rare combination of baseball knowledge. He knew the facts and figures, the settings, and the frame of mind of both the ballplayers and fans. Sharon and John hung onto his every word, but in the end they still didn't have any answers. Was there a connection between the injuries? Maybe, they thought. But what was it? Both John Greco and Ben Johnson certainly must have suffered, after spending all of their young lives chasing a dream that wasn't to be. Coming so very close only to lose it had to be hard to deal with, though you'd never know it from John. Maybe the same was true about Ben Johnson. But Sharon and John felt there must be a further connection.

"Do you know what happened to him?" Sharon asked, desperate to know more.

"He was a transit authority bus driver. Had a family—hard working man. I used to see him and his boy at the games. The boy was a good-natured kid, used to joke about how he didn't have a lick of his dad's baseball talent. Huh, I remember exactly what he said. He said, 'I can't pick up a bat without tripping.' And I can remember how that made Ben chuckle. He loved that kid. I could see that. Didn't really know Ben Johnson, just knew who he was. Seemed like a decent man. Ya know he's dead, don'tcha? Heart attack. Oooh, three years ago, I think. Still see his son at the games every so often." Another sad ending to one of Darryl's baseball stories. "Think his wife died the year before 'im. Broke his heart, I guess." Really sad. "Well, I got to get going." Darryl looked at his watch and whistled. "I'm the chief. Gotta set a good example. Nice chatting with ya. Hope I was of some help. You take care of that man, Mrs. Greco." With that he ducked out the door, leaving them with a lot of information and not a clue as to what Natt might be trying to tell them. I suppose they both knew this process could take some time, and

Darryl had given them something they couldn't get anywhere else. It was just a matter of figuring out what that was.

Sharon was already onto another idea.

"Did you ever look up your file?" she asked John. The idea sounded so attractive to her.

"No," he said as he absentmindedly refiled the Johnson documents and hummed a soda jingle.

"I'm getting a little worried about you." She gave John her best school teacher look. "You used to only hum the classics," teased Sharon.

"Sorry. It bothers me, too," he said seriously.

"All these years and you never looked up your own file?" She was surprised.

"Nope. Never thought about it."

Sharon rifled through a file marked, Highlander's of the '60's. "I can't believe this stuff isn't on computer." She muttered, as she eagerly searched for his records. "Ah, here it is." She waved the papers over her head as if she were about to do a fan dance. Then as she flipped through them, her glee soon turned to disappointment. "It's just numbers? Wait a minute. Ooooh, this is nice. A footnote."

*John Greco: The only Highlander to hit a ball out of Ruth Memorial Stadium. A blossoming career cut short by injury. "The LOVE Game."

34

New York City: May, 1982

"I'D GIVE NATTY three bucks to spend on the boardwalk for him and his brother! Ha-ha! They'd go on every ride, play all the games, eat junk food, hot dogs. They loved hot dogs. Hey, anybody want a hot dog?" Mr. Greco ordered four from the vendor and immediately continued his story. "Anyway, by morning Natt would have more money than he started with! Ya know what that kid was doing?"

Kerrins shook his head and pretended to listen as though he hadn't already heard this particular Natt story five times. He secretly wished the Detroit batter would get a hit and put an end to Guy's storytelling. Faye and Sharon and the Moms gabbed away while Guy Greco told stories about his boys to Mike Costa, Kerrins, and Jason, but mostly to Kerrins. The Natt stories were aimed directly at him. He was sure of it. John just watched the game. He appeared to be oblivious to his father's goading, even though the same stories always came out whenever Kerrins was around. Truth was, Mr. Greco thought Natt could still be alive and was the only family member to have strong feelings against Faye's marriage. Kerrins would get angry sometimes, but for the most part he had learned to hold his tongue and allow the man his memories, even if they were meant to jab him.

"He'd bet the milk bottle men on the side . . . you know the guys with the weighted bottles that ya have'ta clear off the table? He'd bet his nine-year-old brother could do it. Hah-ha! And he could! Two out of three times! Yes, sir, even when Johney was a boy, he had a helleva arm. Natt, too!" Mr. Greco said proudly.

Kerrins smiled and nodded politely. 'Yeah, and gambling got Natt killed,' thought Kerrins.

"John," called Sharon, directing his attention to the scoreboard in center field.

"Look, John! Your name is on the board!" shouted Jason, causing most of their section to turn and look.

"And Ben Johnson's!" cried Sharon. It was between innings, and they were running a trivia question to keep the fans entertained:

Question: Who batted .323 in his rookie and last season?

A. Ben Johnson
B. Troy Parker
C. John Greco

The crowd shouted their answers as the scoreboard narrowed the choices to just Ben and John. The majority of the people shouted John's name, because most of them had no idea who Ben Johnson was. The answer came up: Ben Johnson. 1936 was his only year due to a career-ending injury.

The crowd was disappointed. Sharon and John understood how they felt. Guy Greco abruptly finished his story and sadly watched the scoreboard until John's name faded away and the Highlanders came to bat.

35

New York City: Winter, 1989

"DO YOU WANT it? They ask you every year," Sharon said, as she put her book on the night table, grabbed the remote, and turned on the television. Carson was in the middle of his monologue. She turned the sound off just as the camera panned over to Ed McMahon, bowing to his swami.

"I think I'm ready. A lot of my players are coming up through the system now." John sounded as though he were talking himself into it. "Hank said it would be different this time around."

"Oh, that poor man! Why does he do it? Brenner's not going to change. Fired, hired . . . fired, hired, what? . . . five times now? At least you've always had a steady job." Sharon wasn't a big fan of Mr. Brenner.

"Sharon, I'm getting old. This might be my last chance to do some coaching, for the Highlanders anyway. I doubt if Hank Miller's got a sixth time around in him."

Johnny Carson silently laughed. The camera panned to Doc but more so to his suit, an explosion of colors. He seemed very pleased by it.

"I'm not telling you not to. It's just—I don't want to see you hurt. Jack Brenner doesn't have your kind of loyalty. And, sweetie, you're too trusting," she said sincerely. "Besides, I want to see the first female ballplayer." John snuggled himself closer to her in their bed.

Carson did his golf swing into a commercial.

"I'll still look for her. Okay?"

"Okay."

"Hey! Turn on the sound. That's Bill Singer!" John was all excited as if he'd found a long lost friend.

"Who's Bill Singer?"

"You don't remember? He worked for the Highlanders back when I was playing. Public relations man. Nice guy." Sharon turned the sound up.

"This is your 1989 dream come true! And all you have to do is join me, Reverend William Singer and God on: The Pathway to Redemption, Sundays at 8:00 a.m., 7:00 central."

"He's a televangelist?" asked Sharon, rightly questioning the jump from public relations.

"Yeah, I guess so," John replied, not knowing what to think. There was Bill, dressed in an expensive suit, adamantly waving his bible in front of what appeared to be a huge arena size audience. The tag on the end of the commercial, while Bill preached in the background, was for Reverend William Singer's redemption tapes. The voice-over selling the tapes ended, allowing Bill the last word.

"I have witnessed a miracle!" declared the Reverend Singer. The commercial ended as a bead of perspiration dropped from Bill's brow. The screen returned to the *Tonight Show*. Sharon lowered the volume. Johnny's first guest was a young starlet with an impressive body. She was dressed to show it off. Volume wasn't necessary.

"Wow," said John.

"Wow? Who? Her?" Sharon questioned in mock jealousy.

"Reverend William Singer," said John, "and her." Sharon gave him a playful shove.

"Have I told you how much I love you lately," she asked innocently.

"Well, ah . . . not lately," he replied.

"I love you," she whispered. "And if you want to coach third base and be one of the boys again, it's all right with me. Just one thing."

"What?"

"No starlets. Alright?"

"Oh," John mumbled, pretending to think about it. "Okay. I don't think they'll be throwing themselves at me anyway."

The television murmured in the background.

"That's what you think. You're a very attractive man with a very sexy voice."

"I love you, Shar. You're the best thing to ever happen to me." He took her in his arms, and they kissed.

BASEBALL & BENEVOLENCE

"My next guest tonight is one of the world's greatest entrepreneurs. He's the eighth richest man in the world, a class act, and I'm a little jealous about this, known only by his initials." The audience laughed. **"Here's J. J.!"**

Thunderous applause erupted. Smiles were all around, especially from the starlet who seemed unable to contain her enthusiasm as she anxiously waited to give Mr. Jonelli a kiss. Jonelli strolled out from behind the pulled curtain, smiled graciously at his fans, and gave a slight bow to Doc and the band for playing "New York, New York." As usual he looked very dapper, a gold watch and chain hung from the vest pocket of his finely tailored suit. With cane in hand, he slowly guided himself to his seat next to Johnny. This was his crowning moment. He felt he had truly arrived as he shook Ed's hand, kissed the starlet, and made sure not to step on any of his applause.

Needless to say, Mr. Jonelli's appearance on the *Tonight Show* destroyed the mood between the loving couple. Sharon excused herself and went to the bathroom. She couldn't bear to watch him, or read about him, or hear of his exploits in causal conversation. Mr. Jonelli's celebrity had become a chronic problem for Sharon. His fraudulent persona was everywhere, as American as apple pie, part of the popular culture. An appearance on Carson's show wasn't exactly a surprise. John watched on. Over the years his rage toward Mr. Jonelli had taken on a voyeuristic quality. He studied his every move, listened carefully to all of Jonelli's well-chosen words, envisioning the day he would make a mistake. And John would recognize it.

"So, you got the hotels, the spas, the resorts, and now you're here to plug your new line of menswear." Johnny Carson flipped a pencil into the air, a comic act of frustration. **"Don't you know there's a recession!"** complained Carson, jokingly. **"All I accomplished last week was a thorough belly-button cleaning,"** cracked Carson. The audience hooted and applauded, while Jonelli bellowed his hearty laughter and the starlet bobbed up and down in her seat, clapping her hands with excessive vitality.

When the commotion died down, Jonelli sat up straight with his hands aristocratically draped over his cane which rested between his knees and said, **"Recession simply means it's a good time to buy."** He looked serious, but noted a sense of uneasiness in the air. He quickly added, **"Somebody has to employ people!"** to which he received a crushing round of applause.

John considered his statement for a moment and decided it was the one noble thing this man had accomplished. But he had read nightmarish stories regarding Mr. Jonelli's treatment of "the help" and concluded that it was a mere accident of necessity and probably not nobility. The idea that he could give Mr. Jonelli the benefit of the doubt was, to say the least, disturbing. His depravity was absolute. Yet, the people saw what they wanted. 'He has them fooled,' John thought. 'Or had he changed?' "Bull," muttered John, as he fought off what could only be considered a vulgar idea. He understood why Sharon couldn't watch. She wouldn't allow him the opportunity to get into her head.

Mr. Jonelli placed his cane between his chair and the couch where the young starlet sat. Quite unexpectedly the starlet began to stroke the famous cane in a suggestive manner. Carson pretended not to notice while the starlet pretended to be oblivious to Carson's antics. Johnny played the whole situation for one big laugh after another, simply by changing his facial expressions. Mr. Jonelli played along, too, content to plug his stores and allow Carson his laughs. John turned the set off. He had seen enough.

Sharon returned from the bathroom. Her eyes were strained and puffy. She had obviously been crying, but slipped into bed just the same and tried to act as if nothing were wrong. The same scenario had played itself out a thousand times before. Mr. Jonelli was the one subject that troubled their marriage. His constant media presence infiltrated their everyday lives. John needed to be a witness, to study, to learn. However, he also knew he couldn't in front of Sharon, it hurt her too much. Sharon's heart would break at the mere mention of Jonelli's names. That was why the coaching job became so tempting to him. He reasoned the space might do them some good. John would take the position to start the 1990 season. He'd be in Fort Lauderdale in the spring, coaching the Highlanders, and watching Mr. Jonelli's every move.

Sharon knew she needed help in coping with her hatred towards Jonelli. She promised to see a therapist whom Faye had recommended. To Sharon, one of the most deeply troubling aspects of Jonelli and his media campaign was the popularity of his gluttonous lifestyle. She realized that the United States was built on the premise of freedom for all, the American Dream and the possibility that anyone could become wealthy and powerful. But until Mr. Jonelli's arrival, America's affluent had a certain dignity about their good fortune. "A propriety," she called it. And it seemed to Sharon that many of the rich used to want to give something back to their country, to do something noble. New York was filled with such projects of the wealthy, the New York Public Library, Carnegie Hall, the Frick Museum, to name a few. Mr. Jonelli, however, gave only when profitable, a line item built into his business plan. His money never went strictly to charity, only to highly publicized events. Charity to Mr. Jonelli was in reality just advertising and promotion. He was a realist, prided himself on it, and it was that twisted lack of compassion that built the foundation of his popularity. His realism had taken root within the general public, had become fashionable, was admired as shrewd, but above all it was held up as the paradigm of self-empowerment. Mr. Jonelli's motto, *Experience what most can only dream about,* summed up his greed and elitism in one snappy phrase. A horrid amount of people were buying it, each craving what he—their divine J.J.—had, wanting what most don't have, and flaunting what they could manage to get. Brotherhood was not in vogue. That's what really scared Sharon. It seemed Mr. Jonelli was having a profound effect on many lives, including once again the Grecos.

"You all right?" asked John, staring at the blank television screen.

"You know how he upsets me," she said, doing her best to rid the anger from her voice.

"I don't watch him to upset you. You know that, Shar. I gotta believe that all the things we've been through . . . mean something. You need to believe, too. We can't let him tear us apart. He's done enough tearing. I know what you think about him and his ideas, and I don't blame ya, but you gotta remember there's a lot more good in this world. The bad just makes a bigger impression. That's what has to change." He took her hand and held it tightly under the covers. "I had another one of my dreams last night."

"Oh, honey, one of your nightmares?" she asked sympathetically.

"Yeah, only this one was different. I didn't die."

"That's good. Right?"

"Not really. But I learned something."

"Tell me."

"Well, it was like my other dreams. I'm looking for somebody or something. There's a bad feeling in the air. This time . . . I'm going through the house searching for the intruder. I find open doors and windows, locks that don't work—he could be anywhere. But I know he's in the basement, so I go after 'im. I take my bat with me. I'm in the basement and there's nothing down there. Then all of a sudden I feel it. It's all around me . . . a presence, as if it's trying to scare me to death, not letting me move. Hard to breathe. Finally I yell, 'Show yourself!' Everything stops. And then it appears, some sort of demon, real ugly. But he just stands there, like he's waiting for me to have a heart attack. And I wanted to, but I didn't, so I started swinging my bat in self-defense, getting in some real good hits. The demon turns into Mr. Jonelli and he pleads for mercy. But I haven't got any mercy. I just keep swinging 'til he's dead." John rubbed his eyes as he tried to erase the image of the bloody savagery he had created.

"So, did it make you feel better? You're usually the one dying in your dreams."

"Yeah, it did at first. Then I remembered how I never really died in my other dreams. I mean whether it was bullets or stabs or falling off a cliff, my spirit—me—was always rescued by some unidentified force, and I was okay. Better than ever. But this time I did the killing, and it wasn't for me to kill. It wasn't my decision to make. It was like robbing myself. This time I truly died. I felt nothing, empty. There wasn't any angel to pick me up. I had no spirit, no soul. I was dead," he said softly, as he lay in their bed staring at the ceiling, wishing it possessed Jason's galaxy. Sharon nuzzled herself against John and kissed his neck.

"How can such a nice man have such terrible dreams?" She kissed him again. He didn't say anything, but appreciated the attention.

"I don't always have terrible dreams."

"What do you think it means?" she asked. He looked confused. "The dream, silly!"

"Oh, yeah . . . ah, I guess I feel guilty. How can I let him go unpunished? How can I live knowing he—" He couldn't say the words. The shocking brutality of Jonelli's crimes rendered him speechless as he suddenly recalled the smile of their only child. The color drained from his skin; he was pale and still very much heartbroken.

"John?" Sharon questioned, concerned by her husband's appearance and at the same time feeling just as he did. Her voice brought him back to his dream, though his tone wasn't nearly as rich as it once was.

"The dream tells me it's not for me to kill, that I must have faith. There must be reasons why all this has happened. Right? It's telling me not to be like him, not to give up my soul. And then I think, am I just using that as an excuse, because I'm too scared. What drives me crazy is me. I've seen things, and time, somehow time washes them away, dilutes them. So they don't seem to matter so much. I'm a kid who can't remember his lessons, Shar." He battled his frustration with all he had but the emotion seemed to have an infinite number of troops.

"You're too hard on yourself, John. All that was years ago."

"And you're not hard on yourself?" he questioned. "Shar, aren't you kinda going through the same thing. Close to twenty-five years now and we're still struggling for answers. It was easier when Jonelli wasn't so popular, 'Mr. New York,' but he's here every single day, and we're not handling it anymore. We can't just forget about him. He won't let us."

"So, what do we do?" She was close to tears.

"We lead our lives . . . and not be afraid to remember. Let's be afraid to forget. We lead our lives because we can't afford to hide from him. That would be our death," he said, caressing her face. Sharon held back the tears as she thought about his words.

"I think you should take the job. It'd be good for you. You could be with Charlie. He'd like that."

John gave her a hug and said, "I think so, too."

"You're right. We can't hide. I had a dream last night, too It made me feel much better."

"What was your dream?" he asked.

Sharon smiled. "It was so simple and beautiful. It felt so warm, cozy. Maya was here, sitting on the rocker. Remember how she loved that chair? She would rock back and forth and back and forth until she fell asleep with her teddy bear. That was my dream. She was just rocking in the rocking chair, smiling at her mommy and daddy until she fell asleep. It was as if she wanted us to know that she was okay. And that she loved us."

36

Winter Haven, Florida: Spring, 1990

"COMING OUT WITH us, Uncle John?" called Charlie Greco, pumped full of adrenaline. He had his dirty uniform half off, but still managed to congratulate his teammates, careful to remember and highlight their contributions to the game. 'He was just like his old man,' John thought.

Defeating the Boston Red Sox always felt good, even if it was just spring training in Winter Haven. Charlie looked as though he were going to get off to a strong start, went three for five on the day with a homer and two RBI. He'd get the start behind home plate this season, just as his uncle did a quarter of a century earlier. Charlie was ready and well-prepared. John made sure.

"Not tonight, I'm driving back to Fort Lauderdale. See ya tomorrow morning . . . and Charlie."

"Yeah."

"Take it easy tonight. Anything happens to you, your mom's gonna kill me. Okay?"

"Sure, Unck."

'He a good kid,' thought John.

ON THE DRIVE down to Fort Lauderdale John thought about how much the game had changed. Hank Miller's voice rang in his ears. Manager Miller was a bit upset with the game's progression and, like Sharon, not a big fan of Mr. Brenner.

BASEBALL & BENEVOLENCE

"It's all money. Every move I make is money," Hank had exclaimed. "Young men in their midtwenties can buy and sell their manager three times over. Everything's a deal. Want a superstar to do something, ya gotta make a deal. Guys like Brenner, he's a good businessman, but is it worth it! Cable rights—half a billion dollars. Y'know a lot of people can't afford cable. So what do they get? Maybe fifty games a year on local TV, when they used to get a hundred and fifty. So much for fan appreciation. Seems like they're cutting out a big chunk of the public to me," Hank expounded. He had become extremely opinionated since his years with Dillon Southwood. Many of his opinions were well-justified with a significant body of support in baseball circles.

Dillon had taught Hank well. He was a fine manager when Mr. Brenner allowed him control, which wasn't often. In 1990 everybody seemed to know the business of baseball better than baseball people, especially the lawyers. They believed their legal skills qualified them to run every business. Seemed to me that most lawyers wanted to do anything other than practice law.

"The owners make their money, so the players demand compensation; the owners pay them what they want, and raise the ticket prices. So much for fan appreciation," Hank Miller had ranted.

These thoughts were not revelations to John. He saw them coming years ago as a scout and had always believed that the character of baseball reflected the mood and attitudes of the American people. The love of baseball appeared to be taking a back seat to the dollar and slipping away from the disenfranchised. John personally had never made so much money in his life. He was one of the fortunate. Yet he didn't feel the quality of his life had improved much, not when he had to step over a homeless person to get to work, not when health care cost too much to have, not when drugs raped a generation, and especially not when Mr. Jonelli was considered an American hero.

John was feeling far from optimistic on his drive back from Winter Haven. He caught a glimpse of himself in the rearview mirror and thought how he had aged. He couldn't stop thinking about Sharon, how she had just started her therapy, and how he missed her already. Only three weeks into the season, and he missed her terribly. John found the adjustment back into baseball difficult, but had to smile when the word "taxing" came to mind.

"I need a beer," he said aloud. Then saw a road sign that read: Tommy's Bar, 1 Mile. 'A good omen,' he thought.

The small roadside establishment looked from the outside more like someone's house, than it did a bar. Only a single neon light in the window identified its form of business. John pulled into the hardened sandlot driveway. No other cars were parked in the drive, and the only sign of life came from the blinking orange light and a near death hound dog who slept by the front door. A yellowed "Open" sign hung from the door. John got the feeling that Tommy turned his light on and off when he needed the money or felt like having company.

The Mets and the Braves were on the television that hung in the far corner. The sound was on softly, a low drone in the background. Nine metal stools with green Naugahyde seats lined the battered bar. Garland, tinsel and Christmas lights filled every nook and cranny of Tommy's, creating the ambience of past festivities. John liked it. It had a relaxing effect on him. He ordered a draft from a very short, but pleasant-looking, man. The man offered John a sincere welcome accompanied by a genuine smile. 'Must be Tommy,' John reasoned. The beer came in a frosted mug with a cocktail napkin that read, 'Tommy's Bar, Indiantown, Florida.' John finished the beer in one gulp.   His second beer awaited him, along with a bag of chips. Tommy watched the game while wiping down the bar. John was his only customer. The Braves went down one, two, three, to end the inning 2 to 1. The Mets were up in the eighth. John took another gulp of beer and opened the chips.

"Aaaaaaaaah!" groaned the bartender in the direction of the television. Mr. Jonelli was appearing in one of his many commercials. Tommy poured John another beer, as his facial muscles contracted into an uncomplimentary expression. Then he rapped on the bar three times, signaling a freebie.

"That man is a menace!" he blurted out.

"You don't like him?" asked John, beginning to feel much better.

"And you do?" asked Tommy, casting a knowing glance.

"Ah, no. I don't like him at all," replied John, feeling a bit defensive.

"I didn't think so, Mr. Greco."

"You know who I am?"

"You are a public figure, sir."

"Yeah, but I haven't been that public lately."

"Mr. Greco, I'd know you by your voice. The people of Florida are extremely knowledgeable baseball fans. Old fans, like myself, never forget. Never. You're still very much a hero in these parts. It's an honor to serve you, sir." He poured John a third beer, then threw another bag of chips on the bar.

"You look hungry. Want a deviled egg?"

"No thanks."

"Slimjim?"

"No." He sipped his beer.

"This J.J. phenomenon must be difficult for you."

"Yeah. My wife, Sharon, she has days where she won't even leave the house. Afraid. Reads all day. Love stories, nothing else, not even a newspaper. I'm worried about her. Don't even know if I should be with the team . . . coaching. She's always been such a strong-willed woman. It's hard to see her this way."

"Oh, my. That is sad. Is she getting any help?"

"My sister-in-law had the same kinda problem a few years back. They're very close. She used to live with us. Faye, my sister-in-law, is taking Sharon to a doctor who helped her."

"That's good. So she's not alone."

"Nah. She's got plenty of family around. I'm just afraid of losing her." He opened the bag of chips with his teeth, as he recalled a sad memory. "Had a cousin once, same age as me. We did everything together. I thought the world of him. Sixteen years old—his mind just left the planet. There was no getting through. He just wasn't there anymore. Broke my uncle's heart. He was strong, too, just like Shar. Strong as can be and one . . . " His sentence trailed off as he opted to drink from his beer instead. 'Why am I talking so much?' John thought. The ball game murmured in the background. Shades of red and green reflected from the tinsel throughout the room, casting a warm, hazy glow. Tommy wiped down the bar.

"She's even stronger than you think. I'll bet you and her worked through a great deal. Did a lot of good for people. I doubt she'll give up now."

"What if she's just too tired?" He raised his voice.

"What if? 'What if's' mean nothing, John. Are you too tired?"

"No. I'm not. Well, maybe a little. Being back in pinstripes isn't as good as I thought it'd be. Everything's different. Players are capital investments. Baseball fans are customers. Ya can't lose without a scapegoat or win without a superstar. It doesn't seem real."

"What did you expect?"

"I . . . expected baseball. Pure and simple, I guess. The way it used to feel. I expect it to bring out the best in me. Aren't there any more convictions to . . . to . . . plain old goodness? That's what I expected. I've played ball, made a good living, made people happy, made my body strong, and made a lot of friends along the way. Why isn't that enough anymore, Tommy? Your name is Tommy?"

"Yes," Tommy replied, then paused. John awaited his answer, though he had no idea why he thought Tommy might have one.

"What are we doing?" the bartender pondered thoughtfully. "Well . . . I'm serving drinks," he said. "You're feeling sorry for yourself. Would you like some advice?" John looked toward the tinseled ceiling with a questioning glance as yet another Jonelli commercial aired on the screen.

"Yeah."

"Change it," he said. "You think baseball isn't as good as it should be? Change it. Your life's not what you want? Change it. But don't blame it on somebody else. Waste of energy. Baseball is just people—nothing more— just people and a lot of numbers. Your being there makes it better. That's what makes it great—people like yourself. You know that, John; you're friends with most of them. The unselfish people, that is. That J.J. fellow, that's what he's doing. He doesn't like this world anymore than you do, only he's doing his damnedest to change it into something he does like. Following me? Teach the kids about *your* baseball. Those are the first lessons J.J. would change."

John tried to recall the last person to reprimand him in such a constructive and inspiring manner. He was fortunate to have such people in his life. Tommy of Indiantown, Florida, was yet another. He never raised his voice. What could have been taken as an insult came across as concern. His overall tone was respectful, and, at the same time, eloquent and powerful. John finished his beer. He felt the urge to get back to Fort Lauderdale. He needed to call Sharon.

"Thanks, that's good advice," said John. "What's in the beer, Tommy. I feel . . . young again." He left twenty dollars on the bar and readied himself to leave.

"Nice talking with ya, Tommy."

"Same here, Mr. Greco."

Just as John stepped out the door, Tommy called, "Not in the beer. It's in ya-ya-you."

'Funny,' John thought. 'For a moment he sounded just like . . . Nah.'

37

New York City: Summer, 1990

"I CAN'T BELIEVE this horseshit!" shouted Hank Miller, as he slammed down the receiver. His phone line lit up immediately, and he just picked it up and slammed it back down again. He took a swig of beer and unbuttoned the top three buttons of his jersey. "Did we win tonight?" Hank asked in an irate tone.

"Yup," answered John, knowing he didn't have to answer, but he did.

"You know who that was?!" Hank screamed in frustration, giving the phone the evil eye.

"Mr. Brenner."

"It was Brenner! Ya know what he sez? He wants Toby Redd in the line-up tomorrow night no matter what. How am I supposed to run a team if he's gonna fill out my line-up card for me? Huh?" After another pull from his beer, Hank flung open the door to his office and yelled, "I'm not talking to anybody tonight!"—meaning reporters. Then he slammed it shut. "He wants Highlander pride! Try getting some of these hired guns to act like Highlanders. They don't give two shits! Why should they? They'll be some place else next year at twice the salary. Highlander pride, my butt. Thanks, Brenner. All that adds up to is a so-so campaign slogan. When I think of what we traded away to get Toby Redd, I should have resigned right then and there," said Hank, shaking his head. "Ah hell! That didn't work the last four times I had the job. Huh . . . maybe I should threaten not to quit."

"What are you gonna do?" John said. Hank gave him a cockeyed look. "About Redd?"

"I'm . . . I'mmm gonna play 'im. But if he starts dogging it, I swear I'll kick his butt inside out and out of the game! Screw Brenner if he wants to pay for that bullshit! We got plenty of guys who wanna play ball."

Manager Miller was right of course. Toby Redd was, to put it kindly, a self-centered, egotistical brat who displayed about as much passion for the game as any good mercenary. His commitment depended on financial gratification. He was satisfied only as long as he was the highest paid. When somebody else made more, Toby wanted to renegotiate his deal or he "dogged it" as Hank would say. Toby Redd played left field. He batted above .300 most of his career, could hit fifteen to twenty-five homers a year and steal forty bases per season if he had the inclination, which he usually didn't. Hank Miller disliked him, but the fans had mixed feelings. Redd could be booed all day long for his obvious nonperformance. Then, like a machine, he could turn it on, delivering an incredible fielding play or drive in the go-ahead run. But the skill only came when Toby willed it, which wasn't often enough for a sixth place team in search of veteran leadership.

The silent homer, as it came to be known, happened late in August of 1990. It wasn't absolutely silent, but it was plenty close. You could hear the vendors making change. The Highlanders were fifteen games out of first. The season was a complete wash with few highlights. Mercifully it ended, but not before compiling the worst Highlander record since 1906. However, for John the season was much better than he'd ever thought it would be. He found coaching gave him a renewed vitality. He felt respected and was pleased to find that the Toby Redd's of the world were very much outnumbered by guys who really loved to play the game. By working directly with the kids, he felt as if he was changing things, teaching *his* style of ball. John was as proud as could be about Charlie's excellent play behind the plate and was much relieved when Sharon's therapy vastly improved her mental health. In August right after the silent homer, it was decided by management that the Highlanders were in a rebuilding year, which gave many of John's minor league kids playing time in the big leagues. He was having fun again. Of course, he didn't have to answer to Mr. Brenner. Hank did.

"HOLY COW! AND Toby Redd makes the catch! A Willie Mays basket catch! How 'bout that!" John could hear Rizzuto's call from a fan's radio just outside the dugout. He glanced over to Hank knowing he'd be steamed. He was. The catch was pure theatrics as the ball should have been caught in a much more conventional fashion. But Toby was feeling pretty good about himself that day, and he didn't seem to care that his team was down 3-2 in the eighth. A dropped ball would have allowed two more runs to score. The crowd gave Toby a big hand as he jogged back to the dugout, even though these most knowledgeable of fans knew Toby's catch was suspect. Hank was at the end of his rope as far as Redd was concerned.

"It's always something," muttered Hank Miller, as he paced back and forth in the dugout. Toby slapped high-fives with the fans along the third base line as he casually strolled off the field. You would think the game was over and the Highlanders had won. It just made Manager Miller angrier.

"Redd!" summoned the manager. Toby knew what Hank was mad about. Getting Hank angry was part of his reason for doing it in the first place.

'What's he gonna do? Bench me? Not at $24,691.35 a game . . . or $4,938.70 an at-bat. Brenner would have his head,' Toby figured. Mr. Redd had a head for numbers. Redd sauntered on over to his manager and gave him his best insolent grin, which brought Hank Miller to his boiling point. Hank wasn't a big man, but he was tough, and he did have quite a bark. Nobody could push his buttons faster and with more accuracy than Toby Redd.

"Hot dog!" yelled Hank, maybe three inches away from Toby's ear. "You drop one of those, I'll cut your balls off!" Sometimes Hank could dazzle you with his understanding of the game. Obviously, this wasn't the first time they had talked. If Toby had a gun, I think he would've pulled the trigger.

"Get the fuck away from me!" shouted Redd, as he pushed Hank back. Hank's face turned blood red. John and a few other players grabbed him, sensing he was about to do something he might regret. The cameras panned to the action in the Highlander dugout, feeding the disturbance to a national television audience while Toby Redd calmly picked up a bat. The possibility that he might attack Hank seemed very real to Johney, but then Redd picked up his batting helmet and walked to home plate; he was due up.

Hank was raging. Somebody brought him a glass of water, or something that looked like water, to try to relax him. Colorful, but truly unrepeatable, language burned from his lips. Hank had had enough. By now more attention was being paid to Hank and Toby than the game. The people at home saw the pictures as the people in the crowd could feel the intensity radiating from the Highlander bench. News traveled around the stadium quickly as folks with radios informed those without.

Some people say you can spend a lifetime in baseball and never see it all. They are right. Hank was so angry he wouldn't allow Redd the green light to take a swing. John, as the third base coach, had the dubious task of relaying

Hank's signs to Toby. The first three pitches were balls. Toby looked for the green light from John, but didn't get it. He watched a hanging breaking ball cut through the center of the plate for a strike. The count went to 3 and 1. He wanted John to send green, but all he got was red. Toby gave John a less than friendly look and called for time. Then he marched back toward the Highlander dugout and shouted at Hank, "If you wanna win, you'd better let me hit!" This approach didn't go over well with the manager.

"Get your ass back to the plate!" ordered Hank, beginning to regain his wits. It was then that Toby Redd said something he probably regretted for the rest of his life or, in his case, might have thought about on occasion. Redd walked straight into never-never land when he insisted on the last word.

"I don't care what you call; I'm swinging!" He waited, stood his ground, but to his surprise didn't get much of a reaction, which infuriated him. Toby made sure he had the team's full attention before he dramatically placed his entire foot in his mouth. "I wouldn't want you to have to depend on these bozos to get the job done!" Redd spewed with all the venom he could muster.

Luckily for Toby the home plate and third base umpires had just arrived in an effort to get the game moving. But even their presence couldn't keep most of the Highlander bench from emptying and beating the daylights out of Mr. Redd. Toby wasn't very popular in the clubhouse to begin with—and now this. John watched from his third base box in disbelief. He'd never seen players attack their own teammate before, not in a game anyway. Quite a few punches landed before the umpires and security guards were able to restore order.

The name "bozo" spread through the crowd like wildfire. Toby picked himself up, dusted off the dirt, and walked back to the batter's box. He was determined to have his at-bat, to show up his teammates. A trickle of blood ran down from his nose. By the time Redd steadied himself for the 3-1 count the crowd started booing and chanting, "Bo-zo—Bo-zo—Bo-zo," right back at him, not even yielding for the pitch. The pitch was a called strike. Applause erupted from the crowd, which only made Redd more determined. That was the second thing John had never seen before. They wanted Toby Redd to strike out. Their own player late in a 3-2 ball game. The count went full and the crowd turned up their discontent a few more notches. Just when Johney thought it couldn't get any stranger, it did.

The pitcher was halfway through his wind-up when the home plate umpire jumped out from behind the catcher, his arms extended, calling for time. The bozo chant continued, then just as suddenly broke into a shower of laughter as Jezebel came bounding out of the stands heading for home plate and Toby Redd. Jezebel, a large blonde with a tiny waist, gained popularity and notoriety through her ample fifty-something bust and her passion for kissing chosen ballplayers during the games. Jez, as the players called her, wanted to be a star, and this was her method for drawing attention to herself. Today was Toby's lucky day. After Redd was promptly smothered by Jezebel, the chanting started again. The young lady was escorted out of the stadium as she smiled and waved to the crowd. Jezebel had made the sports pages once again—maybe even the people pages. John had seen her act several times before, but it never ceased to amaze him.

"The pitch. Swing! It's back . . . way back! Deep into right! Holy cow! It's out of here! Upper decker job! Toby Redd has tied the game!!" announced Phil Rizzuto. But the all-forgiving Rizzuto was only one of few who felt the excitement. It was too late in the season for a single game to matter. And Toby had crossed the line one too many times. He could never come back, not even with a timely homer. John felt bad for the young man, for who and what he had become. He thought how alone Toby Redd must have felt, as if he were running the bases naked. Few people celebrated. When he touched home, none of his teammates was there to greet him. They had turned their backs on him. Much the same way he had on them.

"I've seen friendlier faces after a successful pick-off play at third with the game on the line," John later told me.

The silent homer was yet another new phenomenon John had never seen before. And he wished he hadn't. There was more—the topper. Redd walked back to the dugout from home plate and, just before disappearing into the clubhouse, he sarcastically tipped his cap to the fans, effectively alienating almost everyone.

Toby Redd was traded at the end of the season. Hank Miller was fired again. Mr. Brenner decided he wouldn't have a manager who couldn't relate to superstar players, and he couldn't have a superstar who was hated by the fans and teammates alike. Word about Redd spread throughout the league, and whether he admitted it or not, he could never live down that homer. Maybe Toby didn't learn anything that day, but it just reaffirmed something John had always known: Talent can get you there, but heart makes it worth something. John returned to the clubhouse after he had somberly contemplated the disturbing home run in the Highlander dugout.

Toby Redd would die a very lonely man with the very least baseball had to offer—money. 'Maybe it'd all be different if Walter O'Malley hadn't moved the Dodgers from Brooklyn to Los Angeles,' thought John, sipping beer in the quiet Highlander clubhouse after witnessing Toby's infamous hit.

The 1958 Dodgers broke many hearts on Flatbush Avenue. Brooklyn became a baseball town without a baseball team, and the people wouldn't have been more surprised, or more devastated, if a bomb had been dropped in the middle of Ebbets Field. John had nothing against baseball in the West, but the phrase "the American way" took on a conflicting new meaning for him in 1957 when the Dodgers left town for a bigger market. After all, the Dodgers were a very successful team with dedicated fans. O'Malley was making plenty of money, but it still wasn't enough. Just like Toby Redd, what he had was never enough. John remembered Mr. O'Malley and wondered if anybody should have the right to sacrifice history, tradition, and the people, simply because the price was right, or in Toby Redd's case the "idealism of the ballplayer." His blatant disregard of good sportsmanship, his selfishness made John feel ashamed and at the same time saddened for what this very rich man didn't have, didn't know, or more likely what he couldn't understand. After all, Toby Redd came of age during the advertising renaissance of the eighties, during the time Mr. Jonelli repackaged greed as common sense. Madison Avenue informed us who and what to like and dislike. Never before had their ads so targeted human weaknesses and shortcomings; the underlying message being how easy it is to achieve these new and relatively simple goals. All you needed was money. What they didn't say was that none of what they had to sell mattered. And no matter what you drank or drove, it wasn't going to make you happy unless you were originally. 'Had people forgotten the basics,' John wondered, 'that contentment comes from within.'

How much is enough? Toby Redd couldn't answer that question. He just didn't know. He wasn't there yet. He, just as so many of Mr. Jonelli's admirers, believed what they were told and practiced a cruel form of emotional sacrifice—their own. In Mr. Jonelli's case the sacrifice was often human. 'The cost of doing business,' he would say . . . if he were honest about it, which he never was. He didn't have to be.

"Never do anything you don't have to, but if you must, do anything to get what you want . . . anything." That was a much repeated quote from Mr. Jonelli's man-of-the-year interview, a magazine article entitled "Secret to My Success." He said it as a joke, but he lived by it, much like Mr. O'Malley did with his Dodgers.

Walter O'Malley said he needed more parking—in a town that traveled by subway. He said, "Ebbets Field was outmoded and inadequate," when he could have said, "rich in tradition, charming, and intimate." He could have, but instead he chose to rip the heart out of Brooklyn.

"You okay?" asked Charlie. "Crazy game. Huh?" He had his bag in hand, ready to go.

"Yeah," said his Uncle John, obviously distracted.

"C'mon. I'll give ya a ride home. No subway for you tonight. Okay?" He patted his uncle on the back and noticed the dazed expression on his face. "What are you daydreaming about?" Charlie asked.

John came to. "Oh . . . ah, ah . . . the Brooklyn Dodgers."

38

New York City: May, 1991

"HONEY, WHAT'S THE matter?" Sharon asked, groggy with sleep. John sat on the edge of their bed staring down at his hand.

"I'm okay. It's nothing. Go back to sleep. It's only five o'clock." Throbbing pain in his crippled hand had awakened him. Twenty-six years had passed without much more than a tingle from the damaged limb, and now the pain wouldn't allow him to sleep. He went to the bathroom and took some aspirin, then ran cool water over it which seemed to ease the pulsating.

A blue jay chirped just outside the bathroom window in the red maple tree, where John had placed the birdhouse meant for sparrows. 'The hole's still too big. The jays chased 'em out again,' he thought, as the cold water numbed his hand.

'No point in sleeping,' John muttered as he went to the kitchen to make a cup of instant coffee. He brought the steaming mug to the living room and sat at his piano where the warm rays of sunshine filtered in from the nearby window. The piano looked dusty in the pure sunlight of dawn. John ran his finger across a cigarette burn and glass rings that suddenly became so obvious on his neglected instrument.

It was Saturday, in May, and the Highlanders would play one of their few afternoon games of the season. Hank Miller had been replaced as manager by Jerry Owens. John was the only coach retained by Manager Owens from the retired staff. Jerry O., as he was affectionately called by his players, was a mountain of a man, six foot eight, 365 pounds. At sixty-three years of age, he had spent most of his career with the Pittsburgh Pirates. He started at first base when he played the game, then worked his way up through the management ranks with the Texas Rangers, St. Louis, and back to Pittsburgh where he managed from 1975 to 1988. Jerry won a few pennants and was always considered one of the sharpest minds in baseball. Mr. Brenner liked men of stature in his organization, which was one of the reasons why Brenner and Hank Miller never really got along. Hank didn't look like a manager to Brenner, but Mr. Brenner continued to rehire him because he achieved the best results. Then the Toby Redd fiasco happened, and Hank Miller was pushed over the edge.

For all practical purposes Jerry Owens was retired, but he couldn't resist the chance to manage the New York Highlanders. Mr. Owens had been invited to live out a boyhood dream as his last hurrah—to be a Highlander, an opportunity he couldn't resist. John appreciated Jerry's frankness and wit, and Manager Owens couldn't say enough about the modest Highlander, John Greco. The two men quickly became good friends.

The blue jay reappeared in the living room window, casting his presence on the wall like a perfect hand shadow above the piano. John played a chord, and the bird began to sing as though waiting for accompaniment. The yellow-orange light of day cut through the city as the ache in John's hand dissipated. He played another chord, and the jay continued to sing. When the chord resolved, John found himself absent-mindedly humming the bird's melody. Then realized it was one of his own, a lullaby he had written some thirty years ago for his daughter. He stopped playing. The blue jay gave him a disgruntled glance and flew away.

"John, you all right?" That seemed to be the question everyone was asking him lately. Sharon stood in front of him. She pulled on the hem of her nightgown like a little girl adjusting her dress. He caught himself mindlessly wiping the dust off each key and creating truly irritating music in the process.

"I couldn't sleep," he said. Sharon sat herself on the piano bench next to him.

"And you're gonna make sure nobody else does." She smiled and took his hand in her own. "I heard the lullaby. You're thinking about them." *Them* always meant Maya and Natt.

"Yeah. I guess I am." She nodded her head knowingly. "Shar, something is happening. I can feel it." He looked worried.

"What's happening?" She asked in a reassuring tone.

Her nuturing voice was good to hear. 'She's getting better,' he thought.

"This morning . . . my hand was hurting. That's what woke me." He moved his left hand into her lap as if to say, *this one.* "And . . . and, ah, the lullaby. I thought I heard a blue jay singing it just outside our window. Maybe he did. I forgot all about that lullaby." Sharon gave him a quizzical look.

"Did we make the birdhouse hole too big again?" she asked.

"Shar, I'm serious."

"I know you are. But . . . maybe something good is happening." She took his face in her hands and gazed into his eyes to show him she wasn't teasing. "You're getting feeling in your hand again. A blue jay sings Maya's lullaby. Honey, how could that be bad? No. I think those are good things. Something wonderful, if anything, is going to happen. I'm sure of it." Then she kissed his crippled hand and placed it over her heart.

39

New York City: Summer, 1991

THE MORNING SUNSHINE had disappeared behind dark, gloomy cloud cover by the time John arrived at the stadium. By noon it was pouring rain. The game looked doubtful to everyone but the few thousand faithful who turned up early to watch batting practice or visit monument park to pay tribute to the Babe and all the other Highlander legends.

The Highlanders weren't off to a fast start in '91; they were already two games below five-hundred ball. Most of the guys waited out the rain by playing cards or getting taped. The buzz in the clubhouse wasn't about baseball, as usual, which may account for their poor start. The talk was about Mr. Brenner's Houston-based oil company having severe financial problems and the rumor that he was selling the team to bail it out. After all, he was an oil man and a Texan first and foremost. John didn't pay much attention to the rumors. It wasn't baseball, and it wasn't any of his business. What they didn't know was that Mr. Brenner already had his buyer, and the due diligence process had been in progress for months.

"Excuse me, excuse me, gentlemen," Beverly Katz called in her most official tone, which could get very official when she so desired. Ms. Katz was Mr. Brenner's personal assistant and nothing more. She didn't date Brenner. She didn't date ballplayers; something Mr. Brenner appreciated. She was in her midthirties, tall, blonde, attractive, conservative, an excellent assistant, and engaged.

"Mr. Brenner has an important announcement he'd like to make at this time. Will you all please gather around," directed Beverly, all business. "And feel free to put some clothes on." She added as she spotted naked buttocks in the distance.

"Beverly, how 'bout letting your hair down. Just once, for meee," called a young hotshot named Zack Lombardi, getting a laugh from some of his teammates and a non-response from Beverly.

"Shut up, Zachar-eee," mocked Jeff Martin, the veteran center fielder, to a bigger laugh from his teammates and a slight smile from Beverly. Mr. Brenner made his way through the crowd of ballplayers like a politician running for office, pressing the flesh, stopping for a second to whisper something into Manager Owens' ear. Jerry gave him a pleased look as Beverly Katz waited impatiently with clipboard in hand. Obviously she needed Brenner to get on with it, so she could get him to his next appointment.

"I'll keep it short and sweet," began Jack Brenner, surrounded by his team. "I wanted you all to know first, before it makes the papers. As of midnight tonight, control of the New York Highlanders baseball team, my fifty-one percent, will be in the hands of J. Jones Enterprises." A loud murmur rose from the team. "That's right. J.J.'s your new boss. Oh, uh, and if you don't call him J.J., you'd better call him Mr. Jones. . . . This thing's a done-deal, valued in the three hundred million neighborhood. Now . . . now you'll be happy to know that J.J. is a lifelong Highlander fan, born and raised right here in New York City. Why, I do believe his daddy actually worked on the ground crew in Babe Ruth's day. How 'bout that!" Brenner put his hands on his belly and chuckled to himself. He was so overjoyed about the three hundred million he could hardly contain his emotions. Most of the players laughed along with him, unsure of how else to react. John took a seat on the nearest bench as Brenner continued his farewell speech. "For myself, its been a wonderful sixteen years with the Highlanders' organization—the most winning club of the eighties!" That's how he wanted his era to be remembered, not by pennants, not by the goals of baseball itself, say, the World Series, but by the only thing his money was able to buy him: the most wins in the past decade.

In the end Jack Brenner must have realized that he could buy the ball club, he could buy the players, but he couldn't buy the chemistry to create a championship team. What hurt most was to see all the ex-Highlander farm hands doing so well throughout the league. Many of them were John's prospects, traded away for the quick fix. Mr. Brenner was given credit for trying, but even he realized he was better off in the dying Texas oil business with his one-hundred-and-fifty-million-dollar profit on his Highlander investment. He said, "Thank you and good luck" and was ushered off to his next appointment by Beverly Katz, a joint press conference at the Mayhouse Manor Hotel with Mr. Jonelli.

The game with the Angels was rained out. They scheduled a doubleheader for the next day, Sunday, but that was rained out, too. The baseball gods were crying.

THAT NIGHT JOHN watched on the news as Mr. Jonelli informed the world of his newest and grandest accomplishment. Sharon tried her best to confront him and comfort her husband, but after a short while she needed to leave the room. It was much more than she could tolerate.

"Doesn't anybody remember?" she shouted at the television. John turned the sound down on the set.

The crowd at the hotel chanted: **"J. J.! J. J.! J. J.! J. J.! J. J.!"** The unbridled support for this man turned John's stomach, but he had to watch. Mr. Jonelli gave the appearance of a general about to address his troops. He then extended his arms in a regal gesture.

"Thinks he's the Pope," muttered John. Under intense pressure John's half empty can of beer exploded in his hand, dousing his face with suds. Then Jonelli spoke.

"Ladies and Gentlemen," he said so softly that I thought it was certain not to have an effect on the vocal crowd. But in a way, it did; he was affecting some sort of implied modesty, becoming almost endearing, even to John. Jonelli was in control, charming as always, elegant. A master thespian, he raised his hand again to ask the audience for quiet. This time he meant it. **"Ladies and Gentlemen."** He smiled, savoring yet another triumphant moment. The crowd was silenced. **"Ladies and Gentlemen . . . where do I begin?"** He took a sip of water and gazed over the sea of faces. He would not be rushed. **"This is a dream come true."** His words were met by a huge burst of applause and whistles. **"Though my deep pockets aren't what they used to be."** He pulled out the white lining of one of his pants pockets, showing it to be empty, generating yet another warm round of applause and laughter. **"When I was a younger man, I knew someone who was a part of the ground crew at Ruth Stadium, and I thought . . . that was the best job a young man could have. And so did he. Now that I'm older and wiser I know what is the best job a young man can have! Let me tell you this, it's not on the ground crew!"** Hoots and hollers sounded all around. **"Like I said, this is a lifelong dream."** Enthusiastic applause . . . **"Now,**

now, please, let me finish. To be a part of . . . to control the Highlanders is to be . . . well, an intrinsic part of American history."

"You don't know how hard he's worked to control the Highlanders," said John, muttering madly to himself. He could hear Sharon weeping upstairs in their bedroom. A drop of beer clung to the tip of his nose. His eyes wouldn't release from the television screen.

"I'd like to make this new era the most important Highlander era ever! All my life I've heard how the Highlanders have set the standards for baseball, idealism, and excellence. I've learned from their heroes and used them to inspire my own passions. Ladies and Gentlemen," he paused for the greatest possible effect, "I'm delighted to have all of you here today to share in my dream, my greatest achievement, my proudest moment. Let's play hardball! Thank you." He smiled his most ingratiating smile. Oceans of foot-stomping, balloon-popping applause cascaded down around him. Brightly colored streamers floated in every direction. Confetti rained. Jonelli waved his popular cane at his adoring fans as he tried to make a quick exit.

John was about to turn off the set; he'd seen enough. Sharon needed him and he needed to get away from the news. He grabbed the remote off the coffee table. It, too, was soaked with beer. John shook it as a nurse would shake a thermometer before taking a temperature, only he was unable to stop himself once he started. He wanted to throw it across the room and almost did, until a commanding voice cut through the carnival atmosphere of Jonelli's gala, like fingernails scraping across a chalkboard.

"Mr. Jonelli!" The voice was loud, but emotionless. The name caught J.J.'s ear. Nobody ever called him Mr. Jonelli—not anymore. That was of another era, long ago. He turned to face his questioner.

"Mr. Jonelli, in 1965 John Greco testified against you in front of a grand jury. The charges were for the murder of his four-old-year daughter, Maya Ann Greco and for the murder of his brother, Natt Greco. Also charges of kidnapping and racketeering." The camera panned to the questioner. John couldn't believe his eyes; it was Brian Kerrins and standing right next to him was his best man, Lieutenant Max Weinman. The remote dropped from his hand as though a release button had been pushed. He slumped back into his comfy chair and called, "Sharon, Kerrins is on TV . . . Max, too."

"I know," she replied. "I'm watching up here." Their voices sounded entombed.

Max Weinman followed Kerrins' statement with a question after what felt like an eternity of reaction shots. Mr. Jonelli displayed little emotion. He expected the dredging of the past to begin sooner or later and gave the impression that sooner would be fine. The festive atmosphere died. Many of the people in the room had never heard the allegations before this moment.

"Our question is, sir," Max drew out each word, each heavily laden with sarcasm, **"now that John Greco is, in effect, one of your employees, how will this affect your working relationship with him, and would you please make a comment on the charges he brought against you?"** Max tried his best to keep a straight face, but he just couldn't keep his upper lip from curling into an ever-so-slight smile.

Mr. Jonelli returned his smile, along with the slightest glimmer of personal recognition to his old, "unsuccessful" adversaries. His expression read, "I've anticipated your question." It didn't make putting him on the spot any less enjoyable for Kerrins and Weinman. Their plan was to embarrass him as much as possible, and maybe, just maybe, he might make a mistake. At the very least they felt they could provide an education for the city and the country regarding their beloved J.J. It wasn't going to be easy. The people, at least many of the people in Jonelli's Mayhouse Manor Hotel, didn't want to hear such nonsense. Weinman's question was greeted by icy silence, and then a smattering of catcalls and boos. "It felt just like a ball game," Kerrins later said, "after a knockdown pitch in an away park."

"My heart goes out to John and his family. John knows that." Mr. Jonelli's tone actually conveyed sensitivity and understanding. For a moment it looked as though he might even shed a tear. **"As the Grand Jury found, I can't be held responsible for another man's actions just because I was his employer. Yes, I knew Smithy Lango had his problems! Most men out of work have problems. That's why I gave him a job . . . a job as a painter. In hindsight, he was obviously a very disturbed young man. The Grand Jury heard all the evidence. They decided there was no case. This sad chapter in my—and John Greco's—life has been closed for over twenty-five years. Please, for the sake of the Greco family. . . let it be."** His cane hit the floor hard, striking an exclamation point. The faithful applauded. Mr. Jonelli's tactic was to air the dirty laundry and blame the dead man. It worked on the grand jury.

"As for Highlander staffing, all positions within the organization will be up for review. If the job is merited, the man will be retained."

"J.J.!" shouted the pack of reporters. This was precisely what he didn't want. He wanted to make his statement, get out, and answer reporters questions in a more intimate, controlled environment. He called for a glass of water. Alan, his bodyguard, had it for him immediately. Jonelli momentarily turned his back on the crowd to get his drink. He took a sip. His expression went from humble to infuriated, and then back again as he turned to face the horde of questioners. He then acknowledged a young female reporter, assuming her question would be easier.

"Isn't it true that you were at one time a bookie and that Smithy Lango, the alleged murderer, was in fact your strong-arm?" she asked.

"No, there is no truth to that," bristled Jonelli. **"Ladies and Gentlemen, I have no record! I am an honest, law-abiding businessman."** He wanted to kill her. Jonelli pointed to a man, the biggest, toughest-looking man he could find.

"J.J., can you tell us some of your ideas for the new golden Highlander era," asked the reporter in a sardonic tone. Jonelli didn't mind fielding this question at all.

"I'm not prepared to make any announcements right now. All in good time, all in good time. Let me get my feet wet." Jonelli smiled graciously, thinking, 'You insolent asshole.' His supporters produced phony laughter and polite applause to back their man.

"J.J., it's still very early in the season. Don't you think all this talk of reviews would be counterproductive for the present '91 baseball season?"

"This club hasn't made it to the series in over twelve years. I don't think an honest assessment of our talent at any time is unreasonable. It's good business. I'm a businessman first, and I plan to operate the Highlanders as such."

John could see Mr. Brenner cringing in the corner of his television screen. Jonelli's last statement appeared to be a backhanded slap-in-the-face at Brenner's abilities. John didn't agree with many of Jack Brenner's methods, even though he was a good businessman with his heart, for the most part, in the right place. Brenner had wanted to bring a winner to New York, and he made a lot of money for the organization through some shrewdly negotiated deals. Maybe not the best deals for Highlander fans, but Mr. Brenner truly believed in the combination of experienced players and marquee names to get the team and the fans excited. Unfortunately, his business plan wasn't a very successful baseball formula, and he paid for it, in more ways than one. Baseball-wise, that is. Business-wise, he did just fine. His philosophy cost him a fraction of his profits and most of John's best young talent, who were used as trade bait. It didn't work, and Jack Brenner had plenty of critics. John Greco among them. Still, John found him to be a hard man to dislike, because deep down he knew Jack Brenner would have traded most of his profits for a winner if he could, as long as the oil business was doing fine. John also knew the Highlanders were looking at a completely different animal in Mr. Jonelli. His plans, his grand ideas, he refused to contemplate.

"J.J., given your company's vast holdings, can you tell us how much time you'll personally commit to the club?" The expected answer was, "very little," that he'd hire a good baseball man to run the operation. They didn't get the expected answer.

"I plan to run the day to day operation of the Highlanders." The reporter followed up his question. The whole press core seemed surprised.

"Hands on?"

"Yes, yes! My hands will be on the very pulse of the operation."

"That's comforting," muttered John. He rubbed his eyes, finished the remaining drops of beer, and stared at the television like a zombie. John considered having a cigarette to complement his depressing picture, a desire he'd managed to suppress and disdain for some twenty years. Suddenly it sounded appealing. Most people assumed the greatest impact Jonelli would have on the team was a discounted hotel rate, just a jewel in his crown of achievements. They were wrong. He was going to become a full-fledged baseball man. The phone rang. Nobody answered; the machine picked up. It was Jason. He was upset and wondered if they were watching Mr. Jonelli on the news. John grabbed the phone.

"Hey, Jason. Yeah, I'm watching . . . Kerrins? He's something, huh? Well . . . I don't know—thinking about it. Come over if you're not feeling good, okay. I know, I know . . . well, you're welcome anytime. Yeah . . . we both need some rest. Hey, listen now. . . . If you want company, call a car service. I'll pay for it. Okay? Like family, don't forget. Good. We'll see ya later then. Okay. I love you, too. It's okay, just come over."

"Thank you all very much! No more questions, please. Thank you all! I really must be going. Thank you, again," Jonelli called, as he made his turn to attempt a quick exit. Kerrins' voice cut through the applause, freezing him instantly.

"Can you tell us where Natt Greco is?" he inquired with an insinuating tone.

Mr. Jonelli did what he wished he'd done right off the bat. He pretended not to hear and walked away.

Rain fell all night long. Jason arrived at the Greco house an hour after his call. He sat in the kitchen and had a root beer with John. Neither one of them said much, both were just glad for the company. Sharon cried herself to sleep just minutes before Jason's arrival. John stroked her hair until she was able to take refuge in her dreams.

The rain continued into the next day. Sunday's game had been canceled by early morning, so folks wouldn't have to go all the way to the ballpark for nothing. Mr. Jonelli's first game as Highlander owner, the new era, was postponed until Monday when the Highlander's would play a twilight double-header. None of the three and a half inches of water that fell on New York City over the weekend made it into the upstate reservoir system, continuing the severe drought. That was just the beginning for the "new and improved" Highlander era.

"GET MY DECORATOR on this! I will not have those insatiable blue and white strips on everything!" shouted Jonelli. His voice could be heard bellowing through the canons of Ruth Memorial Stadium by anyone who cared to listen.

"Yes, sir," answered a meek-sounding assistant, as Mr. Jonelli barked out his orders in time to their walking rhythm. He was critical of everything and approving of very little. The hits of his cane echoed off the concrete bunker walls of the stadium, like artillery in the distance. It could be heard by the players halfway across Ruth Memorial.

"John, hear that?" asked Jeff Martin, meaning Mr. Jonelli's raging. Martin had played center field for the last eight years. He was a tough, gutsy ballplayer but not quite Hall of Fame material, one of John's recruits.

The day was glorious, especially since the rain had revitalized the grounds. The grass never looked so green, though a black cloud hung over the Highlander clubhouse. Martin knew it would be his mentor's last day. Everyone in the clubhouse knew it couldn't be any other way. History could not be changed.

"Yeah, he wants to redecorate the place," John replied matter-of-factly.

"Maybe a nice shade of lavender," Martin joked angrily, as he massaged his aching shoulder.

"How 'bout polka dots!" suggested Al Walker, their ace pitcher.

"That works for me," seconded Martin.

"Yeah, polka dot uniforms. We just stand in one place and rotate our hips. Might make 'em dizzy," reasoned Wid Barrett, the second baseman; then he proceeded to perform the hula in his underwear, a sight nobody wanted to see. "They say every movement has a meaning," informed Wid, as he rolled his sizable gut. The rest of the team threw gloves, towels, balls, jocks . . . anything they could find as they shared their last laugh of the 1991 season.

BASEBALL & BENEVOLENCE

The laughter subsided quickly when Mr. Jonelli along with his associates, two lawyers, one assistant, and one bodyguard, entered the clubhouse. The assistant wrote down everything Jonelli said. The guard stood directly behind Jonelli, covering his back; from what, was hard to tell. The lawyers stood in the background and looked every so often at their expensive watches as though they had much more important things to accomplish. Mr. Jonelli didn't bother to introduce anyone to anyone, and he assumed that everyone knew who he was. He forced a smile in John's direction as the assistant brought him a chair. John didn't return his acknowledgement. Jonelli sat himself in front of his ballplayers, crossed his legs, and handed his cane to the assistant. He then pulled a handkerchief from his breast pocket and wiped his brow. He always made a gesture before he spoke. The unannounced meeting began.

"Gentlemen, as I'm sure you're all aware, I am the new managing and controlling partner of the Highlanders. I plan to be as straightforward with you as possible concerning all company policy, player-management questions, negotiations, etc., etc."

"Really warm opener," somebody mumbled. Mr. Jonelli pretended not to hear.

"After all, I wouldn't want to impede or," looking toward John, "interfere with the progress of your prospective careers. My only interest is what is in the best interest of the Highlanders and J. Jones Enterprises." He stood up. The assistant handed him his cane, removed the chair, and waited to jot down his next words. One of the lawyers used a handheld tape recorder; every so often he would mumble something into it, which assisted in creating a sense of paranoia. Most of the players looked toward each other for help, wondering "what the hell J.J." was talking about. They were used to the typical warm, fuzzy baseball speeches.

"New beginnings are not always easy. Tough decisions often need to be made by me and, of course, by yourselves. After all we are all employees, and as employees we are responsible to the shareholders. If I can't do what's right for the people whose investments I'm entrusted with protecting, I will step down. And I would expect that your personal commitment to Highlander tradition would fill you with the job satisfaction so many Americans strive for, but rarely achieve. I'm sure this union will be a successful one. Good luck to you all. I wish you a prosperous season."

"What?!" somebody said, voicing a collective opinion. To the players Mr. Jonelli sounded like Casey Stengel without a sense of humor. As usual, Mr. Jonelli had made his statement and wanted to leave. The lawyers seemed especially anxious to adjourn and looked annoyed when John asked a question.

Jonelli didn't expect to be questioned, because he didn't ask for any questions. He appeared surprised at first, then saw it was John Greco asking; so he paid him his complete attention.

"Yes, John," he said in his most affable voice. Charlie Greco positioned himself next to his uncle. Paul McMahon, Highlander shortstop, dropped one of his lucky Indian head pennies onto the tile floor. The sound as the penny spun seemed to last forever. When McMahon stopped the spin by stepping on it, John asked his question.

"Mr. Jonelli—"

"J.J. Please, everyone calls me J.J. Or, of course, you could call me Mr. Jones as so many of my friends do, John-ney," Mr. Jonelli said with a lingering taste of patronization, still trying to act cheerful, though he just couldn't resist adding the "ney" on the end of John.

"Alright . . . J.J. Can you explain what you said right after you said you wanted to be straight with us?" It might have been the funniest line John Greco had ever delivered. The room broke up with laughter. Manager Owens nearly fell off his bench. The only player not laughing was John. He was serious. Jonelli composed himself, even produced a chuckle. "If you really want to be straight with these guys," John opened his arm to his teammates, his friends, "why don't you come back later without the office party, have a beer, and explain it." The lawyers squirmed like snakes as the team gave them the once over. In an instant their confidence melted away. John scanned Mr. Jonelli for a reaction. Nothing. It really didn't matter to John; this was his last day of work.

"Yeah, Jones-y, why don't you cut the bullshit," said big Jerry Owens. All 365 pounds of him stood up and loomed over Alan, the bodyguard. Owens' hulking frame dwarfed the man.

"This is a baseball team, not a board meeting," continued Owens. He smiled a fatherly smile, trying to keep it light. "We'd all like to hear your ideas, but we're about to play two today, so you'll understand if we can't hear them right now. We have our own meetings to attend." Jerry smiled again. He didn't care about the repercussions any more than John did. Owens was Jack Brenner's man, and knowing baseball and managerial changes, he was as good as retired after this rebuilding season.

"We have every right to be here," said one of the lawyers, arrogantly. I suppose he felt the need to say something. Manager Owens seriously considered hurting the man. The clubhouse was his domain, so he treated the lawyers to one of his famous speeches. Manager Owens was an impassioned speechmaker.

"Know how many big league ballplayers there's been since 1876?" questioned the manager within inches of the lawyer's face. He wasn't looking for an answer. "About 13,000. That's it! What are they graduating? About 35,000 lawyers a year? Where you're standing right now, son, is a place reserved for only the best ballplayers in the world, for boys who grew up chasing the dreams of men. This clubhouse, this ballpark is a living monument to all would-be ballplayers who have loved the game of baseball. And these men—your team, J.J.—have elevated this sport into something beautiful and glorious. A game played in the past and the present, a living history of our nation. An idea from the bosom of our people." The manager turned his back on the lawyers, walked over to Mr. Jonelli and sat on the bench directly in front of him. The young lawyers looked relieved. The bodyguard positioned himself between the manager and the owner. "So gentlemen," Jerry continued. "The only way to get into this clubhouse is by living the dream . . . or invitation." The manager pulled a ball from his pocket and tossed it to John. Johney's impulse was to catch it with his natural hand, his crippled hand, which was impossible. The ball hit the tile and rolled under Mr. Jonelli's chair. The manager had made yet another point. Mr. Jonelli was far from pleased by the theatrics. Owens went on, "All of these men work very hard to get invited back each year. So don't tell me you have a right." He stood up and looked Mr. Jonelli squarely in the eye. It became painfully obvious to "J.J." that nobody in baseball had forgotten John Greco's miracle home run or the events that had preceded it.

Mr. Jonelli took a deep breath and asked his associates to wait outside. The lawyers made for the door first. The assistant was the last to leave.

"Well, well, well, Mr. Owens. I must say it certainly is reassuring to hear how highly you regard your chosen profession," snipped Mr. Jonelli. You would think after spending three hundred million dollars he'd want to get on the good side of labor. Quite the contrary, Jonelli seemed almost determined not to, as though it were part of a plan, a sabotage. He reached into his breast pocket, pulled out his wallet and held it up in the air for all to see.

"Let me make this simple for all of you." He waved the wallet like a flag as he staged his own theatrics. "This is your paycheck. If you want one, you had better produce. Does everyone understand me now," he smiled. It wasn't a question. If looks could kill, Jonelli would be dead. He walked slowly to the clubhouse exit, the hits of his cane beating time. At the door he paused for a moment, as though considering—or more likely reconsidering—an idea he had. "I'd like to see you in my office after the games, John. Good day, gentlemen," bid the new owner, as he slipped out the door like a ghost. Mr. Jonelli had succeeded in demoralizing his own baseball team.

"I thought he was supposed to be a nice guy?" complained Merv Hook, the left fielder. He was a rookie, twenty-two years old.

Jerry Owens wanted to say something comforting, but he was at a loss for words and desperately wanted to pick his team up. He began slowly. "Guys, you know what they say about baseball, about how you can see things you've never seen before?" He walked over to John as a few smiles started to appear. "Now, I don't know what this man thinks he's doing. Maybe this is how he gets results in his world. Maybe he's just a—aaaaah!" He was about to make a disparaging remark but decided against it. "We have to put our feelings aside, pick our heads up and play ball, not for him, but for the fans, for yourselves, and for your teammates. Because . . . because that's what we do." He sounded like a man who was trying to set broken bones with band-aids. "And, John," Jerry put his hand on John's shoulder and said, "sorry about that ball thing." He wanted to say good-bye but he didn't know how. John came to his rescue by saying his good-byes first. He stood to address the ball club that he loved so dearly, the club Mr. Jonelli was determined to keep from him.

"Listen, I've got a real bad history with our new owner," he said. The understatement seemed laughable but nobody dared. "I'm handing in my resignation tonight, and I'm gonna live happily ever after with my wife. I guess what I'd like to say are all the things our new owner should have said. Only he didn't. It doesn't matter. He wouldn't have meant them, but I do. Baseball has been very, very good to me." Johney produced a slight smile to inform them that he had in fact made a joke. The players laughed. The tension eased because of it. "I'd like you all to know how proud I am of you. A lot of ya, Jeffrey, Paul, Wid . . . Charlie, we've been together a long time. All of you guys have always given me your best. That's what I'll remember. I'm going to tell ya something I've only told my wife." After a few snide, but good-natured, comments the clubhouse quieted; the players were anxious to hear his next words. The soft-spoken John Greco had a mystique about him matched by few players. When he had something to say, they listened. "In my last game I wrote 'love' in the dirt, and I hit that home run, straight out of the park. My life was changed forever. At that moment I knew there was a God, had to be. I'm not that talented." As so often happened to John, his words came out sounding humorous, but he was serious. "And God lives where the good people gather—in places like this old ballpark. There are many souls in this house, and there is something sacred about this small patch of green in the Bronx. Maybe the angels live here . . . I don't know, but I do know there's something going on. Here's the part only my wife Sharon knows about. When I hit that home run . . . the house became perfectly quiet. There was unimaginable energy and at the same time, silence and peace. It's true. I know I sound crazy, but you guys know I'm not. Maybe if Babe Ruth was still alive he'd tell ya the same thing. What I'm trying to tell ya is . . . that you're not alone . . . that the spirit of humankind lives within the love of this simple game. Baseball is energy; a positive concentration of love and hope. For many folks it's all they got. You're all they have. Don't let an owner's bottom line get you down. You have'ta play; the world needs play more than ever. People need the respect that your hope gives them. If you give into Mr. Jonelli, you're looking at the other side of the coin—the dark side. I don't know why, but that's what he's about, what he wants. Don't give him what he wants. Play the game the way you played it as a boy, the way you'd play it in your heart . . . for the pure joy of it. Believe it can happen— believe in it. Accept the peace." John ran his hand through his hair, trying to cull his thoughts. "I love all of you guys, some more than others," he joked. John smiled and laughed along with his teammates, as he had done so many times before. "I'm gonna miss the play again, but I'd sure like it if you'd go out there and give us your best."

"You're welcome in this clubhouse anytime," stated Jerry, an angry frustration topped his tone of voice. There was a lot of handshaking, a few hugs, and a couple of well-hidden tears. The Highlanders took two that night against the Angels. It was a perfect night with a warm breeze blowing from the south. And stars, real stars, lit up the sky around a magical blue moon. 'Like heaven,' John thought.

The Highlanders played good ball the first half of the '91 season. Maybe it had something to do with John Greco, maybe not. Jerry Owens thought it did.

"JOHN, COME IN! Please, please sit down!" greeted Mr. Jonelli, graciously. John approached with great caution. He wasn't expecting a warm reception. Of course, he had learned to expect the unexpected from Mr. Jonelli. He motioned for John to a take a seat in a brown leather high-back chair, similar to the one he sat in behind his massive oak desk, only Mr. Jonelli's chair swiveled. The office, Mr. Brenner's ex-office, had been completely redecorated from the paint on the walls to the rugs on the floor in a mere two days. The office looked as though Mr. Jonelli had owned the team since its conception. His desk was adorned with glass encased autographed baseballs; shelves were lined with them. Signed bats and gloves hung from the walls. Photos of famous ballplayers were everywhere. A two by three foot aerial blowup of old Hilltop Park in a gold leaf frame graced the wall directly behind Mr. Jonelli's head. 'Nice photo,' John thought. Shots of league presidents, American presidents, British royalty, and hundreds of celebrities all sitting in the stands of Ruth Memorial Stadium cluttered the wall to his left. To his right, mint-condition collector baseball cards of Cobb, Joe Jackson, Ruth, Satchell Paige, DiMaggio, Williams, Jackie Robinson, and Willie Mays covered the wall, each individually framed in what appeared to be carved ivory. John felt as though he had just arrived in Cooperstown. The artifacts took his breath away. For a moment he was actually dizzy. And then he saw it . . . there, as in a museum exhibit, encased in glass, was a bat. It stood vertically as if suspended in air—beautifully lit. It was John's bat . . . with his name imprinted on it. He'd recognize it anywhere. The bat that hit *the* home run.

"I see you like my collection." Mr. Jonelli smiled approvingly.

"Where did you get—"

"Ninety-five percent of it was my father's. Oh, yes, he was a real baseball fanatic. I had it cleaned up a bit. You know, the frames, that sort of thing. I thought, finally a place to put dear old dad's prized possessions." He unleashed a sardonic chuckle. "Of course, there is my prize possession, too." He nodded his head in the direction of John's bat, then swiveled his chair around to get a more satisfactory look at the bat and John's expression.

"How . . . did you get it?" he asked slowly, dazed.

"Paid twenty-five thousand dollars to a man named Bill Singer. You remember him? I understand he used the money to start his own ministry. Haaa-ha!" Jonelli said. John looked as though someone had just shot him in the foot. "I'll pay just as much, " Jonelli went on, "maybe more for the ball, John. Do you have it? Do you know who does?"

"Why do you want these things?"

"Oh, sentimental reasons. Does that surprise you, Mr. Greco?"

John didn't know what to think, and even if he did, he wasn't about to voice his opinion. More than anything else he just wanted out of Jonelli's office. Nothing made sense, as if someone had confused the parts of two different puzzles. He grabbed a piece of paper from Mr. Jonelli's desk and wrote: *This is my resignation. You know why.* He signed it, dated it, and place it in front of the murderer's face. He had one foot out the door when Mr. Jonelli called to him.

"John, we have more business to discuss."

Alan, the bodyguard, blocked John's path, shoved a can of beer into his chest, and showed him back into the office.

"I don't want your resignation. You've done an excellent job for the organization . . . for many years. True, I don't see you as my third base coach . . . I want to make you the manager. What do you say . . . interested?"

John wished he was smarter. He wished he were Natt. 'Natt would know what to do,' he thought. At a loss, John said, "What do you want from me?"

"I want you to be my manager. Say . . . half a million a year. Think about it, John. I need a baseball man. Somebody well-liked, like yourself. The players, the press . . . they don't have to like me. He sat back in his chair and folded his hands over his belly. I'm just letting them know whc's in charge. You, John Greco, would be the skipper. Think of it. Manager of the Highlanders . . . restored to their former glory, the greatest ball club on earth. And they will be." A bead of cold sweat rolled down John's back. He was paralyzed with fear by the mere thought that he could even consider such an unconscionable proposal. As though reading his mind, Mr. Jonelli replied, "I didn't kill your daughter, John."

"Yeah, you did. You wanted a life for your precious losses, and now you're collecting souvenirs for twenty-five thousand—"

"I didn't lose anything, John," he replied smugly, losing patience.

"What'd ya mean! The game . . . "

Alan poked his head around the door frame.

"It's all right, Alan," said Jonelli, waving him off. Then he leaned forward as if he were about to tell a secret. And he was.

"The second time we met, I believed you—when you told me you wouldn't do it." He spoke in a deep, hushed tone. "I wasn't happy . . . my pride, I suppose. You know about that, having so much of it," he said bitterly. "Haaa-ha-ha! No-no-no, Mr. Greco. My money's been on you; :t always has been. On the nose! Haaaaha! Built my first hotel with those funds. Well . . . what could I do? I'm an honest businessman. You would have received your fair share if you just, pardon the expression, played ball."

"You killed my baby because you didn't get your way?!" shouted John, a plea for Jonelli to say it wasn't so, rage screamed through every pore of his body. Alan rushed in, awaited his orders. Jonelli stopped him once again.

"Now, John, that is an oversimplication," sighed Jonelli, losing all thoughts of recruiting this forever unrecruittable man. John possessed the deranged look of a madman. "Besides, I never killed anybody," Jonelli stated. He open his top desk drawer and pulled out a gun. "Get out," he said, angry at himself for even trying.

John turned as if to leave, then pivoted like a bullfighter. With great strength and agility, he threw his still unopened can of beer at Jonelli's chest—a fastball that knocked the wind out of him, as the gun fired into the ceiling and then fell to the floor. Alan went after John, intent on killing him. John spun and rolled to the floor knocking over the display case containing his bat. The bat miraculously tumbled into his right hand. With one tight compact swing, the bodyguard's jaw was shattered to pieces. He fell to the floor, writhing, now harmless. The bat slammed down and pounded the oak desk, scattering balls and photos and knickknacks about the room like atoms.

"My brother! Is he dead—alive—where is heeeee!?!" demanded John, directly into Mr. Jonelli's face. John's neck was red and blue and bulging, as though he were bench-pressing an ungodly weight. Jonelli coughed and wheezed and did his best to breathe in some air, but he couldn't or wouldn't answer. When he regained his wind, Jonelli arched his back and sat in stone cold defiance, as the bodyguard moaned in agony. Jonelli was right; he was a good judge of character. He knew John Greco wasn't a killer.

The rapid patter of footsteps bounced off the cinder block walls. 'More security guards,' John thought as he left the office carrying his bat. 'It was never Bill Singer's to sell,' he reasoned.

"Mr. Greco!" shouted Darryl, the guard, surprised. "What happened? Thought I heard a gunshot!" Two other guards followed close behind.

"I'm fine. He missed me."

"J.J.!?"

"Yeah."

"What'd he go do a thing like that for?"

"He wants me to manage the team," replied John. "I'm not doing it." He moved past the guards, using the bat as a walking stick.

"Stop! Or I'll shoot!" called one of the fervid rookie guards.

"Go ahead," said John. The rookie pulled his gun.

"Put that down!" yelled Darryl. "Yah gonna shoot John Greco?! Damn!" Darryl gave him a look that said, 'You are dumb!' The rookie holstered his gun while the other guard hid his weapon at his side, not wanting Darryl to see that he too had drawn his pistol.

"White folks," Darryl grumbled, as he watched John disappear around the bend, his bat pounding like a heartbeat.

"You leaving?" called Darryl.

"I'm leaving." John's voice came back softly, a faint reverberation from inside a mammoth shell.

BASEBALL & BENEVOLENCE

RESTLESS, THAT'S HOW John felt when he returned to the clubhouse, unsatisfied and restless. Everybody was long gone from the sad party, an impromptu farewell from the guys which John had attended, before attending to Mr. Jonelli's needs. The locker room was a ghost town. Now was when he really needed them, wanted them. He found some archive boxes and started to clear his desk. An anxiousness pulled at his heart and tightened around his rib cage, leaving him with the lonely feeling of helplessness. He wanted to cry, but couldn't.

He found an Easter Day Parade snapshot of himself, Sharon, and Maya, in the top drawer of his desk. The tears came. Thoughts, sad lonely thoughts flooded his head. He was feeling a bit sorry for himself, but not overtly so. John realized that the photograph had been taken just weeks before her death and that Natt had been the photographer. They all smiled so easily then, father, mother, and daughter, walking proudly down Fifth Avenue, mother and daughter in matching outfits, wearing bonnets . . . bright sunshine . . . a perfect time. He recalled how he had flown to New York from spring training to be with his family on Easter, and how Sharon thought he was crazy, but loved him for doing it. He flew back to Florida and camp that same night. It was just something he wanted to do. The picture brought back all the feelings of the day. They ran through his hands and fingertips like a rare and now forbidden power. He remembered how homesick he used to get; how he always missed his family. 'The only down side to baseball,' he thought. And, then again, there was always the other six months when they were free to do whatever they wanted. He remembered how he loved being a full-time parent half the year.

As he cleaned out his desk, he found still more old photos; he always meant to put them in a book, but never got around to it. They were mostly baseball and family pictures, a few high school snapshots, and many from his bush days. Most of John's minor league buddies never made it to the show, but their smiles filled the frames with the hope and joy of the moment—a moment John was sure none of them would ever give away, no matter what the outcome. He stared at the phone on his desk and had to fight the urge to start hunting down the ghosts of his past. A trickle of blood ran down his hand; a shard of glass poked out between his thumb and forefinger. He removed it, while thinking of the past and beseeching the powers-that-be for compassion in a voice that was saddened beyond recognition. "If I could be with them . . . one more time, we could . . . could . . . maybe the feeling . . . the life we shared would seem so much more complete. If we could just take the time to look at it, think about it . . . about all the things we felt in our hearts, maybe we'd feel better; not so lonely, isolated . . . just knowing the good-hearted are still out there in the friends we let slip away, the loved ones that—just . . . knowing it could still work out."

Before he knew it, he was dialing Dillon Southwood in Maine. One, two, three . . . on the fourth ring he picked up.

"Dillon?"

"I've gone fishing. Tell me who you are. I'll call ya," the machine beeped. John hung up before he could even think about leaving a message.

"I don't wanna worry him," he said, talking to the phone as though the telephone itself had questioned his motives. 'He'll think there's something wrong. Is there something wrong? Yeah. I'm afraid. I'm afraid there's gonna be nothing, nobody, after all this living is said and done. I'm afraid I'll never see my brother and daughter again. I'm afraid I'm losing my mind or lost it long ago. And I'm scared to death that Sharon might lose hers. That's what's wrong. What's wrong? Is it wise to ask questions concerning mortality of an old man? Is it polite?'

His anxiety-ridden monologue played on in his head as he flipped through the photos, stopping only to take a closer look at a picture of himself and Natt. Natty wore a Brooks Brothers suit with a vest and chain. John was in his Highlander uniform. They were shaking hands and smiling for the camera, like the owner welcoming the promising young rookie to the team. It was the day after John got his call to the big leagues. The day after Smithy Lango welshed on a two hundred dollar bet. John used to call Natt "Dr. Greco" when he wore that suit; he said he looked like a doctor. Natt liked the title. Even more, he liked the idea that some people might think he was a real doctor. John remembered, could feel it even now, how proud his brother was of him. 'He wore the doctor's suit to the stadium just to get this picture,' he thought. 'It was hot that day. Too hot for a suit.' They stood right behind home plate a full hour before batting practice. Natt's usually surgeon-steady hands trembled before the shot was taken. John gave his brother a firm handshake and the trembling stopped.

After their photograph was taken, Natt declared, "This is the greatest day. Look at you, John! Look where you are!" Natt stepped up to the pitcher's mound, made a pretend pitch, and laughed at his own silliness. John put on his catcher's mitt and threw Natt a baseball.

"C'mon! Throw me one! You can say you've pitched in Ruth Memorial Stadium," he kidded.

John sighed at the memory of his brother's elation, then continued to examine photos.

BASEBALL & BENEVOLENCE

"Aah . . . Thanksgiving day," uttered John, now thinking and speaking and reliving aloud as he flipped to a favorite holiday photograph.

"John, hon', would you get the leaf down from the hall closet for me?" he heard his mother say, as she prepared the turkey. Dad would make the stuffing. The table would need two leaves that Thanksgiving; the whole family was coming over. First time in the new house. John would have to sit at the kiddie table. Natt was on the borderline.

Mr. Greco took the boys that weekend to see his old high school football team, Barringer. Barringer vs. East Orange was the third oldest football contest in the country. At least that's what Dad Greco said every year, trying to build the interest. Barringer lost that day, not that it mattered a whole lot. They'd have to wait until next year . . . on to Ferrara's Bakery on Bloomfield Avenue in Newark, for pastry—cannolies.

"Mom! We're home!" screamed young Johney. Thinking back, that was the very best moment of the holiday. The smell of turkey and good food cooking the second he opened the door. 'It was amazing how mom always seemed so glad to see us return,' thought John, 'as if she actually missed us.'

John held the photo under the light for closer scrutiny. The table set so perfectly at the onset, now resembled a war zone. John's mom laughed uncontrollably at something her sister Marie had said, while Dad hugged his sister Anne, and his brother Steven stood at the head of the table. He appeared to be giving a toast, or maybe he was just telling a joke or a classic family story. The grandparents smiled at their children's antics. Cousins seemed to be everywhere. Grandma, or Big Nana, would play poker later with the uncles. Her winnings always went to the grandchildren, and she often won. Natt held a turkey leg in the air and pretended to be King Henry the Eighth. John thought how his mom was always herself, but it took a special occasion for his dad to come into his own, to be himself, relaxed, without concern over his jobs, the bills, and the fear of not being able to do enough for his family.

"What's the matter, Johney? Why are you crying?" Betty Greco asked softly, trying her best not to embarrass him. Of course, he had no way of telling her. He couldn't possibly understand the complexity of his feelings at such a young age. So she just held him for a moment, and he was all right. Johney could see that a child's pure spirit is so sensitive to pain, yet so easily comforted by love.

John was grateful for the goodness of his parents. He placed his photos into a manila envelope and the envelope into the archive box. John knew now why he'd cried and why the Thanksgiving picture was one of his favorite photos. His father was free from burden—heartened to just be himself. It was as though John were seeing his dad for the first time and loving him all the more.

John emptied his locker, packing a duffel bag with his baseball equipment. He didn't want a reason to come back, yet he couldn't leave without a proper good-bye.

THERE WAS A chill in the air when John stepped out from the Highlander dugout. He shivered—the same shiver that ran down his spine when Mr. Jonelli offered him the manager's job, a position that would have made his family a negotiable commodity. The tarp covered the diamond and home plate. Auxiliary lighting lit the field, casting an eerie stillness over the park. The odor of plastic from the tarp fought the smell of freshly cut grass. John walked around the plastic cover and into the lawn that was center field. The city with all its sounds and sights loomed quietly in the background, as though not wanting to disturb the tranquility of the serene ballpark. A subway train could be seen snaking through the opening in right center field, just before the 161st Street station. A lone straphanger caught a glimpse of paradise, complete with a man who resembled Adam, as his train cut through the earth and onto the elevated tracks. A warm breeze eliminated the chill. Stars and a crescent moon shimmered like a Van Gogh. John laughed aloud as he thought about stars and moons, immediately transforming them into singles and triples. Gulls flew overhead and seated themselves in the upper deck. They seemed curious about the stripped man in the middle of their field and patiently waited for the show to begin.

Time meant nothing as hours passed like minutes. John laid on the warm earth of center field and traveled into his past, replenishing his soul by revisiting all the people who had made up his life. He saw Tommy and Two Face Pete, Gail Richardson, Carla Smitcht and Karl Page, poor Aaron Frost and Katie Evans, Steve Schneider, Doc Gills, Dillon Southwood, Hank Miller, James Darwin, T.C. Golden, Mr. & Mrs. Gooding and Buddy, Angela and Jason Wheeler . . . countless ballplayers and friends. Thousands of cards and letters with identities and hearts attached flashed through his travels. His mind raced from school to the minor leagues, from holiday to holiday, to the major leagues, scouting, to signing a fan's ball. All the people that a life can touch, John touched again. He hugged and kissed his daughter, who arrived hand in hand with Natt, whom he also hugged. No words were spoken; there was no need. It was Thanksgiving again. For the young and old, the dead and alive . . . and the forgotten. For they were not forgotten on this night, as the parents gave goodhearted laughter a chance, and the grandparents smiled their relief. John wrapped his arms around Sharon and they became one. They drifted on a current, they waved to Jimmy Jackson the Cleveland angel; they marveled at Ben Johnson's speed; they recaptured all the moments that made their lives worth living. They remembered the love after the miracle homer, the beauty it created . . . and the shutters of St. Jude's.

"That you, Mr. Greco?" called Darryl with his hands cupped around his mouth. He stood in the dugout, scratched his head and adjusted himself like he was positioning an outfielder. I guess there's just something about dugouts. The sun was just rising. A trail of clothes led from first base to where John lay in shallow center field. He rolled over and seemed just as surprised to discover himself.

"Yeah . . . It's me, Darryl," he said, trying to act normally. Darryl took a long, hard pull off his pint of whiskey and mumbled something about New York City.

"Ah, ah—you're gonna catch something not dressed like that," he said. And he walked away, turning his back on the buck naked man in center field.

40

SHARON WAS UNDERSTANDABLY upset when John arrived home the next day at seven thirty in the morning. She was wired from a night of coffee drinking, calls to friends, hospitals, and overall panic. He could do little more than reassure her he was all right and put himself to bed. He needed to rest. John slept most of the day as well as the following week with few interruptions.

The newspapers ran the story of his resignation along with the usual history between John and Mr. Jonelli. None of the articles mentioned John being offered the manager's position, and the story itself had been diverted by the same day hiring of Frank Jacky as the new third base coach. Frank was a well-liked baseball man who had spent most of his years in the Mets organization. Frank also happened to be a black man who had been looking for the right coaching spot for quite some time. His hiring was well-received and well-deserved. The news media got tough on Mr. Jonelli for letting John Greco go, but he also received high praise and accolades for hiring Frank, just as Mr. Jonelli had planned.

When the reporters were unable to get a comment from John, the focus of their story naturally turned to Frank, and by mid-June the whole matter was forgotten history. Mr. Jonelli was delighted.

BASEBALL & BENEVOLENCE

To: Mr. John Greco
Fm: J. Jones
Re: Contract
Date: June 19, 1991
John,
I am writing to inform you that I cannot in good conscience honor the remaining two years on your New York High-lander contract. In view of the fact that I have your signed resignation and you were in fact offered a considerable job with the new Highlander organization, your contract is null and void. However, because of your many fine years of service I am enclosing a check for one quarter of your yearly salary and would be willing to add additional funds in the amount of one quarter of your yearly salary pending the return of the bat. These completed monies, one half year salary, would be considered your severance package. I assure you this is a very generous offer, and I imagine that you will feel the same. Best of luck in your future endeavors.
Regards,
J. J.

"What are you going to do?" asked Sharon, after she finished reading the letter. It was sent on the new image Highlander stationery with the darker, tougher shade of blue that was really just black, no pinstripes.

"I'm gonna cash the check. It's mine."

"I meant the bat."

"Keeping it."

"Good," cheered Sharon. She pinched the letter between two fingers, as though not wanting to catch anything from it, and dropped it on the coffee table. Just reading his words felt dirty to her. "You never told me he offered you a job," she said curiously.

"Does it count if he knows you can't take it?"

"Was he serious?"

"I don't know . . . maybe."

"He wanted you to keep the third base job?" she questioned, sensing he was holding back.

"No."

"No? What was it?"

"He didn't see me at third base. He said he wanted me to be his baseball man." John sipped on his scotch and soda—second one of the day that she knew of, and it was only early afternoon. John had been drinking more and more lately. She suspected vodka in his morning orange juice, but said nothing.

"Baseball man?"

"Yeah, he wanted me to manage the team."

"Manager?" The word spilled out of her mouth like a foreign substance.

"Uh-huh, wanted to pay me half a million bucks a year. Can you imagine that?"

"Ooooh, John, honey; I am sorry, so sorry. He's a cruel man," she whispered in his ear, then gave him a loving kiss and gazed into his eyes, wishing she could think of some way to comfort him. "He's caused you— us—one heartache after another. I know it's something you've dreamed of," she consoled.

"It wasn't real, Shar. He knew I wouldn't take it," he repeated in a barely audible voice. "You know what I mean."

"I know, you're right," she said, as she rocked him gently in her arms.

"Hey, remember what you said about the feeling in my hand and the lullaby? Good omens. Right? Even if what happened to me at the stadium was all just fever dreams, they were good fever dreams. Right?" He sounded as though he were trying to convince himself, but she didn't let on. She was glad to hear his optimism again.

THE NEXT MONTH and a half felt like a century to John. He wanted to do something, but nothing held his interest for more than fifteen minutes. At age fifty-four he was out of a job, and the thought of having to move for a new job worried him. He didn't want to leave the area. Sharon was just getting back on her feet and enjoying her work at City Hall. He couldn't imagine taking that away from her.

The past five years had been tough for the Grecos. Their lives had been out of sync since the day Jonelli had emerged as a national celebrity. One or the other of them was always dealing with some sort of illness, and John couldn't remember the last time they were both well. Now it was John's turn.

He spent his days at Tommy's, drinking, talking, and playing one-handed piano; none of which, as I said, held his attention for long. One day I saw him come into Tommy's seven different times. He started at noon for lunch and didn't stop until four in the morning. His visits lasted about half an hour on average. He wasn't one to park himself at the bar and drink for hours on end. He didn't want Faye and Kerrins to think he was drinking heavily, even though I knew they did. He'd taken to wandering about town, as though searching for a sign, anything that would help him believe. At Tommy's, John would scan the bar as if one day he would walk in and Natt would be waiting for him, ready to buy his brother a beer.

"George, want a drink?" John would ask me after he examined every inch of the bar.

"Ssh-sh-sure," I would say, and we would talk. John didn't have much to say about baseball, but admitted he had heard about the constant battle going on between Manager Owens and Mr. Jonelli.

"Sounds like they hate each other," was his only comment.

After the All-Star break, the Highlanders season took a nose dive. They had a wealth of talented young players, but they lacked experience, and the pitching had burnt out by mid-July. Their manager did his best to provide them with outstanding instruction on the fundamentals of baseball. He also protected them from Mr. Jonelli's callous daily outbursts which was something John and many other baseball people respected in Manager Owens. When attacking the players seemed to have little effect, Mr. Jonelli got personal by calling his manager, among other things, a drunk and a troublemaker. Manager Owens was unaware that it was all part of a plan, a demented scheme to demean and belittle the importance of his own team.

"The young players need discipline and the old need diapers, including Manager Owens," stated Mr. Jonelli in one of several famous quotes that appeared daily in the news media. John couldn't help but hear about it.

The question most often asked throughout the country was why didn't Jonelli fire Owens if he disliked him so much? And, why did Jerry Owens, a well-respected baseball man, put up with the abuse? They both had their reasons. The manager felt a responsibility to his players, especially the young guys. They became his cause.

"Mr. Jones can get on me all he wants, but I won't let him go after the team. Major league careers are fragile, especially for the kids. J.J. knows that. He should be ashamed of himself," said the Highlander manager. Jerry Owens wasn't about to quit on his team now, not unless the owner fired him, which, apart from Mr. Jonelli's bizarre and abusive behavior, he had shown no sign of doing. His behavior was incomprehensible, as though he were having fun mocking his own team, his own manager.

Attendance dipped to nothing—seven to thirteen thousand per game since the beginning of August, while the Mets did a gate of forty to fifty thousand across town. Mr. Brenner's lucrative cable contract expired at the end of the '91 season. Yet negotiations to recontract were stalled. Mr. Jonelli wanted even more money for his sagging ball club and would only provide brash, belligerent reasons for his hard-line stance.

"You'll pay me now, or you'll pay me even more later," Jonelli told the cable company. His other partners were up in arms and asked the Commissioner of Baseball to investigate, but nothing came of it. The Commissioner agreed that Jonelli had every right to conduct his negotiations as he saw fit. "After all J.J. is an extremely successful businessman," the Commissioner explained.

Through it all Jonelli's antics didn't seem to bother many folks. His swipes at the Highlanders and Manager Owens just made for entertaining reading in most towns. New York City bashing always helped to sell a few papers. So at the onset, his personal popularity remained intact and unaffected, even though Mr. Jonelli was running the ball club and his three-hundred-million-dollar investment into the ground, or so it seemed.

Jerry Owens had another private reason for seeing the season through— what he secretly called "his morbid curiosity." Figuratively speaking, he wanted to touch the dead body; he needed to feel the texture of its flesh; there was no other way to understand. He, like many in the Highlander organization, had heard the rumors—something about the new Mayhouse Manor Hotel complex, built just outside of Las Vegas with little or no fanfare, not Mr. Jonelli's style at all. That was just the beginning of the manager's morbid curiosity. Jerry Owens had his reasons. Mr. Jonelli had his plans.

"Kerrins, another drink for me and George," requested John, intoxicated. Faye gave Kerrins a disdainful glance. She wasn't pleased with him allowing John to drink so much. The door to Tommy's bar swung open. Faye's stoic expression blossomed into a smile when her sister-in-law entered. Sharon was sharply dressed, beautiful, a high-powered executive coming in for a drink after a hectic day.

"Hey, stranger, haven't seen you in awhile," teased Faye.

"I'm here to collect my husband," replied Sharon, relieved to see him sitting at the bar. "How many times today?"

"Four . . . if you don't count the time he stopped in to use the bathroom."

"How are you, George," Sharon said pleasantly. I greeted her with a smile.

"Oooh . . . Shar. Uuuh, hi. Hey, have a seat." John patted the open stool next to him, a little shaky and a bit surprised. He shouldn't have been; it was the third time this week Sharon had come in to bring her husband home.

"Brian, a beer please." Kerrins served the beer.

"Sure look pretty today, Ms. Greco," said Kerrins, trying to make her smile. She did. John was glad she decided to have a drink. She took a sip, felt her husband's gaze. He gave her his complete attention. She blushed a bit. Sharon thought he was pretty cute when he had a bit too much to drink. The way he'd try to hide it. But she could always tell he'd had a few when he got that hound dog look. His big, sad, sleepy brown eyes said how happy he was to see her. She had to smile.

"John, I've been thinking—"

"Yeah."

"Honey, I think you need to get out of the city. Take a vacation."

"Sure . . . we can take a vacation. Vacation, yeah. That'd be great," he said. He sounded unconvinced, but enthusiastic nonetheless.

"No, John. Not us. You. I want you to take some time. Go somewhere. Do something you always wanted to do. Be free. Think, rest, get into the country or go to a beach. Do whatever you want. I'll be here when you come home." He looked pitifully sad.

"What fun would it be without you?"

"Plenty of fun. You just haven't thought about it enough," she insisted. "C'mon. Think about it. You need to get away. There must be something. Besides . . . "

"Besides, what?"

"I'm not going to be around much the next few weeks. We have some very important . . . important business that Mayor Weldon needs taken care of. The whole staff is working overtime. I won't be here to drag you out of Tommy's every night. Please, John, think about it. It'll do you good," she asked sincerely.

"Well, if you're not gonna be around . . . well, I . . . I could . . . You're gonna think this is crazy!" His idea made him anxious and excited as if he couldn't fathom why he hadn't thought of it sooner. Sharon was right, he needed to get away.

"What?"

"I wanna take a baseball vacation. Ya know, visit my old buddies . . . take in a bunch of games, but as a fan—no cares, just baseball. I know, I'll take in some minor league games, too. Maybe even . . . I'll sit in the bleachers! Maybe even a few Highlander games." Sharon gave her husband a wary smile. She thought he might be better off laying on a beach, soaking up some sun. But this was obviously what he wanted to do.

"Great," she said hesitantly.

THAT NIGHT JOHN planned his trip, still buzzing with excitement and alcohol. He would start in Oakland, California, fly out that Friday and work —or play—his way east, flying or driving depending on how much energy he had and where he wanted to go. After the Oakland/Highlander game, his formal plans would end, and he would be free to do whatever he pleased.

THE NEXT MORNING the alcohol wore off, and the idea didn't seem nearly as fascinating, or romantic, or attractive as it had the night before. But after making a few calls and talking with his friend T.C. Golden in Boston, he decided it wasn't such a bad plan after all, and dutifully set off for California following his not-very-detailed itinerary.

The one constant reminder of home was the ongoing feud between Jonelli and Manager Owens, which was well-documented in the sports pages of every hometown paper he saw during his travels. Just reading the verbal volleys was tiring day after day. The only end in sight seemed to be the last day of the season. 'Was this what Jonelli had in mind when he offered me the manager's job?' John asked himself. Of course, the most confusing element of the bickering was how pointless it all seemed. Did Mr. Jonelli honestly expect a championship season from such a young team? Unlikely. Yet it all appeared to be so deliberate, so by design. The unnerving thought was a source of great concern to John and, I'm sure, Jerry Owens.

The day after John had met up with T.C. Golden in Boston when the Sox beat the Blue Jays in an 11-1 laugher and the day they had met the young lady who looked so much like Sharon, John drove from Boston to Baltimore. This was the last stop of his vacation, where he would watch the Highlanders and Orioles play their final game in Baltimore's Memorial Stadium. The Orioles would move to their new Camden Yards Park in 1992 where, in another time, long ago, the Babe's dad tended bar someplace around second base. This was also the last road game for Jerry Owens and his hard luck Highlanders, a Wednesday afternoon contest with a day off on Thursday. Jerry and John planned to have dinner together that night, then go back to New York the next day.

The vacation had had its ups and downs. John wouldn't say that it qualified as relaxing. However, the Carolina league games he had seen went a long way in bolstering his confidence in the game overall. The foundation seemed so strong and pure in those small towns. Everybody knew each other. The games were tough battles and, at the same time, so easygoing. In Durham, North Carolina, John saw the Bulls play Prince William, a Highlander farm team. The Bulls won it 6 to 4. The game included a one hour rain delay which didn't seem to bother anyone—the party atmosphere only intensified. John had made friends with a group of businessmen who were out for the night and an older woman who told him she never missed a Bulls game.

"Don't I know you?" asked one of the businessmen with a friendly southern drawl. "I never forget a face."

"I don't think so," replied John.

"From up North. Yankee, huh?" the man said with a pleasant smile.

"New York," said John.

The Bull's Dave Poland whacked a two run shot, igniting an enthusiastic hometown cheer. One of the businessmen dropped his beef burrito on his shirt in the process.

"You sure I don't know you?" The man kept asking, eyeing John up and down.

"I don't think so," John said, diverting his gaze back to the game.

"You're somebody. I know you're somebody," the man insisted.

"Jimmy, leave the poor man alone. You don't know him," laughed one of his friends.

"I do, I do so know him!" declared Jimmy, as the vivid memory revitalized itself. "I don't believe it . . . I doooon't believe it!" He kept saying until he had everybody's attention.

"What don't you believe, Jimmy?" called the man wearing the burrito stained shirt.

Jimmy swatted at one of the eighty billion flying bugs that didn't seem to annoy anyone else and yelled, pointing at John, "Ya know who this is?!" Everyone in the small grandstand turned around to see who it was. "That's John Greco! Remember? John Greco! Only man to hit one clean out of Ruth Stadium! 1965. I was five years old," he said proudly.

"Ooooh, my God! He's right!" exclaimed an elderly lady, nearly fainting.

John looked around at the sea of faces and felt embarrassed. He didn't look or feel in top form, and attention was the last thing he sought. John was known in New York, but here you would have thought he was a celebrity, a movie star.

"Huuuuuuu . . . " sounded through the crowd that surrounded Johney, as if they were gasping for air and had swallowed an insect instead. The game all but stopped. "John Greco—John Greco—John Greco . . . " burned through the tiny ballpark. He wasn't sure if he should run for it or pretend the man had been mistaken. Many of the faces in the crowd appeared to be perplexed, bewildered, maybe even shocked. John confused their reactions with his own paranoia as expressions of anger, though he couldn't think of one rational reason for them to be angry with him.

"Mr. Greco! John Greco . . . I'm Doreen!" called the elderly lady who sat a couple of rows behind him, as though he should recognize her. "I write you every Christmas! Doreen . . . I'm Doreen!" The attention shifted to John as though a tennis match had begun. "You and Sharon always sent me such pretty cards," she sighed, so very pleased by the thought. The ball was in John's court.

'Cards and letters. Cards and letters,' he thought, and then it came to him. 'The mail, the letters of love and support. Doreen from the Carolinas, Doreen! She never forgets us at Christmas time. Doreen Calvin from Durham, North Carolina,' he recalled. 'Her boy was killed in a car accident a week before Maya died. The Love Game, she claimed, had turned her life around, given her faith and a will to live.'

"Doreen? . . . Your boy . . . Bill," said John slowly; his throat swelled and tightened. He knew this lovely woman.

"That's right, John. God bless you," she called and started to cry. He made his way to her seat, wrapped his arms around her and wiped away her tears.

"I prayed someday we'd meet," she said.

"It's all right, Doreen," he whispered.

"I can't believe you're here," she smiled as if he were her son.

John made many friends that night. Doreen gave him a renewed sense of usefulness as he was once again reminded of the power of a single life. He promised to visit the next time he passed through.

"And bring Sharon along," said Doreen. "I'd love to meet her."

As John drove from Boston to Baltimore, he thought about some of the amazing moments of his trip from Durham's Doreen Calvin to the young man in Chicago who had him sign a baseball. But most of all he thought about the young woman in Boston who wanted only to meet him and who looked so much like Sharon. As he recalled each scenario, he found the possibilities to be both magnificent and disturbing. The throbbing pain in his bad hand had returned. He pulled the car over to the shoulder of the road and took a couple of aspirin.

'It would be good to see Sharon, the Highlanders, Charlie, and Jerry Owens,' he thought. 'I can't wait to get home.'

41

"I DID THE whole interview while dusting the lobby of The Toronto Mayhouse Manor," joked Jerry Owens, chewing on a piece of T-bone. A clap of thunder shook the charming, turn-of-the-century steak house at its foundation, producing an unsettling eerie quality. John laughed and smiled politely. He knew Jerry was hurting. This wasn't any way to end his respectable career. "Hell, if he's seen enough ball games to be a baseball man, well, I've certainly lived in enough hotels to be a hotel man," cried Jerry. He was getting very drunk, often did when he had the day off.

Manager Owens decided calling an extra practice seemed like a perfunctory idea at best. The Highlanders were thirteen games out of first in fifth place with one week left to the season. So on the last day of John's vacation it seemed to both men that the only proper thing to do was to get drunk. And they did, or tried to, knocking back repeated rounds of whiskey and draft beer. Unfortunately, it was the most sobering drunk either of them had ever experienced. And the drunker they got, the more solemn they became. That had never happened before. Conversation quelled by the time they had finished their meal. They were reduced to talking about the weather. Thunder clapped once again, the loudest one yet.

"Lucky to get the game in," said John, referring to the rain. He tipped back in his chair, maybe a quarter of an inch from flipping himself over.

"Yup," said Jerry. He threw a hundred-dollar bill on the table. "Let's go to the bar."

Both men obviously had much on their minds. They would concentrate their efforts.

"Aaah. . . . Bartender, another round!" demanded Jerry Owens, not intending to shout. Then he turned his attention back to John and said, "Ya know what a kid in Boston said to me last time I was there?"

"No, what."

"He said, 'Baseball isn't much fun if you can't hate the Highlanders.' Shit. That's what I live with! Pity from Boston!" Jerry cried angrily. It occurred to John that he and Jerry had something in common besides the Highlanders. Their names, like it or not, would forever be linked with Mr. Jonelli. "Well, he can't take the history," groaned Jerry, staring into the bottom of an empty shot glass. The bartender poured the next round just as Jerry was about to pick up his head and bark for another drink.

"But he'll try," replied John. Jerry enjoyed John's understated commentary.

"You don't know how right you are, buddy!" he exclaimed. His expression quickly passed from light to dark, as if he had just remembered an unpleasant experience and considered dealing with it right then and there. John did his shot. Jerry seemed about to share. "Listen, you gotta keep this under your hat, 'cause I don't know how true it is." The blood drained from his face, as if he couldn't say what he had to say without looking like an alien.

"What, Jerr? What's wrong? I'm not gonna like this . . . I can tell. You look terrible," said John, as he downed his drink.

"He wants to move the team," said Jerry, gripping John's arm as if pressure was needed to back up his words. John needed some time. He had to think. He knew the correct response, but the alcohol had wiped out legions of brain cells. Finally, it came to him.

"C'mon, Jerry," he smiled, trying his best to put on a good face. "Jack Brenner threatened to move the team to Jersey all the time. It's just a ploy . . . to get more parking or some sort of renovation. It's nothing," he said, although he didn't believe a word of it even as he spoke, and he could tell Jerry wasn't buying his hardball theory either. The manager said nothing; he just stared vacantly at John. John kept trying to convince him, "Jerr, Jersey doesn't have the money. They'd have'ta build a stadium. It's not gonna happen in a recession."

"This is the first you heard?" Jerry asked suspiciously.

"Well, yeah," said John, defensively. "Where am I going to hear if not from you?"

"Your wife."

"Sharon? What are you talking about?"

"She works as an aide to Mayor Weldon. Word is they've been negotiating with J.J. since he took over the ball club. I thought you might know something more, that's all."

The words *important business* ran through John's head. She called it *important business* in Tommy's Bar after she asked him to take a vacation. 'Working late. She wasn't ready to tell me. Couldn't tell me,' he thought. "This is crazy. It's not gonna happen," said John, and then the words *not gonna happen* flowed through his head a thousand times as if caught in limbo, a thought glitch. "Where did you hear this?" he questioned the manager in a dispirited manner. The pieces were all coming together, starting to make sense. Fear led to outrage, outrage to impotence, as Jonelli began to get the best of him once again.

"The office. Memo here, fax there. Someone overheard a phone conversation. But lately, damn, it's just getting louder. And, John, it's not Jersey. It's Vegas."

"Las Vegas. How—" The words, he didn't want to have to use these words, ask these questions. He thought of Jason, how he would feel. He thought how it would crush so many people. "Bartender, another round!" yelled John. Most of the bar turned and glared in his direction. He didn't notice.

"They say that Jone-sy has built—"

"Who's they?"

"People! Aaaah—Joyce, executive secretary—"

"Yeah, I know Joyce. What'd she say?"

"I'll tell ya!" hollered Owens in an anxious whisper. "She said that she's seen blueprints of the new Vegas Mayhouse Manor. She said the only reason she looked at them was because of how odd J.J. acted when he looked at them. She said they made him smile." Jerry leaned over the bar, plucked a lemon wedge from the fruit tray, bit into it, and found the proper taste for his story. "Joyce said they were the only hotel prints to ever show up in the Highlander offices. Now listen, the Vegas Mayhouse is not just a hotel; it's a complex: shopping mall, health club, spa, gambling—the works."

"And?"

Jerry paused to catch his breath. "What looks like a twenty-thousand-seat ballpark. Lots of luxury boxes." Their drinks arrived. The shots were gone before the bartender could turn his back.

"Jerry, you can't have gambling and baseball at the same place; the league won't allow it."

"Don't be so sure about that . . . times are a changing. Jone-sy's got a lot of friends. What's baseball without the Highlanders. Besides . . . believe me when I tell ya, he's got a few screws lose when it comes to New York and our ball club."

"Yeah, but what good's a tiny ballpark?"

"Think about it! Wouldn't you love to see the Highlanders in a brand new, tiny state-of-the-art ballpark? Every seat is perfection. Exclusive. Prices: expensive to ridiculously expensive! High rollers. Exclusive. Did I say exclusive? They stay in your hotel, shop in your mall, gamble at your tables. And I got another theory. He buys the best players on the free agency market. Say seventy-five million in payroll. What does it matter?! He sells cable rights straight across the country! The team America loves to hate! And with good reason. Think of it! With the Giants and Dodgers right next door in California, it will be like old times!"

"That's crazy! You've lost your mind, Jerry. They won't let him make that kind of move . . . not to a gambling town! The owners, the commissioner, the congress—can't happen! Can't happen! Impossible!!"

"We march single file out into the hall, hands over head, head against the wall," said the teacher in a singsong voice. "This is what we do in case of an air raid." John could feel the coolness of the wall, the fear in his heart. "An air raid?! Why would anyone want to bomb us!?" he thought, listening for planes, scared to death.

Johney felt the same way listening to Jerry Owens' theories. It was crazy, but was it possible? The one thing John had learned in this lifetime was just how many things are possible. An idea, bad or good, can easily take root in the proper environment. Had Mr. Jonelli created the proper environment?

"That's the problem, John. Don't ya see. He doesn't care. He wants the Highlanders out of New York. That's his goal. He's one of the richest men in the world. It's about money, but it's more than that. I wish I had lost it, Johney. Maybe I wouldn't care. I feel like the ship's going down on my watch." He sipped his beer and gazed into his mug, trying to read the future within the golden spheres, but the bubbles were too small for an effective reading. He ordered more drinks. "It's just a theory," said Jerry, trying to lighten things up.

'A real good theory,' thought John. "Why?" uttered John, not really wanting an answer. But the manager offered his answer nonetheless. He had asked the same question many times and hadn't had a decent night's sleep in weeks because of it.

"He doesn't wanna spend his nights in the Bronx. Money. More money.

Sunshine. Girls. Showgirls . . . the friggin' Vegas Highlanders! That has a ring to it?!" Jerry paused for a moment, trying to figure out whether it had a ring or not. "Ya know, I don't think he's much of a Highlander fan," joked Jerry boisterously. The bartender delivered their drinks. Jerry glared at him like a mad dog, still fighting the demons his statement conjured, then recovered, pulled a twenty out of his pocket and gave it to the man.

"Here," offered Jerry, "for putting up with all our shit."

"Thank you, sir," the bartender said politely and continued about his business.

"Excuse me, Manager Owens. Brad Coleman, *Baltimore Tribune.* I don't think anyone in the bar could help but overhear your conversation regarding a Highlander move. Would you like to make a comment for the record?" The young reporter had an interesting sense of timing, though his cocky expression told Mr. Owens that he knew he was sitting on the story of a lifetime.

"You listening in? Ya little bastard!" shouted Jerry, infuriated. Mr. Coleman dashed out of the bar before the terribly drunk Manager Owens could lay a hand on him, dancing on air all the way back to his office.

'By tomorrow's paper everyone would know the rumor,' John realized. He felt as though Mr. Jonelli had turned the tables on them once again. Having Jerry break the news was just one more uncomfortable task he didn't have to do for himself. After all, they would have to know eventually. Jonelli would simply deny the allegations until the moving vans prepared to steal away into the night, leaving behind only the memories and the ghost.

As John and Jerry would soon find out, Brad Coleman's article wasn't kind. And it was obvious that he had only heard bits and pieces of the conversation. He'd heard the words *Highlanders* and *move,* but he wasn't sure whether or not he'd heard *Vegas.* He'd misread Jerry's drunken energy as a celebration and insinuated that the public might have been fooled by the bickering between Jonelli and Owens, that they may, in fact, have orchestrated the whole affair "to tear down the public's affection for the team."

Jerry would be devastated when he read the articles. The idea that his name would be forever linked with Mr. Jonelli's and the fall of the New York Highlanders would break his heart. As I said, Brad Coleman was young, a rookie. Many of the older and much wiser reporters who knew both Jerry Owens and Mr. Jonelli wouldn't believe a word of Mr. Coleman's accusations. However, the Highlanders alleged move out of New York was an entirely different matter. Like John, they understood that even the unthinkable could be possible. Mr. Coleman had himself a big story, but like most rookies who find a Great White on the line of their trout pole, he had no idea how to net it.

As I listened to John and Jerry talk on that stormy night in Baltimore, I thought about how Jerry Owens would open his press conference two days later by saying, "I just wanted one more season." One look at his saddened, tired face, and anyone would see he was telling the truth.

Like two wounded soldiers, John and Jerry propped each other up as they exited the Baltimore restaurant. Mr. Jonelli had a way of doing that to folks, draining the life from them as though ringing out a dirty washcloth. John helped Jerry into a cab and gave the cabby the name of Jerry's hotel—The Mayhouse Manor.

"You're a good friend, Johney. I might need a good friend in New York," mumbled Jerry with a drunken despondency.

"I'll be there." John watched the cab pull away until it was gone from sight. The street was still slick and shimmering from the earlier rain.

He was alone, his head splitting with pain as if someone had just cracked him with a bat. His hangover, he realized, had arrived several hours early. There wasn't another cab, car, or person in sight. It was late. And through his pain all he could feel was hate. From the center of his being hate festered like cancer. Johney was consumed by a maddening anger that could only lead to explosive conditions with unpardonable consequences. He hated himself for it, but it was all he could feel. "I can't take it anymore!" he cried, trying to walk. I wanted desperately to reach him before it was too late. John tried to catch his breath; he was overcome by a tight gripping pressure that gathered strength about his chest and rib cage. He felt as though he would die, but his will fought on as he slashed out at the powers that be. "How could you!? How could you let this happen!!?" he screamed to the heavens, then stumbled and fell into the gutter, cursing love and baseball and everything he had believed in, everything he'd held dear, while the tightness around his heart wouldn't give in.

As John lay there, the city of Baltimore went through a complete metamorphosis, a transformation in only a heartbeat. Paved streets turned to cobble stone, electric lamps to gas, cement sidewalks to slate. A sign across the street hung from a post and read in gold letters: Clark Apothecary & Chemist. The smell of horse manure triggered his violent vomiting. John struggled to get to his feet, but couldn't. The long shadow of a large man loomed over him; John felt his presence before he noticed the difference in light and time. He told himself he didn't care and, unfortunately, he believed himself.

"Feeling any better, kid?" asked the man. At first John was scared, then he realized that he knew the voice. "I've spent a few nights in your condition," the man said, letting loose a deep, raspy laugh. Then he grabbed John's hand and with amazing ease pulled him to his feet, until John's eyes were level with his own and their faces within inches of each other.

"Babe?" whispered John, certain he had gone mad or, at the very least, been poisoned by the alcohol. Standing before him, holding him up and dressed in his number 3 pinstripes was Babe Ruth, "Jedge" to his teammates. A dense fog rolled in, creating a hazy yellow glow about the gas lamps that lined the street. 'Where am I?' John thought.

"Don't worry. You haven't lost your mind, kid. It's your innocence that's the concern," Ruth smiled. "Hey, that was one heck of a homer you hit, John."

"Who are you? Who put you up to this? You're good—real good—too good! Was it Jerry? This whole night! It's one big joke?!" But he knew it wasn't. "Tell me it's a joke! Tell me the whole thing's a joke," John pleaded. Then shook himself free from Ruth's grasp. A stream of sweat ran down from his brow. His eyes bulged as he circled the mysterious man. Ruth stood completely still, never turning to follow John's path.

"I am, who I am, chap."

"How—"

"See what I mean about your innocence. Last week in Durham with Doreen Calvin, you would've believed me. But tonight, well tonight's a whole new ball game." That statement stopped Johney cold. Nobody knew about Doreen Calvin but Doreen Calvin.

"Innocence? I lost my innocence a long time ago."

"You lost your brother and your baby a long time ago, John, not your innocence. What? You think innocence is gone after your first dirty magazine or after you swipe a candy bar? No-no-no, Johney," proclaimed Ruth, good-naturedly. "Innocence is faith in the unknown and the belief that the unknown is infinitely good—only you don't know you believe that or anything else, because you're innocent!" he laughed, pleased by his definition.

Ruth removed his cap and wiped his brow. His mood quickly changed from lighthearted to sober as he conceived a more meaningful definition. "It's the way kids should feel about their parents, adults about their lives. It's decency. It's your dreams. It's a billion different ideas about love and passion. For us, Johney, it's baseball." He took three quick steps back as if he were shagging a fly, then set himself in his invisible batter's box. Babe lost the smile from his large round face. As his eyes focused, he swung. He performed his pantomime without a hint of lunacy and not a shred of humor. For all John knew he just may have shagged that fly and hit the pitch. Ruth seemed pleased with his at-bat.

"You've had your share of tough times, but you've never stopped believing 'til tonight."

"Tonight?" uttered John, as he took a seat at a conveniently located bench.

"Uh-huh. That's why I'm here," said Babe.

John watched the weather change from foggy to a clear, pristine night. Seeing the moon and stars felt reassuring and somehow removed any doubts about his meeting with The Babe. Ruth appeared to be squaring off against the North Star, as though it were about to race down to earth, a meteoric fastball. He took his swing. John was sure it was a hit. Ruth spat on the cobblestones and took a deep refreshing breath of air.

"See, baseball has come a long way. It's grown into something special, something for folks to believe in when so many things seem to have failed. It may not seem like it, but it's a much cleaner game nowadays. More just. Healthier. The game itself has always been perfection," said Ruth as he weighed each word carefully. "This is an important time; people need it more than ever. They need to know the goodness behind the idea is real, to understand that the quality to all life is within the soul of each of us—our shared soul. Baseball is humbling. It is filled with grace and needs to be benevolent. But only the people can make it so. Only the good folks can help a neighbor, teach a child, care for the sick, and find hope for the impoverished. Only the decent folks can rediscover their own innocence and find benevolence in the heart of a game. Most folks, I'm glad to say, are honest, hard working people. Baseball and benevolence, John—that's what I'm telling ya. It's time. It's possible. Lots of things are possible." His tone took on the quality of a double edged sword. "You always had it, kid. You had it big time. Remember the game you hit the homer in?"

"Yeah?" John whispered.

"Remember how it felt? It was different, right? I mean than any game you've ever played. Wasn't it?"

"Well, yeah."

"C'mon. What about it?!" pushed Ruth, trying to draw him out.

"Aaah . . . it was quiet. Peaceful."

"Uh-huh."

"I remember how clear, focused the ball looked. It would've been harder to miss it. Impossible to miss it."

"Ya see? Do you know why you played ball that day?"

"Because I could count on it, trusted it . . . I guess it made me feel safe."

"That's right, and you believed with all your heart that baseball could turn the ugliness you felt into something good, something positive. And it did. And that helped a lot of folks over the years. But now—" The Babe raised an eyebrow, then reconsidered his pitch. "C'mon, kid, let's toss the onion."

"I—" John was about to say, "I can't," when Ruth pulled a couple of gloves out of thin air and tossed him one. John caught it with this left hand, the crippled hand, only now it performed as well as the day he was born. "How did—" John cried as he worked his fingers back and forth, bending his wrist to and fro. Tears swelled in his eyes, a lump formed in his throat as he thought of swinging a bat, playing the piano, and holding Sharon extra tight again. He wanted to have that catch but his body shook, overwhelmed by the generosity of the gift and paralyzed by decades of pent-up grief. Ruth put his arm around John, doing his best to calm him down. Babe made Johney take a seat, benched until he was ready to take the field.

"Easy, John. . . . You've had a tough time of it lately. A lot of people have. I wanted to give you something, not kill ya," he laughed.

"You gave this to me?" John strained to get the words out.

"No. Not me personally. I'm the messenger."

"What are you, Babe?"

"I'm just a man, John. Right now I'm a man," said Ruth. He seemed unsure, as if he really didn't know. "C'mon—" He smacked the ball into the palm of his glove. "Let's have that catch! What'd ya say." And they played catch. Each throw, each catch was more priceless than the next, until Babe Ruth declared himself almost out of time. "I got something to tell ya, John. It's very simple." Ruth's smile never deserted him. "Keep your faith. Believe in baseball and those who are dearest to you, and it will be all right."

"That's all?"

"That's all." Babe turned and started to make his way down the street.

"Is this some kind of religion?" John called after him. Babe turned and chuckled.

"Baseball is a tool . . . a path to the positive . . . one of many good reasons to live . . . and a small part of the incomprehensible."

"Why me, Babe?" Ruth removed his cap and scratched his head.

"You really are a bit of a simpleton, aren't you, John? Well, I guess I was, too." He tossed the ball high into the sky and it never came down.

"You could have made a great deal of money; possibly saved the lives of your daughter and your brother; led, as they say, the good life. And nobody would have faulted you for it. They didn't fault me. I don't know, maybe that's why I'm here. But what you did was right because it was best for everyone. Your not giving in made the world a better place. Most of the time folks do the right thing, and there isn't even someone to pat 'em on the back for it. But you, John, you even had'ta pay a high price to do it. Only one thing's certain, it ain't easy to look at the big picture and do what's right. That's 'why you.' That's why we're here together, because a chap like you can't do it any other way. And me, I'm here to help. We've all been tempted by the easy street. In your last game, folks saw a man they could depend on, a man they could back with all their hopes and dreams—show their kids what a hero, a real hero, looked and acted like. Maybe I didn't set the best example, but my heart was right. I loved the kids. You, John Greco, you are a flesh and blood man who has sacrificed to do what is right and just," said Ruth, sincerely, as he adjusted his cap, and put his hands in his back pockets. He waited for the sign.

"I don't know . . . if I knew—I mean, about my brother and daughter— I don't think . . . "

"Don'tcha see? There's never any way to know. You can only account for your own actions. You followed your convictions. You can't blame yourself for not knowing how dark the souls of others are . . . were. And you shouldn't discount your actions in hindsight. With more information you might have made another choice, but it probably wouldn't have meant giving in. You feared for your brother's life, so you didn't go to the police. Now ya know that really didn't matter. Right?"

"Do you know about my brother, Babe?" he asked hopefully, nervously stretching his fingers wide and gazing into the palm of his now perfect hand, still very much afraid it was all just a dream.

"It's no dream, kid. You'll wake up tomorrow and be able to use it for the rest of your life," Ruth said reassuringly. "About Natt—"

"Ya know 'im?"

"I know of him. But that's about all I know. I can say this, he's in a good place."

"But is he dead?"

"To your way of looking at it, yeah, he's dead," replied Ruth, not overly sympathetic, confirming what John had long dreaded.

"Babe, do you know about Maya, my daughter?" Ruth grabbed a baseball from out of the sky, or maybe the one he threw earlier had just returned. He tossed it to John.

"She's special, John, very special . . . and in a very good place," he sighed.

"They love you and Sharon and the family a lot. They think about you often." Ruth took several quick steps back.

"Wait! Babe, don't go . . . we haven't even had time to talk baseball," called John. Ruth laughed and set himself in the batter's box once again.

"That's all we've been talking about, kid. C'mon! Let's see your stuff. Give me your best pitch. Let's see what you can do. Let's see if the Bambino can take ya home!" John hustled to his imaginary pitcher's mound.

"Now you can say ya pitched to The Babe," he said merrily. John thought of Natt at Ruth Stadium when he had said something similar. "Of course, nobody will believe ya!" Ruth laughed again, then regained his concentration to focus on the pitcher and the pitch. The dim lighting, culled from stars, lamps, and the moon, didn't appear to bother him at all. John went into a big wind-up and let it fly. Babe swung his invisible bat and launched the ball into orbit. It sailed across the sky like a shooting star, while John made a wish, a wish to believe in baseball and the people he held dearest. And never again would he forget that wish or the night when he met Babe Ruth.

"Need a little work on your fastball, Johney! You pitch like a cousin o' mine," shouted Ruth, excitedly. He raised his brows high, making a silly, jubilant face and practically danced around the invisible bases. Then doffed his cap at the completion of his trip.

"Cousin of mine?" questioned John. Ruth smiled. The old expression brought back fond memories for him.

"In my day, a pitcher that was easy to hit was referred to as a cousin o' mine. Haaa-ha." John laughed along with him.

John thought how Ruth and Natt would've been great pals. They both loved life so . . . they both loved to laugh. 'Probably would have died a lot younger, too.'

"Nice shot," said John, not overly surprised by the hit. 'Nothing would surprise me,' he thought.

"Thanks," said Babe, as he filled his lungs with fresh cool air. He seemed to be enjoying the visit back to his hometown. John wasn't sure why, but he got the feeling Babe didn't get out much. Then again he wasn't sure if there was anything to "get out of."

"Babe, what'd ya think of the Highlanders? We don't win 'em the way you used to." Ruth seemed amused by John's modesty.

"Or the way you used to, John," he said sentimentally. "They'll win again, and they'll lose again. I'm proud of every Highlander team that ever took the field," he said confidently. "With few exceptions the uniform has always been worn with pride. That's what counts—not wins. I'm proud of all ball clubs; every town, every city, every sandlot team filled with kids and joy. And though the Highlanders are the greatest in my heart, it's important for everyone to be a winner at least once in their lives. And I think the great Highlander ball clubs, like yours and mine, taught people how to win. Showed 'em what it takes. And that's what is best for everybody, especially the kids. The wins, they go where they should go, no place else. They go where the hearts and minds tell them to go. And that's not always New York," he said with a smile.

John could tell this was one of Babe's favorite subjects, as if it were his duty to contemplate such questions. Ruth sat himself on the bench. John sat alongside him, and Ruth continued his talk.

"Funny, sometimes the losses are better than wins. The feeling of losing, I think, stays with ya, makes an impact, can really get ya thinking. May even make you a better player, a better person. A loss brings people together as much as a win. They're both perfect. Without one there can't be the other. Either way the point is not to suffer or celebrate alone. Ya-know-what-I-mean? That's the point. Wins, losses, numbers—they're not the point. Folks spend most of their lives working just to have some time to play. Win or lose, the time to play or the time to watch chaps like us play is winning, no matter what. Folks deep in their hearts, they know all this. You know this, too, John. That's why you couldn't turn your back on baseball. It's more than wins and losses. It's how we feel about ourselves, our friends, our family, folks in general. Times are changing. There's a need in us to get over the wins and losses, who's right and who's wrong, that kinda stuff, and to simply better ourselves. But before you can do that ya gotta come together. Some folks might think baseball is just a game, a sport, a business. And it is all of those things. But when the focus is on the pleasurable moment that we're sharing, it's good and right and balances laboring. It's our hope manifested in a game. See what I mean, John?"

"Yeah . . . " he said, as his hatred began to dissolve. This wasn't the Babe he had read about. Ruth walked back to his imaginary batter's box, set himself, and took a swing at the moon. John could feel the breeze from his bat. The current of air it created transported him back to his childhood, a time before he knew hate.

Fourth of July, Mountain Edge, New Jersey. . . All the neighbors were over to watch the fireworks in the Greco backyard. The local fire department would shoot them from on top of the small, but beautiful, Watchung Mountain range. Mr. Greco grilled hot dogs and hamburgers. The adults sat at the long redwood picnic table, laughing, talking, and having a good time as they waited for the fireworks to begin. John could feel how comforting those happy adult sounds were as a child. While the parents talked, John and Natt and the other kids ran about catching fireflies and making windmill circles with their sparklers. Later, when completely exhausted, they fell asleep on the blankets their moms had laid out to cover the soft grass.

The Greco property had the best view, because it didn't have any of the towering oaks found in most of the neighbors' yards. John's dad wanted his yard open. "So the boys could play ball," he'd say. Whenever a window broke, John's mom would jump with fright, while his father would be filled with pride that his boys could hit a ball that far—the first few times anyway. Then the boys learned how to fix a window, and it didn't happen as often. Their dad had an interesting way of teaching bat control. John remembered those summer nights as so warm, they often went barefoot. He recalled the sweet taste of Jersey corn on the cob, and how they would throw the cobs in the tomato garden to create a mulch. Then it was time for watermelon.

"You had a nice childhood," said Babe, his voice pulling John back.

"Yeah, I did—what just happened?"

"You were reliving." Babe pointed to his head. "The mind can do so much, so much more—" He stopped himself in midsentence as though he had just been given a directive.

"Are you telling me I was there?" asked John. Babe shrugged his shoulders and changed the subject.

"You're lucky. You had good parents; you got a nice family. A lotta kids don't. Some people seem to wanna shut out the world, which in a way is understandable. Information coming at ya from every direction can really dull the senses after awhile. But folks have'ta remember that the little things are really the most important. Ya know, playing with your kids . . . talking with your teenagers . . . remembering what it takes to make your wife smile or even yourself when things aren't going so well. Folks need to forgive each other. That's important. Nothing else really." He put his hands on John's shoulder blades and looked him square in the eye.

"Have you ever forgiven yourself for not avenging the murders?" Ruth didn't wait for John's reply. "Of course, you haven't. You've seen too many movies. Another murder is not what is best for everyone. A hero, you're a hero, that's what they need—not a guy wearing a cape with all the knowledge of the world at his fingertips. They need a guy just like them, an honest-to-goodness hero. Darkness can't be fought and conquered with more darkness, John. It just makes it darker. Darkness is fought with light. Show them the light! They wanna see it! Give them what they're looking for. Remember the message, and the rest will come naturally," Ruth told John. "Do you understand?"

"I think," said John, "but should I forgive him or fight him?" He was sincerely confused, which made Ruth smile.

"Now you're asking questions," he declared. Babe grabbed another baseball out of the sky. He inspected it carefully, like an umpire checking to see if it was doctored. "Forgive him in your heart for the sake of the people. Then fight him by your own rules, John—by the rules of light and faith. Only then will the battle truly mean something. Otherwise, all you have are more casualties in an unending war. See what I mean?" Babe handed John the ball and slipped his hands into his pockets.

"Your Mr. Jonelli is a very dark soul and a visionary to boot. He truly is a gambler. His plans could have serious repercussions. Baseball would be just the beginning. Snapping the back of baseball would be like breaking the spirit of a magnificent stallion. Not easy to do, but the rest is just riding. Remember how he was looking for the edge in the Love Game. He didn't get his way, and he made you pay for that. But in the end he still got what he wanted. Didn't he? Don't try to outthink him, John. Just believe. If it's right in your heart, it's right in your head. Say, there's a nice little slogan for ya to remember. 'Right in your heart, it's right in your head!'" Babe laughed, and through his laughter John heard him say, "Don't worry, I'll put you in a good place."

John drifted back to the Fourth of July in the valley of the Watchung Mountains, just below where the silent movie stars once lived. Only now he was sixteen and with Carla Smitcht, his lifesaving partner. They desperately searched for a place to be alone. All the neighbors were over to see the fireworks, as usual. The mortars pounded the night sky as the little kids screamed and squealed with every bang, every explosion of color. The adults had a contented ease about their admiration, as the kaleidoscope rockets decorated the town of Mountain Edge. John and Carla found a quiet place on the screen porch, where they kissed throughout the display.

Babe Ruth hugged the earth good-bye and called to the sixteen-year-old boy, "God is where the people gather, to better themselves." His happiness, his laughter echoed off the mountainside and disappeared in a blaze of glory. Just what you would expect from Babe Ruth.

"You hear that?" asked young John, nervously.

"There's no one here, silly," Carla replied playfully, without a care in the world. A warm breeze covered them as the sky lit up blue, green, yellow, and red.

"Hey! Get up. Get your ass moving."

John slowly opened his eyes to Emory Street in Baltimore—paved, no cobblestones, no gas lamps. A policeman kept hitting the soles of his shoes with his nightstick, barking at him to get up. He looked relieved when he saw John's eyes open. The officer didn't want to deal with a body at six in the morning.

"Sorry, sir," mumbled John, apologetically. "I had a long night. I'll be getting back to my hotel now."

"You do that," said the grumpy officer, as his coffee steamed the window just above the dashboard of his cruiser. He longed to get back to it. John picked himself up. One look at his hand, and it all came flooding back. He wasn't hung over and had the energy of a teenager.

"Hey!" shouted the officer. "Is that yours?" He aimed his stick at the baseball in the gutter.

"Yeah . . . it's mine," said John, and he picked up the ball. There was writing on it with tiny stars that circled the sphere. It read: Good luck, Kid—Babe Ruth. 'Still signing autographs,' John thought.

WHEN JOHN ARRIVED home, a gang of reporters were camped out in front of his house. The news had hit the air waves and every reporter in town was scrambling for a statement from Jerry, John, and Mr. Jonelli. By Monday morning the front page headlines read: "Highlanders Packing," "The New Deal," and "Say It Ain't So!" *The Times* announced, "Highlanders Consider A Move." It was the only topic of conversation around town and was quickly becoming a do-you-remember-where-you-were-when type event. John recalled Babe's words as he was mobbed, stepping out of a taxi.

"A comment!"

"Please, John, what are you thinking?"

"Is Owens working with J.J.?"

"Is this why you were fired?!"

"Are the Highlanders leaving New York?!"

"Where are they going?!!"

Microphones, video cams, and cameras were pushed and shoved and thrust at him from every direction. He was completely surrounded as he tried to push through the crowd while carrying his suitcases. Sharon waited for him at the top of the stoop, glad to see that the police had arrived to help her husband.

"C'mon, John, just one statement," shouted an aggressive reporter.

"Okay. . . . Just take it easy. I have one thing to say." He waited for the shouting to stop. The buzz of the hive diminished to a less annoying buzz of the hive.

"I don't know if there's any truth to this thing, but I do know Mr. Jonelli, J.J. to you, is capable of anything. And I know Jerry Owens is one of the very best people in baseball, incapable of conspiring with Joe Jonelli." A hundred more questions were fired at him as he muscled his way up his own front steps. John smiled at Sharon as she gazed at him in astonishment; he carried a suitcase in each hand.

"John?!" she cried, cutting through the clamor of questions. Her hands rushed to her face, as she tried to contain the tears of joy while catching her breath at the same time. All activity came to a stop in an instant. Sharon's reaction shocked them into obedience. He dropped his bags, and she fell into his arms. The cameras snapped pictures of the elated couple.

"I got a lot to tell ya," he whispered.

"I guess you do." Sharon whispered back, as he held her tighter than she could ever remember. Before going into the house John turned to the people, held up his hands and arms and wiggled his fingers.

"Look!" he shouted. "Two hands!"

The few who understood applauded; the rest were filled in on the story. John's story, dating back to 1965, ran in all the major papers on the following morning. Long forgotten details of love, murder, tragedy, and unassuming bravery were resurrected. And, as the Highlander archivist phrased it, "A promising career cut short by injury," was remembered.

42

"JOHN, I HAVE something to tell you," said Sharon. He turned his attention from the piano, still reeling with the joy of playing again.

"You don't have to," he replied. "I know about the negotiations. I understand why you couldn't tell me. It must have been very upsetting for you, Shar." He was certain that would be her confession.

"John, Jason called this morning," she said, looking distressed.

"What? Is something wrong? Did something happen?" he asked, concerned.

"No, no . . . he's fine. He saw the Baseball Man—Natt—last night. I'm worried about him. He's working double shifts again. I think he's lonely," she sighed. "I don't like it when he works so late."

"Tell me what he said."

"He said he got off work around one in the morning. You know Jason walks home every night; he must have a guardian angel." She considered crossing herself. "John, he sounded scared. He said things had changed before his eyes. One minute everything was normal—cars, streets, the all-night bodega. Then he felt tired, rubbed his eyes, and when he looked up, he said it had all changed. That everything looked older, but at the same time new, cleaner. He said even the ballpark seemed different; the lights and the streets that surrounded it, like an old picture he has in one of his Highlander books."

"And?"

"And he said that's when Natt appeared. Jason said Natt told him not to lose faith in baseball—"

"And believe in those dearest to him?" John couldn't help but interrupt.

"That's right. Something like that. How did you know?"

"I got the same message last night," he said. "I bet Natt is Jason's guardian angel. Humph, got himself a job."

"Did you see Natt, too?"

"No. Babe Ruth."

"Babe Ruth." Sharon made herself sit down.

"Yeah." He flexed his hand and smiled like a little boy with one heck of a secret.

"Are we—could we really be talking about this," uttered Sharon. "Conversations with dead people." She put her hand to his head to see if he was running a temperature. He wasn't and, in fact, never looked healthier. "Why you? Why Jason?" she asked.

"I don't know. We wouldn't be my first choice in a crisis," replied Johney.

Sharon tried to reassure herself as she thought, 'At least John doesn't think he is Babe Ruth.' She questioned him with a weary glance, "John, don't you think this is the slightest bit strange?"

"No."

"Did Babe tell you about the ball?"

"The ball?"

"Yeah, Natt told Jason to bring it to the stadium for the last game of the season."

"Oh," said John. "I guess I'd better get tickets." Sharon allowed herself another questioning glance.

"Look, Shar. I don't get it either. But maybe we have'ta stop looking for explanations. I've lived most of my life wondering if I'm some kinda nut job. I figure guys that think they're Napoleon must really believe it, too. 'Why' doesn't make any difference now. Something's gonna happen; something can happen, and I have no idea what. All I know is that me and Jason could somehow be involved. Babe said everyone needed to win sometime."

"Babe? John—" She cut herself short. "I'm sorry, what did Babe say," she said softly.

"He said the Highlanders taught folks how to win and lose—not on a battlefield but in a park and in their hearts. He said people are better because of baseball. Shar, I want to believe that. . . . Maybe I can go to bat for the good guys. I did it once; I could do it . . . maybe I'm going to bat again, Shar." He said, as he examined the palms of his hands. "Ruth said I should fight by the rules of light and faith. I'm not a smart guy, just an old ballplayer. The rules of light and faith . . . I don't know? He sez they're in me. Crazy, huh? What do I know. Babe Ruth tells you something, ya listen. You just take his word for it. Something's happening to me—to us—it's been happening all along. Okay?" asked Johney, practically begging his wife, fully aware of how crazy he sounded and very much afraid that she wouldn't understand.

"You know we're not just talking about Natt and Babe Ruth, right?" she asked. She couldn't help but wonder how much thought her ballplayer had given the subject.

"Yeah . . . I know," he said. John pulled back the curtain from the living room window just in time to see a policeman remove a reporter from their tiny rose garden.

"You're asking me to believe a lot."

"I know. He said it was part of the incomprehensible," replied John. Sharon stood behind him and gazed out the window at the thinning crowd of reporters; then wrapped her arms around his waist and hugged him.

"Oh," she said.

"They have no idea what the real story is," John sighed, referring to the media.

"And we can only guess," Sharon replied.

"JOHN, JUST GO out there and tell 'em I have a brief statement to make. Then I'll answer questions," said Jerry. He was nervous and kept adjusting his tie that wasn't tied all that well in the first place. The Sheraton Hotel pressroom was filled far beyond capacity, so crowded that they had to move the entire event into their banquet room. Reporters and media people from all over the world showed up with the same enthusiasm they might have for covering an American war.

"I don't know why I'm so nervous. I've done this a thousand times," said the manager in a voice that barely resembled his own.

"You have nothing to hide," said John. "Tell 'em the truth."

"John . . . your hand? How . . . ?"

"We'll need a few drinks for that story."

"Must be some story."

"One of the best."

Jerry nodded, then said, "Ready?"

John made his way to the podium and gave Jerry's announcement. Questions bombarded him from every direction.

"I'm only here as a friend and supporter of Jerry Owens," John said calmly. He stepped back so Jerry could take the stage.

For the first time big Jerry Owens looked unimposing. Gone was the ever-present smile, the good-natured persona, the fortress of optimism. Hollywood couldn't have cast a more perfect Highlander skipper. Jerry's massive presence could build the confidence of an entire city. He was the teacher with unlimited patience, always reassuring, always inspired. Jerry played a game for a living with full comprehension of his own good fortune. 'But that man wasn't at the podium today,' John thought. 'Not yet.' This was some other man, a prizefighter too dizzy to walk and too proud to sit down. It was a tough season for Manager Owens, a year Mr. Jonelli would've loved to put John through—an expensive entertainment, perhaps—the destruction of a hero and Highlander savior, more likely. Today Jerry surprised everyone by just looking like a man. He held a plain piece of paper in his hand and began to read from it.

"I just wanted one more season," he began, his voice weakened by fatigue and the tragic moment of history he was about to make. "Yesterday . . . the *Baltimore Tribune* printed . . . an article . . . a report . . . saying—" He sounded as if he were running out of gas, sputtering. "Yah, shoot," he groaned as he crumbled the paper into a ball and dropped it on the floor. "Hell, you people know what it said—probably better than I do." He was beginning to act and sound like the old Jerry O., the skipper of the ship. "I've always been straight with ya. I know what you wanna know. Is he moving the team? I don't know. It's a rumor—a big rumor, and I've heard it. That's what I know. I'm gonna quote a friend of mine, John Greco. Read it in today's paper, and I agree with him. Your J.J., 'is capable of anything.' I don't think it's any secret that me and J.J. don't get along—a lot. That's what pissed me off more than anything in Mr. Coleman's article. Just the idea that we could be pals sickens me. I gotta tell ya . . . why I haven't been fired is a mystery to me. Maybe one warm body is as good as the next to The Boss. Ah . . . ah, maybe I'll be fired right after this conference. But I won't quit!" He gave them his first smile, and they gave him a smattering of applause. "I took this job to fulfill a dream of mine, to be a Highlander—wear the pinstripes. In baseball you always wonder what it would be like. And that part of the experience I wouldn't give away for all the money in the world. Hey, I'm an old guy. What've I got, two, three days left in the season? I'm retired after this one, and not because of the team; those guys made me proud. And in a couple of years they'll all be men, and New York will have a great baseball team again. They gave me everything they had, every day, through all the bullshit, the ridicule, the abuse, and yes, folks, even the sabotage. They played hard because they loved baseball. I'll tell you this—those kids will win because they've learned, learned to win and lose with respect. Your team's gonna be okay if you can keep them." He paused to let the thought sink in.

"I just wanted one more season, a dream season. Maybe it didn't work out as I'd planned—seems nothing ever does, but I got part of my dream nonetheless, and . . . and I thank you and the people of New York for it. Thank you." He wiped his brow, adjusted his tie, and waited for the barrage of questions to come firing from his audience. Jerry pointed to a reporter in the front row, a real screamer with a high, screeching voice.

"Manager Owens, do you know where he might move the team?"

"I only know the rumors I've heard, and I don't think it would be responsible of me to repeat them. You guys have'ta find Mr. Jonelli and ask him. I'm here to tell ya I have nothing to do with his plans, and I'm retiring at the end of the season."

"Is it Vegas?" screeched the screamer.

"Hey, it could be Vegas; it could be Beverly Hills. What's it matter if it ain't the Bronx? And it ain't the Bronx. You should be more concerned with getting to the bottom of this thing. Find ways to make sure the Highlanders stay in New York, even if ya have'ta write it into the Constitution."

"Why do you think you still have a job?"

"Probably because I detract attention, like I'm doing right now. There's a man in this town who knows all the answers to your questions. Ya-know-what-I-mean? Why isn't he here? These are serious allegations. If you were him, wouldn't you want to put the fire out as soon as possible?! Especially if it wasn't true!"

Where was Mr. Jonelli? That was the question on everyone's mind. And yet, there was an uneasy tension in the air, an energy that begged Manager Owens to tell them that everything was going to be all right, that he was drunk and made the whole thing up to bad mouth a boss he despised, that Brad Coleman got the story all wrong. They would have been satisfied enough with that story, happy even with that story. The media people, especially the New York media, seemed excited and terrified at the same time. The biggest sports story of the century, and nobody really wanted to cover it. After they asked Jerry about fifty more questions that he couldn't answer, somebody finally asked one he could.

"Jerry, if it's true, the move, how does it make you feel?"

John considered his own jumbled mass of emotions and thoughts and prayed Jerry would come up with something better, more coherent, than his own. Jerry took a sip of water and a long, hard look across his audience. He had made up his mind. He decided this was something he needed to get off his chest.

"I think the Highlanders moving out of New York would be a crime. I would want to protect baseball the way the game protected me. I'd battle it . . . I'd consider it an attack. It's an idea filled with mean-spirited greed. And . . . if I can do something about it, I will. It would be an honor to give something back to baseball and this incredible town." Jerry spoke his words with such conviction that he had earned an ovation.

For a second John felt as if things weren't so out of control after all. But the euphoria only lasted an instant as Mr. Jonelli appeared midway through the ovation, snuffing it out like a cigarette butt. He made his way to the podium flanked by two bodyguards, one wearing a neck brace. The single moment of joy was over as Jerry Owens allowed Mr. Jonelli the stage. They briefly crossed bitter glances. The second act was about to begin.

Jonelli cleared his throat, handed his cane to one of the guards, and slipped off his suit jacket. Maybe he was feeling the heat. He examined the crowd, trying to find the pulse, the mood. How far could he go with them?

"Bravo, bravo . . . Mr. Owens . . . how very inspiring. Now, let me try." He tempered his words with a hint of sarcasm.

"I heard you've been looking for me," Jonelli joked. Nobody laughed, and he immediately found the pulse of the crowd.

Reporters fired questions from all sides.

"Please, please! I also would like to make a statement," requested Mr. Jonelli. "Then you may ask your questions." He had no idea what he was about to say as he often relied on what he considered to be his superior instincts.

"The first thing I'd like to say is . . . " Jonelli spoke the words slowly waiting for an idea to present itself. "Is . . . " Then it came to him. "I'd like very much to apologize to all baseball fans . . . to the country for that matter. In a time when role models are scarce, I hold myself responsible for Mr. Owens' behavior, and the season's long drunken rampage he's conducted all across America." These remarks were greeted with icy silence. Mr. Jonelli knew his personal and moral attack might not play well in New York, but he also knew that this press conference was national, and it would play in Peoria. 'Keep the big picture in mind,' he thought. "Because of the well-documented and ongoing problems between myself and Mr. Owens, I regret to say that I cannot in good conscience extend his contract."

"Old news. He's already retired!" shouted someone in the back.

Jonelli raised his hand, gesturing to let him speak. "However, out of respect for his otherwise distinguished career, I would like for him to do as he wishes and finish out the 1991 baseball season." *Distinguished* slithered off his tongue with mock recognition, pity, and contempt. Mr. Jonelli had a knack for making everything and everyone seem trite and inconsequential by comparison to his more worldly concerns and objectives. His tone insinuated a higher sense of values and personal righteousness.

"Needless to say, I am not as impressed with this Highlander season as Manager Owens. And . . . if I recall correctly, most of the writers in this room agree with me."

"Are you moving the team or not?"

Jonelli ignored the question and continued speaking. "I would also like to announce that I am presently negotiating with the City of New York to dramatically improve the stadium. We need more fan support, and that means a better equipped ballpark, more parking facilities, easier access, private boxes, and a gourmet restaurant. . . . That will bring the fans out! That's what the Highlanders need—what they deserve! And I'm doing my damnedest to get it!" He was half expecting applause, but it never came, though he was pleased with his little off-the-cuff speech all the same. 'Peoria,' he thought. 'They'll buy it.'

Mr. Jonelli took a step back and in a soft whisper said to John, "I'm still interested in the bat; heard you have the ball, too. One hundred thousand dollars." He smiled devilishly, knowing John would never give them up. 'Principles,' he thought, shaking his head, amazed at the fool who wouldn't sell a bat and ball for fifty thousand a piece.

'He's just trying to get under my skin,' John told himself as he tried to repress the unspeakable thoughts that flashed through his head, although a trace of them must have registered in his expression.

Alan, the bodyguard wearing the neck brace, moved in closer, looking once again as if he wanted to kill John. The story of John breaking the bodyguard's jaw ran through the clubhouse like wildfire, providing hours of entertainment for the team. Jerry Owens stepped in front of the guard, all 365 pounds of him, and whispered in Alan's ear, "Touch him, and I'll snap your neck off." Alan retreated.

Questions flew around the room and landed nowhere. Questioners fought to be heard as Mr. Jonelli pretended not to be able to hear. As if he were the President standing under the blades of his helicopter, he waved, and smiled, and pointed to his ears but did nothing to remedy the situation. The whole event started to look rather foolish. Some type of action was required which

Jerry Owens was more than happy to provide. Manager Owens removed his shoe, approached the podium where Mr. Jonelli stood, and proceeded to pound the podium with the heel of his shoe, doing a pretty fair impersonation of Nikita Khrushchev. The crowd came to order, a bit shocked and slightly amused.

"You have the floor," Manager Owens said to Mr. Jonelli. Jerry returned to John's side while Mr. Jonelli followed him with a laser-like gaze. John raised a brow and managed to give Mr. Jonelli an ever-so-slight smile.

"Always wanted to do that," said Jerry. Mr. Jonelli put on his best face and turned to his questioners.

"Mr. Morely," pointed Jonelli, acknowledging Phil Morely, the writer from *The News* in the third row. 'He's a wise guy, but he usually asks safe questions,' thought Jonelli.

"J.J., let me see if I understand you correctly. You'd like the City to build you new roads, parking, luxury boxes, and a four star restaurant in the middle of a recession?" He got a big laugh from his peers. "And! My sources at City Hall tell me you want it done in a completely unrealistic time frame. Isn't this just blowing smoke?"

"I assure you, Mr. Morely, this is what I believe is needed to bring Highlander baseball into the twenty-first century," replied Mr. Jonelli.

Phil Morely followed up his question with, "Or you'll move the team?"

"There are no plans to move, Phil," assured Jonelli, like a dad talking with his worried son. He flat out lied. And most everyone knew it.

"Is a deal or plan in the works if you don't get what you want from the City?" asked another writer.

"I am confident the City understands our problems and a solution will be worked out."

"You didn't answer the question. Is there another deal in the works?" asked the writer again.

"Ladies and gentlemen, I am in intense negotiations with the City of New York, nobody else." It became obvious that he wasn't about to tip his hand, especially as the questions became even more pointed.

"J.J., many people around town, many right here in this room, believe you bought the Highlanders with the sole purpose of moving the team. That you in fact, just wanted the Highlander name. Many people think that's why you won't spend any money on players and promotions and have publicly beat up on your own team and manager. A few think you wanted to drive down attendance, blame the whole thing on the City, and leave. Would you please comment on those allegations?" asked the writer from the *Post.*

"Preposterous!" shouted Jonelli. "Absolutely outrageous! To suggest that I paid three hundred million—million—three hundred million, mind you, to sabotage my own team?" bristled Jonelli with yards of contempt, as he grew violet and red in the face.

'Positively his best performance to date,' thought John. Not since the grand jury hearing had he witnessed a more righteous act. Not only did Mr. Jonelli seize the opportunity to appear virtuous, "picked on," and almost underdoggish, but he was able to declare the ungodly amount of money he paid for his team twice. He seemed very upset and angry on the surface but not so deep down. He was practically gloating.

"The worst thing that can happen to him is the City gives 'im everything he wants," said Jerry to John.

'One more question,' thought Jonelli. The whole affair went much smoother than he had planned. 'Five more minutes and this tedious task is over. The seeds are planted. The hardest part finished,' reasoned Mr. Jonelli. He was beginning to feel all tingly inside. 'I'll celebrate tonight,' he thought, while still playing up his condemnation on behalf of the folks in Peoria.

"Mr. Jonelli. Joe Manning, *New York Times.*"

"Yes, I know who you are, Mr. Manning," replied Jonelli, acrimoniously. He wasn't happy about Manning referring to him by his birth name. He had an image to keep up, not to mention that he was embarrassed by his Italian heritage. He saw himself as an aristocrat—refined—a blue blood, and not at all working class . . . or loud . . . or ignorant . . . or naive . . . or a baseball fanatic like his father. Joe Manning was a smart old reporter; he understood Jonelli's egocentricities. Joe cleared his throat, and a hush fell over the room. Mr. Jonelli waited impatiently for Manning to ask his question. Joe was in no particular hurry.

"Mr. Jonelli, do you have any idea what you're doing?" Jonelli was about to speak, but Joe Manning raised his hand to wave him off, and Jonelli yielded.

"Just a rhetorical question," smiled Manning, as he got a laugh from his peers, but Mr. Jonelli never revealed so much as a hint of a smile. He was angered and intimidated by Joe Manning's blend of New York sophistication and Missourian folksy charm.

'Peoria would understand him,' Jonelli reasoned bitterly. Manning possessed a sharp wit, commanding intellect, and didn't believe a word Mr. Jonelli said—never had. They'd met before, Mr. Manning being one of his most outspoken critics.

"I've always found that New Yorkers attended the ball games to watch baseball, good baseball. They probably would've watched your young club rebuild if you stopped berating 'em and acting as though they should win the whole sha-bang. You're trying to sell the most educated baseball fans in the country a bill of goods, Mr. Jonelli. And they're not buying. I'll admit the stadium could use some work, but a fancy restaurant? I think you got us confused. That's what it takes to get Canadians into a ballpark, way up there in Toronto." The reporters snickered. "No, no, no. New Yorkers go to the games by subway. They eat hot dogs and drink beer. They want to smell the grass, hear the sound of the ball hitting the bat. You can't do that in a booth. I, for the life of me, will never understand why anybody would want to go a park and sit in an enclosed box." More laughter and applause. "Oh . . . I admit, when I go to the ball games, I'm in a box. But they pay me to do it! If they didn't pay me, I'd be outside in the fresh air doing my damnedest to stop the wave!" The crowd broke into a chorus of gut wrenching laughter.

Mr. Jonelli had heard enough. "Do you have a question, Mr. Manning?" asked Jonelli, his bottom lip quivering. He was unable to disguise his irritated tone.

"He might break yet," whispered Jerry to John.

"Why yes, Mr. Jonelli. I do. When are you gonna stop this little masquerade? Every single person in this room knows you haven't a shot in hell of getting the nonsense you're pretending to want. There's my question: What do you really want?" The crowd awaited Mr. Jonelli's response. His eyes narrowed, brows furrowed. Mr. Manning could plainly see what Jonelli wanted to do. Jonelli gripped the podium with both hands as though to steady himself. He wanted to lash out—rebuke them—put them in their place. He wanted to hurt them, hurt them badly, as he balanced on the edge of saying and doing something he would regret. His eyes darted at Joe Manning. Joe grinned. Jonelli opened his mouth and then shut it, almost in the same motion, recoiling, regrouping, setting himself again so as not to give in to Mr. Manning.

'He almost had me,' Jonelli said to himself as he collected his wits.

"I want a better baseball team and a more comfortable park to see them in," Mr. Jonelli said candidly, as he stared in the direction of Joe Manning. "I thank you for your time, ladies . . . and gentlemen, though I'm afraid that's all the time we have for today. But please allow me to share this brief thought: I would deeply appreciate the public support of my endeavors to get these crucial basic improvements. After all, I am working most diligently with their . . . our, best interest in mind. Thank you." He smiled for the cameras and started to make his exit from the stage. The loud and discordant voices of hundreds of disgruntled writers filled the air when out of the din came Joe Manning's voice, loud and clear and strong.

"Seems to me you're just looking for an excuse to leave town and make a lot of money. Why start now, Mr. Jonelli? You've never needed an excuse before!"

And that was the general feeling of the press and most of the people of New York. By not laying the issue to rest with a complete denial, he had confirmed their worst fears. Some people thought Jonelli was only interested in getting one, maybe two, of his demands from the City, but that was only wishful thinking. The rumors began to mount about Las Vegas, the Mayhouse Manor Hotel complex, and the twenty-thousand-seat ballpark. The papers even ran pictures of it, while Mr. Jonelli dismissed the whole thing as ridiculous, and the talks with the City appeared to be at a standstill.

How Much Is Enough?　　　　　　　　*10/4/91*
By Joe Manning

I know a man who would like to make Ruth Memorial Stadium into a great tourist attraction. Unfortunately, his idea has nothing to do with playing baseball—only the memory of it. Maybe he thought of it while traveling through Rome, Italy, when he first laid eyes on the Roman coliseum. Pay a few bucks, see the ruins where the games were once played in a late, great civilization. No upkeep necessary. 'Sounds good,' he thought. 'Maybe I can sell this idea to the City of New York.' Of course it would never last that long. Eventually, the City would tear it down to make a parking lot, a parking lot in a forgotten part of the Bronx where nobody wants to go, where only the ghostly myths of heroic ballplayers drift in the wind, and the good folks of the city try to make the best of yet another bad situation. How much is enough? How much money? How many hearts, spirits, and souls go along with the deal? How many jobs? How many neighborhoods? How much hope is thrown in for next to nothing? How many dreams are lost so one man can make his deal, make his money, make himself feel better, more powerful, more in control? Sell this dream, this small piece of real estate, this idea, and you've sold the hearts of the people, given away a part of us—the better part of us, the part that wishes on a shooting star, prays for peace, and longs for summers of innocence, the part that allows us to feel love . . . and maybe, just maybe, a little closer to each other.

43

A LOT HAD happened in the weeks before the last game. The Highlanders were ready to lay claim to a decisive fifth or sixth place finish in the American League East, a slight improvement over their 1990 season when they recorded their worst record since 1912 but, considering what Mr. Jonelli put this team through, still amazing.

It wasn't much of a year for the City. New York's crime and murder rate sky rocketed in the summer of 1991, fueled by crack cocaine. Mr. Jonelli seemed perfectly content to let the pot boil over in his negotiations with the Mayor's office. The country was in its second year of deep recession, and everyone knew about it but the President. The best the City could do to save its legendary baseball team, was an offer to build a parking lot on the site of the baseball fields next to the stadium, which would leave the people—but mostly the kids of the area—no place to play. For the first time in my memory the rest of the country actually felt sorry for the Highlanders and the folks of the Big City. Maybe they knew it was the beginning of the end. 'The Vegas Highlanders?' they wondered. 'Surely wouldn't be as much fun to beat.'

By now everybody had heard the rumors. They reverberated across the country, shaking everyone more than a little. "Could we be next? Will someone tear away a vital piece of our neighborhood?" people asked. A foundation—a cornerstone—was being removed from their lives, making a once venerable institution inconsequential and most everything else suscep-tible.

BASEBALL & BENEVOLENCE

The Toronto Blue Jays had already clinched the AL East pennant, which made the last game of the season between the Highlanders and Red Sox a mere formality, a contractual obligation—on paper anyway. The fans viewed the game in a much different fashion. To many it would be the most important ball game ever played, simply because it held the distinct possibility of being the last game ever in "the house that Ruth built," in the American League, in New York City. Though the rumors flew, Mr. Jonelli held his cards close to his vest. He wasn't saying "yes" and he wasn't saying "no," not even when his friend, the Commissioner of Baseball, stepped in demanding to know just what was going on. But little more was said or done. Mr. Jonelli was a gambler, a very rich gambler, who envisioned change.

"HEY, JOYCE. JOHN—"

"Please hold!" she snipped, cutting him off in midsentence. John held the line feeling a bit slighted and a little embarrassed. 'She's real busy,' he told himself, and the touch of anger dissipated. Then he just felt embarrassed.

"New York Highlanders!" announced Joyce with all the urgency of a blocked fire truck.

"Joyce, it's John Greco."

"Ohhh, hi, John." Her tone softened.

"Listen, you sound real busy. I need some tickets for the last game on Sunday, October 6th. Can I get sixteen? The whole family wants to go."

"Your family and everyone else's, too. Joe DiMaggio just called. Wants forty-three! We got 56,000 seats and over a million requests."

"Wow. You must be going crazy. I guess everybody's thinking the same thing, huh?"

"They must be. We usually don't get a million requests when we're battling it out for fifth place." She made herself laugh.

"Well, can I get any?" John asked, willing to settle for anything.

"John Greco, you can get whatever you want. You're my favorite Highlander," she flirted.

"Well, thanks," said John, blushing.

"I'll never forget that game," Joyce said, as if she were talking to herself, reminiscing—suddenly with all the time in the world. "There was something in the air that day. Ya know I can't remember the last time New Yorkers treated each other so nicely. Did I ever tell you I met my husband at the Love Game? Can you hold?" She left the line and returned within the same second. John thought of basketball for some reason, probably the way they break seconds down to tenths. She continued.

"I was there with my two girlfriends in the left center field bleachers—right where the ball went out. We were having so much fun. And when you wrote 'love' in the dirt—we couldn't see it, but we heard it on the radio—we cried. Lots of people were making fun of you for doing that, but not us, and not my Ben. Why he stood up and shouted those people down. 'How can you?' he shouted. I fell in love with him on the spot. 'How can you?! After all he's given you and all he's lost!' He was angry. Wow. Nobody said a word back to Ben Johnson."

"Ben Johnson is your husband?" John replied, lost in thought, amazed.

"That's right. You know that. We were married a year later to the day. I never told you?" she asked warmly. He was stunned.

"No. I thought your name was Turcotte. Joyce Turcotte?"

"Oh, John, you are an old ballplayer! You still remember my maiden name," she laughed. "I've been Joyce Johnson for twenty-five years now. Can you hold?" She didn't wait for John's response, and when she returned three tenths of a second later, she just continued her story. "When your baseball sailed over our heads, everyone turned and looked at Ben like he was some sort of prophet. He made a lot of friends that day! My girlfriends thought he was soooo cute. I decided to do something about it. I walked straight up to him and said, 'Hi, I'm Joyce Turcotte.' I'd never done anything like that before in my life. I knew he thought I was attractive. He was looking at me during the whole game. Would you listen to me go on!" she declared.

"Joyce, is Ben related to *the* Ben Johnson who used to play center field for the Highlanders?" He nearly lost his breath waiting for her answer.

"Oh, yes! Ben's so proud. Used to go to the games with his daddy after the accident."

"Shattered knee," John said.

"Ya, that's right. What a lovely man he was. Ben said his dad could have been one of the greats. Had all the tools, he likes to say. Ben still laughs; sez his dad had the tools but didn't give any to him. My Ben, he's a sweetheart—ha-ha—but he's soooo uncoordinated. Now our sixteen-year-old, Peg, she's a ballplayer! You should scout her, John! Ben thinks she can really do it. She made the boys' high school varsity team this year over at St. Xavier. Runs like a deer! And what an eye! She can hit like there's no tomorrow. Pretty, too!" exclaimed Joyce. "The school wouldn't even give her a tryout 'til she challenged their best hitter to a batting contest. So sad she had to embarrass the boy. But after that, Peggy was on the team! The first female ever! Isn't that something!" cried Joyce, full of pride. John could hardly believe what he was hearing.

"I'll definitely take a look at her," he said. "If she's any good, I'll make sure she gets a tryout." He was a bit dazed by the possibility of finding both Ben Johnson and a female ballplayer, though he still hadn't any idea of what it meant or how it could help.

"Aaww . . . thank you, John. That would make Peg so happy. Me and Ben, we knew it could happen. We didn't know how; we just believed, and now it all seems so simple. I don't know why I didn't think of asking you sooner."

"Guess it just wasn't time," said John.

"Guess not," she said, pleased by the thought.

"Joyce, what does Ben do . . . for a living?"

"He's a carpenter."

"He'll be at Sunday's game?"

"He wouldn't miss it for the world."

'Interesting choice of words,' John thought.

"You introduced me to Ben, John. That's why you're my favorite Highlander," she laughed, enjoying the memory. "You sure I never told you this before? Funny . . . I can't help but think of it every time we talk."

"I guess I wasn't supposed to know until now." It seemed to me that John was starting to get it.

"Ooooh, John!" she cried, as though he were teasing her. "I'll have your tickets ready for you. Maybe we'll see you at the game. I can introduce you to Ben. He'd like that."

"Thanks, Joyce. That would be great. I'm sure we'll see each other." 'Very sure,' he thought. The moment he put down the receiver the phone rang. It was T.C. Golden, calling from Boston.

"Hey, John! It's T.C.!" announced T.C. Golden.

"Stop yelling into the phone; this isn't a ball game," said John, glad to hear from his buddy.

"Going to the game on Sunday?" asked T.C.

"Isn't everyone?"

"Yeah, I heard Yogi's gonna show. What do you say we meet in Monument Park around noon. We can hang out before the game, and depending on how we feel, you can invite me to your house for dinner." T.C. was trying his best to sound optimistic, but there was an undeniable note of sadness in his tone.

"You're invited for dinner no matter what," replied John. "Sharon would love to see you. We're having the whole family over." The mention of Sharon's name reminded T.C. of the young woman they had met in Boston. John thought about her, too.

"So, has anymore strange stuff happened lately?"

"Yup."

"Tell me!" T.C. was always a bit of a busybody.

"Later. Even then you'll think I'm a nut. So, I'm keeping my mouth shut for now."

"Hey, John. Don't forget. I was there. I saw her! . . . Did you tell Sharon?"

"No. I don't know why."

"I understand. Well, ah, Sunday at noon then." There was a moment of silence; both men were unsure whether to hang up or not. "John?"

"Yeah."

"Nobody in Boston wants this to happen."

"I know. Thanks. See ya on Sunday."

ON SATURDAY MORNING Sharon's brother Mark flew in from Colorado with his wife Debbie and their children Thomas and Karen. Mark wanted the kids to see their Cousin Charlie play in Ruth Stadium. Even though money was tight, it was a trip they had to make. Thomas was twelve and hadn't stopped talking about the trip to New York since it was planned a month and a half earlier.

"He started to get the full impact of having a Highlander uncle and cousin a few years ago," said his dad, "when the school coaches started to follow him around the halls trying to get him interested in their sport. Don't know why . . . they know he's not a direct bloodline." Mark laughed while Thomas squirmed out of his arms. He was too old to be held, he thought. Thomas slid to the floor and silently watched every move his Uncle John made. "I guess they figured the talent would just rub off," Mark joked. Thomas was thrilled and fascinated and scared to death of his Uncle John. He'd heard many stories about him—and not just from the family. Everyone seemed to know his Uncle John. He was famous.

"Thomas, wanna have a catch? I've got a couple of gloves," asked John, trying to make the boy feel more comfortable. His eyes lit up, and then an avalanche of questions poured out of him.

"You played for the Highlanders, too? Right, Uncle John? Were you really in the World Series? How many years did you play? My friend Kenny said you know Dillon Southwood. I told him you know Joe DiMaggio. Do you? My father said you hit the longest home run ever. Did you?" He asked, not in any way concerned with concealing his suspicion or excitement.

"Yup, I know Joe," said John, feeling flattered. "C'mon, let's have that catch and I'll tell you all about it."

BASEBALL & BENEVOLENCE

Karen, now ten, was much more interested in exploring the intriguing townhouse. She wanted to see every room, go into every closet, and look out every window. The city completely enthralled her; she begged her parents to take a walk with her so she could see more.

"I think we have a city girl on our hands," teased her mother. Debbie was an attractive woman. She wore her sandy blonde hair tied back into a ponytail. She was a petite five foot two with a sharp school teacher's "sixth sense," effortlessly anticipating the request, thoughts, and needs of her family. She and Mark enjoyed jogging the rolling hills of Golden, Colorado, chopping firewood, reading, and cooking—the simple life.

That night, the Saturday eve before the game, Faye and Kerrins and Jason came over for dinner, expanding their family. The unity provided John with great comfort and courage to face the unknown peculiarities that the final game appeared to possess.

"My, my!" greeted Sharon as Faye and Kerrins arrived. "The two of you here at the same time! We haven't seen that since you bought into the bar." She gave them each a big hug. 'It feels good to have the company,' she thought.

"We tried to make Tommy feel guilty," said Kerrins. "It didn't work."

"So we told him if he didn't work tonight, he wouldn't have a ticket to the game tomorrow," cracked Faye. "John, did you get a ticket for Little George?"

"Uh-huh, Tommy already has them," said John, smiling. "And here's your three." He handed the tickets to Faye.

"Three?"

"Aaah . . . I thought if John could get them, Max would love to go," confessed Kerrins, sheepishly. "Thanks, John. I know how hard these are to get."

The doorbell rang. Jason had arrived.

Faye gave Kerrins' arm a squeeze. "That's nice," she said. "We haven't seen Max in awhile." And gave him a kiss. Kerrins was positive he had the best wife in the world, but was easily embarrassed by public displays of affection, and Faye knew it. The "ah's" and "oh's" from Sharon and Debbie turned Kerrins' face a deep shade of red, so much so that it caused Jason to ask if there were something wrong with him.

That night they sat down to a wonderful dinner of fresh garden salad, corn on the cob, peppered crab, steamers, and lobster tails. John wanted to pull out all the stops for this far too infrequent gathering. The beautiful October evening was perfect; the air so crisp, the leaves starting to turn gold and red, a lovely New York early autumn. John covered the picnic table with newspapers to allow for the accumulation of shells. 'Nothing like a messy dinner to loosen everybody up,' John thought, as he prepared the meal in large boiling pots on top of the outdoor grill, the one that Natt had built.

Thomas and Karen attacked each other with crab claws and later ate chocolate layer cake with vanilla ice cream for dessert. Thomas talked about his Cousin Charlie, whom he had never met, but had seen on television "a thousand times!" He didn't sleep well that night, thinking about his first major league ball game, all the things his Uncle John had told him, and meeting his other hero, Cousin Charlie. Karen fell asleep in her Aunt Sharon's lap. Sharon brushed her silky hair and sadly thought of her own daughter. It was one of those moments when I wished I could have changed what was.

Later, when things began to wind down, John and Jason were able to have a talk in the study. Jason would stay the night, so they could all go to the ball game together the next morning. John's mom and dad would drive in from New Jersey to join them. Sharon's parents would meet them at the stadium— no doubt, anxious to see their grandchildren.

"I heard you ran into the Baseball Man again?" asked John. "Does he still wanna buy the ball?"

"No, he wants me to help you," replied Jason, not seeing anything strange about the Baseball Man's request.

"How?"

"I don't know. He just said to help you when you needed it. I told him I would always do that. Oh! And he said to bring the ball to the game," said Jason, as he pulled it from a pocket of his new Highlander leather and canvas jacket. "See!" He held it up for John.

"May I?" John asked. Jason gladly handed it to him. John examined the ball carefully, as though looking for a message. But it was just the same old ball with the splinter and his autograph—only now it was yellowed with age. He remembered Angela's shock trick and how it made Dillon Southwood laugh. He smiled at the pleasant thought. Above his desk was the small corked bottle of earth, the home plate dirt that had formed the letters, the dirt that once made a difference, the dirt Dillon Southwood got on his knees for and scooped up himself; his gift, a remembrance of the event, a sequence of events that all seemed to be leading toward tomorrow's ball game. 'How can this ball help?' John wondered.

"He didn't tell me. He just said to bring it," replied Jason.

"You read my mind?"

"No. You just said, 'How can it help.'"

"Oh . . . I guess I did." He handed Jason the ball.

"What did he say . . . after you said you'd always help me?"

"He said, 'I thought so.'"

"Anything else?"

"No, not really. Except . . . it all felt kinda funny. Things looked weird—but nice . . . old—but new, too."

"I had something like that happen to me once. It felt good. I fell asleep and had dreams that seemed real."

Jason's eyes sparkled as he discovered that it was okay to talk about it. "You did!?" he exclaimed.

"Yeah, felt like a kid again."

"Wow! Me, too! My mom and dad . . . they were both there!"

"Where?"

"On the roof. I was little, three, maybe four. We were on the roof of our building waiting for the fireworks to begin at Ruth Stadium. Dad had the game on the radio; it was the ninth inning! They were winning 5-1 against . . . I don't know. They were winning . . . and after the last out—the sky would be beautiful! It was the Fourth of July . . . everybody in our building was up there, waiting. Mr. and Mrs. Walters, the Domingo family, Rafael, Juan, Mr. and Mrs. Morales, everybody!! They all made food. My dad ran the barbecue. It was the only time I was allowed on the roof. The air was so nice; clean. Ya know? The way the wind blows . . . I always got the first hot dog. And, and Mom, she'd hang the Christmas lights on the clothesline—in the middle of summer! It was so pretty, John. Oh, John." He started to cry. "I was there again! I was! The other ladies made nice flowers and put them on the cable spool tables we had. And they hung paper streamers that floated in the wind and lit candles in empty peanut butter jars. It was like our own beautiful restaurant . . . . all those pretty colors against the black tar roof! All our friends . . . it was so good, all those nice people. I've missed them all so much. It was like I was really there again . . . my mom and my dad together . . . like it never stopped happening. Always together. Nice," he whispered. "Always together," he repeated softly.

"Where the people gather," said John, as he recalled his own journey.

"What does that mean?" Jason asked.

"Oh, it's something a very wise man told me . . . "

THAT NIGHT THE Greco house was fuller and richer than it had been for quite some time.

44

BY ELEVEN A.M. the entire Greco family along with a few of their friends had boarded the number four train at the Union Square Station. The day was cloudy and overcast when they entered the subway at 14th Street. The train was already crowded, even though game time wasn't until one o'clock. It seemed as though the people wanted as much time at the park as possible. They understood what the game meant, the implication, the loss. Yet, no one discussed the darker side of this October day—no mention of the move, or Mr. Jonelli, or the end of baseball in the Bronx. The subway car, filled with Highlander fans wearing their ball caps with pride, rattled through the underground tunnel. When a man boarded the train with a Boston cap, most of them smiled politely; after all, he was a baseball fan, too, and on this day that would be enough to gain respect. John observed his fellow passengers and thought how somber and melancholy the adults appeared. Only the children experienced the pure joy of just going to the ball game. 'They have the most to lose,' thought John, as he recalled Babe Ruth's definition of innocence.

"Thomas, Karen," called their Uncle John. They sat snuggled against their parents, maybe a bit afraid of the subway. "Look out your window," he said.

"Go ahead, kids. This is great," said their dad, as he remembered what was about come. "Look, Deb," called Mark, pointing out the window. The kids turned themselves around, their knees on their seats, and stared into the blackened tunnel with wonderment. John's eye caught his father's as they watched the children waiting for the unknown. The same scenario had occurred between them some forty-five years ago. Other parents held their kids up to the window to get a better view. And then it happened. The conductor announced 161st Street. As if by magic, the darkness exploded into sunshine, and the giant ballpark was suddenly so close it seemed touchable. The passengers were treated to the glorious sight of Ruth Memorial Stadium, awash in bright sunlight and covered by a solid blue sky. A jet plane had etched a single white line, cutting the blue in half. Through a briefly glimpsed opening in the stadium, the passengers saw the beatific expanse of brilliant green grass, ballplayers in pinstripes, flags and pennants, a majestic grandstand, and people from all walks of life. The scene had a formidable presence.

"Woooow!!" exclaimed Thomas and Karen, as well as about a hundred other kids. Nothing more needed to be said. John's dad smiled awkwardly; he had heard it a thousand times before, the exclamation point at the end of the ride, never dreaming that one day it would end.

"One of those players is your cousin Charlie," Debbie said to her children who were too dazzled to speak.

When we arrived at the station, John took Sharon's hand as they led Guy and Betty, Mark and Debbie with the kids, Faye and Kerrins, Jason and Max, and Tommy and me into the ballpark. Many people recognized John Greco as they made their way in and nodded appreciatively. They had read the stories about his miraculous hand and knew the history, though writing "love" in the dirt seemed unimaginable even to John at this moment. An unusual energy hovered about the already massive crowd; they were strangely introspective. They seemed to be cherishing each second, honoring every minute, respecting what was and could still be. The demise of the Highlanders was all too imminent to be ignored, but they were at a loss as how to fight, unable to locate the battlefield—or the enemy. John wanted to tell them that he would know what to do.

The truth of the situation was still not known. Mr. Jonelli continued his charade until the very end, pretending to do what was in the best interest of the people, though he didn't say what exactly that was. On the last game of the season Jonelli took a back seat to baseball. The people wanted the day for themselves and their families. They wanted to enjoy the game within its historic setting one last time and hope for another. For the moment they managed to relegate Mr. Jonelli to his rightful place, into the ranks of the forgotten.

"Hey, John. How'ya doing!" shouted Freddy Greene, surrounded by a rambunctious gaggle of grandchildren.

"Freddy!" The two former teammates gave each other a hug. They had lost contact over the years, but found each other's presence reassuring.

"Shar, you remember Freddy?!"

"Of course, I do. How are you, Mr. Clean." She smiled, using his nickname.

"Thomas, Karen, this is Freddy 'Mr. Clean' Greene, one of the great home run hitters in the history of baseball," introduced their Uncle John. Freddy turned to his kids and said, "Listen here . . . this is John Greco. He hit the longest homer ever." The kids were polite, but more impressed by the energy of the stadium.

"Why do they call you Mr. Clean?" asked little Karen.

"Well, now . . . because when men were on base I'd hit a homer and clean 'em up!" said Freddy, releasing a jolly laugh, "Ho-ho-ho!" Karen giggled.

As they walked, John continued to see past teammates and friends, coaches, media people, even celebrities, none of whom were there in any official capacity. They just wanted to see the game. The Hall of Famer and Highlander broadcaster, Phil "the Scooter" Rizzuto, shook John's hand and said hello to the family. Then he patted Jason on the back and asked, "You gonna work some magic today?" Scooter and Jason had become friends. Scooter Jr., his wife Anne, and Phil's wife Cora were all at the game with Phil; they wanted to be there, even though the telecast was going down to Florida.

As the Grecos found their seats, seldom-seen events were taking place just outside the stadium. The scalpers weren't scalping, the bleacher line wrapped around the block with a civil attitude prevailing, and folks who knew that the game was long sold out came to the ballpark anyway, because they wanted to be there, hoping it might make a difference. When the ball game started, there were sixty thousand people inside the ballpark, as well as one hundred thousand in and around the streets surrounding Ruth Memorial, listening to Mr. Rizzuto's broadcast on the radio.

"John, are you all right?" asked Sharon, anxiously. He felt his knees buckle as they walked through tunnel fifteen and out into the open air. Not from sickness, it was as though he'd gotten up too quickly after drinking beer in the hot sun, shaky but feeling no pain.

"Yeah...yeah. I'm, ah...okay," he said, trying to regain his balance. It was as if he had just received a shot to calm down, a patient before his operation.

They arrived at their seats just to the right of the Highlander dugout. A group of thrilled Japanese businessmen sat to their left. Joe DiMaggio sat just behind them. John caught Joe's eye and gave him a wave. They had met a few times. Joe acknowledged John with a two finger salute to the brow and smiled. 'Class act that DiMaggio,' admired John. It seemed as if every Highlander in history were there. John spotted Hank Miller talking with Muddy Ames, saw Bob Goldstein with his wife Rachel, Whitey and Mickey and Reggie . . . Willie Moran . . . and of all people, Hughie Doolan, about a hundred pounds heavier. Even Yogi came back to the ballpark with his wife and family. John pointed out each of these people to the kids and introduced them when they were close enough. But it wasn't just Highlander players; he spotted Walt Rose and Clay Allen from the Oriole team of his day. He was surprised to see their skipper, Manager Matt Connelly, after all these years.

"Mr. Greco!" called the first base umpire. "Remember me?" The man came over to the railing and extended his hand. John shook his hand and greeted him respectfully, but had no idea who he was. "It was a long time ago. I'll give you a hint," he laughed. "Touch my bat for luck," said the umpire. "I'm quoting you."

"Touch my bat . . . the bat boy? Ah . . . ah, James!"

"That's right. James Darwin, sir. My first season in the show. I never forgot that game or how you helped me, Mr. Greco. Changed my life, it did." They shook hands again.

"I'm happy to see ya did so well for yourself," congratulated John. He knew the odds of making it to the majors and was sincerely impressed. Fred Dailey, Darwin's crew chief, called for his umpires to meet behind home plate.

"Well, I gotta go. Enjoy the day," called Umpire James Darwin.

"Yeah, you too. Good to see ya."

Charlie took a break from his warm-up to say hello to his mom and family. I thought Thomas would faint when the man in pinstripes introduced himself as his cousin. Charlie gave Thomas a firm, friendly handshake and little Karen a kiss on the cheek.

"Karen, isn't Charlie handsome in his uniform?" asked her grandmother. Karen blushed, nodding her head shyly.

"Oh, don't embarrass her, Joan," said Betty Greco. "Karen, Thomas, how about some ice cream?"

"I'd like some," said Joan. Joan Costa had an infamous sweet tooth.

"I'll see ya later," said Charlie with a warm, charming smile. Betty noticed he had his father's smile. Charlie jogged back to home plate, glad his family had come to the game.

"Will we really see him later?" asked Thomas, dying to know.

"Sure will. He's your cousin," said his dad, as he bought the kids hot dogs.

When Jerry Owens dropped by, Thomas' jaw dropped, too.

"He's never seen anyone that big in a baseball uniform," laughed his mom. Jerry Owens was quite a sight.

"Get his autograph," suggested Jason to Thomas.

Jerry was happy to oblige. He said hello to the Grecos and several other friends and fans in the area. He, like everybody else, just wanted to enjoy the day.

"Here goes something," Jerry said to John and returned to his duties. John gave him a good-luck nod and watched Jerry lumber back to the dugout.

"Shar, I promised I'd meet T.C. over at the monuments. You wanna come?" asked John.

"No, thanks. I like it right here," she said, feeling relaxed.

"Oh, Shar. I invited T.C. for dinner, okay?"

"The more the merrier."

"Thanks. I'll be back soon."

Faye scooted over into John's empty seat.

"I've never seen anything like it—the people! Not even for the World Series," said Faye, anxious to get Sharon's ear.

"Why's DiMaggio sitting out here?" asked Kerrins. His eyes searched the crowd as if he were a secret service agent.

"He sits out here or in the owner's box, which would you pick?" replied Max, a bit preoccupied as he smiled at the beautiful woman sitting across the aisle.

"The dugout," answered Kerrins.

"I can't believe the people here for batting practice!" exclaimed Mike Costa to Guy Greco.

"Boy, you'd think this game decided the AL East," commented Guy.

"Th, th, thesee are grr, greee . . . great seats," I said.

"Enjoy them, George," said Tommy, tapping his beer cup against mine in a toast and said, "To Natty."

WHEN JOHN ARRIVED at the monuments, he was taken aback by the sheer number of people already gathered in what appeared to be a solemn procession of mourners. Flowers covered the area near the Ruth, Huggins, and Gehrig stones. Cards, pennants, handwritten notes, and tiny flags from numerous nationalities littered the Highlander blue flowerpots at the base of the retired numbers wall. Johney was relieved to see the pots were still Highlander blue. 'They didn't bother to repaint them Jonelli black,' he sighed. It all seemed so crazy and sad, like a trip to Graceland on Elvis's birthday—a baseball wake.

"John, do you believe this?" He turned, expecting to see T.C. Golden. But he wasn't there. Nobody he knew was there, yet it wasn't a stranger who spoke the words. He recognized the voice. His heart pounded; adrenaline raced through his system as he desperately scanned the area. He didn't see him anywhere, then at the entrance to the park he recognized T.C. and standing right next to him was Natt. Natt smiled warmly and gave his brother the Joe DiMaggio two finger salute. His expression saddened as he disappeared around the bend into the stadium's honeycomb corridors. John ran after him, practically running over T.C. in the process.

"John! What—" called T.C. as Johney dashed by. Mr. Golden thought his friend was chasing a pickpocket and ran to help. John stopped cold when he reached the main corridor. 'So many people—everywhere,' he thought. 'They look lost, like me.'

"Ya lose 'im?!" shouted T.C., out of breath.

"Ya see 'im?!" shouted John.

"No. What'd he get?! Your wallet?" John immediately understood what T.C. was thinking and left it at that.

"Nah, he tried," replied John.

They walked back to the park. T.C.'s eyes widened when he viewed the morose atmosphere surrounding the monuments. Aside from the cards and notes, people began to leave their caps, even a few gloves, as though they wanted to leave a part of themselves in the Bronx. The lonesome caps were scattered among the flowers like so many Highlanders on the day all of their numbers would be retired.

"John, look at this," said T.C. in disbelief. He picked up several cards and read:

> *My son wrote from the Gulf. He wanted to know how his team, the Highlanders, were doing. It broke my heart to tell him.*
>
> Ms. Fran Gilholey — Green Brook, New Jersey

* * *

> *God help us.*
>
> Cindy & Dinah — Brooklyn, N.Y.

* * *

> *Say it ain't so.*
>
> Philip Papa — New York, New York

* * *

MARK ALLEN VALENZA

Remember 1965. Life is a miracle.
Angela Wheeler — Bronx, New York

"Let me see that! I know her! She's dead." Johney grabbed the card from T.C.'s hand and read it again and again and again. His face turned pale as he flipped the card over; her note was written on a Ben Johnson baseball card, just like the one Jason received from Natt. His hands trembled and perspired as he shoved the card into his back pocket.

"Wwwhat is it . . . this whole thing is making me nervous," stammered T.C. Johney gave him a disturbing look. It had become more than obvious to John that the house that Ruth built was full on the inside, outside, and the other side.

"Listen, T.C. Hope you don't mind, but I'm gonna get going. I'll see ya tonight, okay?" John said in the calmest voice he could find.

"No . . . hey, I got to get up to the booth," replied T.C., a bit shaken. He wanted out of Monument Park. The sanctified piece of center field grew in intensity the closer it came to game time.

On the way out John impulsively picked up another card which, again, was a Ben Johnson. He read in a maddened hush, "I love you, John. Natty." He automatically put Natt's card in his back pocket along with Angela's. As John roamed the stadium corridors, he became spellbound by his thoughts of the Ben Johnson card collection. "Ben . . . Natt . . . Angela," he muttered, then began babbling incoherently. "I'll know what to do . . . when the time comes. I'll know what to do—to do . . . a do . . . to do . . . a do . . . do . . . Just have faith—that's all I got to do . . . to do . . . You're all here! Why don't you just tell me what to do!" he shouted at the walls. People started to move out of his way as his babbling grew in intensity. John was consumed, sweating, twitching, fighting his way through the crowd. "Tunnel fifteen . . . Ben Johnson . . . he's our man . . . hah . . . gottagottagotta . . . have . . . stormy weather . . . faith . . . believe . . . haah haha . . . haaaaaaaaaah."

"You better get it together, son!" Two large hands clamped down hard on his shoulder blades, halting his delirious chatter and any forward progress. He lifted his chin slowly to witness the next amazement.

"Dillon?"

"Yeah, Dillon!" yelled Southwood. His blustery voice ricocheted off the concrete walls and smacked John in the face, reviving him.

"What are you doing here?"

"Same as you—same as everyone else. I'm here to be a part of it."

368

"A part of what?"

"Whatever it is! I don't know. What'ya think?! To see the Highlanders capture fifth place!" laughed Southwood. "Because it's right, I guess."

"Something gonna happen?" John asked passively as though giving in.

"I hope so."

"What?

"Johney, you of all people shouldn't have so many questions. Huh . . . must be too close to it, lost your objectivity." Southwood grabbed John's hands and shouted, "This! Would ya look at this?! Look, Johney, look . . . don't you see? I can't even tell which was the cripple. When I heard about this, I had to come. I knew it was possible. Don't you see? This! This hand of yours is a miracle! I know. We had the best doctors in the world telling us there was no hope, that you should have it amputated. Look at it. It's as though nothing happened. That's why they're here," cried Southwood, opening his arms to the people around them. "Don'tcha get it? It's you," said the exuberant manager, as he stared into John's blank, expressionless face and decided to take another route.

"Here ya go," Dillon explained. "A little girl is murdered. The world thinks, 'no hope.' The next day her father writes 'love' in the dirt and hits the longest homer ever; and ya know what? Suddenly there's hope again. Rumor is the Highlanders are moving. 'No hope.' Then out of the blue that same man sez, 'Look—my crippled hand, it works just fine,' and suddenly there's hope again. Don't you see, Johney. Somebody's looking out for you—for us—all of us!" exclaimed Southwood with a twinkle in his eye, full of life.

"You don't know the half of it," said John, bewildered but coming out of his funk. He felt as though a great burden had been lifted just knowing his manager and long time friend understood and believed.

"Hah-ha! I'd bet I don't!" chuckled Dillon, slapping his knee. "Tell ya one thing, if something happens, I'll bet my home in Maine it takes two hands!" He gave him a confidential wink, holding his own hands in front of John's face, smiling as he waved them to and fro.

"Ya know what I mean?"

"Yeah," said John, thinking he was probably right, and then not thinking at all, on automatic pilot. "You wanna come over for dinner tonight?" he asked in a daze.

"Already am. Sharon invited me."

"You have the address?"

"Yeah, kid. I got the address."

"Tonight then," he said in a monotone.

"Uh-huh," replied Southwood, as he gave him the once over. "I'll be there if you need me. Ha! I'm gonna go bust Joe Di's balls; the Japanese are driving him crazy. Hah-ha!"

John watched Southwood disappear into the men's room as Mr. Jonelli's voice shocked him to attention.

" . . . **what most can only dream about,**" Jonelli announced, promoting his hotels. It was only the television. Johney continued to view the monitor that was suspended over a beer concession stand. The commercial ended and Alan Swinger, a Penn Garden Broadcasting announcer with a dry sense of humor, began his interview with Jerry Owens. Monitors played everywhere, the sound of the broadcast echoing through the innards of the stadium. It gave Ruth's house the quality of a living, thinking entity.

"Why do you think there are so many people here today?" asked PGB's Swinger, playing dumb.

"To see a baseball game," replied Jerry, playing dumber. John nodded in agreement and made his way back to Sharon.

"YOU SURE YOU'RE all right?" Sharon asked John when he returned. "You look tired."

"Yeah . . . ah, just saw Dillon."

"I invited him to dinner," they said simultaneously, making each other laugh.

Harry O'Dell, the Red Sox pitcher, was loosening up right in front of them. He was throwing some soft tosses to his catcher Brad Petrocelli. Kids gathered at the railing screaming for an autograph as Sharon and John quietly watched the ball go back and forth, back and forth until it nearly hypnotized them.

"He's here," Sharon said.

'Who isn't here,' thought John. He said, "Who's here, Shar?"

"Mr. Jonelli." She pointed to the boxes above home plate. "In the owner's box. He's with the Mayor." John glanced up and saw his large, unmistakable frame silhouetted behind glass, propped up by his cane.

"Huh," uttered John and asked himself, 'Why?'

"He hates the Highlanders," stated Sharon, coolly. "The Mayor's still trying to talk reason, but he hates them and this city. It's more than money. It's an obsession for him. Revenge, I think."

"It will work out, Shar," said John as he stared straight up at Mr. Jonelli, who stood stoic at the window, while the Mayor appeared to be fidgeting about him.

"I'm sorry. I don't see how. He wants to move. He's enjoying the whole thing. I know what he's thinking right now."

"What?"

"He's thinking the people will see him with the Mayor and they'll think he's still trying; that there's still a chance. And I know there isn't; I've sat in on the negotiations."

"Shar, remember what Babe—"

"John, what can happen?" She cut him off in a tense, hushed tone. "And, hon', we've been under a lot of stress."

"You don't believe me? My hand—isn't that enough?" he pleaded, feeling himself pulled in two directions, first from Southwood and now by Sharon.

"I want to," she said, pressing her head against his chest.

"I can help," he whispered and pulled the cards from his back pocket. "Keep these quiet 'til . . . 'til whenever it's right to show 'em. Okay?" At first he couldn't tell what she was thinking. He told her what happened at Monument Park as she handled each Ben Johnson card, flipping them over and back, inspecting every crease and corner like a kid trying to decide which one to buy.

"It's their handwriting," she admitted cautiously. "What's going on?"

"Something good."

"Uncle John!" shouted Thomas. "I got Harry O'Dell's autograph! And . . . and know what?"

"What?" asked John, playfully.

"Dillon Southwood's coming to dinner tonight!"

"I know," he said and smiled at his wife.

"Ladies and Gentlemen, directing your attention to the home plate area, Manager Jerry Owens," echoed the voice of Bob Sheppard, emotionless, with perfect diction. Jerry made his way to the microphone, his hands in his back pockets, a bit of a gut hanging over his belt.

"Hello, folks. I know this is a little unusual. That is, me coming out to say a few words before a game. But, well . . . these are unusual times," said Jerry, apologetically. He had Mr. Jonelli's undivided attention, even as the Mayor danced around him. **"I'll keep it short though."** Owens took off his cap and wiped his brow. Then he held the cap above his head. **"Remember, this symbol is very powerful. It means more than just New York. . . . It symbolizes the best we can be, even in the worst of times. It brought us together in the good times, and now in the not so good times. I ask you to think about that, appreciate it, and enjoy today's game with**

that same sense of brotherhood in mind. I don't know, maybe even shake your neighbor's hand if the feeling hits ya, but what's most important is that we recall what brought us together. And no matter what happens, please, never forget it." The applause rolled in like the slow building rumblings of distant thunder. **"Let's play ball!"** shouted Jerry. And with that, energy and passion ran through the crowd. The clapping, cheering, and foot stomping from both inside and outside of the ballpark shook the earth. The heart of the Bronx was beating strong under a beautiful autumn sun. Robert Merrill sang the national anthem. Fred Dailey, the home plate umpire, yelled the official, "Play ball!"

On the mound for Boston was Harry O'Dell. Harry featured a 92 m.p.h. plus fastball, a slider, a curve, and an occasional forkball, all of which he threw for strikes. Harry's record was twenty wins against five losses on the year. He was widely considered to be the best pitcher in the league. On the mound for New York was Al Walker, forkball, forkball, forkball, curve, and an occasional fastball. Al's record was thirteen and thirteen; he was in trouble if he didn't get his forkball working. Luckily he had it going pretty well for the last game; unfortunately, so did Harry O'Dell. So much so that there wasn't even a hit until the top of the third when the Boston shortstop, Berry Keating, crushed an 0-2 hanger into the right center field bleachers, driving in himself and right fielder Gary Williams, whom Mr. Walker had walked on four straight pitches to lead off the inning (Boston: 2, New York: 0, no outs). Before the inning was over, Walker, living up to his name, walked two more batters and threw a fifty-seven foot forkball which bounced to the backstop, allowing yet another run to score on a wild pitch (Boston: 3, New York: 0).

"C'mon, Wid!" shouted Jerry from the dugout, clapping his hands and offering the young Highlander second baseman, Wid Barrett, his encouragement. "Good eye, good eye!" Wid had two good cuts at O'Dell's fastball, but couldn't catch up with either one of them. On Wid's last pitch Harry pulled the string with a slow curve and made Wid look foolish while swinging off balance. First baseman Ernie Adams didn't fare much better. Ernie was called out on strikes while watching O'Dell's forkball break off and then into the strike zone. He stood frozen at the plate as Dailey rang him up. Jeff Martin, the center fielder, got a rise out of the huge crowd when he ran the count full, only to be struck out by a 94 m.p.h. fastball.

In the fourth Al Walker settled down and was able to get Boston's left fielder Ralph Collins, first baseman Don Jefferson, and second baseman Stan Betts all to hit ground ball outs to the infield. Harry O'Dell lost the strike zone in the fourth, walking two, but he got veteran catcher Charlie Greco to hit into a double play, and then struck out left fielder Merv Hook to finish the side. New York still had no hits. Thomas, along with most of the crowd, was very disappointed in his cousin and the Highlanders.

"That Harry O'Dell's a great pitcher," said Mark to his son. "You got his autograph, right?"

"Uh-huh," said the boy as he looked around at all the long faces in the crowd, sensing the energy drain from the stadium. The magic seemed to be slipping away with every O'Dell pitch.

"Charlie will get a hit, Thomas," said Faye. "He always does when his mother is at the game," she laughed, but I knew it happened to be true.

Boston scored another run in the fifth on a solo homer from the designated hitter, Dick Jasper, (4 to 0, Boston). The Highlander's right fielder Karl Warner, shortstop Pete Kater, and Wid Barrett went down, one, two, three— ground out, strikeout, pop out. Wid Barrett's pop fly was the only Highlander ball to make it out of the infield. He received a sarcastic round of applause for his effort. O'Dell's no-hitter continued into the sixth. The crowd had been silenced. Only abusive remarks directed at the umpires and boos for three time strikeout victims cut through the depression. The fans had so little to cheer about that they cheered the bat boy for simply collecting bats. They came to the park wanting something to happen, needing for something to happen. Why they assumed winning had to be a part of it, was . . . I suppose, very American of them. Even John had to remind himself that the wins and losses didn't matter, that this day was much bigger than the final outcome of a ball game.

In the top of the sixth the Red Sox went down, one, two, three. Walker's forkball was working so well, it made his 80 m.p.h. fastball look good— ground out, pop out, strikeout. Al Walker brought some life to the crowd through his quick work.

"Jerry, put me in the game," said Dale Runson. "I'll get us a hit." Jerry gave him a dubious look. Dale pleaded, "I'm not kidding."

"Oh, I know you're not kidding. You can't walk. How are you gonna swing a bat?!" shouted Jerry, completely frustrated. Runson was the team captain and Manager Owens' best player, destined for the Hall of Fame. He was also injured, hurt—severely hurt. He should have been on the disabled list, but he wanted to finish the season, maybe his career, as a New York Highlander.

"I'll get it done. DH me," shouted Runson. With that, he retrieved his bat. He was in the game. Jerry didn't bother to argue. He knew him too well for that. Dale was the best player to come through the Highlander system in ten years, a John Greco find from Indiana. If nothing else, the fans would love to see him . . . as long as he didn't further damage his already fragile back.

"Your attention, Ladies and Gentlemen. Now batting for Ernie Adams is number 23, Dale Runson. Number 23, Dale Runson."

Shawn Burke, the Boston manager, nearly choked on his chew. Nobody figured Runson to play. 'What's Owens trying to pull? Was I tricked? Outmaneuvered . . . nah. The guy can't even walk,' thought Burke. 'Or can he?'

If nothing else, Dale gave new life to the people, and they in return gave life to him. He walked to the batter's box, standing tall, looking strong, while in reality every step caused him spasms of agonizing pain. The applause seemed close to deafening for Dale Runson's unexpected appearance. O'Dell spit, adjusted himself, pushed some dirt around, cleaned his cleats, spit again, grabbed the rosin bag, and finally looked for a sign from his catcher Brad Petrocelli. Dale took a fastball that split the heart of the plate. Harry O'Dell felt much better being up in the count, but he still didn't know if Runson could swing a bat. The crowd clapped and chanted, "We wanna hit! We wanna hit! We wanna hit!" before each pitch, as if the tying run was at the plate. The count went full, and Runson still hadn't taken a swing. Harry was getting jumpy, but he didn't want to walk him. And Runson didn't want to walk. The infield was back.

"The pitch," called Phil Rizzuto from Jason's ancient transistor radio. **"A bunt!"** shouted Rizzuto. **"A perfect bunt! Runson can walk to first on that one!"** And he nearly did. **"That ends Harry O'Dell's bid for a no-hitter!"** The crowd roared its approval. They were absolutely delighted by the sight of a man standing at first base. It was a start.

Jeff Martin got to O'Dell for a walk, moving Runson to second, then Paul McMahon, who went from designated hitter to first base on the Runson move, easily doubled into the left field corner to score Dale. Unfortunately, Martin was gunned down at third base when Ralph Collins, the Boston left fielder, decided third was a better play than the plate. Charlie Greco sent a long fly ball to the deepest part of center, only to have Jack McQuillan make a sensational diving catch for the first out. McMahon tagged up and moved to third. Charlie got the sacrifice, giving Thomas Costa renewed pride in his cousin. Unfortunately, the seventh ended abruptly after Merv Hook smashed a line drive right at Red Sox third baseman Frank Crawford. Frank gunned a throw to the plate that had McMahon cold (Boston: 4, New York: 1, after six).

The camera panned through the crowd and flashed their images on the giant screen above the darkened bleachers in center field. An estimated one hundred and sixty thousand people sang "Take Me Out to the Ball Game," even though a hundred thousand of them weren't even in the ballpark. After getting just two hits and scoring one run, the Highlander fans felt they had Boston just where they wanted 'em. "Lulled into a false sense of security," as Lieutenant Weinman so aptly put it while making an effort to chat up the woman in the neighboring box. Kerrins sipped his beer and thought, 'Sinatra better not sing *New York, New York* if they lose.' Faye kissed him affectionately on the cheek, as though reading his aimless thoughts.

Karen loved the singing, while Thomas thought it was kind of corny. Her grandpa held her in his arms as they sang. "Maybe we'll get on the screen," he said. They watched, but little babies with tiny Highlanders caps received most of the honors, along with sexy women, young lovers, little league teams, bare chested teenage boys, and, of course, the Phil Rizzuto fan club. Banners draped the ballpark with messages from the simple, "Don't go!" to the more reverent, "God help us all."

"Shar, look!" John shook her arm, requiring her immediate attention as he pointed to the large screen in center field.

"What?" she asked, not seeing anything out of the ordinary.

"Do you know who that is!"

"No," she said passively. "A woman singing 'Take—'"

"That's Joyce Johnson! She works for the Highlanders. Her husband is Ben Johnson, Jr. That must be him!" Standing next to Joyce with his arm around her was Ben Johnson, he held a sign that read: Have Faith.

"You mean—"

"That's *the* Ben Johnson's son."

"No! Really? How do you know? Why didn't you tell me?" she asked suspiciously.

"I have no idea, Shar. I found out when I called Joyce for tickets. I guess with all the stuff—Hey! They have a teenage daughter who's a ballplayer." He interrupted himself as Joyce's words came back to him. "They met at the Love Game." 'How could I forget?' he asked himself.

"There they are! I see them—just across from us on the third base line!" exclaimed Sharon, very much excited. A perfect straight line existed between the Johnsons, the mound, and the Grecos.

The seventh inning went by in the blink of an eye—three up, three down, both sides. By the top of the eighth New York's Al Walker still had his good stuff, striking out Ralph Collins and getting Don Jefferson to sky one to Karl Warner on the warning track in right. That was the good news. The next batter, Stan Betts, put Al's first pitch into the seats down the left field line, a hanging fork (Boston: 5, New York: 1). Jerry Owens hopped out of the Highlander dugout; that would be all for Al Walker. The crowd gave the disappointed pitcher a nice round of applause as he left the playing field. Manager Owens signaled for his left-hander, Danny Caruso. Danny was young and had an excellent fastball, though he could get wild at times. But when he was on, he was nearly unhittable.

Caruso made quick work of the Sox right fielder Gary Williams, striking him out with only four pitches. The first one, a ball, zipped under Williams' chin at 96 m.p.h. The next three pitches were strikes. Umpire Fred Dailey punched Williams out on a 99 m.p.h. blazer that had the outside part of the plate. He was caught looking, felt embarrassed, and put up a real stink. Umpire Dailey was one not-so-harsh word away from throwing Williams out. Some players have a sixth sense about these things, and Gary turned his back just as Dailey was about to cock his arm to give him the boot. Maybe that prompted Ben Johnson to hold up his sign again and yell to the people. His efforts appeared to go unnoticed. John could hear his faint voice if he listened carefully.

In the bottom of the eighth the Highlanders—Hook, Warner, and Kater— went down in order. Harry O'Dell was masterful—pop out, pop-up foul ball, and then he ended the inning by striking out Pete Kater. Harry was finished for the day. Law Sazor, the formidable Boston closer, warmed up in the pen. He would pitch the ninth, all but guaranteeing a Red Sox victory and a sorrowful conclusion to New York Highlander history. However, the sad Highlander eighth wasn't able to dampen the spirit of Ben Johnson. Even as those around him appeared defeated and uninspired, he persevered. A few people got up to leave the park. Their seats were quickly taken by those who had paid to stand.

"Get off your hands!" Johnson shouted. "It ain't over!! Where's your conviction!!" Ben Johnson stood on his seat, pleading, begging the people around him with all his passion, his sincere heartbreaking passion. "I love this all too much. . . . Please, fight with me!" he called. Joyce Johnson stood on her seat in a show of support for her husband. An unattended tear rolled down her cheek. She cried for him, she cried for the forgotten, for all of us. Normally, Ben and Joyce Johnson would have suffered harsh ridicule for their zealous actions, but there was nothing normal about this day. And the people around them understood the depth of their emotions and felt an affinity for their heartache. Not an abusive word was uttered in their direction as Ben Johnson persistently attacked their despondency. The people sat, listened, and agreed, but weren't sure what to do about the emptiness most of them felt in their hearts.

"Should I take him down?" asked the tunnel sixteen security guard.

"No," ordered Darryl, scratching his head with the walky-talky, searching for his faith. "Let him be. He's all right. . . . It's almost over."

In the top of the ninth Caruso struck out the Sox shortstop Berry Keating, making it two in a row for the young pitcher. Then Caruso got wild, and so did Ben Johnson as he preached straight through the eighth inning, the commercial break, and into the ninth. He was relentless, frantically preaching through Keating's entire at-bat. Beads of sweat streamed from his brow, his Highlander T-shirt soaked around the collar. There was no stopping him. More and more people stared in his direction, straining to hear what he had to say. His pepper made the Boston batters nervous, unlike anything they've ever heard before. Johnson wasn't after them; he was after everyone and gaining a following.

Caruso got wild and walked Dick Jasper. Caruso got wild and hit Brad Petrocelli. Caruso got wild and busted one in on Jack McQuillan's fist. The bat snapped in half, and Jack's strength alone looped a little flair into shallow left field. The bases were loaded. Manager Owens and Charlie Greco paid a visit to the mound while the Johnsons' chanting continued to grow in intensity.

"You're overthrowing, Danny."

"HAVE FAITH!"

"Take a little off the fastball, you'll see. Get better movement on the ball."

"MAKE A DIFFERENCE!"

"Relax. Try to keep the pitch low. A ground ball to the infield's all we need," said Manager Owens. He patted his pitcher on the butt and slowly walked back to the dugout, listening, but not looking.

"BELIEVE IN BASEBALL! BELIEVE IN YOURSELVES!!"

"How ya feeling, Dan?" asked Charlie.

"Like something strange is about to happen." He pounded the ball into his glove.

"Yeah. I feel it, too. This stuff is always happening around my Uncle John. He's had a weird life." Charlie tapped Danny on the shoulder with his glove. "Fastball, low, paint the inside." And he walked back to home plate.

Quite unexpectedly a woman not fifty feet down the right field line from the Grecos stood on top of her seat and joined Ben Johnson as "a preacher."

"This may be all we have left! You came for a reason! Come on, people!" she besieged the fans in her section.

"The pitch, hit sharply to Kater at Short! He fields it, makes the throw to Barrett at second; Barrett throws to McMahon—in time! Double play!"

The top of the ninth was over (Boston: 5, New York: 1). The crowd rejoiced. When they settled, several more converts had emerged, each rallying the people in their section.

"Why doesn't security do something about those people!" Mr. Jonelli barked into his phone. "They have their orders!"

"I've never seen anything like it," explained Glen Adler, the Penn Garden Broadcasting play-by-play announcer. **"The reports we're getting say that people throughout the ballpark are preaching to their sections with basically the same message: to have faith in baseball and themselves. There must be . . . oooh, two hundred of them standing on their seats as I speak. Now, as I understand it, this is not an organization or anything like that. These are just, well . . . good decent folks, probably, I'd imagine, scared to death of losing their baseball team, afraid they're watching the last game of the New York Highlanders. And who could blame them? The club owner, J. J., has done nothing to dissuade them by his recent non-actions. These fans are looking for answers through their own strength and beliefs. I feel for them. And I applaud them."**

"Listen to me now," ordered Darryl, speaking into his walky-talky. "Ask them to stop. If they don't, just move on and ask the next one. No rough stuff. I repeat—no rough stuff. Over." Darryl's real orders were to have them thrown out.

When the security people asked the zealous fans to sit down, they did; only to have others take their place—sometimes two or three others. The message inspired the people outside the ballpark, in the city, and across the country. Ordinary people were joining the force across the land. They weren't looking for money or some sort of advantage. They just wanted to protect themselves, their country, and the game they loved. Their intentions were noble and pure. They sought a common bond, begging to hold a dream together like the stitches of a baseball, two perfect and opposite sides tied tightly, united. Maybe they felt if the Highlanders and baseball could unravel, so could everything else.

"You're kidding, thanks," said T.C. Golden and hung up the phone. His producer signaled he was on the air. **"It's complete folks . . . they're preaching in bean town."**

In the bottom of the ninth Law Sazor's strikeout of Wid Barrett only converted more optimists. John thought about the hearts and minds of the people and how the wins go where they should. He knew everyone needed this one.

When Dale Runson came to bat, the entire crowd stood to salute his bravery and determination. Runson battled Law Sazor in an at-bat that took the country's breath away. His keen eye protected the plate by fouling off well over ten pitches, building a 3-2 count once again. With each swing of the bat, Runson tried to hide his pain, but the people could clearly see how he suffered. Dale was determined to give something back, something he knew they needed.

"Ball four!" shouted Dailey. "Take your base." The crowd erupted in thunderous applause, laughter, and joyful sighs.

"Caras! Pinch run of Runson," instructed Jerry. Sam anxiously grabbed his batting helmet and ran to first base. James Darwin signaled time-out while the change was being made.

"Not today, Sam," said Runson. "Tell Jerry I'll get it done."

The rookie walked back to the dugout, disappointed, and very afraid of his manager's reaction.

"Why aren't you on first?" questioned Owens through his teeth.

"He wouldn't give it up," mumbled Sam. "He said he'd get it done."

"Uh-huh," Jerry scratched his head. "Have a seat, kid," offered Owens, deciding there was no point in fighting it.

When Jeff Martin came to bat, "the preachers" continued and folks chanted more fervently than ever, "We wanna hit!" Their wishes were momentarily silenced by the lighthearted rhythm of rally music. The huge crowd both inside and out buzzed with solidarity, as they clapped their hands to the magical spirit created by the grand old organ, its tones reminiscent of another time and a reminder of time itself, as it merrily marched along.

"WHY WOULD YOU want to leave great fans like these?" asked the Mayor, impressed by the joyous celebration, though muted by the confines of the owner's box.

"Where were they in the middle of the season, Mayor," rapped Mr. Jonelli in a cool tone, "when I was drawing nine thousand per game?"

Mayor Weldon gazed out the window at the hopeful crowd. The Mayor grew tired of feeling trapped, and decided enough was enough—no more treading lightly or guarded responses.

"Where were they?! Watching on cable. Reading and listening to you endlessly belittle a fine manager with a young team," he explained, sick of it all.

"Your true feelings emerge, Weldon. Well, Mayor, business is business, and I think I've got a better idea than catering to this." He flicked a contemptuous glance at the field and the fans.

"I'll tie you up in court for years, Mr. Jones. Now, if you don't mind, I'm going to find out what all the excitement is about. It looks like fun."

Jonelli slammed his cane across the buffet table. A bottle of vodka hit the floor and smashed, scattering a couple of the Mayor's aides in the process.

"Don't try to cross me, Mayor! This town is going down the tubes and you know it. There's no future here." He waved *abracadabra* across the sea of people as if to make them all disappear. With that gesture he was able to calm himself. "I can be a very good friend, Mayor . . . but you know that."

The Mayor stared out of the darkened window unsure of what to do, and then Jeff Martin smashed a line drive single to right. The stadium rocked. The noise was muted, but the pictures were undeniable. The Mayor witnessed perfect strangers searching each other out to shake hands, trade fives, even hug each other, as though they were clinging to life itself. He watched as "the preachers" pleaded their case with neighborly goodwill and childlike innocence, and the kids, delighted by all the excitement, danced about without a care in the world. 'Happy,' thought the Mayor, 'because their parents are happy.'

"Martin on first, Runson on second, one out!" called Mr. Rizzuto.

"Look out there! Look!" Weldon demanded. He positioned himself in front of the plate glass window to force Mr. Jonelli to see. "This is the country! You can't run from them! They're here, together . . . the way it should be. Making it work would make you the richest man in the world. Don't you see?!" cried the Mayor, caught up in his own words, imploring Mr. Jonelli to listen to reason. He moved to within inches of the glass that separated him from the community and said confidently, "It can work."

"Many things can work, Mayor. My friend the Commissioner thinks so, too."

"We'll see," said Weldon with diplomatic restraint as he and his aides vacated the owner's box to join the revival.

"BOY, THAT KID Sazor's got balls," muttered Kerrins after Law struck out Highlander third baseman Zachary Lombardi on three straight fastballs, challenging Zack on every pitch, even as the stadium seemed dangerously close to imploding on him.

"Martin on first, Runson, second, two outs. McMahon's the batter!"

Law Sazor was feeling pretty good. 'My heater is really humming, high nineties—unhittable,' he thought. The ardent crowd wasn't letting up even after the strikeout, but Law was used to them by now. He decided to put a little extra mustard on McMahon's first pitch. Then maybe throw him a curve or two, and it would all be over. 'Home for the holidays,' he thought.

"The pitch. Wooooo! McMahon is down! Hit by Law's first pitch! Hit in the head! Oh . . . no—looks like the ball shattered his helmet! Paul McMahon couldn't get out of the way. And he's down like a sack of potatoes!" An eerie silence filled the ballpark. Only a baby's cry interrupted the stillness that surrounded the limp body at home plate. Paul McMahon was knocked unconscious, his body carefully placed on a stretcher and rushed to the hospital.

'Ray Chapman. Just like Ray Chapman,' thought John. McMahon never moved a muscle. John looked to Sharon. She was crying. 'Nobody dies for baseball,' she once said, before learning about Cleveland's Chapman.

Law Sazor circled the mound and paced the crosscut swatches of grass, as the medics tended to the downed ballplayer's needs. Manager Burke walked slowly out to the mound to talk with Law, careful not to step on any white lines.

"You okay, son?" asked Burke, pensively.

"I don't know," said Law, truthfully. "I don't feel anything. I wasn't throwing at 'im, Shawn." Burke nodded his head as though he understood.

"I know. Sometimes these things happen," consoled the manager with his head down, kicking over some mound dirt.

"Shawn?"

"Yeah?"

"Why do they think a win will save their team?"

"Necessity, I suppose. . . . It's all they have left." The sun was beating down hard on the mound. Burke started to sweat. "Can you pitch? It's okay if you want out." It was so quiet the manager spoke at a near whisper, otherwise he was sure the fans would hear his every word.

"Yeah, I can pitch," said Law. He pounded the ball into his glove. The sound echoed across the stadium scattering a small flock of gulls. Umpire Dailey approached the mound. The game was about to resume.

The Highlander ballplayer Paul McMahon died the next day, as Ray Chapman had.

"Sam Caras is the pinch runner at first, Jeff Martin at second, and Dale Runson on third. Two outs in the bottom of the ninth. The tying run is at the plate . . . Charlie Greco, Paul McMahon's good friend."

The stadium was lifeless, a motionless photo image of the Bronx' last breath. The fans hadn't any energy left, not even the children, not even "the preachers," not even their leader, Ben Johnson. They all seemed beaten into submission. A photographer captured the essence of the moment perfectly. It was later published with the caption: *No hope.*

MR. JONELLI SMILED, poured himself a drink and downed it. 'One more out,' he thought.

LAW SAZOR COLLECTED his wits and threw two unhittable fastballs in the high nineties. Charlie took both pitches and stepped out of the batter's box.

MR. JONELLI POURED himself another celebratory drink. He raised his glass and toasted aloud, "The last strike." Things were just as he had planned. One last strike, and it would all be over.

JOHN FELT AS though he had to do something. As if by some electrical impulse, he found himself standing on top of his seat. He looked toward Charlie—'Natt's boy,' he thought—and patted his heart three times with his right hand, giving Charlie the sign that couldn't come from the dugout. Then he looked in Ben Johnson's direction and did the same thing. A murmur rippled through the crowd: "John Greco—Greco—That's John Greco—John Greco . . . "

Ben Johnson, tired and exhausted, gazed across the diamond at the solitary believer and from him found the strength to stand, completing the triangle between John and Charlie and himself. Ben returned the sign.

Charlie stepped back into the batter's box, pushed some dirt around with the barrel of his bat, and stepped out again.

"Where have I seen this before," said Dillon Southwood to Joe DiMaggio.

"C'mon, Greco! Let's get it going!" shouted Umpire Dailey.

Charlie stepped back in, barrel to the dirt, and wrote: L O V E.

The message echoed through the air waves and canyons of the park. The image flashed across the giant center field screen. The crowd was on its feet. 'Could it be?' they wondered. The world froze for three solitary beats.

Law Sazor went into his wind-up and gave it everything he had.

"Holy shit," mumbled Max Weinman.

Faaawaaaaaaaackk! The ball hit the bat, sounding like cannon fire, rising—rising—rising—until it cleared the left center field facade and landed on the subway platform of the number four train. The players poured out of the Highlander dugout to greet the tying runs and Charlie Greco. The fans yelled and screamed, stomped and danced, kissed and hugged in a sea of bliss that was felt from coast to coast, hemisphere to hemisphere. News of the second Greco Herculean hit flooded the air waves. The game couldn't continue because the people wouldn't allow the moment to pass. Time stood still. Charlie Greco tipped his cap a record six times, and they still showed no signs of letting up. Thomas and Karen and every kid in the land had found themselves a new hero.

MR. JONELLI THREW his drink against the wall of his cubicle. He wanted nothing more than for it all to end. 'Now look at them! They'll be out there all night!' he seethed, bitterly begrudging the fans their last Highlander moment.

JOHN HELD SHARON and kissed her. Thomas and Karen shouted, "That's my cousin! That's my cousin!" to no one in particular, while Faye hugged Kerrins and Max Weinman hugged the attractive woman across the aisle. Tommy was misty-eyed as he bought me a beer. And the parents, well . . . the parents just felt . . . reassured.

"John! John—do you see 'im?!" Jason cried excitedly, as he pulled and tugged at John's sports jacket.

"See who? Charlie?"

"In center!"

John looked into center field but there was nobody there, not even Jack McQuillan. He was over in left talking with Ralph Collins.

"You don't see him?"

John shook his head.

"It's the Baseball Man—Walt Disney. He's standing in shallow center," sighed Jason, disappointed they couldn't see his friend.

"You're looking at him right now?" asked Sharon.

"Yeah! He's wearing a baggy gray suit, and he's waving." Sharon gave John an anxious look. "He always wears the same thing," said Jason, curiously.

The three of them gazed into the outfield while the rest of the stadium continued to celebrate. Then John noticed Ben Johnson standing at the third base railing. He was staring into center, too, as if he had half a mind to jump the rail and go out there.

"He's gone," said Jason.

'Shallow center field—Ben Johnson played a shallow center field,' thought John. 'I had my dreams in shallow center field. Natt only talks to Jason in the Bronx—'

"Jason you got the ball?"

"Yeah."

"C'mon." John made his way to the railing and signaled for Sharon and Jason to follow. They were over in a second, though security was already after them. John poked his head into the Highlander dugout. His presence snapped Jerry's celebration like a stick.

"Jerry, tell them to let us go," John called into the dugout, as he grabbed a spade from the grounds keeper's area.

"Mr. Greco? What are you doing?!" questioned Umpire Darwin, hoping for a reasonable explanation.

"I'm gonna dig up center field, James," John said earnestly.

The celebration in the stadium died as soon as the people noticed the odd threesome of John, Sharon, and Jason on the playing field.

"What are you doing?!" shouted Jerry, wondering if John had completely lost his mind. He climbed out of the dugout to confront the guards.

"You'll have to trust me, Jerr."

"John, I can't—"

"Let them go, Jerry," called Dillon Southwood, calmly. "You know it's right." He stood at the railing with his buddy DiMaggio by his side. Joe gave Jerry the two fingered salute to the brow.

"I hope you know what you're doing. Let them go," Manager Owens instructed the guards.

"I'll go wit'cha, Mr. Greco," said Darryl, the head of security. John gave him a funny look. "I'm out of a job after today," he smiled.

"He's not going anywhere!" screamed Crew Chief Dailey. "We have a game to finish!"

"He's coming with me," announced Max, flashing his shield. "Lieutenant Weinman, NYPD, Homicide."

"Good!" yelled Dailey. "Get them out of here!"

Weinman turned to John and asked, much to Dailey's dismay, "Where are we going?"

"Center field."

"Great."

"I WANT TO know what's going on! Why has the game been stopped? And why are the guards leaving!?" Mr. Jonelli listened for the reply. "John Greco?!" he screamed into the phone.

"JOHN," PLEADED JERRY Owens. The look in his eyes begged him to reconsider whatever it was that he was about to do.

"Relax, Jerry. We already lost our jobs." He pointed his chin in the direction of the owner's box. The dark figure of Mr. Jonelli stood like a statue at the glass window, an uninspired show and tell shadowbox. Jerry followed John's gaze.

"Besides, you're gonna appreciate this," consoled John, his eyes remained fixed on Mr. Jonelli.

"Is he here?" John asked Jason, meaning Natt.

Jason shook his head. He felt as though he were letting John down.

"That's okay. I know what to do."

"You do?!" exclaimed Jason with renewed life.

"Yeah . . . I want you to throw the ball as far as you can into center field."

"I don't have a good arm," he sighed apologetically.

"Doesn't matter," coached John.

Jason held his most cherished possession tightly. "I never threw it before."

John smiled, "Go ahead, give it your best," he said.

Jason went into a wind-up as if he were a pitcher and let it fly. The throw hit the ground just behind second base and rolled into shallow center field.

"WHAT THE HELL'S going on down there?" Jonelli exploded. "I want them removed!!"

THE CROWD WAS silenced, riveted by the bizarre turn of events. They'd just witnessed a peculiar man make a bad throw of an old yellow ball into center field. John followed the path of Jason's throw; he was followed by Sharon, Jason, Lieutenant Weinman, Manager Owens, Umpire Darwin, and Darryl the Security Chief.

"If you weren't so loved in these parts we'd all be in Bellevue. Ya know that," said Jerry, not expecting an answer.

"You're doing a good thing. Right, John?" questioned Weinman.

"Uh-huh," replied Johney, determined to get the job done.

"Yeah, that's what I thought. Wow, look at all these people. This is great out here!" declared Weinman.

When they arrived at the ball, John stared into the now darkening sky, as though saying a pray or maybe giving a moment of silence. Only the rattle of the number four train echoed through the stadium. The vendors sold their goods in soft voices and hand signals to the few interested customers.

"Now what?" Jerry asked with trepidation.

John planted the spade into the ground and started to dig. Sharon and Jason helped to pull away the turf.

"Oh, Jesus," mumbled Jerry, helplessly.

The ballplayers from both clubs gathered around, not knowing what to expect, yet at the same time, supporting John Greco. They figured he must have his reasons.

The ground was soft. He was two feet down in no time. The sea of players parted for Southwood and DiMaggio. Faye and Kerrins followed close behind. Not a word was spoken; there was just the sound of the spade as it cut through the soil. Resigned to John's actions, Jerry Owens stationed himself next to the hole, fending off the umpires with just a glance, James Darwin assisted him. *Why* was a mystery to Jerry.

"I want this man arrested!" demanded Mr. Jonelli, as he broke through the line of players. He was followed by his own body guards, stadium security, and five New York City police officers. Jonelli pointed his cane at John and then circled it around the entire group.

"I don't know what John Greco is doing down there, folks. Rest assured it's something, ah, important. He's one of the great gentlemen of baseball," broadcasted T.C. Golden to his mesmerized listeners. Similar reports flooded all forms of media.

"Holy cow, I don't believe it," announced Phil Rizzuto. **"He's always been a little different, that John Greco."**

"I want them all arrested!" Jonelli shouted like a madman. "Even you, DiMaggio! You should be ashamed!—American hero!!" He spat the words out as though they left a bad taste in his mouth. Talking about Joe as he did was a very unpopular decision. "I demand these activities cease!"

John continued to dig as the police tried to figure out what to do. With every shovel full of dirt, Mr. Jonelli became more enraged.

"Look what he's doing to my field! What about my field!?" begged the pained grounds keeper.

"Your field?" snarled Jonelli. "This is my field!"

"I'm afraid we're gonna have to ask you to stop, Mr. Greco," said one of the officers.

"He's still digging. Are you going to enforce the law," Jonelli growled into the face of the commanding officer. The officer regretfully took the spade away from John.

"What about my field?" cried the grounds man.

"Would you shut up about the goddamn field. You sound like my father.

The field, the field, the field! Well, I got news for you—all of you!" He lifted his head to the darkening sky and addressed the universe. "I own this—this sad excuse of a baseball team! And I say—no more! Do you hear me? No more! Get this game over with and get the hell out! All of you!" He raised his cane above his head and shook it like a saber. The huge crowd booed while John continued to dig with his hands. When Mr. Jonelli noticed the dirt flying, he marched to the edge of the hole and shouted into the commanding officer's ear, "Stop him!" The officer gave Jonelli a menacing glare.

"My brother is buried here," said John while still on his knees, his hands blackened by the soil. Infuriated, Mr. Jonelli whipped his cane around and hit John in the head, causing him to fall back and into the grave.

The police grabbed Mr. Jonelli before Charlie or Kerrins could get to him. Sharon and Jason rushed over to help John.

The crowd booed and stomped their feet in displeasure. Lieutenant Weinman stepped forward and introduced himself to the officer in charge.

"This is a homicide investigation. Let him dig," said Weinman.

"It's city property," stated Kerrins. "He doesn't even pay the rent."

"You do and I'll have your jobs—all of you!" screamed Mr. Jonelli.

"You don't and I'll have your job!" interceded the Mayor, as he broke through the crowd.

"You'll never make re-election, Weldon!" bristled a shocked Mr. Jonelli.

"DIG!—DIG!—DIG!—DIG!—DIG!—DIG!—DIG!—DIG!—DIG!— DIG!" chanted the people.

"Dig," said the Mayor.

"You can't do that, Mayor! This is my team! Three hundred million dollars! They have a game to play . . . one more game. We can make a deal, come to some sort of understanding. After all we are buisnessmen. I'm sure we can sit down and work this whole misunderstanding out." With every word his tone became more desperate, more unhinged, flip-flopping between begging and cursing.

The sound of the spade cut through Mr. Jonelli's demonic ranting. The sound of the spade pierced a hole through the darkened clouds and provided a ray of pure sunlight. The sound of the spade was taken over by cries of relief from a city's pent-up grief.

Tears streamed down John's face when he found his brother's bones. He removed the gold wedding band with *Faye and Natt* inscribed and offered it as evidence. He removed the broken walking stick with the abracadabra pyramid etched on a silver winged handle, Mr. Jonelli's stick, and offered it for all to see. "The bird that would never fly," he had said in jest. But now there were two wings, one in John's hand and one in Mr. Jonelli's. A pair can fly.

I suppose burying Natt in center field was some kind of poetic justice aimed at the simple-minded ballplayer who refused to play his game, as well as the father he hated. Maybe it was just his idea of a funny joke, probably both. Natt must have put up a wicked fight to take the stick with him. Smithy Lango told the truth—for once. Natt was buried alive for money and power and just for the thrill of it. The extent of a single person's influence on this world can be impressive. Mr. Jonelli's was. But what was most incredible was the blackness of his heart.

Jason said Natt reappeared when John found his remains, and that he cried . . . for his deliverance. John pulled his family close to him and gave a somber tip of Charlie's cap to the fans. He kissed his wife and gave Joe DiMaggio and Dillon Southwood an appreciative nod of the head. The crowd stood and applauded for John "Gentleman of Baseball" Greco and all that he represented. "He's a decent man," they said. And that became a good thing to be.

John picked up Jonelli's broken walking stick and wrote L O V E in the pile of dirt next to Natt's grave in the shallow center field of Ruth Memorial Stadium. Tommy, the parents, and I gathered at the grave site, along with Ben and Joyce Johnson.

"What is it, Jason?" asked John. Jason's eyes were as wide as baseballs.

"They're all here," he said. "Babe and Lou and Thurman and, and, and— they're all here. All the ballplayers. My mom and dad, too. Your daughter. They want to thank you—me, too," said Jason.

John stood in the center of the park, felt the love envelop him, and he knew it could work. For a split second John saw them, too . . . and there among them . . . there she was—the woman he'd seen in Boston who looked so much like Sharon . . . "Maya," John whispered, "Maya." Maybe all the open hearts had let them in. Because on this day, nobody won, nobody lost, like the spirits in the outfield they did the only thing that really mattered. They came to a good place, where the decent folks gather, to better themselves . . . and play baseball.

Epilogue

When the game ended, they all went home peacefully, and for the three hours while baseball was in progress, not a single crime was committed in the City of New York, and every neighborhood felt like a nice place to live. Times Square gathered its souls like never before, creating a spontaneous reverent New Year's celebration. They say folks were just plain old decent to each other and that the people had come to respect John Greco, baseball, and love more than the gun. They say America took two steps back and found its dream; a profound change had occurred—well above partisan agendas and special interest groups. It was that change that gave John Greco a chance—a change of heart that allowed forgiveness and brought folks together. They say it was the beginning of a new era for humankind.

About the Author

Mark Allen Valenza was born in Newark, New Jersey, in 1957 and grew up in Green Brook, New Jersey. At the age of twenty, he moved to New York City where he gathered invaluable life experiences. *Baseball & Benevolence* is his first novel. He now resides in upstate New York with his wife and daughter.